THE JANUS EAGLE

Book One

The Shattered Frontier

By

FRANCIS HAGAN

AUTHOR'S INTRODUCTION

It is unusual for an author to begin an introduction with an apology but that is the position I strangely find myself in now. When I finished 'The Nowhere Legion' last year I had intended to write the next novel about the events leading up to the battle of Hadrianople and the fall of the emperor Valens. This is a period I find fascinating for many reasons - in which the shadow of the last pagan Augustus is still long, Christianity is being torn apart by competing creeds, the Goths are fleeing from the Huns, the Sassanids threaten the eastern borders, and one inadequate man who preferred his farm estates to the imperial throne is thrust into it all. After the fate of the Quinta deep in the deserts of the Oriens, I wanted to move west into Thrace and the Danube border and follow the Eagles down into that day in which the legions became nothing but shadows to paraphrase Themistius. And so I laboured and wrote the opening chapters and these I printed at the end of the last book as a teaser. I should have known that the gods would punish such hubris.

For it was in the middle of all that activity and research that I stumbled over another legion and the more I read about it the more it fascinated me. It was an obscure legion left to rot now upon a remote border but whose past had once been glorious. A legion raised by Caesar himself no less. Fortune is a fickle mistress however and what had once been mighty had now been brought low. And so as I was writing about characters and events leading up to that fateful day in August (how ironic for Valens), I began to wonder more and more what had happened to the men and veterans of this 'lost' legion.

I wondered so much in fact that I forgot Hadrianople and fell instead into another story; a story of betrayal, humiliation, sacrifice and redemption. It was a story that took me out of the empire and into the wild kingdom of Armenia and finally down into a dark place that perhaps no Roman army had ever fought in before. A story I found my pen exploring more than it was those events at Hadrianople. So with regret (but not too much I hasten to add) I stopped work on the novel and threw myself into this story.

Hence my apology now.

This is not the story promised at the end of 'The Nowhere Legion'. It is instead perhaps a bridging story. A story that fills in some of those years after the fighting around the Quinta under Felix and it is a story which will lead better to those last days as so many of the Eagles under Valens fall in a shroud of dust and fire and chaos. We are a few years now after that battle at Akkad and it is no surprise to find that Shapur and his ambition has yet to be fully checked. Here, in this story, we are still in the same rough world of the Quinta though that legion no longer features. Characters and events in 'The Nowhere Legion' echo but only on the periphery. And the more I have written about this story the more I realise that in some manner I *needed* to write this; that in writing it, Hadrianople will only seem more real and more poignant as a result - for I have no doubt that on that bloody day as the standards fall one after the other, as the shield-walls crack apart in mayhem and blood, and as that final guard around a lonely man yearning for his orchards dissolves, characters from both these stories will collide and falter at the last, one hand on another's shoulder.

This then is the story of the Janus Eagle, that strange totem forged in battle out of loyalty and punishment, an Eagle twinned, as it were. It is a story told over three books. The second 'The Fortress of Desolation' will be published in six months time and will chronicle a valiant march into a land besieged with fire and chaos to rescue a lost queen, while the third, 'The House of Caves' will follow six months after that, and will narrate finally that fate of this little legion on the edge of empire - that is, if I don't get distracted again, of course!

For it really wouldn't do to begin a third book with yet *another* apology.

As ever, my thanks go out to all my friends who have supported this endeavour, and who in many ways have acted as sound-boards, proof-readers, and finally crutches: Yuri, for his unstinting encouragement and passion; Carlo, for his enthusiasm and detail; and Geoff, without whom in many ways this story would not exist; also, to Ron, whose support and his own journey as a writer has been invaluable to me. A special mention must go to Jonas who again has designed a cover that reflects exactly this story.

And, of course, finally, Isobel who rides across a rough landscape whereas I only ride within and yet both our horizons always seem to meet.

- Francis Hagan

Prologue

Judea, 66 AD, the Beth Horon Pass

Marcus Clodinus Bassas stood a little apart from the rough singing around him. It was bitterly cold despite the faint grey wash appearing over the mountain tops above and so he huddled deeper into his ragged cloak. He regretted throwing away the thick subamarlis that he usually wore under his mail corselet but orders were orders, he supposed, and if there was no use now for that armour then there was no use neither for the padding that went with it. High above him, that grey stain widened and one by one the little stars were fading away. Here and there on the rim of those heights he could see small fires against the black and he knew that soon those too would fade. The singing faltered for a moment and then he heard the harsh words of the Magister Armorum urge the legionaries on and once again that familiar song rose up about him. It was an old piece of ribaldry sung, it was said, in Caesar's day, when the legion was first summoned to fight beneath its Eagle. That was over a hundred years ago and he wondered now if those first lads under Caesar's gaze had ever imagined such a song being sung now in such a place and by such a final band of men. The words fell over him as he bundled himself deeper into that ragged cloak and he found himself smiling bitterly at them:

> *We 'ave fought the barbari against the dawn,*
> *And held the shield up all forlorn,*
> *We 'ave stabbed the beggars hard and fast,*
> *And ne'er once did mock their past,*
> *For we is Mules, we is Mules, and we bray the day away!*
> *We is Mules, we is Mules, and they feed us naught but hay!*

What he wouldn't give now, he thought, for some of those old legionaries to return with that eternal tramp of the hobnail boot and the rhythmic swinging of weapons and gear. Above him, those ominous lights on the rim of the mountains began to fade, each one a little jewel snuffing out as if a god pinched it away. The grey light was becoming stronger now and out of the night around him vague contours were emerging - jagged clefts, tumbled ravines and rocky slopes, all mired in the detritus of battle and death. Dark shapes were fluttering up into that swelling greyness and he supposed with a fatalistic shrug that even buzzards must have their fill. He tried not to look at the torn shapes scattered all about. Death is no stranger to a legionary but there was something pitiful about those corpses left now as if thrown away especially while that old song echoed up about the stony walls of the mountains around him. He stood amid the leftovers of a tragedy, the torn masks all thrown upon the ground, while a Saturnalia played out about him. Truly, he thought, the gods have a rare sense of humour.

> We 'ave marched the whole wide world all loud,
> And held the Eagle up so proud,
> We 'ave crushed Caesar's foes without a care
> And there is naught we do not dare,
> For we is Mules, we is Mules, and we bray the day away!
> We is Mules, we is Mules, and they feed us naught but hay!

The words had a hollow ring to them that he had never heard before and it shamed him to hear those men sing now. He wondered then on that coldness which seeps not so much into your body but your soul instead. He knew why the Magister Armorum shouted at them in his harsh words - what else was he to do now that he had no artillery or crews left to order around? No, his words were all the ammunition he had now and so he spent them on those legionaries who faltered in the singing of that doomed song. He doubted then if he could have kept up that song himself. Would his heart have remained strong among men already dead but still singing that old ribald refrain? He expected not. Soldiers of Rome should die fighting, gladius in hand, the shield arm forwards, the standards high above, men shouting and laughing despite the terror and the cold rush that always accompanied battle. That was how a legionary of Rome should die - with honour and disciplina; the ancient virtu of arms wreathing his name. Not like this. Waiting for that bloom of grey to arrive and singing that song amid the fluttering of the torchlight and the braziers all cocooned among the leather tents. He swallowed a feeling of bile in his throat and looked up as that last bright spark in the mountain darkness winked and vanished.

The grey light became monstrous then as if the sky above was stricken with a rain of ash and for one moment Marcus Clodinus Bassas lifted up his hand as though to touch it, the rents in his cloak falling apart in a grotesque parody of silk. It was an old hand, scarred and worn now; the hand of a man who had wielded a gladius for longer than he could remember. The skin on the underside was rough and calloused. A white seam split his middle knuckles down to the gold bracelet on his wrist - won, he remembered, for an assault on a mountain fort in which he had thrown his pilum and shattered the skull of a Saraceni phylarch over fifty paces away. The air was cold despite the wash of dawn on his hand and for one moment he enjoyed that simple pleasure, feeling the tingle of sensation creep over his skin. Yet that hand in that light looked now like a dead thing, wrapped as it was in grey. He raised up a dead hand and no small part of him saw the fit of that.

Marcus Clodinus Bassas turned then as the light of dawn fell down upon him from the mountains and he looked back into the rough legionary encampment. Row after row of papillio tents were pegged all about, some lit by braziers from within, others carved out of the fading night by campfires or torches. Standards rose up about the tents, all gilded by those flickering lights, with the shadows of guards about them. Here and there, asses and mules brayed, hungry after the long night, while the few slaves and servants who had remained behind - for whatever doomed whim even he could not fathom - began to scatter feed about, mouthing familiar words and soothing phrases, even as their hands shook as though with an ague. And there within the midst of this cursed camp, buried amid all the tents and the impedimenta of the legion - the little that was left - massed his legionaries. All singing and laughing as those old words and those old phrases rose up into the grey light - in the hand of each one of them lay a naked gladius but in the eyes of each one also, he noticed, rested a dark brittle fear he had never seen before and for one quiet moment then he almost felt like weeping.

He was the Primus Pilus of the First Century of the First Cohort. Before him stood what was left of that Cohort in the wreckage of a desperate camp - yet every one of those singing men had volunteered to remain here while what was left of the legion with its Legate had slunk away deep in the folds of the night to the west and safety. They had all remained, all four hundred of them, while up in the crags and the rocky bastions thousands of Judean rebels waited, thinking the legion was still below shivering deep in its tents and cloaks. These four hundred men - his men - had remained behind even as the survivors of the legion had crawled away, century by century, into the dark like rats. His men had waited here singing and laughing as the night crept past and the shadows within it crawled to safety - and that ruse had worked. Almost a thousand legionaries and those few auxiliaries still alive had vanished west to freedom and safety - including the Legate of Syria himself, Cestius Gallus, the man whose stupidity had engineered this entire disaster, including all his staff and retinue, and including also the Legate's son, Caesennius Gallus, who commanded the legion itself.

The singing faltered even as he turned back to face them. The words sung first under Caesar's gaze fell away into a hushed murmur. Cloaks were shucked off. One by one, the legionaries pulled off their military belts and flung them to the ground. No one wore armour or helmets or carried shields - all had been abandoned a day ago in that desperate flight back through this black pass. Panicked orders had arrived down from the Legate to abandon everything - stores, weapons, armour, artillery, siege equipment, everything, even the wounded in the carts and across the mules. It had been in vain however as these Judeans had rippled up above them over the high ridges and into the crags, scorning the temptation to tarry among the pickings, and so trapping them all here in this pass known in the Aramaic tongue as Beth Horon or the House of Caves. His Cohort was a stripped Cohort now in more senses than one and the men who stood before him shivering in the cold, that grey light bathing them all like ash, looked to his tired eyes as dull and thin as if they were statues carved out of a fog. The only colour to shine among them all was the gleam of the legion's Eagle in the centre. It was the one thing Marcus Clodinus Bassas demanded as the price for this sacrifice - that the Eagle, that sacred heart and soul of the legion, remain with them at the end. Save the men, yes, he had argued, save all your lives if you feel they are worth it, but do not think for one moment that in doing so you will save this legion. It dies here in the dawn with these four hundred men. My men. It will be the price of all your lives and no god - not even that old haggard god who looks backwards and forwards - will ever forget that.

And this Legate of Syria, this Cestius Gallus, had agreed, never once looking him in the eye.

A sudden howl from the mountains about him broke his reverie and the Primus Pilus of the First Century of the First Cohort of the Twelfth Fulminata Legion knew then that their deception had finally been revealed. He unsheathed his gladius, threw away his cingulum belt, and then tossed his ragged cloak after it. A wash of cold air embraced him and he smiled like a wolf. Before him, his Cohort echoed that feeling and the last refrain fell away into an awful deathly silence. He knew that this legion, the Fulminata, named after the Thunder of Jove Himself, would find in its own silence now a roar to equal any coming down upon them from the heights above. He smiled and the legionaries about him smiled back through the grey of their last dawn as they prepared to die beneath a hundred year old Eagle of Rome . . .

INTRODUCTION

It was the day a friend died in the falling snow and I found a doorway into darkness.

I suppose in looking back now that there is a certain symmetry to that - that perhaps it was in some manner an inevitability - but at the time such thoughts never occurred to me. We were tired, of course. It was late evening and the sun was fading. My dig manager, Sally McCarthy, was harassing us about packing up for the night and many of the interns and volunteers were looking at me with expectant faces as a result. Winter was in the air and small flurries of snow were dusting everything - the tools, the battered trucks, the old generators under their tarpaulin covers. Someone had remarked that God's dandruff was about us all but the laughter which followed was tired and perfunctory. Sally was pressing me - dusk was falling fast, she urged, and it was a long drive back to the main camp at the foot of the hills. She lit up another of her Turkish cigarettes and then looked at me with that enquiring stare she always had as if waiting for me to arrive at a conclusion already bloody obvious. It was a stare both patient and accusing. I remember that I laughed while looking around at the dig. I was buying time I suppose from the inevitable. She was right, of course. Night would be on us all soon. And with the falling snow, would come a bitter cold none of us wanted to endure. Not even me - and I was perhaps back then the most dedicated of all of us.

We were in a low valley - a glacial hollow framed now by rounded hills and sharp gullies. A worn path had cut through this valley and we had used it to drive the few trucks and jeeps up here to begin the next round of excavations. A small flat plateau formed our rough camp which sheltered the portable generators and tents. A ramshackle canteen van lay parked over to one side. All about us, up and down the valley sides, lay marks and trenches and half-erected scaffolding. We had not been here over a week and already we had dug and probed almost half of this small valley. I remember seeing Akil, our Turkish guard and a man who had to have been the most ineffectual soldier I have ever come across, lounging by one of the female volunteers and laughing too loudly at a remark of hers. It was his job to remain behind here with the generators and equipment while we drove back each evening. A sudden wind brought a new flurry of snow and both of them vanished from my sight. Most of the remaining volunteers and interns were idling about the trucks, eager to be away. Some had already stowed their equipment and were drinking the last of the coffee from the flasks. High above us, up a narrow incline, I saw Jacek and his small team working hard up against a bleak-looking cliff-face. I smiled at that - he was a Pole from Krakow, deeply Catholic and one of the most erudite people I have ever come across. He was a small man with a round shiny face that never ceased from smiling at you - though whether it was to indulge you or mock you, one could never tell. Sally had once bitingly remarked that Jacek reminded her of a clean-shaven Santa Claus who had perhaps read too much Oscar Wilde. He was turning now and waving down towards us, a little yellow handkerchief fluttering above that shiny head of his and I remember thinking that only Jacek could carry a thing like that - something somehow antiquated and yet so *apt* in his hands. He waved that little yellow rag and I found myself smiling at it even as I turned to Sally to give the order to retire for the night - and that sudden urgent shout cut through everything like a knife.

Sally was already moving, running, throwing that damn cigarette away, her hand grabbing for the walkie-talkie at her belt, even as I half-turned into that shout and saw him collapse among all those interns and volunteers. And for one, absurd, moment I didn't look upon him as he fell, his face white and in agony, his hands clutching at his chest, even as a dozen people surged in towards him. John Atkins, my old friend, fell down by the trucks, a crowd about him, my dig manager already shouting urgent words into her walkie-talkie, and all I saw was Jacek high above waving that absurd handkerchief. Snow fell about me. A gust of wind caught at the collar of my jacket and made it whip up into my chin. And before Sally had even reached the body of John now lying on the ground down by the trucks I *knew*. I knew that he was dead. It was a feeling above and beyond the cries of grief and shock below, beyond the hideous angle of his body, beyond the sudden low urgency in the voice of Sally - a voice which had had all the emotion and love forced out of it, knowing that such things were useless now. I knew he was dead and there was nothing I could do about it. And high above, that yellow rag fluttered through the falling snow - and without knowing why I found myself walking up towards it.

I walked up over the rocks and crags as if in a dream - as though I were being lured onwards - and it seemed to me to be the most natural thing in the world. Death lay below but up there with that smiling Pole I knew something else had been revealed. Something that had become an obsession and a goal stretching back over twenty years. Behind me, I heard Sally shout out something to me, her voice angry and disbelieving, but I ignored her and walked on. The ground was rough and I knew I stumbled over it but it did not seem matter. There was a coolness on my brow - from the falling snow, I expect - and that coolness somehow left me detached from what was happening around the trucks. I felt the sharp cut of rock on my hands as I hauled myself up those last few feet and then found myself standing alongside Jacek, who was laughing now at my toil up the slopes oblivious to what lay below - laughing and pointing with that damnable yellow handkerchief to where his team stood, all exhausted and eager to see my face in turn.

The cold was bitter and sharp, I remember that, as I looked past him and then saw it. It made me shiver suddenly, almost violently, and pull in the jacket about me for protection. Jacek nodded that shiny face of his and patted me on the back as though to warm me up. Then, with a shooing gesture, he ordered his team to step back and I found myself alone in a flurry of snow, its wetness plastering my brow, my eyes screwed up against it.

It stood there before me like an offering. It was a huge stone disc some five feet in diameter bevelled into the cliff-face and for all the world looking like an upright mill-wheel. It was old and eroded and I knew in a moment that it had not been moved for over a thousand years. All about it, lay piles of loose stones and rubble which had been scrapped away by the team under Jacek. In the centre, lay a depression - what had once been a socket - but of the timber pole which had once been used to lever open that stone circle there was of course no sign. I can still see it now all these months later even as I write these words almost as if it is still hanging before me - a doorway into another world - and I suppose that is what it was. A portal to so many other things and a threshold over which so many had passed but which had not yet seen the last of those desiring such a passage. Jacek understood. It was why he had ushered those assistants aside and pushed me forwards. It was why we had all been here this last week.

It was why in the beginning I had assembled a team and funding and why I am writing all this now. That stone wheel - its eroded surface and implacable weight - in many ways hung over us all.

I had finally found what I had been looking for after twenty years of research and digs and here I was standing before this stone wheel up against a cliff in a remote part of eastern Turkey. It was an odd contrast to those many years ago when this had all started. Then I had been on my knees in a little trench lifting up scraps of pottery shards. I remember I had lifted up this one last shard intending to call it quits for the day and then I had paused - seeing on it something so tiny and slight, a little scratch of writing, but which all those years later would leave me stranded now before this massive stone entrance - from the tiniest fragment to this enormous stone wheel and in between such time that all my life before it and no doubt after it will seem as nothing but bookends . . .

The snow fell and through it I thought I heard lost voices. I saw Jacek turnabout in alarm then - sensing for the first time that something was wrong below - even as I stepped forwards and placed my hand on that ancient surface. The stone was calloused and cold to the touch but the feel of it brought out a fierce joy in me and I leaned in against it, pushing against the bulk of it. It did not move of course. I knew it wouldn't but I *needed* to test myself against it - to know that it was real and not just an illusion or a figment of all our imaginations.

It was then that I turned back to Jacek, smiling at the fulfilment of our dreams, to find him white with shock. He stood there, that little round-faced Pole, his face blanched, with his hand held out towards me, offering up that yellow handkerchief as if in consolation, knowing perhaps how futile and meaningless such a gesture was. It is the only time I have ever seen him looking lost and I have always wondered since whether that moment had left him shaken not so much from John's death as from the fact that in his eyes I did not seem to mind. He stood there, his hand bunched up, fat and shiny, that yellow cloth whipping ineffectually in the wind, snowflakes cascading over him, and in his face all I saw was the loss of his faith - his faith in me, perhaps, or in that project we had all embarked upon.

My smile robbed him of his faith and so much more besides. For all his wisdom and mockery and wit, poor old Jacek never saw what I saw as I stood there before that portal. He never understood that in that moment wherein he raised up that handkerchief to signal to me that he had found the entrance, was also the moment in which death arrived to my oldest friend and took him away. Truly, there is a god of doorways and portals and archways and that god is one who always reminds you that to step forwards is also always to leave something behind.

It was the day John Atkins died and I finally found what I had been looking for over twenty years.

It was the beginning of the end in many ways and what you will read now is perhaps not just the story of that journey but also a journey into a forgotten past long since itself buried in obscure places and archives. A past slowly unearthed over the last twenty years which itself has led me and all those with me who subsequently joined as those years rolled past to this very spot here in these remote hills. And finally it is a journey back into that black space behind a stone wheel which has not been opened in countless generations. A black space within which lay the ending I had been seeking - perhaps unwittingly - for too many years.

And as that old shriven god Janus allows doors both to swing forwards and backwards so too did the culmination of my life end also in death . . .

And it is perhaps to his *memory* now that I write the story of what lay behind that dark portal. For what follows is not the old dust of the academic text - that dry report of detail and quotation littered with supposition and query - but instead something more personal. More intimate. Death underpins so much of our lives that often we forget or dismiss it not so much out of ignorance or fear but simply because we are bored by it. It inundates us through the newspapers and the television. We simulate it in the dramas we watch or the films we gawp up at. Death swamps us at every turn of our lives but it is a simulated death and like the ancient Greeks of Athens we prefer that death to be distant and off-stage; hidden behind fake-blood and breathless report. And when death does intrude upon us - the parent fading at the last in a nursing home or the brother torn apart in a car-crash or a friend collapsing among colleagues but with a look upon his face that tells you he is so very apart and alone from us all - we stand and feel as if we have strayed into a clichéd moment on a screen as fake as anything we have seen in the past.

I have spent my entire life among the ruins of the past - searching for something beyond words, that vague sense of *being there*; of touching the ineffable - so that in that moment when my friend fell and died I walked instead not towards him but up and onwards over snow-dusted rocks and flinty edges to stand at the last before that stone wheel. I walked away from the presence of death refusing to allow my friend to become a cliché towards the past as I have always done all my life.

So you see that I cannot write this now as if none of that ever happened. If only as an attempt at atonement - and I can almost hear Jacek laughing gently at that - must I write what follows in a different voice. Perhaps I am seeking redemption and perhaps I am merely looking to justify that moment. I cannot say. I only know that if I were to write the history I have found as yet another academic book would I not be walking away from my friend twice? And that I cannot do even though as I write this I can imagine a figure snorting behind my back at that suggestion as she lights up another cheap cigarette. So, reader, allow me to walk you into a past and a fate in which empires collide and battles are fought and those few men who stood under a cursed standard also walked as I have walked and stood before that which I too have stood - although behind their steps lay far more blood and death than did mine. And so forgive me the hand I extend to you in this writing and wonder not that it is both encompassing and also intimate.

My pen bleeds, as a poet once wrote, and all the paper in the world will not bandage it . . .

Where to begin then, I wonder? I suppose it would be true to say that over the last twenty years or so, I have seen the rise of what might be called the social history of war to the extent that it has now become firmly entrenched in historical and archaeological circles. Ground-breaking works such as Carlton's *Going To The Wars* and Marshall's seminal *Men Against Fire* have allowed a whole host of other works to entrench themselves in academic circles to the extent now that it is almost impossible to conceive of studying war without taking into account the experiences of the men on the ground. In a field where such voices remain recorded long after the conflict is over, it is relatively easy to amass and study the diaries and interviews from these men and place them against the wider views of the politicians and the generals who dictated those wars and battles. However, in more distant eras, such as here in the Later Roman period where my own research is based, for example, these voices are at best provisional or at worst absent therefore much of the research is necessarily circumstantial or speculative.

This work which follows, however, while painstaking and lengthy, goes some way to redress this issue and is, I suppose, my apotheosis - and so it is with both pleasure and a certain bitterness that I write what follows after all the research and the work and the long hard digs. And while it is impossible to resurrect the voice and comment of long-dead soldiers and officers from a period where such things as videos and voice-recorders remained barely a dream, what follows is perhaps as close as we can come to such a record and if, on occasion, I take what might be called an artistic license or even perhaps a blatant imagining, forgive me that license. In disavowing the academic crucible, I am seeking instead a deeper truth. A truth predicated not so much perhaps on factual report as that inner insight into character and motivation. A truth perhaps emotional or philosophical. I am opening a window as much as I found myself later - weeks later, that is, after John's funeral - standing again before that stone wheel and after much labour opening it to cast a light deep into its musty blackness.

So what follows is perhaps what some might call an *imaginative* study on the impact of battle on the soldiers and officers of the later Roman army – in this case, and in particular, the troops from the Eastern provinces during the Sassanian Wars under the reign of Flavius Julius Valens, that ill-fated and much maligned emperor. A study derived as much from surviving documents and records as it is from my own *sense* of that history. Others, those more conservative or critical perhaps, call it a provocation or a fiction. Even a lie. But then they were not there that day we found that portal and my old friend fell in death. It does not matter. I am extending a hand across an epoch both into the past and from that past back into the present. More than that I am opening a portal and that portal is one cloaked in loss.

The Janus Eagle – as I have called this work of history or whimsy depending on your view – has rightly caused a stir among those academics who have read it and one consequence has been to see a certain 'lessening' of the rigorous straightjacket we sometimes accept when it comes to writing or recording the 'little voices' of war in the Roman and Greek period. After spending the better part of twenty years in Iraq, Iran and the Turkish highlands, often in very dangerous circumstances, involved in archaeological digs, supplemented with archival work at the various museums and libraries, I have amassed over fifty documents and inscriptions (many previously unseen) relating to army units deployed in and around the East during the years 367-71 AD onwards - a period when the fighting was bitter and prolonged along the Armenian, Sassanian and Roman borders. These range from papyrus fragments and epistles to inscriptions and even obscure scribblings. What has subsequently emerged is a startlingly detailed and personal account of some of the units stationed in the East of the Roman Empire and their fate in the face of the Sassanian Wars of Shapur II, the *ShahanShan* of the Persian Empire, during those tumultuous years after the death of the emperor Julian.

But more than that it is the story of men and women drawn into one ill-fated moment in history wherein all the threads and actions of great men fell down upon a few shoulders and left those poor souls abandoned before that stone portal as I stood before it with the shadow of death behind me. It is an irony and a humour which has not gone unremarked in those about me and it is why, despite the long lapse of time and fate, I feel a kinship and even perhaps a brotherhood to those desperate survivors and is why what I have called *The Janus Eagle* exists now here on this page as neither history nor fiction but somehow something in-between. And all the better for it, in my humble opinion.

However I am moving ahead of my theme and that simply will not do. For those unfamiliar with this work, then, what follows is a painstaking reconstruction of the events along that tectonic fault-line where Roman, Armenian and Sassanian forces clashed and around which Christian, Pagan, and Zoroastrian faiths merged and fought with a tenaciousness and hostility rarely felt elsewhere on the frontiers of the Roman Empire. Here, up among the highlands and mountain passes out of which tumble the Tigris and the Euphrates rivers, ancient enmities and blood-feuds erupted with startling speed and into which unwary Roman ambassadors and Persian satraps fell, their minds awhirl with confusion and doubt. This was a land in which three great civilizations clashed: the Roman Empire with its newly-burgeoning Christian veneer, the fiercely aggressive Sassanian Empire under Shapur II, that monarch crowned *in utero*, and the oldest Christian state, Armenia, whose king, Arsaces, plays both Rome and Persia against each other in a desperate attempt to preserve his kingdom's precarious independence.

It is a wild frontier populated by hill tribes, studded with fabulous towns enriched by spice trades and silk routes, guarded by remote fortresses and legion encampments, riddled with ruins and empty plateaus, all echoing with past glories and bitter defeats. Here drift the remnants of remote tribes seeking new dominions, old Parthian Houses under Armenian and Sassanian banners, the dry, dusty, echoes of the Greeks under Alexander the Great, venerated Aramaic and Syrian trading houses now intermingled with old Jewish exiles, and under all an even more distant people: the Cordueni, known now as the Kurds of modern times, occupying a land where it was claimed rested the remains of the Biblical Ark itself, and through whose lands the famous Ten Thousand of Xenophon had once passed, a passing beneath which lay secrets even that Greek general could barely hint at. A hint it would later transpire that would indeed perhaps save so many desperate men and lead me and Jacek and Sally and finally John to that fatal portal where death would emerge for one final show.

It is an area little regarded in today's histories of the Roman Empire here in the West, which prefer to detail the troubles of the Gothic migrations or the mighty Vandal invasions around the Mare Nostrum or the Fall of the Eternal City itself.

What makes what follows however so vital is not just the voices of the little figures caught up in a vital epoch of history, it is also the light I can finally shine into a nook and cranny many other writers ignore or forsake and of course reveal a legacy wherein one man fell that so many others might be redeemed. Although in my mind I cannot decide whether I am writing about John Atkins or that poor Roman - ah, but again I find that my pen outruns my story . . .

- Thomas Anderton, Professor, University of Glasgow

CHAPTER ONE

'Corbulo', Praefectus, drills his men like a lazy Aegyptian eunuch.

I still remember twenty years ago stumbling over that *graffito* in rough vulgar Latin. It was inscribed on a pottery shard unearthed from a dig at the Malatya site back in a hazy Summer. The light was fading, as I recall, and the shade amongst us was growing cold. We had paused amid a refuse heap and had been sifting it all out into tiny trays and wire meshes. This was old school archaeology - on our knees in mud and dust, our hands all grimy but eager to feel the remnants of the past. And there it lay - caked in grime. It turned out to be one of a number of pottery shards, now recycled as writing surfaces, and was probably circulated among the low-level tenements which serviced off-duty soldiers and wanderers in this decadent and volatile region of the Roman Empire. The terse humour on it captivated me and without realising it at the time was to propel me on a life-long quest to track and record these 'little voices' which History in its grand epic often ignores. I still don't know why it was this particular piece which captivated me. It was not that unusual, truth be told. I had held and read dozens similar to it. All covered in rough Latin or Greek; all recording sarcastic observations, or meetings, or crude jokes. On the surface this was no different. And yet, as I knelt there and scraped away the caked mud to read its faded inscription - something in me subtly changed. If I am being honest now I suspect that it was not the piece at all which changed me but rather something in me waiting for this catalyst to come along.

I had spent the better part of ten years, you see, most of my professional career as an archaeologist, amid such ruin, finding objects and sites and lost records and yet always remaining curiously distant from it all. It was not that I lacked interest or even failed to find new and provoking remains but rather that somehow in all that detail and mass of data, I seemed to always stand alone and apart from it all. My colleagues back then always remarked that I was efficient and even cold and I had always scoffed away those suggestions while perhaps wondering if they were not right. We dug and recorded and annotated and then we moved on. Those among us who published gained renown while others who remained on their knees as it were stayed anonymous but somehow closer to the past and its dirt. And I? I drifted between those two poles, I suspect, never comfortable in the wider academic world but also restless among those who remained always in the trenches and pits. I was seeking something more but like all seekers did not yet know what it was I was looking for.

Then one day there I was in that mud and holding that ubiquitous shard, scraping away the dirt, reading that Latin, my lips stumbling over the translation, and finding a slow grin spreading over my face. And I knew then what it was I was really seeking. Here we all were - my colleagues and friends, all grimy and tired - digging up and recording the past like a large illumination for posterity and yet within it all we *reduced* such men and women down into anonymous faint footprints easily lost or forgotten. Here with this shard in my hand I held a voice - the implacable presence of a solitary will - and the faintly absurd notion seeded in me that rather than seeking to record *history* - its forces and structures - I should instead seek where this single thread - this little voice - took me. I rose up from that trench holding not a piece of the past but the echo of a person. And it was his story and the stories of those about him that was beginning to grow in me. It was a slight shift in intention but it thrilled me at the time - to dig not for objects and ruins but instead for the remnants of one man's shadow. I know this reads as perhaps ridiculous or even a little absurd but at the time it seemed so natural. I did not question it. I *knew* that what I was doing was something which would fill that void I had been holding in me.

And so it was that I fell away from Tacitus and Ammianus and Procopius with their sweep of history to take up residence instead with a hundred other names, all minor and insignificant, to find in their rough humour and laconic comments another Rome, a darker and less civilised Rome, which paradoxically seemed much closer to our own world now with its perhaps cynical *mores* and lax moral attitudes, if you will forgive my nostalgia. These were real men and women who did not always act out the fine passions of Homer or Virgil or embody the upright ethics of Cicero or Marcus Aurelius – but instead seemed to live a rough-and-tumbled life where everyday concerns revolved around pay, equipment, loved ones, feuds, and the petty laws of discipline and taxes. These were names which bore Syrian, Persian, Greek, Armenian and Arab antecedents and it was a world in which Latin remained an imposed language, steeped in officialdom and legalese.

To say, I was drawn into this world would be an understatement. Little did I realise, as I embarked on that journey twenty long years ago, just how many stories were to merge together in this underbelly of Roman history thanks to that single pottery shard but in time, it would be true to say, I came to know those names and the characters behind them better than some of my own colleagues here - and finally as for 'Corbulo', that lazy officer, whose *graffito* started me off so many years ago, I will only say now that had those words on that dry, cracked, pottery shard been the only testament to his remote character then History herself should have bowed her head in shame. Instead in a perverse manner that little shard would one day lead me to stand smiling before a large stone wheel behind whose portal waited all the final answers to all the questions and queries which that tiny shard had started . . .

So it was that the dusty frontier town of Melitene, or Malatya as it is known now, a few days' march from Amida in the east, provided an unlikely introduction to our Corbulo for not only was it during the dig here back in 1991 that I found that shard, it was also here that I was later able to examine in some detail surviving papyri from a legion's headquarters building as they emerged one by one from that excavation. Those papyri, it would later turn out, were intimately connected to the writing on the pottery shard and so in some small way endorsed my change of heart.

We were a combined team back then - part Turkish, part Polish and part British, all scavenging like ants over bits of ruins here and there. Funding was always incomplete and precarious and the joke soon spread among us that each beer we bought was Polish in volume, Turkish in price and British in its flatness. It was here that I met Jacek for the first time and fell in love with his colourful and witty character. We had arrived fresh from the embassy at Ankara and still a little amazed at this provincial town. Two Universities - Glasgow and Edinburgh - had combined their funding to launch a project dig among the slight remains of the ancient Roman town. Nothing too spectacular but we hoped to yield interesting data on civic planning and development - or its decline - in the Later Roman period. Good solid archaeological work but hardly newsworthy. Our Polish and Turkish colleagues were already onsite but excavating what was thought to be the remains of the ancient legionary fortress outside the walls of the town. Of course such a dig received more attention in the press and their finds always made the local newspapers.

It was Jacek himself who first made the introductions, sauntering over to us as we were lining up our initial excavation lines, a ruddy smile on his face, an overlarge Panama hat tilted at one angle on his head, and twirling what looked to be an outdated parasol. We did not know whether to laugh or take him seriously at first and no few of us wondered later in one of the bars if he had not aped the persona of the eccentric Englishman abroad to mock us. Over time however we realised that if there is one nation able to out English the English in their eccentric mannerisms it is the Poles. And so it was with Jacek. He was a Krakovian, deeply erudite, and as with all those who have read too much and understood perhaps too deeply he carried about him an affable but always slightly mocking air. The world for him was old and sage but also broken. I remember once standing outside one of the tents with him during a sunset, marvelling at the colours on the low distant hills, when suddenly he raised an imaginary glass and shouted 'bravo!' and I knew then that for him such wonder was old and jaded and now nothing but an endless pantomime for those who looked but did not see. It was the first time I ever saw him glance at me with a complicit wink in his eye. To say I warmed to him would be an understatement. Together, the two of us acted as the glue which bound the two teams together - our British endeavour in among our low walls and scattered pottery shards and the combined Polish and Turkish team deep in the much more impressive legionary remains outside the modern town.

And it was of course those remains that yielded up my further steps after this 'Corbulo'.

It was the evening, if I recall correctly, that Jacek and I were mulling over the days' events with a glass of beer or two - both of us grimacing at its quality - and I had showed him that pottery shard and told him how I was determined now not to record artefacts but instead hunt after the voices behind them. I had expected him to scoff in his usual mocking manner - after all, was I not in some fashion turning my back on his own vocation - but instead something else happened. Something entirely unexpected. Jacek bounded up and grabbed my arm in an excited fashion and then proceeded to drag me out of our tent and into the large archival pavilion we all shared. I barely had time to put the beer glass down such was his enthusiasm. Moments later, he deposited me beside a low trestle table where two of his assistants were unrolling a fragile papyrus. It was remarkably preserved in the arid northern Cappadocian heat and I remember how both their hands were moving in slow delicate gestures, lifting, opening, revealing the small sections while preserving its integrity. Little by little, the tiny blocks of Latin were emerging, so faded now as to be almost invisible - but under the fluorescent lamps, I could see words and even the beginnings of sentences. Jacek shooed those assistants away in a hurry and then closed a curtain about us so that we were alone. I saw sweat glistening across that shiny brow of his as he took the pottery shard from me and laid it slowly alongside that dusty papyrus.

Before he could even look up at me, I saw it. I saw what had gripped him. The writing on the shard and on the papyrus was by the same hand. And I remember looking down upon that scroll as if vindicated; as if my instinct was being rewarded - and I had the absurd thrill for one single moment that an unknown god was placing a hand upon my shoulder.

Although 'Corbulo' himself is not initially mentioned, the papyri which emerged in the days and weeks to come – scrap by scrap – were written all in this one hand and detailed at some tedious length the regular daily routine of a Roman legion relegated to patrolling caravan routes and maintaining custom posts along the ancient roads of this part of the Empire. It took the Poles and the Turks over a month to unearth it all and then roughly translate it but it was a month in which that single fragmentary voice upon the ostraka opened out not into an historical fact or statistic but instead into something much more interesting: a character. A month later, as the autumn chill fell over the low hills here in eastern Turkey, I spent a long weekend taking copious notes and writing up as much as I could before the fragments and scrolls were bundled up and sent back to Britain for minute examination and preservation. There were gaps, alas, and sections too damaged to read but on the whole we had been lucky in unearthing something this detailed - and no doubt other scholars would in time use this find to deepen their understanding of Late Roman army procedure and organisation - but for me, I found something far richer, something far more exciting. I found not an excuse to revise a theory or develop a thesis but a moment in history - a collision of events and people whose threads I could follow in more detail in the years to come.

That shard was a portal to a new world; a world opening out for me alone - at least in those early years.

First, however, allow me to set the stage. We are sometime in early Spring of 367 AD. Hostilities and tensions with Persia have been rumbling on for a few years but no actual conflict has broken out as yet. There have been the inevitable border skirmishes along the Armenian frontier and a potentially volatile eruption of *Saraceni* tribes past Damascus and Bosana - all contained or snuffed out thanks to the diligence of local units and commanders in the area. The Emperor Flavius Julius Valens has moved a sizable portion of the army of the Oriens out of the interior cities and towns and is re-grouping them as a precaution in various detachments along the *limes* – the frontier zone that marks the border between Rome and Persia. Meanwhile, he himself has marched north across the Bosphorus and into Thrace to penetrate the Danube frontier. It is an *excursus* designed crush the Goths in retaliation for their support of Procopius, a now-dead usurper. Whether war with Persia will break out in the absence of the emperor or not remains a heated topic of debate in the local *tavernae* and *agoras* of all the towns in the Diocese of the Oriens - from Antioch itself to Edessa, Damascus, Amida and even up to Melitene and the nameless hill settlements strung out about this remote town. However, the initial papyri fragments recovered from the legion ruins itself remain dry and interested only in assessing provisions, detailing guard patrols and notating those soldiers who were fit for duty and those who were on assignment out with the town itself. Details typical of any army in any period and which would not be out of place in the regimental headquarters of a field camp among the trenches in Flanders or the silk pavilions of Harfleur or even in the prefabs of Kandahar in Afghanistan.

This is the daily world of the Twelfth Fulminata Legion, a garrison and frontier legion, now under the regional command of Brachius, the Dux Armenia, a stolid and career-orientated Illyrian from Sirmium; a man the philosopher Libanius once referred to as 'that dry aqueduct of a conversationalist.' The Duodecima Fulminata Legio – to give it its full title – is no longer, as can been seen from the papyri, a crack legion and is clearly operating now more as a border police force: gathering taxes, hunting down inept bandits, and generally patrolling the ill-defined *limes*. What makes all this interesting however is not the mundane and somewhat regurgitated litany of details in the papyri of the Twelfth 'Thundering' Legion but the surprising fact that the hand-writing in all these reports is clearly by the same hand which wrote the *graffito* on the pottery shard about our 'Corbulo'. It was an observation which not only propelled me on my first steps into this period but also earned Jacek a bottle of single malt whiskey in gratitude as a result:

'. . . First Cohort and Second Cohort remain under-strength and in need of essential provisions in this the Consulship of Lupicinus and Jovinus, the third year since our Sacred Dominus assumed the Purple. Eighteen *milites* remain missing from the lists. Twenty three *milites* are under the care of the medicii. Four died of the flux a week ago. Fifteen *milites* are on authorised furlough to Antioch – may God and His Son bless them – and we still have no *Praefectus* to make the benedictions and raise the prayers for the divine goodwill of our new Imperator. The *curiales* of Melitene resist as ever their requisite hospitality and have lodged several claims for property damage and theft. The Third Cohort remains detached to the frontier fort at Auaxa to the south under the command of the *Praepositus* Cyrion. Scouting detachments of the latter report sporadic hill brigandage of the usual sort. The grain horrae are plagued with rats, may the Forty curse them all . . .'

What do we learn from this first fragment alone? As ever the local population resents the billeting of the legion within its area despite the protection such a force will provide; it consists of three remaining cohorts out of an original ten which gives the Twelfth an effective strength of some two thousand legionaries or so, given that the First Cohort has always traditionally been a double-strength one; and the Twelfth is without a commanding officer or *Praefectus* and has been for some time - a highly unusual position and one that the writer will refer to in more detail later. Another subsequent fragment is worth quoting:

'. . . The Nones of Aprilis passed with ferocious storms and the Melas river broke its bank to flood the main forum of Melitene. The men of the Legion assisted with repairs and celebrated with prayers and offerings to Christ and the Forty. The *curiales* of the town presented watered down wine. Violence ensued. Two legionaries and one centurion, Remus, ever Remus, were placed under the care of the medicii. Nine men of Melitene suffered broken limbs. In punishment, all centuries involved were ordered on a ten day march into the Analaean Hills north of the town and suffered the flies and thirst of Roman *disciplina* . . . The Bishop of Melitene was banished together with his pregnant servant and not just for his heretical Nicene faith. The statues of the gods from the temple of Aphrodite were finally broken up and their marble sold off to the Syrian traders. The latter gifted the Twelfth four amphorae of Alexandrian wine, of the unwatered sort . . .'

Religious tensions, civilian against soldier, the drudgery of manual labour, sporadic violence, celebrations – in other words, typical life in a frontier town on the edge of Empire . . .

Melitene, or modern day Malatya in south-east Turkey, is an ancient town in the Cappadocian hinterland of the foothills of the Taurus mountains. It has an illustrious history having seen Scythian, Cimmerian, Hittite and Akkadian invaders wash over it in previous epochs. A tributary of the Euphrates, the Melas river, washes past the old town. A few Roman miles east lies the Euphrates itself as it tumbles down from the Taurus mountains and seeps into the great fertile lands of Mesopotamia to the south. Beyond that mighty river lie the ancient peoples of Armenia and Persia all mixed together in an oriental stain of history and conflict. Further east amid jumbled hills and knotty peaks lies the upper Tigris, that second great river of the Fertile Crescent. Melitene while old and venerable is now a canton town of the province of Armenia Minor and part of the frontier *limes* of Cappadocia. All along the crowded banks of the upper Euphrates, small garrison forts and river-posts can be found, with the Twelfth stationed here further back. North at Satala can be found the old legionary camp of the Fifteenth Apollinaris Legion, built back in the days of Trajan, while up on the shores of the Black Sea at Trebizond musters the final legion under the command of the Dux Armenia, the First Pontic Legion. In between these three border legions lies a scattering of cavalry regiments and the old auxiliary cohorts. Together, these make up the command of Brachius, that pedant of a soldier, to paraphrase Libanius, who is tasked with patrolling and defending the edge of the Empire here along the Euphrates as it tumbles down from the northern Taurus mountains into the rolling fertile plains further south and east.

The town itself, crowded about with low dusky hills all fringed with apricot groves, olive trees and wild rose, remains a typical town under the Empire in the east in these troubled regions: it is a redoubt of Roman, Greek and Syrian culture surrounded in a hinterland of rough Cordueni hillmen and pastoralists. There are only a few outlying *villae* cast in the Senatorial mould. Small settlements cling precariously to the lower slopes of the Taurus, dependant on fragile crops and roaming herds of goats and sheep. Higher in the mountains, drift deserters, bandits, Christian mystics and the remnants of pagans - the latter now all but banished from the lower plains and valleys. War and invasion have not spared Cappadocia in the past but the town itself remains largely intact and free from devastation. Its people are a hardy mix of Cordueni natives and those Greek and Syrian families whose blood now is so intermingled that a sort of *patois* or *argot* is spoken in which Greek and Aramaic mix and flow like badly diluted wine.

On a low hill to the north of the town itself sits the old legionary camp of the Twelfth - now run-down and dilapidated. Ongoing excavations under Jacek's combined Polish/Turkish team have shown that in the Third and Fourth centuries, the original fort was reduced in size and re-configured from the classic playing-card shape into an uneven trapezoid which hugged the contours of the low hill and so provided better defence. Gateways are filled in, the ditch is widened, and protruding bastion towers able to support mural artillery are added. Jacek has estimated that a garrison of some two thousand soldiers was now quartered in the fort and this is borne out by the papyri records of a legion reduced now to three cohorts. We may conjecture that in the chaos of the Third Century, cohorts from the Twelfth were detached and marched away with various vexillations, never to return, and the legion has remained in its rump state as a consequence ever since.

Life drifts on for the Twelfth and the emerging papyri fragments detail a world which has changed little in over three hundred years as the following various extracts show:

'Ammidas, Optio, is granted ten days' furlough. He has three days' furlough also to return . . . The Centurion, Pamphilius the Bull, of the broad shoulders, Second Cohort, returned from the Dux at Sebestae with *tiros*, thirty in number, all empty wineskins of men . . . The *latrunculus*, Mammertus, together with eleven of his bandits, was caught at the Trident Crossing and apprehended. Two *milites* were slain and four wounded. Appropriate deductions to be made from the funeral fund . . .'

This hand, so methodical and persistent, and which at some point had made that mocking remark about our 'Corbulo', remains curiously detached from those figures about him - there are slighting remarks, for example, about a Centurion named Remus; Pamphilius is nicknamed for his broad shoulders; other fragments refer dismissively to the *curiales*, or town councillors, and also the *coloni* in the wider area or *territorium* of the town. On the whole, it seems, this is a hand which while meticulous is also bored and it does not take a genius to realise that in the daily monotony of life in a border legion, writing up such reports must have been dull in the extreme. A longer extract will illustrate this better than my words can:

'. . .The patrol returned late and under the command of a centurion clearly drunk. I refrain from naming him. In his wake filed a century of worn and sullen *milites*, all glowering at his back. Whether from resentment or jealousy, it was hard to tell. His report as dictated to me was confused and contradictory and left me with the distinct impression that the ten day march up and down the Melas river as ordered by the Primus Pilus Strabonius only covered a few days and the rest were spent idling about along the riverbank out of sight. I put it to him that he was in dereliction of his duty and he laughed openly in my face before spitting onto the papyrus and walking out. When I mentioned this later to Strabonius, he shrugged and told me to report it to the *Praefectus*. That has become a refrain now - any infraction or lapse from duty is coded with the phrase 'report it to the *Praefectus*'. In other words, shut up. And so I shrug too and write the reports and put them away for no-one to read. There is a joke here among the *veterani*: a dog with no master has an easy life . . .'

It is an irony, of course, that this hand which has left us so much detail and event in these fragmentary reports remains largely anonymous outside these papyri. It is possible to glean a little of his personality and his background (which I will leave for the reader to appreciate as it emerges in the extracts) but on the whole we know little save his name and his current posting. We may conjecture that he is educated for he writes in Latin and knows both Greek and that Aramaic/Syrian tongue prevalent in these regions. He is ambivalent about the Christian dogma being fought over in these intense times and yet also remains aloof from the old pagan traditions. There is a nagging sense in him that he has missed something or that something has passed him by - and that now he is idling in a faintly dismissive manner in a life which gives him no joy. Or is it that our reading of these dry Latin reports misconstrues his words? It will perhaps be impossible to know for certain. What is certain however is that this man - an *Adjutor*, or senior notary, in the Twelfth who is excused a battlefield commission as a result - pens and reports and observes as if he himself is never involved in it all. This is the hand of one Optatus, a man and an adjutant who, along with so many others in that old legion, hides a secret which his writings alone allows him to allude to - and it would be perhaps not unfair to state that in all things else this Optatus remains aloof but in these scrawls - and even then just a little - something of his heart emerges.

April is memorable not just for the onset of the storms and the river-flooding but also for the appearance of a troop of Arab federate cavalry, arriving towards the end of the month with sealed orders from the Dux Armenia. These rugged and olive-skinned nomads from deep in the arid tracts beyond Palestine and Arabia have been riding for a month north and west, under the care of

Roman supply masters, intent on reaching their new posting here at Melitene.

We know a little of the background of these desert fighters thanks to the surviving correspondence from their leader preserved in an annotated manuscript. I owe this discovery to none other than Sally McCarthy and her research into obscure Christian Arab literature. I first met her that following Winter in Turkey when she had heard about our papyri findings. I think, if I am honest now, Jacek had alerted her privately but when I challenged him about it, he merely shrugged and pulled that panama hat over his eyes against the sun. Looking back, I am surprised I was not more suspicious at the time but I think I was still wrapped up in this new insight and revelling in the joy of reading more about this Optatus and the shadow of 'Corbulo' which lay behind him. So it was that one brittle evening, Sally arrived in a trail of cigarette smoke to drag me out into a local tavern without so much as a formal introduction or a greeting smile. I warmed instantly to her manner - brusque, efficient, focused. She reminded me of those academics who have dug so deep into their own tiny niche that everything else in the world is nothing but a distraction. Within minutes she had grilled me about the papyri and Optatus and the sections where he writes about the arrival of the Arab federates. After I had finished mentioning what little I had read so far, she had leaned back in her chair, lit up another of her cigarettes and exhaled deeply, flicking the ash away. Then she looked me in the eye and smiled like a feline. It was then that she told me about her own research and one particular manuscript she was translating for the first time into English.

This manuscript had collated several ancient texts into one large tome with the intention to preserve something of the pre-Christian and pre-Islamic Arab literary traditions. Among the collection lay a series of letters written in Greek from one 'Ubayda to his father - a man who clearly had once been an important tribal leader of the Bani Al Jawn, who were active as Roman federates opposing Persian advances across the Harra and into Syria. With the demise of Julian amid the debacle of his Persian *excursus*, Arab loyalties had faltered and even reversed. This was then further exacerbated through the Arian tendencies of the new emperor Valens which had alienated the remaining Christian Arab federates. It seems however that one Arab tribe in particular had remained loyal and so suffered the persecutions of its rebelling neighbours as a result. In consequence, those remaining warriors have drifted north and west under Roman protection and have been organised into a cavalry *Ala* of some hundred or so light cavalry. These bear no Roman military ceremonial and present only savage faces as they ride into the main (now rebuilt) forum of Melitene. Their *Praepositus*, an Arab with the nominal Latin name of Obedianus, records his arrival in the first of many letters sent back to his father, a retired *phylarch* now living in the deserts south of Palmyra. It is worth quoting at some length for the light it shines on Melitene:

'. . . What is Rome, father, if all she presents now are no more than lazy soldiers in dull armour and faded crests? This little dusty town here where Roman and Greek names glide through the hills like phantoms lost and confused shows little spirit or mettle, I swear. My Arabs rode like *daemons* through the night and as we arrived into the forum of this town we roused only sleepy eyes or bored looks. The guards at the main gate were drunk as the morning sun rose and we were past them before they had even donned helmets and fumbled for their long spears. This town of Rome seems wrapped in a dream. A wisp of glory fading even as it is reached for. I know you fought for Rome for many years and sing of the glory of fighting under the Augustus Constantine but, father, I do not see this glory you mention. I see only thin men in torn tunicas and whose standards and banners seem as faded as this hymn of Rome itself. I know you urged me to seek service with this new Emperor in his war against Shapur, that Sassanid dog, especially after his Arab hirelings savaged our desert oases last year, but I wonder now whether I have brought my warriors here to fight only for a dying Empire too wrapped up in its past to forge a new future? I am your loyal son, father, and will honour my pledge to you, this I swear. Remember this however: we will fight for Rome to revenge our fallen, no matter how dull and old the camel of Rome is now, for you alone, father, for you – Obedianus, once 'Ubayda, of the tribe of the Al Jawn, may Ishtar and Ailat shine down upon us all . . .'

A terse entry from our Roman *Adjutor*, Optatus, a day later reports the Roman attitude to the new arrivals:

' . . . An *Ala* of *Saraceni* arrived commanded by the *Praepositus*, Obedianus. Sealed orders were presented and opened under the standards of the Twelfth and in the presence of the Primus Pilus, Strabonius, and the senior centurions commanding the two cohorts. It was a struggle to understand Obedianus' Latin . . .'

No record remains of exactly why the nomad federates had been posted specifically to Melitene so far to the north and their desert homes. However, given the huge logistical re-ordering of troops and supplies all across the Diocese of the Oriens to counter the Persian threat of invasion, even if only as a bluff, it is probable that these federates were relocating further towards a *limes* where its loyalties would not be tested against Arab brethren. Be that as it may, an interesting tension builds up as the lack of a commanding officer for the legion, now filled by the Primus Pilus, or chief centurion, Strabonius, means that technically, Obedianus or 'Ubayda, as *Praepositus* of the Arabs, outranks all other Roman officers in the town:

'. . . Five amphorae of wine requisitioned by the *foederati* under express orders of Obedianus. None left for the Fulminata . . . Obedianus reprieves a Jewish merchant from flogging by the Centurion, Remus, of the First Cohort. Much olives and honey is lavished upon him by this merchant . . . The *foederati* excused from deep patrol of the Analaean Hills due to pagan rites. Twelve later arrested for drunken behaviour . . .'

This tension, as we will see, is only to get worse.

CHAPTER TWO

The month of April then brings only an increased friction among the soldiers of the Twelfth Legion as they share their billets and supplies with a small cavalry troop of Arab federates. Reports sent back to the *officium* of the Dux Armenia, Brachius, allude to the indiscipline of the desert riders under Obedianus and their continual dereliction of duty. Fights occur. Supplies are requisitioned unfairly. Billets are taken against the wishes of the soldiers. All sealed with the orders of the Arab *Praepositus* against whom the legion can only muster a senior centurion, the Primus Pilus, Strabonius. It would seem that this Arab commander, Obedianus, once called 'Ubayda, is skilled in enlisting the townsfolk of Melitene against the men of the Twelfth for we have a solitary epistle from one Ennadius, a *curialis* of the town, who writes to his brother in Antioch, praising the newly-arrived federates over the incumbent men of the border legion:

'. . . And what prayers have been answered, my Florentius, that brought such doughty fighters into our desert town? What offerings pleased the gods to bring such fierce fellows into our walls to provide for our defence in these uncertain times? Truly the Sacred Emperor is blessed to have such men under his Imperial standards!'

While reports from the legion filter back to the Dux ensconced in the provincial capital of Sebestae complaining about the behaviour of the Arabs, it seems that 'Ubayda has already wooed the townsfolk of Melitene and turned them against the legionaries. We must remember however that all this ill-will results not from genuine mistrust between Arab and Roman, christian or pagan, but rather from a broken military hierarchy which allows the federate allies of the Empire to usurp the legion's status in Melitene.

One report – again written in the same hand which wrote the *graffito* – sums it up:

'. . . These *Saraceni* roll through the town and the legion castra as if they owned it, overriding the *milites* of the Twelfth like a wind blowing rubbish about. What can the legion do if there is no head to guide and order it? The Primus Pilus, Strabonius, knows he is merely an incumbent with no power while the other centurions in among the cohorts bicker amongst each other like Gallic fishwives. What is a Legion with no *Praefectus* over it? What is an Empire with no Augustus to rule it? Plant a head upon us that we may raise our eyes to our standards once more, illustrious Dux . . .'

The unspoken question which has been hovering in the background regarding this legion must surely be what exactly occurred to deprive it of its commanding officer in such a manner that no replacement is found? What happened that left this ancient legion languishing in Melitene in a time of imminent invasion? The Twelfth itself has had a chequered history, it must be said. One which does not lend itself to glory or honour. It was originally formed by Caesar himself in preparation for a campaign against the Helvetii along with its sister legion, the Eleventh. Over the years and centuries, it saw action at Pharsalus with Caesar, at Actium under Mark Anthony (where he honoured it with the sobriquet *antiqua* for its veteran status), and was part of Lucius Paetus' expeditionary force into Armenia to shore up the collapsing regime of Tigranes.

It was here that the first of its many misfortunes began.

Mismanagement, arrogance and timidity allowed a Parthian force under Vologases to defeat the legions under Paetus' command such that each one, including the Twelfth, had to swear under their own Eagles never to invade Armenia again. It was Gnaeus Corbulo - and it is perhaps no surprise that this name occurs here in the past - himself who later invaded Armenia in retaliation with several legions under his command and won spectacular victories over the Parthian and Armenian troops opposed to him. The Twelfth was not among those legions, however - judged by Corbulo to be 'unfit for battle.'

It subsequently acquired a further tarnishing of its reputation a few years later during the ill-fated Judean campaign which saw the Legate of Syria, Cestus Gallus, march the Twelfth up to the walls of Jerusalem itself only to retire in utter disarray even as those walls were about to fall. What followed was an unmitigated disaster wherein the Twelfth not only abandoned it baggage, artillery, and supplies, it was also butchered in the notorious Beth Horon pass and lost the Eagle itself to the Jewish forces. Again, as with Corbulo, a Roman returned in vengeance and this time it was the future emperor Vespasian himself. Due to desperate measures, he did not have the luxury of allowing the disgraced Twelfth, the 'Thundering' Legion, to languish in shame but was forced to bring it along even back to the walls of Jerusalem itself. There it fought wrapped in bitterness and dishonour even to the moment when it was cut to ribbons by the very artillery it had abandoned earlier. Once the Jews had been vanquished and Judea brought back into the Roman fold, Vespasian relocated the men of the Twelfth to garrison Melitene as a punishment for this once glorious legion. Here it has remained now for some three hundred years and in that time it has passed from shame and ridicule to neglect and poverty.

The Twelfth is a legion habituated now merely to garrison and patrolling duties here along the dusty and rugged frontier which nestles up against the mighty Euphrates river. It is graded as a *limitanei* legion and as such receives lesser pay and status than the field army legions in the interior. Only the left-over recruits are allocated to its ranks and it rarely receives fresh armour or weapons from the state fabricae. It is an old legion now, still holding to the ranks and the grades we recognise under the Principate - the *Praefectus* commands the legion, centurions swagger along the files and ranks such as this Remus mentioned above or the bull-shouldered Pamphilius, cohorts and centuries still muster under the old disgraced Eagle (although how and when it was returned, no writer has told us). Unlike the newer legions, smaller and tactically more flexible, the Twelfth remains a static and moribund legion.

It has not marched abroad for over a hundred years and, more interestingly, with its ranks filled with thin Cappadocian and Anatolian farmers, all from a land deeply Christianised, the Twelfth is now emerging as a revered legion in the burgeoning annals of Christianity. Who in the east of Rome has not heard of the Forty Martyrs of Sebestae from the Twelfth and their awful fate upon that frozen lake, for example? Not to mention the myth perpetuated by Eusebius himself wherein the legion was trapped in a parched defile, under siege from Sarmatians, and is driven in desperation to pray to Christ. And it is Christ alone who sent a mighty thunder-storm in their honour and so drove away the barbarians in fear and terror? A deed revered in the memories and annals of this legion so much so that the crossed thunderbolts of Jove that grace the shields of this Legion is surmounted now by the frowning face of God Himself. No, the Twelfth now is honoured by Christian writers of this period - such as Basil and Gregory, for example - both for the martyrs who shadow its ranks and also the miracles it has seen in its past. One is tempted to wonder on the *psyche* of a legion such that it moves from shame and poverty to embrace a religion which elevates forgiveness and rebirth above all - and also on a legend wherein a legion is saved not by martial valour from its enemies but instead a resort to *prayers* . . .

All of which brings us no closer to the specific situation the Twelfth now finds itself in. While historically both Tacitus and Josephus illuminate this legion's past dishonours, our only real contemporary historian, Ammianus, remains silent on our legion and so provides no guide to us for an answer to its present state.

We have two pieces of the puzzle already in place however: namely, the *graffito* found at Melitene besmirching a certain 'Corbulo' and also the reports from the *praesidium* of the legion written by the same hand. We can deduce that the men of the Twelfth are hardly front-line crack troops, given that the Emperor is already mobilising several field army regiments across the Diocese into potential jumping off points around Edessa and Amida and the Twelfth is not among them (as yet) and that a small Arab cavalry force is able to bully them around. We can also surmise that the administrative officers of the Twelfth (amongst whom is our *graffito* writer) are desperate to receive a new commander only to be rebuffed time and again.

For another piece of the puzzle, I want to move us south and west some one hundred Roman miles, across the dusty roads of Cappadocia and the high plateau of Anatolia, towards the remote villages and farmlands north of Arabissus, deeper into the rugged Taurus mountains among which dwell the Isaurians. Here, amid all the turmoil of imperial forces toiling against these brigands and mountain robbers, we find a small elite legion marching along obscure paths eastwards. It marches with full *impedimenta* not along the main Roman road east to Edessa and Amida but instead along mountain paths and goat-tracks and dry, dusty, riverbeds away from the small hill villages and fortified villas. It marches with discipline and order and it marches in newly-minted armour and weapons from the State Fabrica at Caesarea itself.

We must thank Sally McCarthy again whose dedicated work has allowed my own research to join up with various papyri and records she herself had been working on for quite some time. Already, her work on the Arabic documents had allowed her to link other works and papyri and those efforts led now to the small presence of this legion and the connections it will allow me to make to that poor and discredited legion of the Twelfth, now languishing at Melitene . . .

This legion is the Solenses Seniores, or Senior Sol legion, the Legion of the Sun, and is enrolled under the Lists of the Notitia Dignitatum as a front line field army legion. It is graded as a *palatina* unit - the highest grade in the imperial army structures of Rome. We know little of the origin and history of this legion but can deduce that it was formed by Julian from his Gallic recruits early in his accession due to the fact that it carries the Sun or Helios emblem as both its name and the design upon its oval shield. This emperor, before he fell in the Persian deserts, was devoted to the worship of Sol and it is from around this period that this legion first makes its appearance. It can be reasonably conjectured that rather than transferring entire legions east for his Persian adventure, Julian instead enrols volunteers from those Gallic and Rhine legions into newly-created units. Units named after Sol, for example, and therefore favoured by him. We also know that with the election of Valentinian after the demise of Julian and then Jovian, this new emperor had been urged to nominate a partner to aid him in ruling the vast empire. This Illyrian had chosen - against much advice - his brother Valens, and then together they had divided the attendant field army and civil staff into two halves - one for the West under Valentinian and one for the East under Valens. We can surmise that the original Sol legion formed by Julian was split at this time into a Senior and a Junior unit with both units then being recruited back up to full strength. In a gesture of surprising generosity, Valentinian further ceded Illyricum to Valens with all the tough recruiting grounds it afforded and where the Senior Sol Legion was now stationed. Hence this legion's presence now in the East under Valens rather than with his older brother in the West.

This legion, then, is one of the newer field army legions, smaller and leaner than the old bloated legions of which the Twelfth is an example. Here, in its ranks, we find titles and grades which are unfamiliar to the student of traditional Roman military history - gone is the centurion, the *praefectus*, the optio, for example, and in their stead stands the centenarius, the tribune, the primicerius and the biarchus. This is a legion which still fights under an Eagle but stands at around a thousand men in strength, ordered in six maniples or *numeri*, each made up of two centuries of around eighty men. As such, it would normally be twinned with another legion of equal status and together they would stand side-by-side in a battle line. Now, however, in the re-organisation prompted both by Valens' *excursus* over the Danube into Gothic territory and the movement of troops around the Syrian and Armenian *limes*, we find this legion alone and marching east and north over mottled hills and dry rugged valleys, the proud 'Sol' emblem on its shields all dusty and faded, while the old Latin marching songs litter the air in its wake and crude jokes hang lightly about its fringes. There is a confidence in the ranks and files of the Sol legion which speaks both to its status in the *exercitus* of Rome and also to the fibre of the men under its standards.

Being a newly-formed palatine army legion, recruited from volunteers and veterans from other legions, all outfitted in the best weapons and armour the state factories could manufacture, it may be asked what it was doing marching in the hinterland of Cappadocia – a march surely calculated to add several days on to its itinerary in an atmosphere where speed and dispatch would seem to be of critical importance. The answer may be found in the following report from one Scorpianus, a Ducenarius, or commander, of the Third Maniple to Asellus, the Primicerius, or second in command, of the legion:

'. . . The men are wearied but remain steadfast under this Cappadocian heat and the high sun, *Dominus*. Of that there can be no doubt. Of the ranks in the Third Maniple, scarcely one hundred and thirty men remain at the standards however. This long march in the fringes of this hinterland bakes the men and causes them to falter like *coloni* in the fields after a drought. The urging of the centenarii is rarely needed each mile to force them on but no one among this Maniple has ever laboured under such heat before. *Dominus*, I know our Tribune daily reinforces this need to march but know that my *milites* suffer. Truly we lament the soft stars of a Gallic sky and the sighing waters of the Liger and the Rhenus in this empty iron land . . .'

These men, all born in the green and lush lands of Gaul or along the tangled banks of the Rhine, or, lately from the tough verdant mountains of Illyricum, are being inured to the desert lands of the Orient and are learning again what it is to march and fight in bright armour under a molten sun. There are no Saxon barbarians hiding in dank woods and forests now, glowering at them from within deep shadows, but instead olive-skinned bandits or skirmishers, all faint and evasive in the distance. These men of the Senior Sol Legion are being re-trained methodically in desert and hill warfare by a cold and distant task-master who is broking no soft quick route to the staging posts ahead around Edessa and Amida. Not only is the legion marching to a new posting in the east, its Tribune is using that march to school and inure his men in a new and merciless climate.

And you can imagine my surprise when, one evening with Sally at my side pointing out phrases and connections, I soon found out that that solitary report from the Ducenarius of the Third Maniple alludes to a Tribune who, it turns out, is none other than our 'Corbulo' himself, that man dismissed so sarcastically by Optatus on the pottery shard. That is not his real name, of course, and therein lies most of the mystery surrounding his character and the cryptic *graffito* found in Melitene . . .

Flavius Anicius, Tribune, commanding the Solenses Seniores Legio Palatina, on route to Amida from Arabissus in full marching order, is referenced twice in relation to the Gallic-filled legion as 'Corbulo' rather than his usual title and name, that of Tribune Anicius, and both references are typical of a western Gallic or Germanic morbid humour:

'. . . 'Corbulo' suffers this heat as a pup hyena takes to rancid meat, I swear (*from a fragment of a letter to a brother in Lugudunum*) . . . Daily he struts around the men in full amour and wielding his officer's staff without let. The Celts and Germans in the Legion begrudge him not his cold discipline and eye for detail but find his reverence for the old Romans gods and ways ill fitting now in this supine heat. Drink well of the wine, my brother, for here in the arid hills we lick at best only our own sweat . . .'

Again, in a dispatch to the state weapons-factory at Caesarea, an unnamed legion subaltern mentions:

'. . . Our arms break and bend in this incessant drill. Pray amend our toils with fresh provender and urge the slaves and craftsmen of the Fabrica to work without let that we may re-arm and re-kit with all haste. This 'Corbulo' chaffs at all delays and enquires of me where his re-supplies are. His youthful brows, I swear, thunder like old Jupiter's in a storm and render his face more a comic mask than a tragedian's leer! Yours, ever felix and faithful . . .'

And so I had him.

In less than a year since that fragment had been found in the dirt, I had 'Corbulo' in my hands, so to speak. In the Prosopography of the Later Roman Empire, we find that Flavius Anicius Bassas, is a scion of the ancient *gens* of the Anicii in Rome. Around him and before him stand a clutch of powerful and rich relatives who have moved and coloured the Empire in various ways and always to the advantage of the Anicii. His father held the Consulship some seventeen years earlier. One of his relatives was the immensely powerful figure of Sextus Claudius Petronius Probus, whom Ammianus Marcellinus disparages so much in his history, and who is about to assume the post of Praetorian Prefect of Italy. In future years, such names as Symmachus, Boethius, and two emperors, Petronius Maximus and later Olybrius, will all emerge from that powerful *gens*.

As to Flavius Anicius himself, son of an ex-Consul of Rome and commanding one of the elite legions, we find that he is deeply pagan and so at odds to the later Christian Emperors after Julian. He has risen from the Domestic Protectors to command first an auxiliary cohort on the *limes*, then escort an ambassadorial mission to the Bosporus kingdom - one which earned him a promotion and a glowing letter from the Senator Themistius which was read out to the Senate of Constantinople, suggesting the success of that mission - before being re-assigned and fading from our scant records. Some years pass and he has resurfaced now as Tribune in command of a palatine army legion en route into the east and the city of Amida at the edge of the empire itself. In these slight references in the Prosopography, however, there is no mention of a nickname nor any mocking references. It falls to the work of Sally who unearthed these later epistles and reports of the Sol Legion and the two references to his tag as 'Corbulo' to add to that record. That and the shard I had found in the dirt.

This is obviously a young if proud officer-soldier in the old mould of Rome, hence the derogatory nick-name of 'Corbulo', after Gnaeus Domitius Corbulo, the legendary Roman general renowned for his discipline and unyielding loyalty to command. It is therefore not inappropriate also that the Senior Sol Legion marches to battle under the Eagle of Rome and to the somewhat mocking battle-cry of *'Axios, Axios, Axios!'* or '(he is) Worthy!' in response to the commands of this young Tribune. Words which were Corbulo's fatal last to Nero when the latter ordered him to commit suicide - words whose grim morbidity must have appealed to certain well-read officers in this legion. As with all veterans, it is a humour well suited to fighting men and it is to be wondered on the reaction of this Flavius Anicius that he both allows it and ignores it at the same time.

What, we wonder then, prompted the scandalous reference to him being nothing more than a lazy Aegyptian eunuch from that *Adjutor* of the languishing Twelfth? Why did this Optatus coin a derogatory name for a young man clearly aristocratic and martial? The missing years from the lapse of his command of the mission to the Bosporus kingdom gives us a hint - for those years correspond almost exactly with a gap in our records regarding the Twelfth Fulminata, toiling rudderless as it were now at Melitene, and that single *graffito* written by one of its headquarters' officers, our *Adjutor*. Is it a sarcastic comment penned in anger to mock an upstart disciplinarian? A desperate attempt to besmirch his character, perhaps? Or a political ploy designed to stir up discontent in Sebestae where the Dux, Brachius, resided? Or something much darker? What we do know is that it is a fair assumption that prior to his appointment as Tribune of the Sol Legion, Anicius must have held command over the Twelfth at Melitene in reward for the success of that mission and that something happened during that time which facilitated his removal with all haste and the subsequent disgrace of the legion by not replacing him. Whatever it was that happened, it left Anicius in charge of a palatine legion, filled with Gauls, Germans and Illyrians, all hard-bitten veterans of the West, while the Twelfth was punished and left to languish in a rotting border town, leaderless and forgotten. Yet it must be wondered on the vagaries of a History wherein what was once sundered in mystery and shame is soon be reunited in the most unlooked for manner.

Looking back now I still remember those first few hints of our Flavius Anicius in those early reports and I can still hold in my mind's eye how I pictured him among his veteran legionaries - striding purposefully among the ranks, his harsh face a curious mixture of imperial haughtiness and that green of youth yet to be burned away in time and experience. I imagined him on foot of course - not for him the comfortable saddle of the Roman nobility - a hard-pressed slave in his wake holding his shield and helmet, his subordinates and officers around him like a phalanx of authority. Behind and to his flanks march the soldiers of the Legion of the Sun, all perhaps eyeing him with a strange mood of respect and resentment. Respect for his harsh discipline and resentment for the unending slog in the Cappadocian heat. Of course I allow a certain romanticism to colour that view now. Now that I know his fate of course. How could I not? Flavius Anicius will march and fight both into a future as yet unknown and also back into a past which still in many ways scars him. A past which the pottery fragment only barely hints at. As the god Janus looks both backwards and forwards and as each step is always also towards and away, so will this poor man travel and cross thresholds like mirrors. As did I many years later when I stood before that ancient stone portal with his shadow so faint and evasive all about me.

So, yes, I imagined him striding on foot among his men. To Sally he was nothing but a key to her Arab federate - a piece of a mosaic she was building up of both him and his doomed tribe - but to me he was the symbol of my new purpose and as such he walked as I did then with purpose and with drive. Only with me I had yet to see that double shadow he walked in and which would one day leave both of us alone and deep in the dark . . .

CHAPTER THREE

That long march through the remote hills and barren warrens of Cappadocia, under the sun and with the dust always lapping at them, is always towards the large fortress town of Amida, of the Black Walls, nestling up against the Tigris. A city taken by siege some eight years earlier by none other than Shapur II himself. The great historian Ammianus Marcellinus leaves us with a gripping and fateful narrative of that siege - one which he himself participated in and which he barely escaped from. Amida had been sacked brutally following a seventy three day siege but by its resistance had halted the ambitions of the *ShahanShan*. Reoccupied and rebuilt under Julian, Amida now bestrides that precarious boundary or frontier which sees the newly acquired territories under the Sassanians abut against the coveted jewel of Armenia in the north. Here, among the flowing banks of the Tigris, the city - famed for its black defensive walls of basalt rock - stands as a lonely bastion and a sentinel of Rome. It is here around Amida in the first months in the new year of the Consuls Lupicinus and Jovinus that sees key elements of the eastern army assemble under various officers, tribunes and *comites* in response to the uneasy state of affairs which exists now between Rome and Persia. Rumblings and troop movements across the Tigris hint that Shapur is now preparing for a massive invasion but whether up into Armenia or west across the Tigris and towards the Euphrates and Syria, no one knows for certain. What *is* certain is that alarm and panic ripples all along the *limes* here - with traders and monks flooding back westwards, mingled in with herders, villagers, notaries, and desperate army *exploratores*, the latter all lathered in dust and sweat. Amida heaves with life but it is a frenzied life speckled now with fear and uneasy tension. Fights break out in the streets. Food requisitions and military drafts provoke anger and bitterness. Long streams of refugees from the great Tigris itself move incessantly by day and night - and they all report that across that river, deep in the newly won lands under Persian suzerainty, the long glittering columns of Sassanian mailed cavalry roam the land under high silk banners, their frozen masks cold and implacable.

We remain on the whole ignorant about Shapur's larger strategic aims regarding the Roman Empire under Valens in these early years of the latter's reign. It is well known that Shapur laid claim to all the old Achaemenid Persian lands even into Thrace itself as an ancestral right but current consensus sees in this nothing more than posturing designed to wring more concessions from a still-green emperor. What *is* certain is that Shapur coveted Armenia - for one of the clauses in the treaty he gained from the previous emperor Jovian after

Julian's death promised Roman inaction should the Persian empire stretch out and meddle in that land. Rome is banned from sending any aid, or militarily intervening, or otherwise intruding into Armenia, no matter what Shapur deigns to do there. This had been a bitter pill to swallow by Jovian but one he had had no choice in. Now Armenia, and its king Arsaces, once a loyal ally, has been all but abandoned by Rome. This is a treaty considered by many Romans as shameful. Already agitators inside the empire are calling for Valens to abjure its terms as ones imposed by force and therefore no longer applicable. Others are decrying Roman weakness and urging revenge. This, we can surmise, would have been known to Shapur's agents and it is no surprise that we see his ambassadors earnestly reminding Valens through his intermediaries that he is bound by oath to honour those terms.

We are fortunate to have a window into this process from the energetic pen of a certain Macrobius, a notary under Lupicinus, the Magister Equitum per Orientem, who, in an earnest and hastily written epistle to Basil of Cappadocia, paints a sharp miniature for him of events late in March, 367 AD, at Amida. Satraps and nobles from the court of Shapur have arrived in that city to protest the build up of troops and materiel while at the same time reminding the Magister of the terms of the recent treaty. It seems that Lupicinus, co-Consul for the year, adopts a certain *tone* in the meeting which is not lost on these satraps, as described by Macrobius:

'. . . The Magister partook of a light evening repast in the manner of soldiers on campaign and received into his illustrious presence the dignitaries from Persia, that land of the fleeting deserts and swift horses, and they, amazed at his stark dress, protested that it was not proper for a high officer of an Empire to sit upon a canvas stool and break bread as a simple soldier. And the Magister smiled at them and said in a soft manner, as if teaching a child, that he did not need more than was provided, and was not the Roman Empire for the benefit not of he himself but of all its subjects under the largesse of Christ and the One God? And as he ate only that which was needed so too did he order, in Valen's August name, all which was only fit to be under his domain and not one province more nor less. These Persians understood then by his manner that this officer of the Emperor in the old Roman austere ways would not grab onto his plate more than was fit nor surrender up from it one crumb that was not his. And so the Persians left, empty of stomach, as it were, and knew that war was brewing upon the horizons of Mesopotamia as surely as if Shapur himself were to shoot the arrow . . .'

Over a month has passed now since the formal cessation of talks by Shapur subsequent to this event. Trade routes have been closed and the great Silk Road is barred from Roman merchants. Nestorian Christians fleeing from

Valen's Arian heresy move eastwards into the dim and unknown lands of Persia and are accommodated into remote communities under Shapur's benediction - a move calculated to inflame religious tensions inside the Empire. Various political overtures are made secretly on both sides but always end in stalemate: Shapur stands by his initial demand for suzerainty over Armenia and the return of the lands around the upper Tigris. Valens responds with firm refusals and then begins to assemble the main Roman field army in the Orient around Edessa and Amida with its outlying towns and forts, under the overall command of his Magister, Lupicinus, known fondly as 'The Wolf' by his troops. By the end of April, Edessa has become a massive munitions and logistical base for the units of the army. The bulk of the field army of the Oriens together with elements drawn from various ducal border commands are gradually assembling in and around Edessa and to a lesser degree, Amida itself. We can imagine many more units being assembled throughout these short months. From Antioch, Palmyra, Bostra, Damascus, and all over the Oriens, troops are being called to the standards and then marched eastwards to join their brethren. Elite palatine legions and cavalry vexillations, the main bulk of the field army, and even the border or *limitanei* troops are all being drafted into what Valen's court panegyricist, Themistius, is now calling the Great Rebuke. Persian hostility and arrogance is being rebuked in harsh terms by Roman martial valour and strict discipline and we might imagine in the hearts and minds of the Romans all swept up in this great mustering a pride and eagerness to once again fasten the Persian snake in the claws of the Roman Eagle.

Except that it is all a gamble, of course.

Valens has no intention of invading Persia, keen as he is to crush the Gothic threat across the Danube. Valen's empire is far from secure and he needs time to stabilise it - time which a massive Persian distraction simply will not give him. This mustering of Roman troops and standards along the desert *limes* between Rome and the Sassanid lands, it has generally been agreed, is nothing more than a show of resolve to compliment the staged evening meal for the ambassadors quoted above. In other words, the Augustus is bluffing and it is a bluff it must be said which has a degree of desperation attendant to it . . .

All of which is of little interest as yet to the Twelfth. All through this, we find that our poor scribe and duty-officer is penning yet more endless reports and tiresome dispatches. Life seems to grind on for the men in this border legion almost as if the wider world outside is passing them by. A little drama is mixed into the pot with the antics of the Arab federates and there is a vague sense that important events are happening - but always, it seems, over the horizon:

'. . . The hinges on the south portus have rusted with under-use and now the grumbling *milites* are complaining that it must be the slaves and farmers who should wrestle the gates down so that new fittings can be placed into the sockets. A crowd of local *coloni* was herded up and cursed into place, under the gaze of Remus, his staff always slick now with blood. Then the *Saraceni* were among them, like wraiths, like desert hawks, and the dust from their horses' hooves caused the *milites* to cough and curse them all. It was Obedianus alone who dismounted and wrenched the staff from his hands and flung it away. I saw Remus shoulder himself up against that Arab, his eyes dark and narrowed, but as the latter remained standing before him, a lion against a jackal, the centurion was then forced to laugh suddenly as if some poor joke had been made and stride away. The *milites* followed him, muttering uneasy threats and curses. The portus remains rusted still. Should I look at that gateway now and see a symbol perhaps? It would be too easy, too easy . . .

. . . The town *curiales* protested at the imposition of Iacob, ordained in Constantinople, a follower of the Arian creed now favoured by the Sacred Augustus. They cited letters from Basil of Caesarea and Gregory of Nazianzus, allowing those of the Nicene creed to be ministered by a priest of their own faith, as allowed previously by the Sacred Valens, Augustus. They were ignored by Strabonius and escorted from the castra back to the town. Many insults and stones were thrown at the escorts. The *Saraceni* looked on, smirking . . .

. . . Sealed orders from the Dux Armenia arrived on the Kalends of Maius with, we hoped, word of a new commander. I saw the disappointment on the face of our Primus Pilus even before he read out the words to the combined presence of the senior centurions of the legion. To the praise of the Forty, Strabonius detailed various orders from the Dux: the cohort under Cyrion is to be recalled from Auaxa and the fort to be handed over to a vexillation of Dalmatian Horse, under the command of the Tribune, Severianus. The new bishop of the Arian faith, now that he is installed over the fickle populace of Melitene, will be given any aid he requests and any rioting or provocation as a result is to be suppressed without mercy. All furlough is herewith cancelled due to the tensions along the frontier. The grain horrae are to surrender one third of all annonae to the provincial collectors by the end of the month. And so on. And so on. This litany of orders remained dry and listless and we all looked deeply in the face of Strabonius for some recognition of this but all we saw was his usual evasive shrug. I saw him lick his lips repeatedly and his fingers seemed to shake as he held the papyri. Around me, the senior staff looked away, bored. A few fidgeted. Probus, the Aquilifer, his waxen hair shining in the lamplight like that of an Anthiochan whore, smiled brazenly at us all - and we, in our torpor indulged him. How could we not? What *Praefectus* was there to report him to? He is Aquilifer in name and not deed - and that deed which is his stains us all now; a curse; a dark thing. And so he smiles alone among us all like a rabid dog all other dogs are too afraid to approach - even as the orders of shame and neglect drift down around us like bitter leaves . . .'

This is the first mention in the papyri of the Aquilifer, Probus. It is clear that Optatus feels deeply conflicted about this man and is using the writings to in some way both condemn him and also redeem himself - but alas he refrains from truly committing to that act. Our scribe however does leave his readers with no illusions about this Probus and his responsibility at having something to do with the removal of Flavius Anicius and the subsequent rudderless state of the legion - despite acknowledging that whatever happened is the responsibility of them all. In some fashion, however, certainly according to Optatus, this Probus is made to bear a larger share. It seems that his presence among the centurions and other senior veterans remains a dominant one which our scribe seems to passively accept.

Unknown to the Twelfth however, as April drags on into May and its legionaries struggle now to repair the north gateway or slouch through Melitene under the sullen eyes of the townsfolk or simply stand idly around the gates of the town or the legion castra, a storm is about to break over the distant Tigris which will change everything . . .

CHAPTER FOUR

It is the first day of May and the weather is unseasonably warm for the year. Tensions all along the banks of the Tigris have remained high with refugees moving west and north all clothed in dust and choused with the squeal of babies and the braying of tired mules and asses. The trading barges moving up and down the river are absent now and the long caravansaries snaking out of the distant Mesopotamian oases have long since ceased to appear. The day begins under a faint purple wash from the east as the last glitter of the stars fade away in a stillness which is preternatural and some would remark portentous. As the oriental sun rises high over the fertile lands and irrigation ditches about the Tigris, a great long shadow is seen to emerge from that purple dusk - a shadow which rustles and gleams under that imperial dawn as column after column of mailed cavalry and lightly-clad horse archers move purposefully northwards towards the river. Mantled by the faint sparkling diadem of a tumult of torches, a Persian army emerges into the day and then heads with one inexorable purpose towards that river with the sole intent to parallel it and then breach into the Roman Empire.

Out of the shimmering haze and the distant sands arises a host of Sassanid steel like a molten river pouring forth from a hot forge and at its head floats the gleaming banners of the Houses of Sassan while in its wake toils the infantry and the slaves and the rabble and all the baggage and train of a mighty army on the move. Above it all, rises the high silk emblem of the Persian *Shahin*, the 'royal falcon', while below and to the right in the place of honour flutters a proud commingled sun and crescent moon - the symbol of the House Karen-Pahlavi, held aloft now by Ardawan Karen-Pahlavi, the *Spahbad* or army commander of Shapur. Beneath these proud silk banners ride the feared Persian heavy cataphracts, the *Savaran* of the noble houses, shining like a host of stars. This great mass, wreathed in silk and iron, moves north from Nisibis, that once proud Roman fortress now surrendered over to Persian suzerainty, up into the banks of the Tigris and then turns with a great shroud of dust in its wake along that river westwards and towards Amida, with the rugged spine of the Masius mountain to its left.

Those too slow to evade that endless army - Roman *exploratores*, perhaps, hiding in low gulches or among the rougher crags of the Masius mountain, or unwary monks still foot-sore from tramping back out of the fastness of prayer and meditation, or tax assessors half-asleep on low carts, a few *limitanei* guards acting as escort - will have heard perhaps, deep in that dust and low murmur of laughter, the *chthonic* moan of the feared Persian elephants as those dark and weighty behemoths strode and ambled leisurely among the mailed cuirassiers, their mahouts shouting out ribald jokes to one another. A brief mention in the Nestorian Church History of Mardessus alludes to the Persian host being three miles in length and covering the land like a horde of locusts. Putting Biblical rhetoric aside for a moment, it is worth noting that our chronicler includes the detail that among the Persians were renegade Christian *Saraceni*, the slit-eyed Hunnic Chionitae of Grumbates and even tall long-limbed Nubian and Auxumite warriors, all clad in antelope skins and sporting ostrich feathers. One can detect in this brief and all too erratic notice the tremor of a man overawed at what he is witnessing . . .

And so it is that five days after the first sighting of these Sassanids pushing west and north up the left side of the Tigris towards Amida, a dusty rider is seen to gallop under the main gate of the castra of the Twelfth at Melitene. This rider, an unattached officer from the *officium* of the Magister, all vexed at the sorry state of the soldiers about him, tumbles from his mount and then thrusts hastily written orders into the hands of a startled Strabonius. This Primus Pilus, a man who evades as much as he commands, finds scrawled in the wax of that tablet three simple Latin words:

'*March to Amida.*'

It is the afternoon, all dusty with the tramp of the returning Third Cohort, now relieved from Auaxa by a vexillation of Dalmatian Horse, and the castra is a riot of tired men, mules, slaves and that endless throng of wives and children who follow the men of the legion from time immemorial. There is a single moment in which Strabonius remains lost for words or deeds and in which he holds that wax tablet with its damning scrawl as though it is a strange object, some dream thing which has drifted unlooked for into his own realm and which he would wish would vanish again as quickly. Men and animals mass past him into the castra, all lathered in dust and dirt, shouting out rough greetings to sweethearts or old comrades, while others exchange rude oaths over money still owed or feuds still hot and egregious. Probus struts about one parapet, his waxen hair gleaming in the sun, a calculating smile on his lips, while in the shadow of a portico leading into the *praesidium*, a small coterie of senior centurions snatch at a wineskin and look askance at the tired Cyrion as he leads the Third back into its permanent camp. No one notices the Primus Pilus alone amid it all with that harsh bronzen tablet in his hands. This man has long ago lost the ability to command attention and inquiry from those officers about him.

It falls finally to Cyrion, Centurion and *Praepositus* of the Third Cohort, to hesitate as he marches past, a gorgeous cloak of Sidonian wool twisted over one arm, the other grasping his vine staff, to reach out to grasp the Primus Pilus on the shoulder. The shock of that physical contact allows Strabonius a small jolt of fear and without speaking he hands over the tablet and its uneasy words.

'. . . I never saw Cyrion smile so much before. It was like seeing a hunter scent a pray which not only has eluded him but which he was not even aware of in the first place. He stood still, that smile cracking his face apart with relish, the cloak wreathed about his arm as he held that tablet, and I swear that I looked upon not a soldier of Rome but instead some mythic figure reborn. And such a contrast - Cyrion, smiling, his face lit-up as if with arcane pleasure, and Strabonius beside him, almost pleading, a vague unease and even trepidation spreading over his face. I stood up from my canvas stool and craned my neck forwards, wondering what it was that had provoked such disparate reactions - and felt a cold hard knot forming in my stomach. Everything was a wash of confusion about those two as the Third in all its tired train moved past them both and yet they stood there as if divorced from it all - complicit yet opposed. Above on the parapet, I saw Probus frown then and bark out an order to one of his slaves - and I knew then that he had seen what I had seen . . .'

A meeting is hastily convened that evening in the legion's *praesidium* and it is a fractious meeting, to say the least. The messenger has gone to deliver more curt orders, no doubt, leaving Strabonius alone with that bronze tablet. Behind a low trestle table and flanked by the cohortal commanders, Strabonius attempts to diffuse a crowd of lesser centurions and other officers of the Twelfth while outside mill most of the legionaries intermingling with their wives and children. Raucous shouts and oaths rise and fall within the smoky hall while slaves move hither and thither with amphorae of wine. Again and again, Strabonius ineffectually holds up the bronze tablet while about him the lesser centurions raise their fists or spit contemptuously on the floor. Ranked alongside the Primus Pilus stands Cyrion, his full title being Pilus Prior, or Senior Centurion of the Third Cohort, while on the other side stands the other Pilus Prior - Mascenius of the Second Cohort. These three leading centurions in turn are flanked by the more prestigious officers of the Twelfth - the Aquilifer, our Probus, and various adjutants and administrative staff or *immunes*, and the few legionary veterans who have remained on after their period of enlistment - here we find Remus, for example, and a few of his *coterie*. Our *Adjutor*, Optatus, of course, being an *immunes* or soldier excused front rank duties due to specialist skills, stands with these men, all of whom lead or otherwise dictate in some way the fate of the Twelfth.

It is the brevity of the order which seems to elicit most anger and confusion and the words which follow are hot and contrary. March, yes, but when and with what part of the Twelfth? Surely not all of it - and if not, then what part should be dispatched to Amida and who should retain command over it? It is folly for the legion to abandon Melitene after residing here for hundreds of years. What of the wives and children, the slaves, the servants? Who will tend the legion's land? It would be madness to uproot the legion wholesale from Melitene - and besides the Twelfth has not decamped from this Cappadocian refuge for over three hundred years and so it should not do so now. And so on and on. Cyrion seems to relish in the confusions and so shouts that he will lead the Third Cohort out as a vexillation - the men are inured to fatigue now that they have spent a month garrisoning and repairing Auaxa - many have been involved in skirmishes with the *latrunculi* who infest the hills and ravines there and all his men are eager for glory and rewards unlike the centurions of the First and Second Cohorts. Mascenius bristles at that and turns on Cyrion as if personally slighted but Strabonius smoothes over the latter's anger. Yes, the Primus Pilus shouts out above the hubbub, of course the Twelfth cannot abandon Melitene, the orders are abrupt but surely do not address the entire legion. Perhaps the Third and the Second should march out under command of both men? Perhaps that is the best solution? Our scribe is polite enough at this point in his report to only allude to the mocking laughter which greets the Primus Pilus. It falls to Probus, deep among his phalanx of fellow centurions, to suggest that clarification is needed. Surely it would be better if a courier is dispatched back to Amida requesting such a thing? Send a rider back to seek clarity, he urges, smiling softly in the faint light, his hair shining like gold. The neat Latin sentences penned by our *Adjutor* are nearly always fastidious but it must be admitted that here at least he seems agitated in his writing for the words are shaky and once or twice are scored out to be replaced with more politic alternatives. Strabonius, sensing a way out of the tension and recriminations, moves to put this suggestion to a vote and so in one fatal moment an old vase is broken into shards which are then passed about the trestle table. Make a mark, he advises, a cross for sending a rider or a circle for marching out - scratch it on the shards, he shouts out, even as Probus spreads out these ostraka on the table and invites all up to it.

'. . . And so now a Greek constitution replaces Roman *disciplina* and the centurions shuffle forwards to snatch up these broken parts. The smell of wine hangs heavy over us all and there on that low table an amphora is knocked over and a red stain floods the ostraka. No one cares and like greedy children who have cracked open a sweet jar, hands dart in and out, all sticky with wine. Strabonius steps back, frowning, thinking now that perhaps this is not such a good idea after all, while near him Probus nods and smiles and preens himself -

and why shouldn't he? We all know that a rider will be dispatched and a rough war deferred. Only Cyrion looks aggrieved as he sees his clumsy grab for glory slipping from his fingers. And so he should - we all know that he throws himself into battle not to gain a thing but to forget a thing or worse even redeem himself from that thing. That thing that stains us all. And I see that *Saraceni* loitering against the far wall, smiling, indulging his desert humour, no doubt at our ineffectitude, and for one moment his olive eyes pass over me and the contempt in them burns in me. It does not last however. How can he know that we all carry a deeper shame than any he can throw upon us . . ?'

It is then, as the centurions sweep up all the little ostraka, and a few senior officers feel that fate has been averted, that the doors burst open to the *praesidium* and a figure enters who will change everything. It is perhaps appropriate to give Obedianus the honour of introducing him and the suddenness of his appearance:

'. . . Do legends ever die, my father, or do they blow forever like the south winds in the deserts near the Erythraean Sea, or shine ever distantly like the stars above our heads? Here in this little dusty and dying castra, its gates all rusted now not by time but by neglect, I have shuddered under the glow of the oil lamps and felt my blood freeze. There, in a little shroud of dark, a man has come to us even as we read the command to march. An old man white with the frost of too many years and laced all over with too many scars. In his eyes lie wars and blood and death and in his voice echoes the doom of too many men. He came to us out of the shadows of the evening and wearing simple home-spun clothes and yet his fist grasped a staff of twisted vine and at his waist hung an old Roman sword – short and broad that the Romans call a gladius. It caught my eye and he smiled mirthlessly at my gaze even as he entered. He came to us as those centurions scooped up the fragments in their eagerness to throw away that command and as he stood there in that archway, shadows playing over that scarred face, I saw all those little men of Rome hesitate a moment and throw a wary look towards this newcomer. He smiled mirthlessly into their faces and before a challenge could ring out, he had marched stiffly through them and up to the trestle table and its stain of wine. I saw Strabonius stumble backwards a little at his presence while those barking centurions nearby rankled but said nothing even as this newcomer with the dark face surveyed them all. Only for a moment, such a brief moment, did I see him acknowledge me out of the corner of his eye and I swear under the shadow of Ishtar and Ailat of the endless deserts that a sardonic light flashed then in his eyes. He reminded me, father, of those ancient *daemons* you have talked about lost in the ruined cities no one visits - the nameless lords of empires all dust now or the shades of heroes whose tales once glittered under marble halls - and I wonder, do you still remember those tales you span under the palm trees in the soft dust? . . . I do not know if myths ever die, father, but I swear by the gods and spirits of the distant deserts that one emerged out of the dusk with the name of Rome upon his lips and an ancient sword at his waist . . .'

Our legionary *Adjutor* however pens a different picture and it is one he goes at some length into:

'. . . I have seen his kind before. Old and brutal men who linger along the fringes of the *respublica* as though lost or adrift. These are men who have outlived their time and persist in loitering - old legionaries or worn-out gladiators; scarred, of course, and bitter deep inside. These are the men who had been marked to fall in battle but on a whim or quirk of fortune have lived on while all about them had vanished into that arena. These men will be found outside the walls of the most remote castra or burgi - half in the shadow and half in the gaze of those who watch them with a wary eye. There is a bitter canker in them - what the medici call a melancholia that no amount of purging with wormwood or black hellebore can cure. It is a stain upon them. Some revere them as bringers of good luck for these men have survived all that Fate or Fortune can throw at them despite their whimsy for death. Others, those wiser perhaps, disdain them as marked by a curse in which all those about them will die whereas they themselves drift on, bleak in soul and dark in eye.

He was one such man. Old and shaven-headed - he looked like one of those ancient soldiers one can see in the marble busts in the forums of the big cities. He had a big nose, broken, of course, thick, beetling, brows, eyes deep beneath those brows, and a thin cruel mouth. His skull was shaven except for a few wisps of white curled about the ears in a careless fashion. Scars criss-crossed his face and his arms and his hands. He wore a dirty shawl knotted over his left shoulder in the Lycaonian fashion. I saw the old centurion's vine staff gripped in one hand while the other rested on the hilt of the oldest sword I have ever seen. I found my eyes lingering on that sword - it was the old gladius, broad, short and vicious. A lethal stabbing blade now no longer suited to the fighting style of the legions. The pommel and hilt had been replaced - many times, I suspected - but the gladius itself hung across his shoulder on a simple leather lanyard tied about the hilt. It had no scabbard and simply hung there exposed; naked. The iron of that blade was dark, almost black, and I found myself wondering on how many battles and desperate fights this weapon had been in. There was a loose blanket now rolled up across his opposite shoulder and I could see it bulging from whatever meagre possessions he carried - food, no doubt, and a little coin. He wore sandals with straps that criss-crossed up his ankles.

He stood there in the archway of the *praesidium* and all the anger and all the commotion slowly ceased. It was as if a wild animal had been let into the space to stand still on that threshold while all about men ceased their cares to wonder at it in amazement. I remember hearing that spilt wine drip from the table onto the tiled floor in the silence which followed his arrival. Strabonius baulked at his presence but seemed at a loss as to what to do. Even Probus looked bemused, his face flickering uneasily from disdain to uncertainty and back again in as many heartbeats. Only that *Saraceni*, Obedianus, sensed this man's true bearing and I saw him make a strange gesture as if warding off an ill omen as he stood unnoticed in the corner. One by one, the centurions and the senior officers of the legion turned to gaze upon him - and this old ugly man whose body stood as a testament to his wars held all their gazes without a single tremble.

It was then that he seemed to sniff the air as if looking for something. He raised his head and he smiled and it was such a cold smile that I found myself shivering despite the heat and the sweat of the bodies about me. Before I knew what was happening - before any of us knew what was happening, I suspect - this aged figure was pushing his way deep in among us and up to the trestle table now slick with wine. Bodies rippled apart about him and I saw one centurion step back and stumble almost in haste. In a few heartbeats, he was up at the table and facing Strabonius and frowning a little and rubbing a finger along the stubble of his jaw.

The Primus Pilus wavered, caution and uncertainty warring across his face - and it was then that Remus stepped forward, a hard look on his face. In the blink of an eye, he had pressed the edge of his vine staff into this stranger's stomach and was about the challenge him - and what happened next was the swiftest thing I have ever seen. I write this and even now seem unable to remember exactly how it happened. I saw the cold eyes of this old man flicker over Remus so casually that I almost missed it and then he looked away even as that vine staff remained pressed into his stomach. Then there was a blur of motion, a cracking noise, the sudden whip of that staff now in half falling across the trestle table, and Remus was face down into the wine and the ostraka, stunned, with this man pushing hard on his skull. For one almost endless moment, I saw blood and wine intermingle as that hand pushed remorselessly down, grinding the side of his face into that sticky wreckage, and then I saw Pamphilius the Bull move forward, his hand darting down to the long spatha slung over his side. Strabonius back-peddled in fear and inadvertently gave space to him but before Pamphilius could unsheathe that longsword, the tip of the stranger's own vine staff was at his throat in one long hard line. The centurion froze in shock and then this old ancient figure, his face a stone mask of contempt, stepped in towards Pamphilius the Bull, forcing him back one step at a time - even as he dragged the face of Remus along that table after him, his hand hard and ruthless on the latter's skull. The smear which was left in that wake on the table was flecked with torn skin. It was then that this stranger spoke and his words were cold and hard.

'Back, *porcini*, or your friend here loses what is left of his face.'

Remus is a large man, of Galateaen stock, thick in the waist and with a chest larger than an amphora, but this man dragged him along that table, his face pressed down into the wine and shattered pottery, as if he were a child or a starving slave. Some said later, those up by that table, that they heard a slight abrasive sound of skin tearing on the shards and of bone grinding against itself but I heard no such thing and I was as close as all of them.

I saw Pamphilius the Bull retreat and then shrug as if dismissing this old man's words. He shrugged but let go of his spatha so that it slid back into its scabbard, all the while that vine staff remained pressed deep into his throat, a cold and scarred face staring him down. Pamphilius sheathed his sword as if it were of no consequence but we all saw the sweat glistening across his brow.

'Good, Centurion - now look after your friend.'

And he lifted up the face of Remus, his fingers entwined deep in his hair, as though pulling up a reed basket even as the latter moaned and reached up to hold what was left of that side of his face. This old man lifted him up and then threw him casually towards Pamphilius. And it was impossible to tell where the wine ended and the blood began. Silence engulfed us all. Remus collapsed onto the floor at the feet of his friend but the latter ignored him, his gaze still locked onto the scarred face of this old veteran. For one moment, that vine staff remained at his throat and then it was gone as if it had never existed. This old man sighed then, as if disappointed, and turned back to the table. I saw him place that staff across it, pushing the broken pottery aside as he did so, and then he looked out at us all. And we in all our fascination, stared back.

'How apt,' he said, 'how apt that all you hold in your hands is the ostraka of a broken thing.' He glanced contemptuously at the Primus Pilus. 'You - are you not the First Spear of the Legion? The Primus Pilus of the First Century of the First Cohort? And look at your hands - covered only in wine and ink. And what mark have you scratched on that shard? A cross, First Spear?'

Of course, Strabonius nodded, no words on his lips, his eyes downcast. He reached out and dropped that shard onto the wooden table and the sound it made was a hollow sound.

'I thought so, as the gods bear witness.'

His gaze fell on us all then and though a dark humour flashed in it, I shuddered. He spoke to all those about him and told us that his name was Stygos and he called out the names of the Emperors he had fought under in all his long life: Maximian, Diocletian, Licinius, Constantine, Constantius and Julian. He told us he had stood under the standards of a dozen legions and travelled from the *limes* of Africa to the mist-shrouded banks of the Rhine. A wife and sons had brought him out of the *exercitus* to settle here in Cappadocia but disease had taken them away and now a fading god had whispered to him that a legion of Rome needed him once more. There in the deep of a sleepless night, alone and forlorn from love and family, this ancient god had whispered dark words, goading him to emerge from that mourning to fight for Roma one more time - and here he was among us and at a table anointed in wine and blood and now, he told us, must come a time for this old legion, once called *'antiqua'* for its tested courage and honour almost four hundred years ago, to choose . . .

' . . . Choose the wine or the blood, *commilitones*, though that epithet ill becomes you all.' He held up that bronze tablet then and tossed it carelessly onto the table. 'What will it be? Three simple words that admit no ambiguity or confusion - or disgrace through the coward's path of clarification and evasion and delay. Which will this legion choose?'

His words hung heavy among us and I remember staring about to see the faces of my fellow officers. Not one among us dared look him in the eye. He stood above us though he was small and compact and we in our shame allowed him to own us. Only that *Saraceni*, Obedianus, leaned in towards him, his eyes afire, his hand tight about the handle of his spatha. This dirty Arabi from the deserts south and east of Damascus and Palmyra smiled then and it was a fierce and hard smile. We, we in our idleness and torpor, remained silent and cowed however.

He nodded then, this Stygos, soldier under a litany of dead emperors and fallen Eagles, and the silence he gave us was back was damning.

It was then that a strange thing happened and which I would never have anticipated. They say that salvation comes in the most unlooked for places. I for one have never heeded that saying for daily have I and others about me looked in all such places and found naught but dust and mocking laughter but now, now indeed, I saw finally that thing I had always sought. For there, beside this Stygos, stood our First Spear, Strabonius, his lips dry and cracked, his eyes fearful - and by the Forty, he stood forward then and snatched up that bronze tablet, stained now in red, and before I or any of us could grasp what he was doing, he had thrust it back into the hands of this ancient and scarred veteran. Words tumbled out of him then - mad words, desperate words, words which poured out of him as though a damn had been burst and such was the passion and the desperation in him that I saw the muscles writhe along his arm as he pressed that tablet back into the hands of this Stygos . . .

'Lead us, then! Take up the mantle of command! Be the head of the

Twelfth and lead us down into war and blood! Take that title no one will place over us - and as God and Christ and all the Saints shelter us, you too will now hold us and damn or save us as you see fit! Lead this legion out, I beg you!' And he pressed and pressed that bronze slick with blood and wine into his hands.

It was a moment I will never forget. Remus, bloodied and groggy, his face shorn apart, Pamphilius beside him, ignoring him, Probus frowning in half-shadow for the first time in how many months I cannot recall as if something beyond his grasp was at his throat, and Strabonius supplicating an old man as if proclaiming him emperor. And this Stygos stood there allowing the Primus Pilus to humiliate himself, testing his desperation, while his dark gaze swept over us all - and not one of us contested the words being heaped upon him. Not one.

Stygos smiled then and there was no warmth in it. He smiled and it felt as if we were being condemned to death in the arena . . .'

The entry ends abruptly at this point and it is to be wondered at our *Adjutor's* deeper thoughts as he writes far in the night, a lonely oil lamp at his side. We do not know for example what happens after this extraordinary offer from the Primus Pilus nor do we know how the other legionaries of the Twelfth, crammed outside in the dark, among their wives and children and slaves, respond to the news that this stranger, this old veteran covered in scars, is now titled *Praefectus* and commander of the legion, despite having no imperial edict allowing him that title. While it is obvious that Strabonius grasps at a straw to save himself from a desperate decision about whether to march or vacillate, it is also clear from the pen of our adjutant-clerk that perhaps this straw is indeed a two-edged thing.

We do know that the next morning sees the Twelfth all a bustle with activity. The subsequent entry in the papyri is nothing but a long dry list of men and supplies under the standards and one gets the sense that it has been written specifically for the eyes of this Stygos. It tells us that all three Cohorts march out from the castra at Melitene but that each Cohort is slightly under strength. Each Cohort musters six centuries, some four hundred odd legionaries with the First doubling that number, but that the last century in each Cohort remains detached from this *notitia* penned by our scribe. This leaves some three hundred soldiers unaccounted for and it is reasonable to assume on the basis of these figures that this Stygos has left behind a slight garrison force to hold the castra. The absence of any further papyri detailing the subsequent march and climax at Amida allows us to understand that the Twelfth's *Adjutor*, our Optatus, remains behind at Melitene, and is himself detailed with the command of the remaining three centuries of soldiers as the most senior officer left. A few papyri follow and these remain solely concerned with stores, discipline (four legionaries are lashed for theft, for example, one is executed for rape, and so on), building work (the gate is now finally repaired, for example), and routine patrols, the longest of which into the Analaean Hills is commanded by a surly Pamphilius . . .

At midday, the long lines of the legion vacates the ancient fort and tramps away into the east and the Euphrates. It marches all mingled in with the *conturburnia* mules and the century wagons. Dust rises high in the wake of the tramping feet, the kicking hooves and the squealing wheels. Among the baggage and *impedimenta* of the Twelfth jog and sweat the army slaves, the *calones* that is, pushing the wagons or urging the mules on over the rutted roads. On either side, canter the Arab federate horse in a careless fashion, as if observing the discomfort of the Roman soldiers, while at the head of this ragged column strides Stygos on foot as if he were no more than a simple *miles* summoned one more time to war.

It is a long and disorganised march, to be sure. Unlike the old discipline in Caesar's day, or that of Trajan, for example, the Twelfth stumble and dribble out of the castra throughout most of the morning. We may wonder on the resentment and sullenness of the average legionary who is now forced to uproot from the environs of Melitene and its outlying forts for the first time in living memory and it will come as no surprise that a great throng of women, slaves and squealing children hang upon the tail end of the march until late in the afternoon. The immediate morning is dull and overcast but by midday sharp breaks in the overhead cloud have brought sudden swift shafts of light down onto the assembling lines of infantry. Sparks are thrown from helmet rim and spear tip. Swirling dust glimmers with motes. The tall poles of the standards sway uneasily in this dust so that it seems as though an uneasy crowd is following a religious procession behind a small array of icons. Only the loud shouts of the Fulminata's centurions and file-closers cut against this impression as the legion drifts inexorably away from Melitene and its rough pastures and vineyards towards the dull hills in the east.

By dusk, any observer on the cracked walls of Melitene, his hand shaded into the dying light would have seen only a faint smudge of dust hanging against the purple swells of the Taurus mountains in the east. A smudge which would soon vanish into darkness and silence. As the last figure from that march walks back under the castra portals, this straggler, a wife of one of the lesser centurions, her hair a mass of curls and loose ribbons, gazes back out for a final glimpse, one hand tugging back a lock of hair from her eyes, and sees nothing but memories and that final gesture from her husband, pushing her away, his face turned from her, closed and distant . . .

CHAPTER FIVE

The Persian thrust out of the desert and up along the Tigris seems to have taken the Magister Equitum of the East, Lupicinus, by complete surprise. The silk banners and heraldic standards sweep like avenging demons over the ill-prepared garrison outposts at Castrum Cepha and Sardeva, leaving them untouched, and then plunge north and west into the cultivated tracts south around Amida. As the month of May begins, the last thing anyone expects, it seems, is a main Persian assault out of Nisibis upon Amida itself. Chaos ensues as refugees tumble backwards from the oncoming Persian mailed horsemen, bringing word of a seemingly endless river of flowing steel out of the desert. Light cavalry blown hither by the Persian storm ride into Amida daily with news that in the wake of the shimmering cavalry of Ardawan toil also massive siege engines all packed up in parts on wagons followed by a host of miners, carpenters and artificers, surrounded by throngs of levy spearmen, all eager to crack the walls of Amida itself and bring into the dust yet another Roman town. The timing of this march and assault is indeed fortuitous for it seems to catch Lupicinus himself with his *officium* and guards inside the city while on an inspection. One is left to wonder if the Persians had some advance intelligence such that the move is a direct response to this opportunity to cut him off from the Diocesan-wide Roman forces. Regardless, he is trapped within the Black Walls and in one swoop it seems the Persians have decapitated the Roman high command in the East . . .

Both the pens of Ammianus and Libanius have painted the Magister and Roman Consul Lupicinus as a lightning tactician and a bold leader, a man who has risen high in the command of the Roman *exercitus,* cunning and possessed of a certain theatricality, but it falls to the youthful pen of one Candidus of Alexandria, a *tribunus vacans*, or staff officer, who perhaps best illuminates these dramatic days as the month turns. His writings survive mainly in fragments preserved in the Byzantine *Suda* and various other epitomisers. They show us a man both fastidious and cultured - one eager to uphold the glory of the empire under the standards. As with all officers promoted to the grade and rank of Tribune, this Candidus has performed *adoratio* to the imperial purple and has now been assigned to the imperial *officium* of the Magister.

If Jacek brought Optatus to me through the papyri and Sally brought Obedianus to me through her work on the old Arabic manuscripts, it remained finally for John Atkins alone to bring Candidus into the web of connections and events now developing among us all. What is there to say about my old friend that does not in some way also remind me of his loss? We had graduated together, of course, and done our first fieldwork together - some poor ditch in Surrey, if I recollect correctly - and dreamed together over wine and beer of exotic digs in the Syrian deserts or some such place. I paint all this with a romantic gloss, of course. His death has done that and the past is now tainted with regret and a certain elegiac quality I will never shake off. John had heard about my shift in intention at Malatya and how certain colleagues of mine were working privately on a subtler project as a result. We were some three years now into the digs here in eastern Turkey and although the finds were prosaic in their nature, funding always seemed to dribble in between the Turkish, Polish and British sources. Interns came and went. The Winters always saw us returning home for more academic work. Spring found us all packing and flying out again to Istanbul and then by train and bus onto Malatya. There in the hot Summers which followed we alternated between digging and cataloguing and packing our finds up for preservation - and slowly collating and deepening these long slow webs of connections which seemed to be springing up with both the Twelfth Fulminata Legion and Flavius Anicius at the centre. Curiosity had got the better of John as a result and one Summer as the days ripened into a long hard heat, he arrived and quizzed us all about our 'secret' work - that hobby we were working on alone and in private.

There was always something warm about John - where I was reserved and solitary, he was eloquent and gregarious - and thus he fell in with us and wooed Jacek and Sally over with his charm in a matter of days. And so it was that we regaled him with our slowly growing web - of these papyri written by Optatus; the letters of Obedianus; the various supplementary material I and the other two were finding alongside these major works. I think it amused him that we were both working on a dig and also researching a history on our own - that in some way, we were all hoarding another world away from the ruins and remains outside in the sun. And so it was a year later, that John returned on a sabbatical and in his pocket lay Candidus now carefully extracted and collated for the first time outside the *Suda* - and what he brought was perhaps the strongest thread in all the web so far . . .

If Optatus is burnt-out or bitter, nursing a secret, and Obedianus is regal but dismissive of the Romans around him all the while ignoring the decline of his own tribe, then Candidus instead is that peculiar Roman Aegyptian: decadent, perhaps, but eager to find something of an old world he has read too much about in the fragments and echoes which lay all about him now. Ruins and licentiousness are his upbringing - the overwrought poetry and satires read deep within the crumbling temples and arcades of a city steeped in art and wealth. Position and pedigree stands behind him as it does behind Flavius Anicius of

Italy but unlike the latter, Candidus bears an older mix of blood - one swilled together from Aegyptian and Greek ancestry. A blood poured from the same mould as Cleopatra some three hundred and fifty years earlier. There is in this Roman officer something *apt* that allows him no place in this world now except as an unattached person; his *vacans* status. A literary upbringing, his cultured Greek leanings, his blood nurtured by the Nile and the fleshpots of Alexandria, all have combined in this youthful but literary man a longing to see outside his collection of scrolls and papyri and into a brutal world so very different from his poets and satirists. I think if I am being honest that it could only have been John who brought Candidus to us for there was something of a *fit* in them both.

His history and account of this period remains fragmented but what John brought is worth quoting in sections for the light it sheds not perhaps on the grand stage but instead, as with Ammianus, on the middle-level echelons of command and their response to this crisis and, as the first surviving fragment also begins where Optatus seems to leave off, it remains for me to quote it now:

'. . . The *consistorium* of the Magister remained locked away in frantic talk far into the night while outside Amida bemoaned its fate like sheep caught out in a storm. Southwards, torches and lamps flared far into the desert towards us in chaos while northwards more torches pricked up only to recede away from us in haste. Some of my fellow officers commented upon the comic element of this while another, Constans, of Damascus, muttered that in time, as in the past, we would not be finding things so amusing. He was right as I am sure all the ancient gods will bear witness, for in art the tragedy precedes the comedy but in life it is the other way around.

They say that the Persian barbarian is like a snake writhing in your grasp and that just when you think you have him where you want him you find that it is the tail and not the head which rests in your grip. Now the serpent of the Persians winds towards us and all our legions and vexillations lie scattered in staging posts and forts around Edessa to the west. Why does Lupicinus not summon them to our aid instead of leaving them alone and separate out here? This ancient and some say cursed city, which saw doom under the Sacred Augustus Constantius, cannot stand long against this oncoming Persian storm. My fellow Tribunes wait anxiously for word from out of the depths of the *consistorium* but nothing comes. Wine, food, reports by the handful, enter but nothing ever seems to leave. Is the Magister paralyzed with fear, we wonder? Have the gods deserted us? Why will Lupicinus not summon the army to aid us?'

Except of course, one legion alone has been summoned. Even as Candidus of Alexandria is penning his overlong sentences within a panic-stricken city, packed with refugees, the Twelfth Legion, in three cohorts, is crossing the Euphrates and marching east towards Amida, along with its accompanying *Ala* of Arab cavalry. Two epistles survive from fleeing wealthy landowners to relatives back in Constantinople which record in some scant detail the passing of this disgraced legion. Nonae, a Christian Syrian, founder of the two monasteries in the province of Syria Secundae Salutaris, and former wife to the Roman Senator, Illus, writes:

'. . . And what of God's Will in this dusty land, I wonder? As the barbarians rampage through Mesopotamia towards Amida and I must flee my beloved houses of God, I find only empty staging posts and abandoned watch-towers. Even my female habiliments are no longer a guarantee of my safe conduct and my slaves must now batter aside the *honestiores* as well as the common folk who attempt to cling to our carriages as we travel west towards Antioch. We fear for our lives but I place my trust in God's Will as always: '. . .You are the first way of the creatures, bliss-bestowing Trinity, You mixing unstable stability and permanence with whirling motion . . .' Two days from Amida, we passed a poor sight indeed. Roman soldiers marching in haste and without respite back towards that ill-omened city. I have seen boys dressed up in war looking better, I swear. Where is the spirit of Rome now? Where are the shining labarums of Christ? Our Emperor seeks to exalt the Arian heresy and all that march to his standard now is a tired legion of wasted men. What hubris of this Valens, now so far away! What nerve! I took pity on the men of this broken legion and bade my slaves to pass out what little honeyed wine I had left but some scarred officer, an ugly looking dog of a man in a faded tunica, snapped at me and ordered my slaves to pass on in haste. The nerve of the man! I can still see his face resting atop that old shift of his like a roughly carved mask of wood, all chipped and knocked about. I swear he must have been a century old at least! I will pray for his soul and for the souls of all those legion soldiers even as they toil towards Amida . . .'

Another epistle is equally unflattering about the Twelfth:

'. . . At the little trading post on the Euphrates known as Juliopolis, Roman soldiers commandeered all the barges and fishing boats to transport their men and mules and supplies over the great golden river. When a small group of traders begged for recompense for the loss of their trade, an officer, with ill-fitting words, scolded them out loud and told them to ask for coin from the Persian barbarians riding now out of the deserts of the Orient. The centurions about him laughed at that but he lashed his tongue upon them also so that they crossed into the boats like sheep. This man stood upon the shore as the boats plied away into the deep currents of the Euphrates and we thought that an old Anatolian god had arisen from the past for he seemed to be as dusty and as dry as the land around us. One of us, Maxentio the Greek, approached him and asked where his men marched and he, all distant and aloof, muttered that they marched where all Roman soldiers marched, to death. We shivered to hear him speak so coldly about his men . . .'

It is an irony of history, of course, that a mere twenty or so Roman miles away even as the Twelfth Legion crosses the Euphrates to close in on Amida, the Tribune Flavius Anicius, with the shining men of the Sol legion, is also approaching the city fully unaware of the impending disaster. Their circuitous route through the empty trails and tracks of the province of Euphratensis has left them somewhat isolated and in ignorance about the wider scheme of things - so much so that the Gallic, Germanic and Illyrian veterans in its ranks are blissfully looking forward to arriving finally at Amida with its baths and wine-houses having missed the fleeing refugees toiling westwards . . .

'. . . The discipline of the Tribune Anicius is stern yet even. We march steadfastly as we did under Julianus at Argentoratum and only now is the high sun finally bearable. Dust cakes everything. Our lips are parched. Our eyes full with sand and flies. The tramp of our feet raises only more dust to torment us. Amida beckons like a siren and we feel its nearness daily. The ducenarii of the maniples do not bark out so much now and even our Tribune smiles a little, although there is no mirth in such a smile it must be said as we mutter *Axios'* to his every command. This 'Corbulo' is stiff like a rod but green, so green! And not even the jokes of the biarchi amuse him. Discipline is all. It is his god and, some would say, his shield . . .'

If History is a stage then it cannot come as too much of a surprise that it has its entrances and exits. And upon this stage named now as Amida, that city caught alone at the edge of Empire and fated to see battles litter its land like rain, among all the confusion of retreating refugees and scouting cavalry, three columns converge: the bedraggled line of the Twelfth Fulminata Legion, the tight ranks of the Senior Sol Legion, and the Persian army of Ardawan, the *Spahbad* of Shapur the Second. And of course if a stage exists at all it exists with a backdrop to frame it and this backdrop is none other than a violent sandstorm which is soon to sweep over all the players even as they move to collide.

What history has subsequently named as the Siege of Amida begins on the Nones of Maius in the year 367 AD. As the last of the scouts and refugees dash inside the old stone walls of Amida, the bright shining sun illuminates the endless banners of the Persian host emerging from out of the distance. Rank upon rank of shining *Savaran* cataphract cavalry all intermingled with the jostling hosts of the other warriors - the Nubians and Auxumites, the Chionitae and the Arab federates - and the trundling and groaning shapes of the siege wagons, lumbering over all like wooden galleys, all emerge inexorably towards the city. Dust shrouds their wake and a soft wind sweeps ahead of them like a herald towards Amida of the Black Walls. Over all rides the silk banner of Ardawan, the *Spahbad* of the Sassanid Empire, and favourite of Shapur the Second. Panic engulfs the citizens of Amida even as the old, iron-framed, gates are strained shut and several centuries of sagittarii take up careful positions along the main south-facing wall. Crowds still sweep out of the open north and west gates, milling with camels, mules and carts. A wagon-load of amphorae containing olive-oil and figs overturns at the Edessene Gate and jams its entrance. Fights break out around it and a panicked cry rises up that the Jews, ever eager to see the Persians, are sabotaging the city. Candidus of Alexandria, our main authority for these events, relates how it finally took a century of nervous legionaries to beat back a vicious mob from assaulting the Jewish quarter - even as the first of the enemy cavalry, savage-faced warriors from the distant steppes beyond the Caucasus, began to cautiously encircle the walls.

Night brings only a subdued tension. The camp-fires of the Persians ring most of Amida like a poisoned necklace, to paraphrase Candidus, and deep in the folds of the moonless dark, soft chants and singing can be heard, praising Ahura-Mazda, the ancient fire deity of Mesopotamia. A muted clanging is heard also and those officers and soldiers who have been in sieges before warn their comrades that towers are being constructed and other engines of war being pinned together. Candidus remains mostly alarmed in his writings which cover this period – perturbed at the supposed inactivity both of the Magister in his midst and also the scattered units of the field army of the Oriens spread throughout the regions around the *territorium* of Amida. There is a palpable sense via his pen that the sudden advance of the Persians into Roman territory has taken everyone by surprise in the manner in which a smoking stick thrust into a bee hive scatters its drones and leaves them disorientated. The first day after the arrival of the Sassanid host, finds him tramping the north wall and its gate which remains open for the last of the refugees. A scattered medley of light Persian horsemen still drift idly out of bow-shot but seem disinterested in the fleeing men and women of Amida, being content to merely show their presence with their high silk banners and animal totem poles. The bulk of the Persian forces have encamped around the south and east-facing walls, erecting a triple line of shields to defend against ballistae shot or sudden sorties. Neither of which, to Candidus' youthful amazement, are initiated.

It is Candidus himself, if we are to believe his pen, who sights the newcomers first, marching down the north road in a long formation. His first intimation of their arrival is the sudden scattering of the Persian light horse - those Chionitae in animal pelts and loose iron caps - away from a rising cloud of dust and then a light but dull gleam which tells him that a body of infantry is on the march. Barking out orders to the sentries below, Candidus sends off runners to the *officium* of the Magister even as he descends to the north gate and anxiously awaits their arrival. By midday of the day after the Nones of Maius, the dull gleam has resolved into the armour and standards of a Roman legion in a long but ragged order and with full marching kit. Even as his eyes alight upon the outline of this legion, Candidus narrates that a dry wind sprang up and with it the sand of the desert brought a veil over his eyes. This wind rises suddenly in ferocity and soon he is blinded down by the North Gate, huddling within the folds of his sagum cloak, a felt cap pulled tight over his eyes, struggling to see who these Romans are. There is a sense of something otherworldly in the description which follows of the wind and the sandstorm, as though judgment is being given by the old gods of the desert. This vignette of the unattached Roman officer huddling into the rough stone of the north gate, wrapped in his great cloak, peering into the blasting sand, looking for fate perhaps or salvation or even just relief is a powerful image - which John had argued was a conceit carved out by Candidus as a wilful piece of literary craft. I defer from that however and wonder why such an intelligent officer, who later achieved Senatorial rank, would paint himself in such debilitating terms if not for the veracity of the scene and the impression it left on him in all his lonely years ahead.

For out of the dust and the wind and the indeterminate wash of yellow which surrounded him at that north gate came not salvation at all but the tired and dull-eyed men of the Twelfth Legion, the old garrison legion of Melitene, with an *Ala* of Saraceni cavalry in their wake, all wrapped up in white cloaks and robes so as to appear like wraiths or *djinn* of the desert. Candidus watches them enter Amida and it is worth quoting his pen rather than summarising here:

'. . . If ever Crassus were to return from Hades or the Lethean realm and bring back a legion of the dead in his wake then these men would be their *imago* now - for what is Rome in this paralyzed city of Amida if not an empty word, a broken banner, a shrouded mummy as we Aegyptian Greeks make? These men toiled through an awful storm of sand and dust, heralded by wind, and battered by a shrieking moan, and not one face of these legionaries could I stare into in thanks. Slaves I have seen who have borne cooking implements with better discipline. What a legion is this that marches here out of the desert into certain death and knows not to flee like the rest?'

The Twelfth Fulminata Legion, a border legion long since neglected and cut-off from honour and glory, disgraced over a nameless deed, left ungeneraled for months, understrengthed, mocked by Arabs, arrives in Amida, a mighty desert storm in its wake, with only the grim face of an aged Roman, a face which is scarred like a roughly-carved mask, to push them on. It is a face which brushes past our Candidus at the north gate as an old hoary dog paces past a cub not worth a glance.

Moments later, Candidus orders the North Gate to be closed, even as the storm washes high over the stone walls in wave after wave of bitter sand.

CHAPTER SIX

The arrival of the Twelfth Legion, under its *Praefectus*, Stygos, together with the white-shrouded *Saraceni*, largely goes unnoticed as the sand-storm sweeps over Amida and renders everything into a dim and distant outline. It is here, amid this unnatural phenomenon, that Candidus of Alexandria unleashes his literary bent - that poetic heritage he has inherited from an upbringing redolent with decadence and stilted Latin - and so begins to describe the ferocious winds and biting sands as the '*Gorgona Spiritu*' - or Gorgon's Breath.

This storm has arisen from the south and west around the barren lands in Mesopotamia and although the lands here about Amida are fertile and cultivated it is not unusual for great sandstorms to sweep this far north. What is unusual is the season. Arab and Greek writers are uniform in allowing late Summer for the seasons of such storms and it must have struck no few of the inhabitants of Amida that such an unusually early storm was nothing but an ill omen. This is no doubt the reason which allows his rhetorical flourish to emerge but perhaps what he designates as the Gorgon's Breath is by no means his own literary label but also a deeper allusion to the forces marshalling outside the city. For it is to be suspected that, given the Hyrcanian origin of the *Spahbad* commander, Ardawan, an area which is also known as Gorgona in the ancient Semitic tongues, that Candidus is indirectly commenting on the Persian presence itself. Regardless, by early evening, with the sun a washed-out orb, and the remaining inhabitants of the city huddling inside for shelter, we find the Tribune bearing news of the arrival of the legion to the notaries of the *officium* of Lupicinus. His description of the events that evening, as he waits in the outer chambers, witnessing hasty arrivals and grim-faced departures, is vivid indeed. Notaries, slaves, high-ranking officers and regimental commanders filter past him on urgent business as the oil lamps gutter low and the shriek of the *Gorgona Spiritu* outside rises higher. A sudden blast in particular sweeps aside a tapestry and causes an oil lamp to crash down, startling all in an antechamber. One senses in him a desperate desire for action; for command instead of this waiting and apparent indecision from a high officer he clearly regards as a hero. Again and again, Candidus edges up to the shrouded inner sanctum, past the ranks of the Magister's guards, only to be politely rebuffed and made to wait outside.

It is only as late evening comes and the gilded tapestries around him seem to whisper in colluding tones, that the stern figure of the Magister Equitum per Orientem, 'The Wolf', Lupicinus himself, emerges with a phalanx of senior officers in tow. This is the first time that our green staff officer paints a physical description of the Magister and it accords well with what other writers - Libanius, for example - have left us:

'. . . A poor slave was attempting to strap the illustrious Magister into a bronze cuirass, all decorated with wreaths and little victories, while the latter suffered the indignities of his fumbling with a scowl. It is said that Lupicinus is a wary man, plagued with conspiracies and designs, all the while defending the edge of the *respublica*. I fear this is nothing but gossip noised abroad in the agoras and whorehouses of the cities. Here in the margins of Rome, I have seen him be nothing but diligent and demanding. He reminds me of that wolf he is often likened too, ever alert, but wary also from his constant watch. His eyes are always restless and I see his hands always occupied with something, as if his drive and ambition knows no rest. Now, as that poor slave tightened the straps too much and made him wince, our Magister snatched at a nearby writing tablet and began scoring small letters into it. His eyes flickered over to me almost as an afterthought and then he beckoned me to him - finally . . .'

Candidus is made to repeat his news about the arrival of the Twelfth Legion and their bedraggled state to the satisfaction of his superior, the overall commander of the diocese of the Oriens. Words are feverishly whispered to his adjutants and then Lupicinus faces Candidus to place a hand upon his shoulder. The words which follow are harsh and unremitting:

'. . . "Tell this Stygos that his legion is to be de-listed from the *exercitus* of the *respublica*, that his legion will suffer *damnatio* as the old emperors were damned, that this Fulminata will rot in the memory of all Romans until not one whisper of its past will remain. Tell him also that to take up the command of a legion in disgrace with no mandate from myself as Magister is to usurp a title that is not his – no matter his past record and deeds, which we all here recall. Do you understand these orders, Candidus? Then tell Stygos this also – that tomorrow morning by the will of the Sacred Augustus, orders will come to his *milites*, his Twelfth, whose cause he has so rudely adopted, and should his legion accept these orders, all dishonour noted above may be expunged, if the Emperor wills it. Garrison them tonight in the Baths of Trajan by the South Wall and feed them like *principes*. *Principes*, you understand?" '

What happens subsequently is difficult to disentangle from his writings for Candidus is clearly struggling with the import of those words. Lupicinus with his *coterie* of senior officers disappears again into the inner halls and only the howl of the wind outside the Black Walls keeps Candidus company. Mad thoughts whirl through his mind and he wonders at the events to come. These confusions remain with him even as sometime later he finds himself in the presence of Stygos to deliver the words of the Magister in person. This meeting,

Candidus is at pains to point out in his writings, is a private one and it is the first time he is able to assess this odd Roman:

'. . . He watched me like an old hoary dog who had seen too many winters and fought in too many packs to be dazzled by baubles and scraps now. His head was shaved and rough like an old stone idol seen in the lands of the ancient Scyth and the Getae. His eyes were black and mirthless. His smile cold. And such scars about him! As if each year of his life was scored brutally upon his face! I saw a hand grasped around a long gnarled vine stick and for one mad moment wondered where one ended and the other began. He saw me shiver at that and rudely bade me repeat the words of Lupicinus. He nodded once as I finished his request and then he told me to damn the food to Hades:

" . . . Bring wine, bladders of the stuff, enough to float the Ark of the Jews and the Christians. Do not stuff a soldier's mouth with food, drown it with wine, instead, if you wish to sacrifice him," he said, and I saw him smile coldly.

I baulked at that. "What sacrifice? The Magister made no mention of such a thing – only that orders would come which might allow the Twelfth Legion to redeem itself on the morrow."

He laughed at that in a way which made my blood chill "- Son, you have much to learn about the whims of Magisters, even ones as gifted as this Lupicinus." He turned then and barked back at me even as he summoned his servants and slaves, "– Do not forget the wine, by all the gods of Rome, you understand? Bring wine!" '

The night brings no respite from 'The Gorgon's Breath' and the Romans atop the city's walls struggle even to see their own watch fires and standards let alone the massed Persians spread across the plain to the south and east. Every so often an erratic ballista bolt would arc out of the sand and the wind only to careen carelessly off a buttress or supporting wall. Stragglers crawling in through guarded culverts in the walls report that the host of Ardawan Karen-Pahlavi, of the House Karen, that great Hyrcanian satrapy, seems cocooned in the desert, the siege towers and rams all bogged down in drifts, the sentries wrapped up in moistened cloaks to guard against the endless sand. Candidus remains awake through the night and it is clear from his writings that unease about the words of Stygos are eating away at him. He cannot conceive what orders will come in the morning nor their import, however, and so no balm comes to his fevered mind. Once towards dawn a slave brings him a flask of wine to refresh his dry mouth but he throws it aside as a bad omen and waits for an unseen sun to rise and end his anticipation.

There is little remaining now in Diyarbakir, formally Amida, of the Baths of Trajan, built in honour of his conquest of Ctesiphon, but archaeologists have determined that it was a magnificent structure as befitting an Imperial statement. No doubt, with the decline in civic patronage which was a feature of the Later Roman period, the Baths were not at their best. The marble would have been cracked and dilapidated; the heating hypocausts perhaps in disrepair; some rooms left to fall in decay even. Having said that – it would still have been an impressive structure and a worthy billet for a front-line legion or cavalry vexillation passing through Amida to a distant posting or far-off battle.

It is only as the first light of dawn struggles through the gloom of the 'Gorgon's Breath', all sickly and pale like glue, that Stygos emerges from out of the darkened hallways and chambers of the Baths and summons the principal centurions of the Twelfth into his presence. In a small adjacent bathing hall, the marble benches slick with old stains and mould, an open cell above allowing a little thin light in, these few men assemble around him. At his side, stands Strabonius, his lips dry and cracked, one hand plucking slowly at an ear, while before him hesitates an uneasy Remus, a rough and caked bandage about one half of his face. Nearby stands the Aquilifer Probus, his yellow hair matted now with dust and sweat. Half a dozen lesser centurions - all *veterani* - shuffle uneasily under the gaze of Stygos. Apart and hesitating a little stands Cyrion of the Third Cohort and also the wary figure of Mascenius of the Second Cohort - both centurions now looking uneasily at the dark figure of Stygos and then to Strabonius by his side. All are drunk from the wine brought to all the men of the Twelfth through the long night and one, Mascenius, is only just recovering from a vomiting bout in the hallway nearby. In the silence which follows their summons, as that pallid light drifts down from above, its motes coating those below in a faint dust, Mascenius coughs awkwardly and feels how parched his throat is - all the while secretly yearning for more wine. Stygos, waiting for them all to arrive, watches them with an impassive face, one hand resting on a vellum scroll he has placed on a marble stand. A scroll whose seal has been broken.

In the shadow of the doorway stands Obedianus apart from the rest. He has responded to the summons but now waits on the threshold separate from these centurions. In that short march south and east towards Amida, this Arab chieftain has remained among his brethren, acting as escorts and scouts for the legionaries all marching along in the dirt and the heat. These Arabs have slept apart from the rigid tents and camps of the Romans, roaming the night in little detachments or sleeping warily near their fleet ponies and desert horses. It is to be wondered why this Stygos has not corralled these federate riders within the ramparts and ditches of each night's camp, but if we read Obedianus' words correctly, there is a strange rapport growing between him and the ancient Roman soldier - a rapport where it seems one does not interfere or criticise the actions of the other. It is clear that this Arab regards the latter as somehow touched or marked by the gods and accords him a certain respect and even wariness:

'. . . I was summoned, father, and yet it seemed not *invited*. He brought me into that small sickly cell, its light dripping down as if from a dank pool above, and even as I made to enter with the other Romans - those awkward commanders and faint warriors - his hand shot up and I hesitated on the threshold.

"Not you, *Saraceni*," he said in that harsh gravelly voice of his. "Wait there - this is something you may watch but not enter into."

"Watch, *Praefectus?* I do not understand."

I saw Stygos tap the scroll at his side and I knew that orders from the Magister had finally arrived and been read. Orders which I sensed did not include me or my brothers from the Bani Al Jawn.

I saw the other centurions stare back at me, some with curiosity and some with contempt. One, Probus, smirked suddenly and turned to face me. I remember his smile being oily in the dim light.

"Yes, Obedianus, know your station. This is a Roman *consilium* and federate barbarians such as you have no voice here."

It was then that Stygos stepped forward a little, his hand dropping without a thought onto that naked gladius of his. The black iron glittered in the faint light. "Wise words, Probus, bearer of the Twelfth's Aquila. I can see why you have held that sacred standard for - how many years, is it now? Five? Six?"

There was something in his voice that made me edge a back a little into the shade of the doorway. Something dark and sinister. Probus sensed it, too, for that Aquilifer moved cautiously a little from the centurions around him. He had a lithe frame, graceful and almost feminine. There was something of the leopard in him - a gliding effortlessness in the way he moved; a grace and ease which told me that this man was a killer, a stalker of men on the battlefield. Not for him the clash of equals over the shield-rim or across the sweating flanks of a horse. No, this languid man, his hair always waxed and shiny, *stalked* and slew as merciless and as swift as that golden predator he seemed to echo. He was a man, father, you would have despised. A Roman who was all calculation and opportunity and who played in the shadows where we Arabs moved in the light . . .

Probus raised his head even as he moved apart. "Five years, *Praefectus*. I stepped into the honour after old Syrenius fell to plague. Five years I have had the privilege of holding the Twelfth's Aquila. God and his Saints have blessed me with this honour -"

"*Bless*, you call it? How much gold did you grease across how many palms, Probus? You haul aloft a broken standard, a cursed standard, and you find it *worthy* to do so? You *paid* for the privilege? The Magister here -" and I saw Stygos glance quickly back at that scroll - "tells me of you, Probus. Do you wonder on why the illustrious Lupicinus pens your name in these orders and what he writes about you? What he writes about that Eagle you so casually hold as Aquilfier? I wonder if you have ever really looked hard into the cold eyes of that Eagle and seen what lies in its gaze. Well, have you, Probus?"

Something shifted in that little room then. I saw men move apart almost without thinking - shifting and stepping back so slowly as almost not to realise it. As I stood on that threshold looking in I saw what they all could not see: a space forming in that way men have of parting for two others who in some unfathomable way, in words so slight as to seem innocent, are now foes. I looked and saw and smiled even as my own hand drifted lightly to the pommel of my spatha. This Stygos was playing a game here and although I could not understand its rules, I and all those about me sensed its presence. And I knew then that the reason I was not invited in was not that I was an outsider but that instead I was now a guard.

I saw Stygos smile slowly even as his body tipped in slightly, one shoulder dropping down towards the Aquilifer. "That Eagle is old, Probus, old and tainted. Its eyes have seen blood and shame while all its claws have grasped is the tattered banners and laurels of hollow victories. Is that the Eagle you really want to hold aloft? A shamed thing?"

"I am the Aquilifer of the Twelfth. What are you that you mock me?" His voice took on a cold hard edge.

"Strabonius? What am I?"

I saw the thin frame of the Primus Pilus hesitate. "You are the *Praefectus* of the Twelfth -"

Probus laughed back at that. "Four days you have held that title and honour, old man, four days! I have been Aquilifer for five years - you will be the third commander of this Legion in that time."

Something odd happened then, father, something dark - for Strabonius stepped forward almost as if starting at something. Fear rose in that dry face of his and I saw him raise a hand.

"Probus - don't -"

"What? Don't *what*, you coward? Look at him, Stygos - the First Spear of the Twelfth - and there beside him, the First Centurion of the Second Cohort and the First of the Third - and what do we have beside them? The other *veterani* of this legion - centurions one and all! And have we not all stood under three commanders of this Legion now? The one who died, the one who broke and this one, the old one marked by battle and death -"

"Death, is it, Aquilifer? Is that what you see in me?"

A shiver ran through them all then. A shiver that left Probus alone from them all. It was as if a wind had swept through them in that little room with its sickly light falling down from above in a drift of dust and in its wake two men were left apart from all the rest. One a liquid predator in gold the other a grizzled old dog and all around them both lay a circle of men as far from them as it was possible to be and still stand in the same room. I saw Strabonius give a quick panicked look about the other centurions and that they all in one way or another returned that fear.

Probus nodded then and the smile he gave was cruel. "You want the Eagle? Is that what Lupicinus commands - that I am to relinquish it? Do you hear that, my *commiliatones*? This left-over wants me to surrender up the Eagle of the Twelfth. It is mine by right, do you understand, Stygos? I alone bear that standard. No other - and you will not take it from me."

"You fool," snapped back the *Praefectus*. "You have paid gold to hold a standard which is nothing but a broken thing. What is this Eagle that it has languished for over three hundred years? Do you not even know the history of the Twelfth?"

"I know the honour that comes from holding it aloft. I am an Aquilifer of Rome. I stand as close as one can stand to the soul and spirit of the Legion itself. I *am* the Twelfth! You will not take that from me. This Eagle *is* the Legion and I hold the Legion!"

"Not any longer, Probus."

Stygos tugged suddenly on that lanyard about his neck and by some hidden contrivance it fell away and the gladius was naked in one gnarled fist. "I know your kind. There is a poison in you and it has infected everyone in this room. You hold aloft a standard ·which is planted in blood and betrayal. The irony is that you do not realise that the Eagle itself is already corrupted. Let it go - this is my last warning."

I looked about them all in that sickly room and wondered on what Stygos was doing. Was he going to slaughter Probus here and now? In front of the other centurions? They would rally to the Aquilifer and turn on this old Roman surely? But, father, I sensed then even as Probus hesitated with a sly look about him that something else was happening here. For now I saw Remus shake his head slowly, his crusted bandage making his face look like a twisted mask in some grotesque *pantomimus*. Nearby, both Mascenius and Cyrion kept to the shadows and seemed to be absorbed by the tension between Stygos and Probus and I knew then that they would never step in to aid the Aquilifer. Strabonius, too, hesitated in the shadows and I saw that the pallid light from that cell above fell over him and gave him a deathly countenance. The other senior centurions all stood back and shuffled uneasily not daring to look Probus in the eye.

He, sensing this, nodded to himself and began to pace about like a caged animal. His hand hovered over his own spatha and for a moment I saw his gaze flit over me, assessing my guard and that escape which lay behind me. My own smile dissuaded him and he turned back in towards Stygos, a dark flame flickering in his eyes. "I have broken better than you - your predecessor, for example, as all here can witness - did we not -"

"Probus!" Again, I saw the startled look appear on the Primus Pilus' face.

"What?" he challenged in return. "We were all there - or have you forgotten? All of you - Remus, Cyrion, you, too, Mascenius. That pup dared to question *us* and we broke him better than all the *daemons* of Hades could have done. Or have you all forgotten that night?"

No one answered and Stygos smiled slowly into that silence. "It is a lonely thing to hold aloft the Eagle, Probus. With that honour comes also an obligation. An obligation to hold it alone and at the last. It is not that I do not think you are worthy of all those who stood before you for all those generations at Melitene - just the opposite - but that now, at the last, it should be held aloft by one who echoes in some fashion that first Aquilifer raised by Caesar himself. I will have that standard from you, willingly or not."

"At the last? What are you mumbling about, old man?"

It was then that Stygos struck - and that liquid form, all golden and lithe in the pale light, fell back in surprise, a moan tumbling from him. I saw that black gladius shift as if it were a shadow between them and a sudden scarlet thread appeared as if from nowhere. Probus moaned in shock and pain as blood spurted from a gash down his thigh. And Stygos stood again where he had been, unconcerned, that blade loose by his side, his scarred face cold and implacable. For one mad moment, I thought his shade had leapt out from him to strike before slipping back again such was the speed and the awful stillness which followed it.

All looked to Probus then and that deep cut in his thigh. For one moment, this man stood there looking uncomprehendingly down at his wound. A slight frown emerged and I saw him lick his lips. The wound was not mortal. It lay deep in his flesh but had missed the artery in the leg which all legionaries are trained to cut in battle should the enemy's shield rim rise up too high or drift out too wide. I wondered then, father, if perhaps this Stygos had miscalculated his stroke - that in the speed of it, he had erred in landing the blow - but what followed showed me that the opposite was the case.

Probus howled then and yanked out his spatha. With a sideways swipe, he closed in on Stygos and I saw his fluidity and grace emerge in one cunning lunge. It was a lunge which I knew had years of killing practice behind it but which I also knew in a flash would never connect. The *Praefectus* was already slipping around him and in a moment a second cut landed across his back, causing Probus to stumble awkwardly. He lashed out in a back-handed move to give him time to recover even as he pressed one hand into that new wound. It was useless. Stygos ducked easily and again scored him - this time around the left forearm - before stepping back calmly.

And I knew then, father, that this Probus was not going into a clean death. That in some manner, Stygos was exercising more than a fight. He was *executing* the Aquilifer.

Probus staggered a little and dropped back, his shoulders hunched in, and I saw him glance fearfully about this little space, even as he raised up his spatha into a futile guard position. Blood ran from him and soaked his tunica. It dripped onto the cracked marble floor. It stained his leg, his back, his arm. His spatha by contrast trembled in the pallid light without a speck of crimson on it. He shook his head and smiled then at Stygos, fighting to push the pain away. "All this for an Eagle? You are mad!" He stumbled then and one foot slipped on his own blood.

The smile that Stygos gave back was distant and empty. "You would not be the first to call me that. Or the last. You took it on the back of gold and bribery, Probus, but now it is time to hand it back on blood and sacrifice. Did you not know that the Eagle of Rome comes with a price greater than coin?"

And he moved again, that gladius licking at him in cut after cut after cut.

Probus is a tall man, elegant in his form, a leopard in grace and cunning, father, his hair golden and preened. In another life I expect he would have been a prince among men, cruel and unsatiated by gold and jewels. His eyes glittered with a hunger for more than material things. He lusted for power and that was why he grasped at the Eagle and why he would not relinquish it now. Power did not lay in command, it lay in the soul of the legion - that body of men these Romans revere above the warrior or the champion upon the battlefield. Probus lusted to hold that soul in his hands and gold had merely been a path to that power and prestige. And now Stygos was stripping him of it in the most bloody and brutal manner I have ever seen. Again and again, that black blade of his cut at the skin and flesh of the Aquilfier as the latter tripped and stumbled about. Crimson streaks appeared like hideous strokes of paint upon him - his back, his arms, his legs. And his breath began to heave forth in great ragged sobs. Probus tried every trick and tactic he knew to land a blow upon that small old Roman but all in vain. Stygos did not so much dance or evade as simply step aside from each blow and in its wake he cut another deep wound. The blood from those strikes splattered his craggy face and I swear, father, that in the yellow light falling from above over them both that the scars upon him became runnels of red like a mask born by the god of Dis himself.

It was the longest time I have ever seen for a man to die.

Stygos cut him again and again in all the little places that drained him of life. There was no mercy and no compassion in what he did. I knew, standing there in that doorway, that this old man was carving out not a death so much as a lesson. A lesson he meant to illustrate with no hint of ambiguity or mistake. And so Probus floundered and gasped as an agony of cuts drained his life away while all those about him watched on aghast. Even Remus, that bully and braggart, turned his broken face away so that only the caked bandage could be seen. Probus bled his life away to that remorseless iron blade and after each cut or slash the horror in his eyes grew larger. I have seen men cut down in battle and put out of their misery when too wounded to live. We accept all this. It is our way, father. The soul is ready for this and that is as it should be - but what I saw that dawn was something different. It was beyond butchery. It was the coldest thing I have ever seen.

At the end, Probus lay quivering on the marble floor, his flesh nothing but a canvas of tears and slashes. He moaned like a newborn and the sound of it struck them all with fear. The spatha lay alone nearby. Stygos stood over him, his face blank and distant. It was then that I saw him look around at the centurions. A little of the pallid light fell over his face rendering it ancient and distant, as if a god watched them . He hooked up his gladius to the lanyard about his neck and then moved to depart.

"He is still alive . . ."

It was Strabonius who spoke, his voice faint, hesitant.

The *Praefectus* paused a little, his back to them all. I remember he was facing me, his eyes on me, his body covered in the blood of another, and then not taking his eyes from my face, he replied:

"Not for long. Watch the life drain out of him or end it yourselves. I do not care either way. Know this - the Eagle is mine now. *I* am the legion."

With that he walked past me.

And like the conspirators against Caesar, I saw all the centurions - Strabonius, Cyrion, Mascenius, Remus and the rest, close in slowly on that pulped mewling thing on the cracked marble but who it was that reached for his blade first, I do not recall . . .'

I have often wondered on why this Stygos left the Aquilifer dying on the marble floor among the other centurions and not kill him at the last. The viciousness of his death is compounded for me in that abandonment. It is not that something personal motivated him - how could it for this old Roman has yet to learn of 'Corbulo' and his real identity - but rather the almost forensic dissection of Probus speaks to a deeper motivation. A motivation which allows him to break the will of the surviving centurions. But to leave him bleeding out his life? The Eagle was his with that man's death. To walk away from him seems to me to move that clinical approach into something much more sadistic. And while it is impossible to know fully what it is that Lupicinus has written in that scroll about Probus, I find it impossible to believe that it included orders to leave him bleeding out on that marble floor. So yes I have wondered on that moment.

That morning, as the sand-storm shows no sign of abating, Stygos assembles the hung-over members of the legion, a mere three cohorts, all now groggy from too much wine and rough humour the night before. A little time has passed since the death of Probus but not enough for the bulk of the legionaries to hear of it. Rank after rank of hung-over men stand before the assembled centurions and standard-bearers as slaves and servants move in and out of them passing water and bread about. Many of the legionaries are wearing wine-stained tunicas. Some are bruised from the rough humour which always gets out of hand among such men. All are curious and eager to know what will come now that they are finally in Amida and among a besieged city. Candidus, attired in his best parade armour and crested helmet, a slave beside him bearing his oval shield, finds himself standing alongside these legion ranks, his eyes scanning the old carven face of Stygos for a hint of what is to come. It is obvious he has had no indication of what has just transpired and instead is eager to see what finally the Magister has planned for all these worn and rough-looking men of the ancient Twelfth Legion.

It is only as Stygos steps forwards to hold up a vellum scroll that Candidus realises that the three commanding centurions of the cohorts - Strabonius, Cyrion and Mascenius - are standing beside this old veteran all looking ashen-faced and wary. One has a nervous look while another seems to flinch at any sudden sound. Curious, our staff officer examines the centurions around him in more detail and to his growing disquiet finally sees that the Aquilifer, Probus, is conspicuous by his absence and that the Eagle of the Twelfth is being held now by a slave behind Stygos. And yet, as if some poorly rehearsed play is being performed, this absence is studiously ignored by the veteran officers now clustered about the *Praefectus*. The single exception, according to Candidus, is the Primus Pilus, Strabonius, who is white-faced and attempting to casually clean his spatha hilt with a ragged cloth. A cloth stained red, notes Candidus . . .

'. . . I watched that man wipe his hilt clean and knew then that blood had been spilt. Where was the missing standard-bearer? Where were his servants and slaves? Why was the Primus Pilus, Strabonius, ashen-faced as he stood next to this Stygos? I gazed into the cold eyes of the legion *Praefectus* and in my heart knew what my mind could not fathom. This *veteranus* stepped forward then and raised up the vellum of the Magister like the fasti of old – his voice was a low rasp and it reminded me of a spatha sliding out of its scabbard – he talked then of shame, the shame of a legion's name in disgrace, the shame of corruption and cowardice, of lethargy and fear, fear like a stink which no man could wash from his clothes. This old Roman named Stygos talked then of other legions and other battles and other honours, all won in the dim past of Roman prestige and yet I swear he talked as if he himself had been there. He talked of soldiers lost in German forests and wild savage lands, of cohorts surrounded and fighting to the last rather than being taken alive and sacrificed to savage gods, of legates and tribunes ordered by corrupt emperors to fall upon their swords and never failing to follow that last bitter order, of standards broken in a river of blood, and of solitary centurions, that old rank of honour, who fought alone in a sea of dead comrades, and always his voice remained low and deadly.

"And what of you?" he asked, finally, still holding that vellum scroll up in his gnarled hand, "What of the Twelfth Legion, now of Melitene, what of this legion and its old honours? What salve could ever come that would wash it clean and place the Eagle again upright in pride?" I saw men look around like bewildered children then and try to find the missing Aquilifer but this Stygos stopped them and barked out that as the Magister had deprived this legion of its head to mark it as shamed so now he, himself, had cut out the corrupt heart which had remained.

"– Do not look now to that standard-bearer for you will not find him, I swear! If you imbibe a poison what is the remedy? You bleed the body and let it out. I have bled this legion and let some of the poison out. I have purged it in the night with wine and iron. Now I ask you all, will you let this legion fade away into dust and bitter loss or will you march out and redeem - not yourselves for you are too stained for that, trust me - but this legion and its Eagle? Will you wash away your dishonour with your lives that this legion may be reborn again as it once was? Will you if only for one day step into the past of this legion and its battle-honours and step also out to doom as your Magister commands?" This Stygos threw the vellum scroll towards me then and trembling I reached down to pick it up. "– Read it out, Tribune," he barked, "read out their doom'"

And I did.

Thus the orders of the Magister Equitum per Orientum bade the legion march out of Amida into the desert and engage the Persian barbarians alone and unsupported so that time might be bought and confusion sown among their ranks. March forth and wipe out the shame which no legion should endure. Bring back only honour and redemption not for yourselves and your lives but for the legion. For the Twelfth Legion, the legion that once thundered. "Restore its name to the rolls of the legions with your blood, my Romans," wrote the Magister, "and by doing so expunge your shame with your death and restore to us a little time to gather our forces . . ." '

Candidus writes that a vast silence entered the old Baths of Trajan then once he had finished reading out the words of Lupicinus and that even the wind of the *Gorgona Spiritu* seemed distant and muted. Without a second glance, Stygos turned and walked out, buckling on his military belt before snatching up the golden Eagle of the Twelfth from the nearby slave - and then the Primus Pilus, Strabonius, still clearly in shock, followed him, dropping the bloody rag in his wake. One by one, the soldiers of the Twelfth Legion too moved to depart, girding weapons and armour, wrapped up in a silence as deep as the waters of Acheron itself. Not one of the soldiers glanced at Candidus as they passed him, some clearly in shock and others too hung-over to collect their thoughts, and he remarks that he is left alone, finally, in the giant Baths, that vellum in his hand, a forgotten witness . . .

We may never know the full truth of what happened in that night, as the Twelfth sank into debauchery, all lost amid the cracked halls and atriums of the Baths of Trajan, but it is obvious that by slaughtering Probus and retaking that Eagle Stygos, on the orders of Lupicinus, has bound the men of the legion with all its corrupt officers to him in a pact of blood. By doing so, this Magister Equitum sent orders which would carry the legion out into its doom and which also had inscribed in them the means to allow Stygos to bend them to his will - and that means was the Eagle won back in blood and butchery. If that is the case, then I suspect that this old Roman walked away from Probus not out of a sadistic design but instead because he refused to bear the burden of that order alone. Of course, I prefer that interpretation. It allows me to redeem him a little and knowing what is to come in the doom of these men's lives, I need that act, I think. So, yes, let us say that Lupicinus in ordering Stygos to march the legion out into certain death also detailed to him how he was to bind that legion to him and that fateful order. And it was a binding Stygos felt unable to carry through to its bitter conclusion.

And, as if in unspoken agreement, the Aquilifer is never referred to again, damned by all those who once stood under his shadow. Blood and wine has once more flowed with the Twelfth and again its legacy is not a happy one . . .

At midday on the second day after the Nones of Maius, two thousand or so men of the Twelfth Fulminata Legion, swathed in wind and sand, under the command of Stygos, march out of the south gate, known as the Mardin Gate, of Amida not to fight barbarians so much as to fight and overcome their own dishonour. They march straight towards the Persian army - an army which even as the Romans emerge pulls back into a serried block of lines to await this presumptuous solitary legion, abandoning their breastworks as they do so. A single officer stands upon the walls of ancient and blood-drenched Amida and this officer for the first time in his career finds himself regretting his *vacans* status and yearns instead to be among the ranks even if such ranks are marching to certain death. For this young officer from Alexandria, it is perhaps the elegy of sacrifice which acts as a lure to his soul and bids him march after them to stand among their fatal ranks. An elegy which causes him for one moment atop that wall, the wind and the sand battering him, to look down upon his parade armour and despise it.

Beyond this Tribune's sight, deep in 'The Gorgon's Breath' waits almost eight thousand Persian mailed cataphracts with their accompanying infantry and elephants.

CHAPTER SEVEN

There are few who mourn the passing of the Twelfth Fulminata Legion as its files out of the Mardin Gate – save the unattached Tribune Candidus upon the Black Wall, surrounded by a scattering of huddled sagittarii all hunkering down into their thick cloaks. No one watches or even cheers. Like phantoms, the legionaries vanish into the sand and wind as if they have never been. Ahead of them, far beyond the sight of Candidus, like a distant roar of a sea that remains over the horizon, can be heard the kettle-drums of the Sassanids as they pull back their lines and prepare to receive this foolish body of men.

It is to be wondered on the thoughts of these oriental warriors and nobles that they perhaps honour this lonely legion in the re-ordering of their lines as if it were indeed some proud and valiant guard marching out on its last fatal remit. For these thousands of Persians indeed do pull back, the ornate silk standards fluttering deep in the sand and the rasping wind, the horses neighing wildly, their eyes all white and rolling, the poor levied infantry lashed back by tall, hawk-faced, officers in high helms and silk tabards. Candidus however later conjectures that the Sassanids, with all the guile unique to that race, are luring this lonely legion on, ever on, into the sand and the dust, out of sight of the dim walls of Amida and those few sentinels upon it, not out of honour but instead so that its fate will remain lost from those eyes within and it will seem that the desert alone has swallowed up the Twelfth like an omen. This inexperienced staff officer, green with Virgil and all the Classical writers, hot romantic Alexandrian blood in his veins, who pens his journal for posterity and laments an end beyond his imagination, mentions also almost as an afterthought the dim outlines of the siege towers visible through the storm, lightly guarded by levied spearmen, standing like beached lighthouses on a sea of sand, and that the drumming of the retreating Persian hooves causes the sagittarii around him to stare uneasily about and pluck at their recurve bows as if warding off unseen demons.

It falls to Obedianus of the Arab cavalry, known as 'Ubayda of the Al Jawn, to pick up in some detail where Candidus leaves off. For his light body of horse archers, born and bred in the distant deserts and oases south of Palmyra, has not been ordered south into the Persian maw with the Twelfth but instead, on that morning, can be seen filing out of the Edessene Gate, all wrapped up against the storm in white robes and long billowing cloaks. The wind is bitter and Obedianus writes that he can taste the smell of almonds in it – surely an ill omen. He looks back along the line of his fellow Arabs, their heads down against the rough wind, their blue-black beards glistening with sand, and wonders on the efficacy of an order to ride north when, even as the gates squeal shut behind him, Roman legionaries are marching south to certain doom:

'. . . What madness is this, father, when Rome throws to the Persians morsels not even fit to grace a jackal's table? These broken Romans march out with that stone god at their head and I remembered thinking that not one shall return. Tonight the Persians will feast a victory feast and much wine and honey will be consumed. Their sacrificial fires for Ahura will burn bright. We file out north under orders from Lupicinus and skirt the walls of Amida to scare off Persian scouts, no more. What a jest! This wind and the endless sands blind and deafen us. I remember years ago the Great Storm which drowned the oasis at El Thaba and how we dug our horses and camels out - those of us that survived. Do you remember that struggle once the sands had died down? How we carved ourselves out of that heavy sand like caryatids coming alive? I will never forget that toil and how finally we left that oasis to its doom. It was from that storm that you said the doom and end of our tribe was marked. This storm is worse, I swear, father. As if we could find scouts in this? As if the Persians would even dare send out riders into this wave and wash of a desert which lies upon our faces? This is a foolish Magister of Rome, I swear! Shapur, that snake, has caught at his neck here at Amida, and now this Lupicinus staggers like a young pup too weak to stand. I will honour your bidding, father, though it doom us all here at ancient Amida, under the auspices the ancient mother-goddess, Ailat. I am always a dutiful son . . .'

The Arab equites, however, are barely a hundred yards from the closing Edessene Gate of Amida when figures loom up out of the blowing dust towards them. A legionary Eagle seems to float above in the swirling dust as if guiding them and in its wake follow columns and columns of soldiers with broad open faces, blue-green or grey eyes, and blond or reddish hair, braided or closed-cropped under iron helmets. For a moment, the lead riders around 'Ubayda recoil as if seeing ghosts or desert *djinn* and mutter strange oaths under the wind but then a sharp command in Latin rings out and so Obedianus spurs his horse forward in response. He finds himself gazing down into the face of a Roman officer, his skin cracked and dry and blistered, and this officer gazes frankly back at the Arab and then gestures past him into the storm.

'. . . "Amida?", he asks of me, father, and I nod dumbly down at these new Romans. This officer, a Tribune, his face cracked like the face in a mosaic, his gaze keen but somehow closed, nods back at me and tells me his men are looking forward to wine and the baths there. That it has been a long and lonely march deep in the mountains and gullies of the Taurus. They are filing past us as we speak and I see broad strong men in sturdy armour. Their shields are adorned with the bright symbol of Helios itself. Yellow plumes and crests adorn their segmented helmets. They shoulder all their food and weapons and only a few slaves, perhaps one to every ten legionaries, move among them. I remember rubbing my eyes as if I am in dream but despite the wind and the raging dust these martial figures glide past still, their tramp unerring and their determination faultless. I shout out to them 'Amida?' and they all nod back, silent on the march, muffled up behind scarves and rags and cloaks, but I can see the eagerness in their eyes to get some relief from the vagrant wind. This officer reaches up and grabs the bridle of my horse and asks me my name and rank – "Obedianus, *Praepositus*, once 'Ubayda, of the *Saraceni*," I shout back through the wind, "but you will find no wine or bathing now at Amida, legion Tribune!" '

'Ubayda swiftly tells the officer all that has happened over the last few days, the surprise advance of a Persian host up along the Tigris to Amida, the imprisonment of the Magister within its walls with his *officium* and guards, the desperate attempt to marshal a defence, and finally he concludes with the news that a disgraced legion is even now marching south into the Persian host to gain time for the Magister and his officers ensconced inside Amida. Though to what effect, none can divine.

'. . . I searched his face as I told him the ill news and the siege and the Persian army which even now lay behind the walls of Amida as we spoke. He seemed thrown for a moment, his earnest face blanching, and I wondered then on how he was so ill-informed. I could see that his mien was an Italian one. It bore that dark stain of pride and arrogance which I have seen oft enough on those olive-coloured men from the lands and cities of Italy - not the deep olive of the deserts and the Syrian sun here but that indolent olive bred under a soft lazy sky. I judged him a Roman from a deeply ancient house who wore his authority and command as a thing born into and bought for rather than learned. There was a sharp edge to him that seemed somehow brittle, as if he aped the thing rather than owned it, and I knew without being told that this Tribune was a man who led men solely because his father or some such relative had procured him this position. Behind the stern gaze and the hard lines of his mouth, I saw a flicker of doubt and he reminded me of the antelope at the edge of the oasis, eager to drink but too proud to dip his head lest he seem weak within the herd. Now, that face was open with surprise even as his immediate *principales* closed up about him to hear my words.

"What legion marches south?" he barked up at me, above the wind, one hand shielding his face, the other one my bridle.

I told him that it was the men of Melitene, the broken legion, the Twelfth Legion, ordered out like slaves into the arena, and he laughed then mirthlessly at that. That laughter threw me for it was black and bitter. He told me that it was good that a headless legion should fall into death and so erase its shame from the lists of the Empire but, father, behind that laughter I saw a flicker of unease in his eyes which told me that a deep scar lay in him. I shook my head at him then and told him that it was not headless now, that it bore a *Praefectus*, a dark and scarred man, an old Roman from out of the desert, a man who carried a vine staff and wore an old short sword on his military belt as if honouring a distant past – and this officer started at that then and gazed up urgently at me with a horrified look upon his face.

"Describe him again," he shouted at me, and such was his urgency that I found myself telling him again of Stygos and his arrival into the Twelfth Legion even as that message from Amida had arrived days ago. I told him of that evening in which a centurion had been scarred for life and another had begged for this stranger to become the head of the legion. And before I knew what was happening, this Tribune had halted the tired men around him and summoned its Ducenarii over to him – orders were shouted out above the wind and the soldiers urgently dropped their kit and rations to unfasten the shield covers and pass out their missile supplies. Before I could comprehend what was happening, father, this Tribune grabbed my wrist and ordered me as if my life depended upon it.

"Ride!," he shouted, "ride to Stygos, and the Twelfth Legion! Tell him I am coming!" . . . '

The Greek writing in the letters sent back to his father is always stilted and awkward, the language unnatural and sometimes forced. It is to be conjectured that the Christian heritage of the Bani Al Jawn points to a past in which Greek rather than Persian first allowed these Arabs to develop a rudimentary literary culture. The few Arabic letters and records which have survived from this period remain bound up in mainly Greek or Syriac - there are a few Latin inscriptions but no real epistles or accounts. Those that do remain evince at best only a clumsy grasp of those two languages. Sally was at pains to point out to me on many occasions that the Arab tribes in Syria and Jordan who adopted a Christian religion remained strongly on the fringes of that religion and, more importantly, the doctrinal disputes and heresies which raged in this period. As a result, most of the Arab tribal groups were strongly Nestorian in their beliefs. Obedianus and the survivors the Al Jawn seem unusually to have been a remnant of pagan Arabs who also had developed a little Greek literacy. I suspect that it was this latter aspiration and the fact that Valens needed what few Arab allies he could find which led to these remaining warriors being enlisted into the Roman *exercitus*. It also in a curious way allowed Obedianus to look down now upon Flavius Anicius and see in him something he has found lacking so far in the Romans he has encountered here at Amida - with the exception of Stygos - something urgent and imperial. For, despite the orders of Lupicinus,

Obedianus wheels his mount about in an instant and shouts out for his warriors and brothers to ride with him.

There is something fierce and wild in Obedianus in this moment which the Greek barely hints at; something primeval wherein all his desert upbringing and traditions crystallise about the urgent shouts of the Tribune. He writes that to see in the face of this young and sun-burnt Roman a passion and fear for that old wardog now marching on foot into the maw of the Sassanids is to look into the heart of someone who *dares* - and that was something he had found lacking all about him. And so Obedianus responds in kind and wheels his Arab mount about, calling his brothers to him, even as a grin covers his face. All about, men are shouting out orders in harsh Latin, arms are being readied, shields unwrapped, the standards raised - and in the midst of it all a small knot of Arab riders swing in on their chieftain, all smiling and laughing at the madness of it, even as the sand and the harsh wind batters at them.

When I look back over those twenty years, over all the fragments we read and translated, the research we did, the evenings and nights spent comparing notes and piecing things together out with the digs and those later months when we moved up into the deep remote uplands of eastern Turkey, I always remember that night when Sally, Jacek, John and myself put Candidus and Obedianus together side by side around the walls of Amida for not only did we connect two key figures in a single moment in time we also allowed both Flavius Anicius and Stygos to become bound together in a manner none of us were expecting. In that night, as we pieced things together and revealed our research to each other for the first time, to our amazement these figures seemed almost to both thanks us and mock us - that in some odd way what we were doing seemed almost fated to happen. Now looking back I find it inconceivable not to imagine Flavius Anicius and Stygos as companions but at the time it was a revelation unlooked for and one that left us breathless.

Behind Obedianus and his Arabs, as they ride now into the dust and sand around the high walls of Amida, lashed on by the urgency in Anicius' words, the Senior Sol Legion tightens up ranks and proceeds in full battle-array after the distant and inglorious Twelfth Legion. One by one, the six maniples open up into long columns of armoured soldiers, the wide oval shields rippling forwards at the ready, even as the rear ranks dust off their bows and pass around the leather shoulder buckets filled with the *spiculi*, the heavy javelins of the legions. This legion moves at the full-step, the *plenus gradus*, the files and ranks re-ordering under the harsh shouts of the centenarii and the biarchi, all the while the dragon standards of the maniples and the red vexillum flags of the centuries rise up into a sheen of dust as opaque as glue. Not a few of the Gallic and Germanic and Illyrian men in this legion's ranks must have glanced bitterly up at the walls of the city as they moved in formation around it, lamenting the wine which was now not to come . . .

It is, of course, always difficult to reconstruct accurately the events of a battle, given, as we must be, to rely on eye-witness accounts or the sober reviews of historians long after such events. For much of the 20th Century, the tendency was ever to dismiss contemporary accounts as hyperbolic or exaggerated but latest research tends to support the figures and details more than it does dismiss them. In many ways, understanding an ancient battle is eerily similar to the very battle about to be fought by the Twelfth Legion in that one stands upon shifting sands and views it through eyes befuddle with a dusty wind. Our main reports of the events that day come to us from Candidus of Alexandria and Obedianus, via the former's diary and the latter's epistles back to his father in ancient Palmyra. This can be supplemented with a meagre scattering of other letters and requisition reports and also by the account of some of the centurions of the Twelfth, one Sergius in particular, for example, no doubt written up for the records of the *officium* of the Magister, so that in the main a comprehensive account can be gleaned but always with the proviso that these men are viewing events through clouded eyes, as it were.

Hung-over, shamed, and still in shock, in a loose sense, by the actions of Stygos and the senior centurions regarding Probus, these men in their old armour and dull weapons, march out into the endless sandstorm and the waiting ranks of the assembled Persians. Behind them, Amida fades from view into a shifting wall of yellow while before them lies only the endless beating of the Persian kettle-drums and a vibration beneath their feet of the tramp of armoured horsemen and endless footmen pulling back before them. Perhaps, just dimly visible, to their left and right, would have been the great siege engines of Ardawan, now left unattended but for their wary guards, all looming out of 'The Gorgon's Breath' like mute sentinels, and perhaps they saw the shapes of the Hunnic Chionitae light horse archers shadowing them as they draw further and further away from the safety of the walls - shadows that must have appeared as if centaurean wraiths were lurking deep in that swirling sand.

Regardless of these suppositions, we know that finally some one hundred paces beyond the rear of the Persian ditches and wicker fences, now all but abandoned, in a low flat tract of land, recorded in the local Aramaic tongue as the 'Hekatontarch's Mark', surrounded by low rises and uneven ground, the Twelfth Legion halts, each cohort forming up abreast of the other. Ranks are dressed and the men of the centuries elbow out into ordered files, *contubernia* after *contubernia*, all eight men deep in the old discipline of Rome. The wind is sharp and vicious and not a few of the legionaries remain swathed in their old cloaks, hunched down behind their wide oval shields. A few men, those near the clustered staff *principales* in the First Cohort about Stygos, look slowly up at the pole atop which rests that ancient Eagle of the Twelfth. An Eagle with a cursed and unpropitious history. It is Stygos himself of course who grasps that pole now in one scarred hand with the other idly twirling the black-ironed blade of his gladius by his thigh. His vine staff is thrust rudely through a military belt. There is a tight closed look upon his face that speaks of an old thing being put finally away and perhaps a few of those legionaries about him - the tuba and cornu players, the Eagle's veteran guard, among whom stands Remus, his face half-swathed in a rough bandage, the adjutants and orderlies and the rest, wonder just on what it is that this scarred legionary of Rome is putting away - himself perhaps or the Twelfth legion.

This shallow plain south of Amida is fringed on the right with a series of rough uncultivated hillocks tumbling down from a ragged gorge cutting into the city's south-west flank. This gorge is studded with a series of ascending watermills fed from deep artesian wells behind the Black Walls. As a result, burrowing down into these hillocks is a meandering river and its smaller offshoots. It was here, up and into this small gorge and its watermills, that the historian Ammianus Marcellinus fought his way into Amida some years earlier when the Persians first besieged the city. To the left of the plain is one long low flood embankment and then the slow roiling waters of the Tigris itself, some two hundred paces across. A few reed-choked islands and mounds could be seen when the great river was at a low ebb but now on this day with the river fresh from rains higher up in the Antitaurus mountains, only the sound of the rushing waters can be heard. About half a kilometre from the Mardin Gate lies the Tigris Bridge now lying roughly parallel with the middle of the plain. The ground itself is wide and even and had once been levelled by Greeks in preparation for a cavalry training ground or hippo-gymnasium. It had never been built and instead the ground has been used ever since for the annual great fairs and trading stalls that the Amidans set up at the end of each harvest cycle in honour of the Great Mother, Cybele.

It is here, all beaten down by the wind and sand, that Stygos brings the Twelfth with all its ragged marching to fan out into a battle-line even as the Persians fall back to lure them on. It is a ground which would seem to favour both sides - a low level plain suitable for a massed cavalry charge but which would also support a fixed line of heavy infantry standing ready to repel such a charge. The Tigris on the left and the rough hillocks on the right would impede light cavalry flanking attempts and would also deter any sudden rear century or cohortal oblique moves.

Around them all, dust and sand will have rendered everything into a soft and vaporous gauze and will also perhaps have left these soldiers wondering if they have not marched uncertainly into the Underworld or perhaps a dream or even some mythic realm lost to all now. The booming of the kettle-drums and the endless tramp of the distant armoured horsemen before them would have framed this uncertain world and done nothing to dispel that unease. An unease surely heightened by that most fearsome sound of all - the low *chthonic* moan of the Sassanid war elephants, echoing through the dust like the unearthly cry of the dead.

It is just as the last of the lines of the Twelfth Legion are being dressed by the centurions and the optios, that the Arab *foederati* arrive from out of the blowing wind and sand in a sudden and unexpected flurry of hooves and billowing white robes. Even as Obedianus reins in his small Arab steed to arrange his riders on the exposed flanks of the legion, a guarded smile on his face, a distant pulsation is felt ahead of the Romans – a deeper wave in 'The Gorgon's Breath', as if it is alive and now bunching itself forwards in one slow roiling motion. Before the last of the rough Latin commands echo around the lines and are swallowed up into the sandstorm, before even Obedianus can dismount and pass on his urgent message to that chipped and aged *Praefectus*, all ensconced in the ranks of the First Cohort, dim shadows emerge from ahead and the muted tramp of a host of horse blossoms into a martial din. Obedianus, in a terse letter, later captures that moment:

'. . . They came, in their thousands, out of the sandstorm the Romans called Gorgon, as we stopped, in the desert, in the heat, our steeds blown from that furious ride around the Black Walls. They came upon us, a wave, a surge, of steel and horse and bright silk and we felt the world itself revolve down upon us and that little legion, alone before Amida . . . And, father, I wondered on the command of a strange Tribune, that I flung my Arab brethren into this maelstrom of dust and wind, knowing that only death would follow . . . And Ailat herself came then, her cloak dark and her breath all-consuming, her breath about me like a golden rain . . .'

The host of Ardawan falls upon the Twelfth Legion even as the *Saraceni* halt to dress ranks and pluck at their lances or bows, eying the dazed legionaries about them as if they were face to face with dead men. That host in all its shining glory, like a veil of stars, descends to the thunder of its drums with the glorious silk panoply of its standards - the falcon, the gryphon, the hawk, the moon - wreathing it like wings while far behind it tower the awful black monsters of those elephants . . .

'. . . Do not we Arabs know, father, that to catch the Sassanian in all his slippery coils one must set other snakes upon him? Did we not learn this in those endless wars in the deserts and oases of our people as we fought for our survival against their mailed cataphracts and elephants? Had not Petra, that jewel in the desert, and Palmyra, too, wove around themselves cunning coils which had often ensnared the Persian? How sad then that this ferocious storm which fell upon us even as we rode out of the desert and into the city was named 'The Gorgon's Breath' - that awful Hellene *Djinn* with stone-fixing eyes and a head encrusted with a weave of snakes like no other - for that storm alone seemed to ensnare us and not the Persians. And were not these Romans all stony with sand and frozen like statues now before this storm and if that is so one must ask where are the snakes to writhe and hiss about the head of this Gorgon that she may bind these men of the Twelfth together into their unholy doom? Where are the serpents of this endless storm? And I will tell you, father, they came upon us in all their shining doom, writhing out of the dust and the wind, and their breath was silk and their venom the pounding of drums . . .'

So wrote 'Ubayda, also known as Obedianus, native commander of a small *Ala* of indigenous mounted archers, a man who from his writings has had a long and bitter experience of warring with the Persian Empire. This 'Ubayda must have had barely enough time to form up on the Twelfth's flanks even as the Persian host under the glorious banner and standard of the *Spahbad*, Ardawan himself, advances, in rank after shining rank, down upon this isolated and lonely legion, all lost behind the Persian breastworks. In the swirling sand and dust, the Sassanians advance upon the legion and the little Arab troop of cavalry, their drums pounding and the hooves of the horses reverberating, such that it seems as if the desert itself is opening up to swallow them all away.

CHAPTER EIGHT

It is in this moment of conflict and collision, where the desert vomits up a host of war and death, that Stygos, under the shadow of the Twelfth's *Aquila* grasped now in his knotty fist, barks out what would seem to be a final and fatal order.

For there, as the thunder of the advancing cavalry catches at them all, he shouts out the command to half the ranks as though the cohorts and centuries are to extend in shallow order - and up and down the lines, the tubas and cornus echo that command even as the confused centurions turn about and shout at their own men to open up the ranks. In an uncertain rippling, as legionary after legionary steps slowly out to each side of the other, the three cohortal blocks begin to shift into a longer and leaner mass, all the while the Persian host emerges in its glory - and no few of those poor men of the Twelfth must have stared back at the Eagle within the First Cohort and wondered on the madness and horror of it all . . .

It is this surprising order - to open rank into an extended formation and in effect double the length of the legion - that causes confusion and disorder up and down the lines. As each centurion barks out the requisite command - *primani hold your ground, secundi step out!* - to the urgent squealing of the tubas within the cohorts, the lines and files ripple with a sort of uneasy hazy movement. Lost deep in the swirling sand and dust, the vexillum standards fluttering like impaled *daemons*, words and shouts snatched away in the gloom, legionary after legionary stumbles about as if caught in a mad dream or prophesy from which there is no release. More than a few heads strain about into the *Gorgona Spiritu* in a vain attempt to grasp at some sense - even as within the storm a wall of shadow pulls itself in towards them all like an oncoming wave of darkness, kettle drums framing it all in an unending nightmare . . .

In moments, the First Cohort under Strabonius has doubled its facing, with all four *secundi* legionaries in the eight-man file stepping out to the left and moving forwards to sidle up to their respective *primani* in front. Oval shields all emblazoned with the ancient thunderbolts slot into place even as the long spears or *hastae* of the front rankers level down towards the oncoming darkness. This cohort, the First and prime Cohort of the Twelfth, stands in that most prestigious place in the battle-line: the right flank. It anchors that battle-line and now accounts for half of the entire length here in the 'Hekatontarch's Mark'. The Primus Pilus, sweating intensely under his scale armour and segmented helmet, his nervous face blanched in shock now, screams out again and again for the men about him to half the facing even as the centurions to his left and right urgently seize on that command and drive it down in among their own centuries. It is a credit to Strabonius - if to nothing else but his nervous energy alone - that he manages to effect the command in time and all six double centuries of the First Cohort re-form into a formation four men deep.

The legionaries of the Second Cohort under Mascenius are not so fortunate, however. The wind and the sand obscure the commands and while this Primus Prior understands what Stygos has ordered, his own incredulity and the effects of the wind deprive him of precious moments in which to put it into effect. Standing at the edge of the first century in the Cohort, he feels more than sees the legionaries under Strabonius edge towards his own and while it is obvious that to preserve the integrity of the battle-line, he must also extend his own lines, both the onrushing thunder of the Sassanids and his own mounting disbelief cause him to doubt his eyes. All around, legionaries stare anxiously at him even as the centurions of the Second Cohort edge forwards ready to bark out the command to turn. That command, however, hovers too long in Mascenius' mind and with a dawning horror these centurions realise that in moments the enemy will be upon them in their thousands despite their wavering lines and loosening oval shields.

It falls to Cyrion of the Third Cohort, ever eager to bluster his honour and courage, despite the stain he and so many of his rank bear, to realise that if he does not double the facing after Strabonius the battle-line will be dangerously broken. In doing so, he must have known that Stygos is not effecting a solid strategy but is instead throwing the legion upon the lances and swords of the enemy as a sacrifice - and so something in him snaps then. Something wild and dark which perhaps has been festering in him for too long. In a sort of mad abandon, Cyrion barks out for the *secundi* to open out and fall to by the *primani* and then he begins to laugh out loud at the madness of it all. Sergius, a centurion in the Third Cohort and not far from his superior, remarks on what happens next . . .

' . . . It was a dark laugh, that sort of laughter a man throws out when drunk or goaded on, and I looked to him, the Cohort's Centurion, our First Centurion, and saw a black humour in his face even as the tubas cried out against that awful drumming. Sand and dust fell between us like a shroud of the Martyrs, but still his laughter fell over us. I swear by all the Names of the Forty that in that moment of madness I knew that his feyness was for death not honour or victory and wondered again on this Stygos - this ancient Roman more an idol than a man - that he could infect us so. The wind buffeted into me but I spun about and shouted out to the file-leaders and file-closers under me to half the files. I think in my voice was an urgency that may have sounded as fey as

Cyrion's was now. It was an order of madness - an order of death - to half that depth from eight men to four - and against those cursed cataphracts of the Persians! - but I knew as Cyrion must know that we were nothing but a sacrifice now, a lamb to the slaughter, and as all good Christians do, we must open our arms to receive the blow . . .'

Sergius is voicing what many if not all must have felt as that order rippled down the ranks of the three cohorts, all wrapped up in that desert storm. The Sassanid cataphract, armoured in iron leg and arm manicas, his chest covered in a great corselet of scale, his face enclosed in a cassis complete with a frozen mask, mounted on a proud Nissaean warhorse bred especially for battle, is a fearsome opponent - so much so that Rome has incorporated its like within her own armies - and as with all opponents the cataphract has been met and challenged on the field of battle by the legions. Again and again, the long stolid lines of the heavy infantry have held fast against these armoured horsemen, deflecting their long two-handed contus lances only through the mass behind those shields. The shock of a cataphract charge is one few infantry can withstand and those that do are able to only through the depth of their lines, as legionary behind legionary braces forwards with his shield. It is a doctrine unquestioned here in the Oriens and one now that is thrown to the wind by Stygos.

In moments, then, the long line of the Twelfth buckles unevenly across that flat plain, with the First Cohort and the Third Cohort extending in time along the left. The Second under Mascenius, however, remains inert and dangerously jumbled and so drifts backwards in confusion even as the swearing legionaries under Strabonius collide into it. Panic begins to seed among the men of the Second Cohort and those in the rear ranks - the sagittarii and the light javelin men - step away from the lines and look wildly about as if to find some order in it all. Seeing none, more than a few turn to the rear and begin to lope backwards towards the dim monolithic outline of the siege towers in the distance. These shapes, huge and incongruous in the plains here, seem implacable, like titans judging the scampering mortals about their feet. That uneasy hesitancy soon blossoms into something more urgent and no few of the rear rankers of the Second Cohort fling their heavy shields away and sprint backwards under the looming shadow of these moniliths.

It is in this moment, with the Second Cohort wavering under the indecision of Mascenius, the wind buffeting them all without let and the moan of distant elephants shivering all their fortitude, that the long dark stain in the *Gorgona Spiritu* resolves itself into a massive elongated line of glittering cataphracts, their contus lances held low over the crop of the Nissaean horses, hooves flashing in the murk, high silk banners flaring out in abandon and victory - and all along the three cohorts, a great impact is felt as that wave of armoured horsemen collides remorselessly into the lines of the cohorts . . .

'. . . *"Silence! Do not fall back! Do not advance ahead of the standards!"*

- Again and again that refrain spewed forth from my lips as those cursed Persians fell on us. We had little time to loosen what heavy javelins we had before yanking out our spathas and crouching low behind the oval scutums. It was a fall of thunder the like of which I have never heard and before I knew what was happening - before any of us knew what was happening, as Christ is my witness - we were all hedged in under lashing hooves and the long sharp thrust of their contus lances. Poor Nysias beside me fell back, his head crushed into a bloody pulp, the helmet cracking asunder as a great hoof flicked at him. The rider arced high above us, his cold implacable face mocking us all. All along the front ranks of the Third, I saw legionaries tumble and spill backwards in shock and fear even as these Persian cataphracts slammed into us without let. It was a sacrificial toll and we paid it in moments. Again and again I heard my voice, raw and hoarse, shout out the eternal legion command - *Do not fall back! Silentium!* - and that most mocking of all commands now: *Do not advance ahead of the standards!* As if any would dare or even find the space to do so! I heard shields crack like ice on a river about me. The few long *hastae* we had were shattered on this armoured wall of rider and horse. Bodies were rammed and pummelled into a bloody pulp under their contus blades or heavy mace-heads. I remember a fierce pressure against me as I crouched beneath that old scutum, a wall of weight which found me and seemed to want to crush me and me alone. The foul stench of horse sweat fell over me and in one desperate mad moment I glanced up above the scutum rim and saw a Persian cataphract, gilded in silver and gold, a lush tabard of emerald about him, forcing his mount into me. Dust and sand flowed between us so that it seemed as if he were both real and also some wild desert phantom forming before me even as I watched. And there on his left and there too on his right emerged mirrors to this immortal shade of Persia and the Orient. And all up and down the thinning lines of the Third shimmered cataphract after cataphract as if all were no more than copies of this one enemy above me. A harsh clang resounded from my helmet and sparks flashed across my eyes. The force of that blow knocked me sideways and it seemed as if that frozen mask, its eyes black and hollow, the mouth curved always into a leer of victory, was looming down into me - and then a hand grabbed the back of my scale hauberk and pulled me aside. A spatha flashed forwards, knocking that long lance askew, even as the legionary behind me - young Theophanes, his beard always no more than a goat's wisp - barged into that rider with his shield and attempted to manhandle him backwards. I laughed at his nerve and stepped into him, our shields sliding together, locking along the rims, even as we pushed and ducked down from that vicious contus blade. Sweat fell from me in waves but my throat was parched like a eunuch's purse outside the basilica. By Christ, though, as all the Forty bear me witness, we held that front line despite the mass of horseflesh and the licking of the Persian contus blades down upon us! . . .'

Both the First Cohort and the Third Cohort, by a miracle many will later ascribe to divine intervention, manage - barely - to hold the initial impact of the Sassanid charge but at a heavy cost. It is later estimated that perhaps as many as a century's worth of legionaries all along that thin battle-line are swept aside and butchered either on the end of the contus point or crushed beneath a lashing hoof in that first moment of contact. There is no doubt that had Stygos not ordered the Twelfth to half its depth from the old eight man file to a four man one, the entire battle-line would have been able to absorb that shock and perhaps even repel it with far fewer casualties. As it is, however, the battle-line is halved and now as dozens and dozens of front-rankers collapse into the sand before the cataphracts, it seems as if the Battle of the Hekatontarch's Mark is over before it has begun. Screams and desperate shouts ring out all along the front ranks of both cohorts, even as the surviving centurions beat out again and again the mantra of command - and despite all the odds, neither cohort crumbles into retreat and panic. Instead, in a riot of shouted orders, the dead are left where they fall and the wounded hauled quickly out and passed to the rear where the slaves and medici are waiting to catch them up. In places all along both the First and Third Cohort, the Persians affect a penetration almost through the thin lines but never completely and never at once. A single cataphract *Savaran* rider - magnificent in gilded armour and silks, his silver mask splashed with crimson - leaps the last line of legionaries, all scrambling aside from the flicking of hooves, and reigns his Nissaean horse about behind the Third Cohort. In one elegant move, this lord and master of the fertile lands in Mesopotamia, flexes his knees along the flank of his mount, causing the stallion to swerve about, even as he brings that awful contus lance up and over the horse's neck to bear on the rear of the Romans around him. In that single moment however when this rider is caught in that turn, a phalanx of light legionaries or *exculcatores* swarm him, pulling him down into the dust, stabbing and hacking at the iron manicas until blood pours forth, and the armoured body is laid out in the dirt like a sacrifice. The horse bolts into the swirling sandstorm and is never seen again - and all along those rear ranks, as those *exculcatores* rise up scowling and grinning ruefully at their own daring, all that can be heard is the mad laughter of Cyrion deep among his men, all flecked in blood and dark fluids. That moment of penetration is repeated up and down both cohorts but never in force or at once and so they hold, bent, strained and crumbling, but they hold that long fierce charge of the armoured Persian horse.

The same cannot be said alas for the Second Cohort under Mascenius. Although massed in a deep block and with a far narrower front as a result, the Second Cohort remains a ragged undisciplined mass, with some centurions anticipating the command to half files and others hesitating and waiting for the Primus Prior to shout it out. Legionaries waver and drift in and out of position. A single standard - the vexillum flag of the Fifth Century under a certain tall Anatolian named Elias - is actually seen to *advance* into the thunder of hooves and drums all falling now onto the Second, his legionaries moving into a tight wedge or *cuneus*, oval shields slotting together, *hastae* spiking up out. This centurion, Elias, a man renowned for his fiery temper and long spatha reach, has clearly snapped in frustration. The remainder of the centuries however buckle and waver even as the Persian horse falls into them. In moments, everything is chaos and abandon, with the front ranks all dissolving into a crimson wreck. Men scream and vanish beneath the hooves and contus tips of the enemy. Standards topple. Commands to hold fast are cut off in mid-breath. Mascenius and those intimate about him stumble backwards, frantically beating off the long blades and maces of the Sassanid riders. The cohortal standard bearer - a dark bearded Isaurian, his teeth all missing from too many fights - ducks and weaves amid it all, holding desperately onto that standard, his spatha flashing in a dull net about him. In a heartbeat, he is alone in a wild onrush of Persians who all seem eager to butcher him and snatch up that glorious red flag. The dark mound of horses rears up about him, hooves lashing down, even as the long contus lances jab again and again at his jigging form. Mascenius looks once at this Isaurian, even as his comrades trip backwards, yanking at his arm, and then he turns from him into the dust and the sand. The last anyone sees of the Isaurian is his form falling into that patchwork of horses, blood spilling from it, and that broken pole being caught up and raised high in victory by a silvered cataphract rider. To many in the Second Cohort however the loss of the standard goes unseen. Panic washes over everyone and it seems as if the Persian riders have barely been checked at all by the legionaries under Mascenius. In moments, dozens of armoured riders are through the rear of the crumbling legionaries and into the open ground behind them. Small clumps of Romans hold fast, swirling down into uneasy shield-walls but not many and nowhere near enough to hold a line - and like a dam bursting, the entire mass of the Second Cohort dissolves into ruin and death.

Obedianus alone on the flank sees the danger and flings his Arabs behind the dissolving rear lines of the Second in a futile attempt to check the Persians' advance and buy time for the legionaries to recover and regroup. It is a forlorn attempt but this Arab chieftain sees little alternative . . .

' . . . Beside me, Old Jubyal, his face split asunder with amazement, grabbed my arm to check my orders but I swatted him away and urged my fierce steed on, pulling my brethren after me, as we turned to ride into these emerging Persians. Oh father, you would have been proud to see us all charge into that maelstrom! Gone was the ineffective discipline of these Romans and in its stead was our hot Arab blood and pride! I saw grizzled faces about me, their blue-black beards flecked with spittle, anticipate my orders and already spur their horses forwards, high yells and savage cries echoing the doomed voices of the legionaries not far from us. I heard Old Jubyal shout out behind me 'We will all be dead men now!' - and I laughed back at him over my shoulder, all thoughts of life and old age wiped from me. He shook his head at that and then followed, kicking his little Cappadocian pony after me. We careened about the rear lines of these Romans and slammed hard into the Persian *Savaran* even as they spilled and erupted out of the rear of the last lines. Everything was a mess of falling bodies and legionaries running hard away in fear and terror. I saw spathas and scutums being thrown aside in haste. One legionary stumbled even as he wrenched away his scutum to fling it from him - and in that moment of hesitation a Persian rider reined about and caved in his skull with a mace blow. Another fell forwards hoping to lie inert and remain undetected as the wash and wave of the enemy fell over him but an alert cataphract rider saw him and stabbed that awful long contus down into his form without a second glance.

And then with a high yell, we, the sons of the Bani Al Jawn, the shades of our ancestors at our shoulders, fell in among these cursed Persians, our spears unerring and our steeds never faltering in that charge. We were wraiths of the desert, the white of our cloaks blinding them, the nimbleness of our ponies dazzling them, our laughter mocking them, even as those Romans tumbled and fell and scattered about us. It was a glorious moment, father, as Arab bested Persian here deep in the swirling storm of the Gorgon, and for one long heartbeat it was all ours. I felt the blessing of Ailat herself on me, her dark cloak and breath wreathing me, her veiled gaze upon me, honouring me, and I shouted into the madness of it all.

And I remembered in that hot work the stain of the Sassanid, of how his ilk had broken our ancient deserts and oases, burning our palm groves, salting our villages and sacred places, and how this Shapur himself had breached the ancient lands and threaded his iron chains through the shoulders of his captives, to our eternal shame. All this flashed through my mind, hot with battle and rage, even as we collided our fleet horse in among their heavy mounts. In moments, we were hacking and stabbing at them, flying past in a whirl of dust and rippling white, our mad laughter dazzling them and causing no few silvered masks to twist this way and that. Old Jubyal reared up his pony and thrust down with his long spear into the neck of one *Savaran* noble, cutting deep into him so that crimson spurted up into the dust. That armoured figure toppled sideways from his horse and vanished into the chaos of the fleeing Romans about us all. A wedge of Persians swept between us then and Old Jubyal vanished from view. I pulled hard on the reins and twisted my horse about into those Persians and in a mad moment hurled my spear into the faceplate of one. It clanged fully from his helmet, snapping in two, barely making a dent in him. Before I realised what was happening, my spatha was out and I had slashed it about him - and, father, furious then was the play of spatha and mace against each other . . .'

It is no use however despite the madness and desperation of that charge. The light unarmoured Arab horsemen stand no chance against the cataphracts who are pouring through the lines of the dissolving Second Cohort in ever increasing numbers. Scores of white-clad Arabs are cut down or simply bowled over by the heavy Nissaean horses. Others are baffled as their spears shatter or snap against the iron armour of the riders. In their hundreds, the Sassanid riders sweep aside the bulk of the Second Cohort and pour out into the rear of the Twelfth Legion, even as the legionaries of the Second break ranks and tumble backwards in panic. Only a few pockets of legionaries remain intact, forming desperate knots of defence, oval shields overlapping, spathas and *hastae* thrusting out in panic, the odd remaining centurion or optio barking out breathless commands. In an odd irony of battle, that single century - the Fifth under the tall Anatolian named Elias - its rankers and file-leaders intact, finds itself alone in the wake of the Persian charge, the wind buffeting them all and the sand hiding all, even as this Anatolian sweeps his gaze about in a determined attempt to divine what is happening. The *Gorgona Spiritu* baffles Elias however and in a moment of frustration he orders the century to halt and form an *orbis* about the century flag. Elsewhere, however, apart from this oddity, the Second Cohort in effect has ceased to exist as a battlefield unit; its legionaries in desperate retreat or wounded or already dead under the hooves of the Persians. Despite the actions of Obedianus and his light horsemen, the line of the Twelfth is breached and the centre of the Persia advance erupts into the rear of the lines.

It is now, as the Persian riders sweep around and begin to pour into the rear ranks of both the First and Third Cohorts, that the madness and doom of Stygos' command to halve the lines becomes apparent for, with only a depth of four men, there is no opportunity for the files to split and form a double shield-wall or *fulcum* facing both forwards and to the rear. Even as those first Sassanid cataphracts slam into the rear rankers of both remaining cohorts, wild-eyed centurions and file-closers spin about in a futile attempt to form some sort of defence - but to no effect . . .

'. . . The laughter of Cyrion was maddening but I knew there was nothing to be done about it. A great wall of sand buffeted us on all sides and it was as if shadow-shapes emerged to assail us from the drifting desert itself. This endlessly moving wall of shadow, of dark figures, all wrapped up in flowing silk and fluttering standards, charged about us and I knew then that somewhere to our right the Second under Mascenius must have been breached. There was a momentary flash of white out of nowhere and then I saw one of those cursed *Saraceni* tumble backwards into the ground, tipped out of his saddle by a contus thrust. Blood gouted out of a chest wound and his long dark beard was tipped up at a grotesque angle. For one solitary moment, I gazed upon his ashen face even as that blood poured out of him and wondered then on these desert riders that they were holding our backs against such fearful odds. It was no use though - and even as I heard again Cyrion's laughter echoing about us, I saw that wall of shadow close in about us all and knew then that we were doomed. We had held them at the front but only just - each *miles* shoving desperately into the back of the man before him - but now with these Persians to our rear, we stood forlorn under God's eyes and all about me, man after man could be heard whispering whatever prayers or oaths he knew. I threw a desperate glance to Cyrion at the corner of the Cohort but all I saw in him was death and mockery. That and red flecks all across his face but whether that blood was his own or another's I could not tell. And above that laughter, above that endless wall of shadow and dust, as if a maelstrom of horse and rider swept about us as insubstantial as the storm itself, I looked up and saw then the blessed Forty shining in a radiance as glorious as anything I had ever seen, and I think I was smiling then - as were so many about me - smiling at that divine light now enveloping us all as if we were being lifted up by the grace of Heaven itself . . .'

This Sergius is not the only Roman that day to remark upon this ethereal light and the presence of the Forty Martyrs of Sebestae in it, all gazing serenely down upon the dying Romans. In the chaos of the slaughter and the panic, with legionaries frantically running back towards an unseen Amida, all lost in the storm, or hunkered down behind wavering shields, it seems that no few of them see a glowing light as if from Heaven itself and held within this light shine the faces of those Martyrs of Sebestae, those most iconic of Christian martyrs here in the East, and owned by the Twelfth as their patron saints now. This light seems to grow out of the lashing wind and the rippling waves of sand and is possessed of a divine radiance few have seen before. Many of the legionaries in the Third Cohort pause from their desperate defence even as the Persians surround them in a river of dark shadow and heavy drums to gaze in awe up at this light - some crying out in praise all the names of the Forty like a litany - while over within the First Cohort, its centuries bracing hard in turn against more of the same Sassanid riders, men look up and wonder on the providence of God and His Son, that the Saints and Martyrs of this Legion should appear now to welcome them all up into Heaven. Some break out into tears of joy and throw their weapons down to embrace martyrdom, others fall to their knees in fervent prayer, while still others advance willingly onto the arms of the Persians, their eyes rolling with ecstasy even as the centurions about them wonder at this madness. All along the lines and ranks of the First Cohort a sort of religious frenzy stirs and amid the blood and the death, wonder and joy emerge, that the Forty have come and through their intercession all will be made martyrs to God, the emperor, and the *respublica*.

It is perhaps Stygos alone, that disgraced Eagle in his hand, surrounded by those few veterans elected to defend the standard of the Twelfth, who stares about to assess what is happening. The frown on his old and scarred face is an ugly one, his eyes dark and pitiless - and then in one single moment of inspiration he is seen to spit and curse contemptuously at it all. Stygos curses into the religious faces of the legionaries about him even as that glow ascends higher over them all. Nearby, Remus, his face broken and bandaged, one eye permanently blinded, swears in bafflement and then moves to step closer to the *Praefectus*, his spatha edging upwards. We will never know what the intention of this burly Galateaen was for in that moment a Sassanid rider rears up over the Eagle of the Twelfth, his contus lance long since shattered and now bearing a heavy ornamented mace in one armoured fist. That implacable face turns triumphantly towards the glittering Eagle of Rome - and in one surprising move this *Savaran* slides from his warhorse into the path of the cursing old *veteranus*. It is a moment which startles all about this Sassanid noble as he lands in the dust and advances towards Stygos, one hand wrenching up his silvered faceplate, the other swiping hard with the mace into him. The latter, that harsh curse still about him, crouches down into the old guard position, the gladius in low and close, the Eagle held before him as both a shield and a lure. A swirl of sand washes suddenly over all, battering both the Sassanid *Savaran* and Stygos, blinding them both, and then, in its wake, there is a savage crunching noise, a spurt of bright crimson, and then the Persian lord is tumbling backwards screaming, clutching at his severed arm, as Remus stands by, that spatha flecked in fresh blood. Those nearby swear that Remus shrugged then, blaming his one eye for missing Stygos and hitting the stupid Persian instead, before he turns away into the dust and wind, hefting his oval shield up higher into his shoulder. The face of Stygos remains a mask, however, his eyes dark and inscrutable even as he, too, turns away from the vanishing Remus and looks again up at the growing sheen of light flowing about them all. And that contempt in him rises again above the prayers and ecstasy and the murmured ritual of name after name after name of the Forty . . .

It is those fleeing from the remnants of the Second Cohort, back towards an unseen Amida, their weapons and armour flung away, that seem to find themselves most in the heat and depth of this rising light. These panicked legionaries soon find themselves apart and alone in the Gorgon's Breath as the Persian riders wheel their mounts about to fall on the rear lines of the First and Third Cohorts. It is a moment in which a sort of frenzied panic recedes momentarily and those stumbling legionaries slow a little, unbelieving of their fate, even as it seems that a wall of light flows up about them and not a few wonder then that fire as well as snakes should emerge from the breath of the Gorgon . . .

'. . . I ran and lost my *contubernales,* my tent-mates, in that panic and rout, the breath heaving from me like a ragged streamer, and then I was on my knees. The wind and sand battering into me without let. I fell and began praying like a *monachus* atop a pillar of rock. Words tumbled out of me - mad words, incessant words, words I could make no sense of, even as that wind hammered me and made me bow my head in shame and humility. Christ and God and all the Saints I prayed to even as I saw about me nothing but corpses and the dying. A hand reached out to me but behind it lay nothing but a shroud of sand sliding and fastening on whatever dying *miles* lay beneath it. And still words tumbled out of me unchecked. My eyes were veiled in confusion. My mind awhirl as this Hekatontarch's Mark was awhirl with dust and sand. I prayed and prayed and prayed and, lo, a miracle came unto me, unto us all . . .'

Looking up, this poor legionary of the Second Cohort sees a wash of light like a glow from Heaven fall all about him as he kneels among the dead and the dying. He describes it as a pillar of flame ascending unto Heaven, pure, golden, and so tall as to make his head crane up to follow it. This unnamed legionary lost in the storm, shriven from his *contubernium,* looks up in awe and traces high into the heavens a tall pillar of fire:

'. . . It ascended like a ladder blazing with the Lord's glory and pierced the veil of the sandstorm like a beacon, a *pharos* of divine light pointing the way to the providence of God through Christ's mercy. I wept to see it and praised the Lord, the One God, His Son, of like Substance, and all the Saints in whose footsteps I was to follow now. I stood up then as if on legs of marble and raised my head up high into that eternal and blessed pillar of flame . . .'

It is then even as this legionary rises out of the dust, seemingly intent on ascending up to Heaven, that he sees another pillar of firing rising up. It shoots up out of the wind and the dust, ethereal and glowing, rising higher, a twin and counter-part to the one absorbing his gaze - and even as he turns to wonder on this second pillar shooting high above him, a third and then a fourth pillar flares up and a vast hellish glow suffuses the rear of the Hekatontarch's Mark, a glow irradiated with fire and light, these pillars crackling and hissing as if tormented and twisted under a heat beyond endurance. He hears, as if distantly, a mighty whooshing noise, followed by what he dimly recognises as screams or shouts and then a low long rending sound is heard and that first blessed pillar of flame is seen to waver uncertainly in the sandstorm before toppling in one slow majestic movement down into the ground. Its impact stuns this legionary and makes him flinch, his hands rising to cover his face, and he feels a tremendous wash of heat and noise flow over him. The shock of that collapse causes him to stagger backwards, fear flooding through him, and to his horror he sees, one by one, the other pillars of fire flaring up and then collapsing all wreathed in screams and cracking noises, as if the world itself, the rim and edge of it, were breaking and then melting apart. And out of that maelstrom of red and ochre and yellow, figures are seen to emerge. Strange figures, all marshalled under tall standards and moving swiftly forwards, as if given birth by that hellish wash of fire and now eager to leave it . . .

And without a backward glance, the legionaries of the Senior Sol Legion, yellow crests and plumes tossing wildly in the wind, jog past this amazed survivor of the Second Cohort, their tight faces uncaring of his wounds or exhaustion, their discipline and purpose fixed alone on the Persian horse all ahead and ploughing now into the rear ranks of the surviving two cohorts of the Twelfth. These Germans and Celts and Illyrians jog past in tight order, oval shields in close, the *imago* of Helios himself all emblazoned on each one, long spears gripped tightly in each right hand, even as the rear rankers move up in loose order, readying their light javelins and bows, curt Latin commands piercing the wind, all ignoring the prone legionaries in the sand about them. For one moment, this amazed legionary sees a figure jog past, a heavy crested helmet on his youthful face, his olive-coloured skin cracked now with the cares of the desert, and his lips pursed tight against the demanding pace all are following - and in that moment both eyes meet even as this officer draws level and passes him by. And all the prayers and all the praises to God and Christ freeze then on this legionary's lips and a black chill seeps into his heart such that it wipes away his joy and all his jubilation. The cracked olive-skinned face nods once down to him and the gaze he returns is grim and satisfied indeed.

And behind them all, the tall siege towers of the Persians fall, one by one, wreathed in flame, their timbers cracking apart, sounding for all the world as if mighty titans are being brought to earth and butchered for all time. In the wake of each one, lie scores of butchered corpses.

CHAPTER NINE

All this however is lost on those legionaries under Elias.

Alone within a howling wind, blinded by sand, and all hunkered down behind a triple layer of oval shields, the men of the Fifth Century wait, tense and nervous. Deep within that sandstorm named after the Gorgon, some eighty men peer into that impenetrable wall of shifting dust, each one grasping a long spear or a heavy javelin, all the while Elias, their centurion, strides slowly about an inner pocket of space, rapping his vine stick sharply upon the helmet of a legionary peering about too nervously or perhaps joking too loudly among his *contubernales*. Elias is tall and thin - a wiry Anatolian bred out of the harsh hills and high plateaus - and is known for a hot anger always tempered with an unerring precision in his weapon-play. Among the centurions of the other centuries of the Second Cohort (many now dying or wounded in the bloody chaos of that collapse unseen behind them), Elias is accorded uncommon respect and is rarely mocked or ignored. It is said among them that sooner provoke a scorpion than the wrath of Elias. Now, with all his men kneeling or crouched or standing about him in a tight *orbis* fronted by a triple hedge-row of shields, that respect and even indeed fear is the only thing holding his century intact. The dull rasp of sand sliding over pebbles, of twigs and reeds whipping past in a blur of motion, of the faint rumble of drums and the shrieks of horses in the distance, wraps them all up in an endless wavering shawl but he alone, moving slowly about in that single pocket of space, one hand about his staff of rank and the other casually swinging his shield back and forth, pins the men in place. One legionary, a recent recruit from Sebestae, barely a few months into the legion training and only just tattooed with the *stigma* - the old crossed thunderbolts - of the Twelfth, looks up in trepidation as a certain *deepening* in the roar of the storm seems to wash over them. He looks up and in a flash that vine stick raps off his helmet and Elias is up over him barking at him to maintain his place in the *fulcum*, that old layered shield-wall of the legions. Only a few legionaries about this unfortunate youth note a slight frown of concern over the grizzled face of Elias; a shadow so slight as almost not to be seen - except by those who know him too well. This frown is gone in a heartbeat though and Elias moves on around that tiny empty hollow, his voice cruel and unremitting, but now his gaze is peering deeper into that wash of sand and slowly, so slowly that no one seems to notice, his puts aside the staff and unsheathes the long spatha slung over his torso.

It was the madness of the sudden charge under Elias which allowed the legionaries to find themselves alone and unsupported within the *Gorgona Spiritu*. Expecting to charge into a wall of Sassanid heavy cavalry, all had braced their long spears or heavy javelins for impact as they had rushed forwards into that oncoming charge. It was the last thing it seems that the Persians had expected and as a result many of these riders had simply veered aside to let this impetuous knot of men through, intent as they were on riding down and obliterating the wavering lines of the Second Cohort under Mascenius. Once that thundering body of horse and armoured rider had swept past them and they had found themselves all alone in a swirl of desert, Elias had quickly ordered them into a tight defensive circle, swathed in shields, out of which spiked their spears and javelins. In what had seemed an endless monotony of wind and dust, they had remained there in that desperate pose, waiting, all the while the only identifiable sound was the harsh Latin of Elias, sometimes punctuated with an earthy Aramaic curse or a Greek expletive. Sounds fell on them from all sides and those sounds were of an ilk - death, pain, fear, and all lost as if drifting past in the hands of unseen wraiths. It is a place in the Hekatontarch's Mark where, unknown to Elias, his Optio, and the file-leaders under him, the first line of heavy cavalry has swept past but the second line of the Persians has yet to appear. It is a lull and a space from the battle and the slaughter and, as with all spaces, it is soon to be filled.

And the first thing to fill it is that deepening sound in the sandstorm which had prompted this young legionary to look up, bewildered and tense.

There is a moment after the hearing of that sound, followed by the sharp tap of *vitus* over helm, that all seems again to be no more than the eternal rasp of the storm - save that Elias is slowly placing aside the vine staff of office and sliding out his spatha. Then that sound is heard again - a low dolorous moan wafting past them - only this time it seems to arrive from far over on the left, away from the young legionary. It falls over them all in that little huddle like a tease and in its wake vague shadows drift towards them, flitting here and there - figures in Phrygian caps, bearing light javelins and small wicker shields - a few at first and then more and more but always loosely and passing them at such a run that they neither pause nor stop, only dodge away from the Romans deeper into the darker folds of the Gorgon's Breath. These figures appear and then vanish as if from a dream - one only pausing long enough to gaze upon the tight shield-wall before smiling bleakly and vanishing as if he had never existed - but in their wake comes the echo of a third low moan. A long rumble or squeal, deep and sonorous.

And then it appears, a high wall, bristling with spikes and heavy plates, monolithic but swaying slightly in its gait, close enough to seem as if the sandstorm itself has thickened into a monstrous desert leviathan. This ancient enemy of Rome, once the terror of the Latin lands itself, sidles past the legionaries of the Fifth Century in a long slow drift; a mass of dark movement broken at the edges by the turret and the trunk and the tusks and the long thrusting contus lances angling down now left and right. Another appears athwart the century, walking slowly as though unconcerned, the mahout driver and those spearmen in its turret all looking down at them with blank oriental eyes. A third and then a fourth elephant emerges from the wind and the sand, all swaying in long gentle gaits, their trunks curving slowly back and forth as if without a care in the world. These majestic beasts, reared and trained far in the east of the Persian lands in the K'ushan valleys, their riders all small dark Gupta warriors with kohl about the eyes and teeth painted crimson, move past in row after row as if the Romans did not exist, ignoring them, avoiding them, their human cargo looking deep into the storm ahead, heavy cloaks pulled tight.

It is Elias alone, his voice low and harsh, his commands unflinching, who holds the Fifth Century together lost as it is from the legion with its lines now all crumbling behind them. He stands in that little empty hollow of the *fulcum*, his shield loose by his side, the spatha raised slightly into a half-guard, and he does not look once upon the shadows of these Persian elephants as they pass them all by but instead talks to his men, naming some, cursing others, reminding a few of past deeds, mocking those few he trusts with his life, and as he does so the low overlapping shield-wall remains intact. Against the squeals and moans of these elephants, he musters the cold Latin of the *exercitus* of Rome, that discipline which embodies the Legion, as he orders them to hold over and over again; the *'Silentium'* of his command and authority anchoring them all as the monstrous shapes sift past them and vanish into the haze of the storm. In the momentary silence which follows the last Persian elephant, this centurion, Elias, allows himself a slight smile. A smile which is not reflected in his eyes however.

To these legionaries, all lost deep in the swirling sands of the storm, that moving wall of dark flesh and ivory consumes them and so it is no surprise to hear that in their world, there is no vision of the Forty wreathed in flames, no ecstatic light or halo, nor indeed any urge to thrown away their arms or armour and give themselves alone into the embrace of martyrdom. Nor also, it must be said, is there the sight of the siege towers of the Persians all falling in a crescendo of flame and sparks . . .

One by one, these impressive works, buttressed with Cyprus wood, bound in iron strips, spiked at the top with staves and batons all roughly sharpened into points, flare up into columns of fire. Long sparks shoot up as if racing each other. The timbers crack apart with a boom which echoes across the Hekatontarch's Mark. And then, one by one, each siege tower subsides in a long slow topple to the ground below, shattering the area about it and spraying out shards and debris, all afire as if the heavens themselves are falling down. No tower is spared. No guard is left alive. No slave pouring water over the iron joints is allowed to escape back into the Persian lines. And the grim silent soldiers of the 'Sun' legion, on whose shields rests the symbol of a deity favoured by the Augustus Julian himself, move forwards in tight formations, maniple by maniple, dragon standards high and triumphant.

The speed of the assault upon those siege towers must have taken all the guards and slaves by surprise, intent as they would have been in following the fate of the Twelfth Legion to the rear of the breastworks. One can imagine their fear to find scores of armoured Romans in among them without warning, hacking and cutting them down, even as the legion's *exculcatores* were up against the great base of each tower with lighted torches and arrows. The dry wind of the *Gorgona Spiritu* would have inflamed those torches in moments and the subsequent conflagration must have been unstoppable. The few guards - poorly trained levy spearmen behind oblong wicker shields - would have fled in an instant before the wrath of these Sol legionaries and their tight-lipped ducenarii. It remains unknown who originated the idea to strike first at the siege towers but whether it was the idea of Flavius Anicius himself or one of the *principales* under him - the Primicerius, for example, or the Campidoctor - the effect was immediate and devastating. In moments, the tall towers roared up in a conflagration which lit up the entire interior of the sand-storm in a hellish glow. And out of that glow, that harsh vermilion weal inside the sand and the dust, the outline of the emerging legionaries, maniple by maniple, took everyone by surprise:

'. . . These were dark shapes cut out of that light, silhouettes bristling with spears and shields, all inky and fluid against that wall of flame, and for one moment, as I stood there, dumbstruck, that vision of the steps to heaven fading, I wondered on these *milites* of the Light, that they emerged as if born from it. All across my vision, all along that flaming horizon, came a long shimmering rank of legionaries - and here and there, rose up the snarling heads of the standards of Rome . . .'

In moments, the fleeing and the wounded legionaries of the Twelfth Legion have been passed by and left alone in the sand-storm. Deep among the ranks of the First Maniple, cloistered among his staff officers, Flavius Anicius is barking out sharp orders which send the orderlies and *principales* scurrying in all directions even as the tight maniples advance at speed down upon the collapsing lines of the legionaries ahead of them. Whatever might be said about this 'Corbulo's' youth and obsessive addiction to discipline, no one can doubt his grasp of tactics for in moments, the men of the Senior Sol Legion ripple out into a double line of maniples and then advance, shields locked in a tight *fulcum,* directly into the shattered lines of the Second Cohort. Like a thick wall, buttressed sixteen men deep, long spears projecting forwards, these legionaries shout out a harsh battle-cry and slam into the rear of the Sassanid heavy cavalry even as it is falling onto the crumbling rear-rankers of the First and Third Cohorts. That tight ordered charge under the mantle of the legion's battle-cry of '*Axios!*' achieves complete surprise and like a dam stopping a flood the *Savaran* wheel about in disorder and chaos. Horses collapse, riders tumble out of their horned saddles, standards waver and then topple as if being swept away by an unseen wind. Overhead, a sudden volley of lead-weighted darts and arrows arc up and fall with deadly accuracy into the disordered horses and riders. It may be doubted as to the effectiveness of this volley, launched by the rear-rankers of each century, given the armoured nature of rider and horse but if in nothing else but confusion it sows many seeds. Down in among the front rankers an altogether different battle is being waged however. Here, as the legionaries in the front rank overlap shields and push forwards in a long packed line, the *hasta* comes into its own. This is a long thrusting spear some two metres in length used either over-hand or under arm depending on the tactical need, which allows a legionary to create either a spiked wall of spear-points to defend a line or a triple layer of horizontal spears in the ancient manner of the Greeks while advancing. It is this latter arrangement which is used now as up and down the locked lines of the maniples, with the ducenarii and centenarii shouting out the old orders to lock scutums and present spears, rank after rank of legionaries tighten up and thrust out the iron blades. The tubas and cornus blare out the command to advance and to a rhythmic shouting, the front three maniples shove forwards deep into the press of the reeling Sassanid horse. The rear three maniples brace their shields, *hastae* upright, and shove hard into the backs of their *commiliatones* in front.

That tactic - of damming the broken cohort in the battle-line - checks the Persian advance in a heartbeat. The *Praepositus* of the Arab cavalry writes of what happens next:

'. . . I had lost Old Jubyal, father, within a swirl of Persian horsemen, dust and wind battering at me, my guards and brothers all swept away in that rough flowing melee, when I heard the deep roar of the Roman horns from behind me. Of course I knew this Tribune was coming with his legion of Helios, of course - but still in all that blood and slaughter, with those poor men of the Twelfth falling like ripe corn, my heart had forgotten and knew now only the hard hot iron of revenge, the *tha'r* we Arabs hold closer than love. I knew they would be upon us but when I heard that low animal growl of their cornus, I raised my head in shock. They came out of that sand in long tight rows of armoured soldiers, all packed behind their oval shields, long spears thrusting forwards, dragon heads leading them on, and before I knew what was happening, they were up into the jostling cavalry of the Persians. In one long heave, their spears were deep into the flanks of the horses while above rained an endless shower of arrows and those little darts the Romans favoured - their *martiobarbuli*, the 'darts of Mars'. In moments, everything was a chaos of squealing horses and panicked cries. Spear shafts snapped. Figures toppled out of their saddles. Blood spurted up into the air, stark and brutal against the vapour of this sand storm. I saw a Sassanian , some elegant *arteshtar* lord clad in red and purple, his faceplate up, wheel his battle-mount around in haste, shouting out commands, even as one of those tiny darts took him in the face.

About me, my Arabs reined in and together we dashed outwards even as this inexorable line of heavy infantry advanced deeper into the Persians. All of us were bloodied and exhausted from that desperate struggle to hold the place where this Second Cohort had crumbled - exhausted from the futility of it and bloodied from the sheer exhilaration of fighting our ancient enemy - and I saw that of the hundred I had flung into that slaughter less than sixty now remained. That knowledge, father, brought a chill into my heart - that so many of my brothers had fallen in so short a time - but before that chill could take root like a canker, I saw Old Jubyal shake free from the hot melee and shout over to me, grinning. He was waving his arms and there wrapped about one hand streamed out a long silken standard, torn no doubt from a Sassanian commander. He laughed like a madman and spurred his pony over to me, shaking that gorgeous wrap like a palm frond of victory. I shouted out to him that for a dead man he was princely looking indeed - and he, still laughing, brandished that wrap even higher.

Then we were lapping about the edges of these newly arrived Romans, our horses slowing, all lathered with sweat. Around me, the warriors of the Al Jawn reined in, wounded and swaying in their saddles - but all looked to me expecting another order to charge again, such was their devotion to me and their hatred for these Persians. The wind blasted about us and we all squinted into the dust. I saw then, behind the massed lines of the Romans pushing forwards with their long spears and shields, this Italian Tribune amid a small *coterie* of officers and orderlies. Slaves and servants near him were dashing hither and thither pulling the men of the Twelfth - those still alive - to the rear to tend to their wounds. A limping centurion of the Twelfth stood next to this Tribune, pointing out where the First and the Third were cracking apart despite a desperate fight, all the while holding one hand against his side as blood dripped slowly into the sand at his feet. I saw this Tribune glance once, almost dismissively, at this centurion and how the latter seemed to flinch under that look as if whipped. I saw then that it was none other than Mascenius himself. Old Jubyal at my side saw it also, father, and glanced quickly at me, frowning.

"These Romans snap at each other as much as they do at the Persian dogs, 'Ubayda!"

"Sooner divine the wind than know the mind of a Roman!" I shouted back over the wind. "Come - let's see what this Tribune plans next!"

We were up among his officers in moments, all riding in around them on a wave of dust, even as his guards moved instinctively between him and us, spathas out and shields raised. Behind us all that infernal glow was receding now and all that marked where those siege towers had stood was a mass of cracking material here and there which occasionally shelved in amid a shower of sparks and fresh flames. I saw soot on many of the faces about me and no few of these Western Romans had pulled off their heavy helmets and were wiping the sweat from their brows. This Tribune saw me arrive and ordered his guards to receive me and in moments I had dismounted next to him. I swear, father, there was a cold hard look in his eyes despite the brittle face he had; a look which seemed to relish this battle as something *owed* to him. I remember the way he turned to me for news and the way in which that badly wounded Mascenius at his side was ignored as if he was irrelevant. And I knew then that this Italian with his olive skin and that little thing behind his eyes which he hid so carefully but never completely cared nothing for the legionaries dying ahead of him - only for that one man he had interrogated me about. That man who alone had brought them all out here to die forlorn in a storm of sand and iron. About him, stood hard-bitten Romans, officers and adjutants, all in tough mail and iron helmets. I recognised their type in an instant - these were stubborn fighters, disciplined and calculating. Romans who were dedicated to war and battle and that old hoary goddess they called *disciplina*. These were men who had marched south into Persia five years ago at the head of the army of Rome - men prized by that dead Augustus, Julianus, and favoured above the soft incumbent oriental legions. Many of whom fell with him in that fatal *excursus* and retreat.

It was then that this Tribune grabbed at my shoulder and pulled me in to him, to shout over the wind, asking after Stygos, that old scarred soldier, and I laughed back into his olive face, father. I laughed and shouted out that no Sassanian *mashrafi* blade would take *that* one's life! And he had the audacity to scowl back at me! This pup who aped command, who held authority like a shield! He scowled at me as if I were a child and made to rebuke me -

But I raised my hand suddenly and looked up, alert and tense.

We Arabs know the wind and sand as if it is in our blood, father. I still remember when you first left me alone at the edge of the Harra, the Black Desert, with only a goat skin and a thin cloak. Do you remember what you said to me before you mounted your camel and left me? 'Three days to the north lies an old ruin, my son. A tower lying broken across the sand like a stave snapped in two. This ruin is where your foster-brother of the Bani Nahshal is waiting for you. He will wait for the fourth day and a night and then he will leave. May you avoid all curses, my son.' And then you were gone into the dunes and the broken stones of the Harra. I walked and walked, sleeping under that cloak at the dead of the day, sipping but sparingly from the goat skin, and marvelled at the desolation about me. It was then - as you knew I would - that I grew to know the desert and the wind; its endless, weaving, dance. And in that long trek all alone I found not just that knowledge but favour from Ailat Herself when She came to me in a vision, her breath warm and comforting, her eyes luminous like the moon. She came in my dreams and wound me deeper into the desert and I knew then such intimacy that I have never walked in fear among the deserts since. So, father, I know the wind and the sand and in that moment when this Tribune dared to scowl at me everything about us changed.

I felt it in an instant, as did my brethren about me.

The wind shifted like a lover's touch upon my face - and then it was gone. Gone so completely that in the silence which followed, in that well of absence, I found myself looking about as if waking from a dream. That wind fell away in a heartbeat and all that sand, all that rough detritus of the desert hanging now in the air about us all, fell away like a veil rent apart. The world itself emerged then as if the breath of Ailat Herself dissolved away to reveal the glorious splendour of a land long since hidden from view. It was a moment of wonder, father. A moment of such glorious stillness and beauty that I knew in a heartbeat that She of the Dark Folds, the Mother of All, was about me then, her mysterious eyes on me, her touch, her breath, willing this rough storm away so quickly it seemed as if it had never existed. The wind vanished. The dust fell. And all about me, my warriors and brothers were smiling for we knew what only Arabs can know about the desert and the Will of She who resides deep in it: that on a whim she had snatched away that storm and left us all now naked to each other on that rough plain known as the Hekatontarch's Mark.

It was a moment which checked this young Italian commander even as my hand rose against him.

All about us men and horses seemed to pause as if startled or thrown. Before, dust hid them all - Roman and Persian - but now a certain clear nakedness emerged. That sudden exposure threw men up and down the lines. It was as if the veil of that sand storm had allowed their bravery to remain unwitnessed and therefore unchecked but that now, out in the open, it stood upon a wider arena and as a result a certain hesitancy grew up around us all. Father, it was a hesitancy which spread up and down the locked lines and even before that dust and migrant sand had settled and vanished, a stillness spread around us all. A silence the like of which I had never heard before. In that dome of stillness, the world opened to us and what we saw took our breath away even as we paused and fell into silence . . .'

Obedianus writes to his father in words which are redolent with a deep mystic impression which is the legacy of his pagan Arab upbringing. His eyes see through a lens shaped neither by the emergent Christianity of the Roman Empire nor a certain Greek or Syrian tradition of anthropomorphic gods and goddesses whose attributes shift and merge in a sort of cultural syncretism. His vision, his world view, has been shaped by centuries of desert tradition in which the moon, the wind, the stars, and the ancient rock formations of the deep deserts hold a special place. For him, the wind itself is alive. The ground beneath his feet is a tapestry to be read. The world around him, a palimpsest of meaning and divination. These forces are occasionally manifested into sacred personages - the moon goddess, Ailat, who brings death as release, for example - but in his world, the great canvas of the landscape in all its myriad forms is for him divinity itself and needs no human idol or statue to stand in its stead.

The Ecclesiastical Chronicle of Mar Simon refers to this sudden collapse or cessation of the sand-storm as follows:

'. . . Then the Divine Word came to the assistance of the Amidenes. The wind had created an intense storm about the two armies and poured it onto the Medians and the Greeks, surrounding them as with a thick darkness at noontime. A dreadful slaughter occurred among the Greeks and one could not distinguish the corpses of the fallen from each other. However, through the mercy and intercession of Christ, the dreadful storm abated as though whisked away and in the lull which followed the Medians were thrown into confusion and despair . . .'

Mar Simeon's curious mix of archaic terms and biblical rhetoric omits mention of the surprise arrival of the legion under Flavius Anicius and the burning of the siege towers which is understandable given his need to emphasise the providence of God. It is that reduction of causal history into a narrative predicated upon divine favour which also allows Mar Simeon to overlook another and far more important arrival that day. One which plays a key role in the subsequent events of the battle more than the collapsing lines of the Twelfth or indeed the sudden arrival of the soldiers of the Senior Sol Legion. An arrival entirely unlooked for both by the Arab chieftain and also the two legion commanders. Sergius, caught up in the lines of the Third Cohort, surrounded on all sides by the Persian - or 'Median' - heavy cavalry, finds himself in a unique position to witness what happens next after the wind and the dust abates . . .

'. . . We all staggered as if struck by a blow though no blow fell on us. That sudden collapse of the wind and the dust caught us all by surprise and it was as if an unlooked for nakedness now stunned us. All about me, *milites* paused from their desperate defence and looked up, wide-eyed and uncertain. The eternal curtain-wall of horse and rider froze about us into a dark and mottled frieze. I saw one Persian rider, his faceplate up, his eyes wide and uncomprehending, even as below him a Roman soldier who had sprawled backwards, one hand thrown up in a desperate block, blink as if waking from a dream, all the fear and mortal terror fleeing from him. The vexillum flags swayed once and then fell still above us all. One glorious Persian banner, long and intricately embroidered with birds of prey, fluttered as if dying and then slowly rippled downwards about the haunches of a black horse. Everything was still then. I heard as if like a chorus the ragged breaths of hundreds of men and animals about me. It was a strange and unknown thing, this ending of the sand storm so soon after the vision of the Forty which had swept through us. Strange in that, unlike the vision, it held us all - Roman and Persian - in its icy grip. As that dust fell like a vaporous silk at all our feet and as the wind shivered into an absence which left us naked, we all became still and mute save for that endless breath. I saw thick black columns of smoke tumbling up into the heavens then from the shattered siege towers - four great pillars which rose and spilled across a startlingly blue sky - shot through with flashes and sparks of fire. Other sights fell onto me - details which seemed to crowd my eyes now no longer blinded by that storm: the distant black walls of Amida and the flash and gleam of soldiery on its towers; the glittering tumble of waters falling down from the mill wheels to my right about the rough ground near the Mardin Gate; unknown legionaries behind us all, boxing the Persian cavalry in like a thorny dam - and then something far off caught my eye. A glint or a flash - I do not remember - but before I knew what I was doing, I broke that frieze and stepped out of the tangle of falling legionaries into a clear space. I stepped out and gazed in wonder far over to the Tigris, to its cool waters, to the low level edge of the bank which protected it - and what I saw made me grin like a fool and I knew then why we had been ordered out to die. I knew what it was our Magister had planned and I understood now why this Stygos was so keen to bathe us all in our own blood . .
.'

Up and down the broken and disorganised lines of the Twelfth, legionaries look up and see what Sergius is the first to see. It is a sight which not only raises dazed smiles on all their faces it also galvanises the tight ranks of the Sol legionaries to their rear to push even harder moments after the *Gorgona*

Spiritu has ceased. For there, on the far banks of the Tigris, in one long and shimmering column, is an army advancing down towards the stone bridge over that river. It is a mounted army on powerful steeds all carrying armoured warriors clad in mail and scale, high plumes and crests adorning them all with a regal aspect. These mailed cuirassiers look similar in appearance to their Persian rivals but there is a subtle and eternal difference between them for these cataphracts bear a hardier mien than their oriental cousins to the south. The faces are sun-burnt but harsh and unforgiving, lacking the long oiled moustaches of the Persians or their kohl-rimmed eyes. And while the armour and the weapons are eerily similar there is a certain roughness to the latter which sets them apart from their Persian cousins. These cataphract riders are not so gilded nor clad in silks. Their maces lack ornamentation. The long contus lances do not sport silk or gold tassels. Those that wear animal pelts or drape them under their horned saddles display the gold of the mountain lion or the speckled yellow and black of the cheetah or the rippling sable of the bear. However what truly separates out these riders, this army, from its mirror over the Tigris, now in among the broken Romans, is not their miens or habiliments but instead their standards - for floating and rippling high above all these mounted regiments and troops is the eternal sign of Christ, the Greek monogram which is his initials, along with the banners and icons of various saints and martyrs. These symbols and woven words shimmer far in the distance above the ranks of these armoured horsemen, so alike and yet unlike to the Persians across this ancient Mesopotamian river.

It is a moment wherein that river would seem to become a maze and a mirror; in which twin forces are cast only to be split asunder in a shift which is subtle and devious. For these opposing armies fight and are organised within a similar ethos - an ethos in which the mounted lord or prince sits astride a heavily armoured horse, himself clad in manicas and cuirass, his head sheathed in a heavy cassis, all the while he rides into battle wielding the long contus lance even as his lesser cousins about him hold the shorter lance or carry the curved bow. These armies both prize martial combat over discipline or the anonymous grind of faceless soldiers; wherein the embodiment of valour and courage is the single combat on horseback before the waiting nobility; in which the sight of two mounted opponents riding towards each other, long lances poised, is held in far greater esteem than the slog and heave of the infantry in the rear with their oval shields or anonymous hedge of spears. And as one army fights forever under the gaze of Ahura, all the while the Persian magi bless each one with the smoke from the holy fires, the other fights under the benediction of bishops and monks who carry before them the relics of saints and vials of holy water.

For what the Romans see even as that sand-storm falls away is an

Armenian army under Artashemeh, sister to Vashak of the Mamikonean House, the *Sparapet* or commander-in-chief of Armenia. She is a powerful noblewoman in her own right, renowned for her warlike skills and blunt diplomacy, dubbed mockingly by her brother Vashak as the arm and mace of the cataphracts. In her wake, and the wake of her picked *Azat* bodyguard - all clad in bronze scale corselets and sporting the sable of the bear - ride hundreds of grim-faced *Naxarar* nobles from the Houses of western Armenia - the sons of the Bagratuni, the Arshakuni, the Aspetians and her own House, the Mamikoneans, to name but a few - those old bloodlines from the ancient Parthian clans scattered and driven into exile by the Sassanians over a hundred years ago. These latter lords of ancient Parthian blood have never forgotten the shame and humiliation of losing the Iranian heartland to the Sassanids and nurture now an ancient hatred bred deep in the Armenian highlands. A hatred fed by a religion which despises the old fire-worship of the Persians as nothing more than the very breath and blood of Satan himself . . .

It is a moment, for Sergius at least, in which the Tigris is both a divide and reflection: one of exile, one of religion; one of destiny and fate   and like counter-posing rhythms, these twin armies face each other even as the dazed combatants raise their heads up into the clear air and that stillness which has frozen all.

'. . . For one mad moment, it was as though we looked not across that river but instead upon some fantastical Greek mosaic; a demented mosaic - one which mocked us all with the martial purity of its lines and spirit. The colours were vibrant. The standards high and emblazoned with the words and signs of Christ. The movement of riders and horses sure and determined. It was a long procession of war and vengeance caught in a single act - a tesserae of glittering cubes - and about me, all around me, wounded legionaries stared in disbelief upon this army across the Tigris, wondering if they were not mad or drunk still on that vision of the Forty. Not I. I sensed in a heartbeat what was before me. That clarity drew me out of the hesitating ranks and left me alone from them all, my spatha limp in my hand, the scutum lax at my side - and I grinned then like a beggar in the agora who stumbles over a dropped purse. I grinned for I saw now what that Stygos must have divined. I grinned knowing that sometimes a sacrifice is not just a sacrifice.

It is also bait . . .'

CHAPTER TEN

A fragment of a funerary inscription survives from Amida which allows us a rare insight into this moment of change and discovery. It was unearthed only four years ago during renovation work on an apartment block up against the northern wall of the city. In the process of that work, a small Christian cemetery was uncovered and a rescue dig subsequently initiated. Some thirty inscriptions were removed and restored as a result. One in particular, using the seven day week inaugurated by Constantine only forty odd years earlier, is inscribed as follows:

'To my well deserving sister, Illyria, blessed under Christ, who lived thirty eight years. She died on the second day of the second week of Maius, at the eight *hora* and five *minutiis* under the mantle of the Apostle, Thomas, whose arrival washed away the bitter storm.'

In Christian burial practice in this period, the twelve hours of the day are now synonymous with the Apostles under Christ, whose body itself is the day and night of birth and resurrection. It is a curious intermingling of pagan astrology and Christian/Jewish mysticism which allows those recently dead to be identified as Christians so that when the Resurrection arrives they will be set apart from those unbelievers about them. This moment of death, which is recorded by the hour and where each hour now is linked to a specific Apostle - in this case St Thomas, the eighth hour - signals that moment when the dead one is reborn again and therefore evades the fate and determinism of the older pagan zodiacal system. It is both an adoption and also a refutation. In the case of Illyria quoted above it allows us a fortuitous glimpse into the time of day when that sand-storm ceased. The reference to minutes usually indicates nothing more than a rhetorical expression of longevity but here in this case the fact that it specifically mentions the storm seems to argue for precise timing.

Five minutes after two o'clock on the afternoon of the Ninth of May in the year 367 AD, the great sand-storm which had raged about Amida and its *territorium* vanishes as if it had never existed. Atop the Black Walls of the city, legionaries and officers blink unexpectedly up into the glaring blue of the sky and marvel at the sight which greets their eyes. For while Sergius fancifully describes what he sees as a mosaic all revealed about him, it is only high up on those basaltic walls that the full effect can be seen. All along those parapets and towers, men crane forwards in astonishment. Some fall to their knees in prayer and others shout out orders and messages to those deep below and out of sight. A single tuba cry echoes around the bastions about the New Gate as one startled soldier blows on his instrument again and again, perhaps hoping that by maintaining that clear sound the wind and the dust will stay at bay.

It falls to our Candidus, alone at a corner of a tower and a wall, a heavy sagum cloak wrapped up about him, his felt cap pulled tight about his head, to rise up in wonder and see the entirety of the scene such that he records it for posterity. Shaking out the dust from his eyes and throwing wide his cloak, this Alexandrian officer, his blood a curious mixture of Greek and Aegyptian, grips the black stone of the wall and sees not the tussled lines of the legionaries and the Sassanians a rough mile out from the city walls in one uneven mass across the Hekatontarch's Mark, nor the smoking ruins of the great siege towers and the hacked corpses scattered about them, nor even the long snaking columns of the Armenian heavy cavalry moving purposefully south down the Tigris and to the stone bridge. What strikes this Candidus is none of these details but instead the slow peaceful roll of the mill wheels and the sparkling water which cascades from each one. To him, straining forwards, dust drifting from his shoulders and cap, his knuckles white against the black stone, that image is what first captivates him - the tranquillity of it, the refreshing cleanliness of it, as those wooden wheels revolve and great spumes of water and foam tumble down from the ravine up against Amida. The *Gorgona Spiritu* vanishes in an instant and to his amazed eyes the relief which fills him is a sweet picture of almost rustic charm. And for one moment, this unattached Tribune feels that sight as if it is a balm to his eyes - and while others around that long circuit wall react in surprise and alarm, and even as that single tuba cry reverberates about the city, Candidus finds himself smiling alone watching those wheels arc up out of the river in turn after turn, the water spraying away from the spokes and slats like diamonds.

Of course it does not last and within moments his pen lifts away from this bucolic scene and all the litany and agitation of battle consumes him for what Candidus sees then is the enormity of war all across that plain to the south and east of Amida.

Around him, confusion reigns as soldiers and monks, notaries and eunuchs, all rush to the parapets in response to the echoing call of that single tuba. Thick ropes of black smoke trial up into the sky before them all like pillars framing a scene wrought with blood and chaos. Strung across the dry plain of the Hekatontarch's Mark is a thin and frayed line of men the centre of which is dangerously bent and twisted. It is here in that chaos of the centre, with the glittering Sassanian horse all pouring forth like a river of iron, that the hard lines of the Senior Sol Legion have made their stand, the *hastae* bristling forwards over their shields, even as what is left of the Second Cohort dissolves into a mess of running men and toppling bodies. Out on the flanks, both the surviving Cohorts are now buckling inwards under the pressure from armoured riders both at the front and now from the rear. Standards twist like saplings in a wind, the plaintive cry of tuba and cornu drifts back to those now watching from the Black Walls of Amida and within those sounds can be heard lost shouts of despair and anger. And there, out beyond the flowing lines of the Persian heavy cavalry all embroiled now with the Twelfth and the Sol legions, stand the dark wrinkled bulk of the elephants - a score of them strung out like enormous brutal statues carved by a hand which knows nothing of elegance nor softness. These black pachyderms shuffle forwards, their mahouts urging them on with fierce cajoling shouts even as the riders in the armoured turrets loosen off waves of arrows and light javelins. A single elephant raises it snout up high and trumpets out a long *chthonic* cry and all along that line it is picked up and echoed so that Candidus writes that even the walls of Amida itself seem to shiver in response. Behind those great behemoths, in one long mob, drift the Persian levied and allied troops - rag-clad spearmen bearing oblong shields, archers in felt caps, the Nubians and Auxumites, marked from the rest by their exotic garb and savage standards, the cruel twisted faces of the Hunnic Chionitae hovering on the flanks, their light steppe ponies nervous and skittish now that the desert storm has passed, and finally the Arabs who always trail the Persian armies into Roman lands for plunder and rapine.

It is of course neither the enormity of the Persian army now toiling forwards in three great lines nor the surprising reveal of the Armenian column forging in a cloud of dust down the left bank of the Tigris only moments away from crossing that river and advancing into the exposed flanks of the Persians which consumes this unattached officer's gaze. All along the parapet, excitement and confusion wells up with many soldiers pointing and gesticulating across that wide river, while others are staring in awe down into the long rippling ranks of the Sassanian foot troops or the auxiliary riders or indeed even those mountainous dark shapes, all crowned with infantry. A few cry out at the imminent collapse of the men of the Twelfth now exposed in the daylight. What seizes upon Candidus is none of this however, alert as he is to the fate of the Romans down in the Hekatontarch's Mark below. Instead he leans in over the black parapet, frowning in shock as he sees *another* legion deep in the dust and confusion of the battle below - one neither expected nor anticipated. Only dimly does he see their standards and the thought comes to him that the presence of this new legion is something perhaps to be wondered on more than the arrival of the Armenian cavalry. Even as that thought emerges, a sudden commotion nearby surprises him and he sees the Magister Equitum Lupicinus arrive atop the parapet. In his wake, shuffle anxious notaries and guards and a whole gaggle of adjutants. This Imperial commander brushes aside the soldiers ranged before him with a brusque order and then peers down into the plain, his dark eyes sweeping all across the lines of the battle. What he sees is not a sight which he seems to find welcoming, according to Candidus:

'. . . The anger on his face was as sudden as it was unlooked for. In one sharp movement, he had spun about and barked out a dozen orders to the orderlies and slaves about him. The Latin of his words was clipped and harsh. In moments, a dozen figures spilled away from him and he remained alone but for a small phalanx of guards. I saw him glance once back out into that mess and confusion of battle below and I knew that his gaze fell not on the dying men of the Twelfth but on those stubborn unexpected troops who pushed forwards now into that long ragged tear in the centre. Noise and chaos fell back to us atop these Black Walls but there was no sense in it. He looked back once and then before I knew what was happening the Magister was striding towards me, his face pinched and pale with anger.

"*You*, Tribune, find out what that unit is!" he snapped at me.

"Me?" I stammered back. "How will I do that, *Dominus -*"

"Ride out, you fool! Ride out and order them to pull back now before it is too late!"

The look on his face brooked no argument and so I hurried myself down the bastion-tower's steps and out into the wide space below it. In moments, Timoleus, my Aegyptian slave, had arrived with our horses and then we were cantering out of the Mardin Gate and towards the Hekatontarch's Mark. Crowds of impetuous beggars and vagabonds were beginning to pour out of that gate in our wake both eager to see what was happening and also share in the booty which they suspected might follow. As we left the shadow of the high black walls behind, however, I heard harsh orders ring out to close those iron-bound gates no matter who was left outside.

Then we were alone and moving swiftly across the rough plain. Behind me, Timoleus carried my shield and helmet if I needed them while I bore only the spatha at my side. The speed of the Magister's order had caught me unprepared and as a result I now wore no armour only the light *subamarlis* used as padding. About us, the landscape was a rolling parchment of abandoned debris - wicker baskets, piles of wood heaped about ready to form defensive barriers, torn cloaks, split boots, and so on. Nearby I saw one of the siege towers now all a heap of charred wood and melted fittings. Great ropes of black smoke rose up from it while below the shadows thrown from that rising pillar roiled across the ground, slimy and vaporous. It was here about this broken thing as we cantered past that I saw corpses - poor things gashed and hacked to death without mercy. One was headless and some legionary in a moment of grim humour had impaled that head alone on a stake, a loaf of bread rammed into its mouth. My slave behind me baulked at that sight but I ignored him and spurred my mare on. Ahead, I saw a veil of dust rising up now to replace the cover of the *Gorgona Spiritu* and through it the gleam of arms. The escort and guide of the Twelfth - those *Saraceni* under Obedianus - were milling about the rear ranks of these soldiers and I could see a small knot of officers and *principales* among them. I veered over towards that knot, lashing the mare into a hard gallop, even as mad thoughts consumed me.

I did not understand what the Magister meant - pull back? But why? And where had these Romans come from? Ahead, within the dust of battle, I saw the sun flash from a score of oval shields but the emblems on them were ones I did not recognise. A spark of gold told me where an Eagle stood deep within the officers and guards and so I knew this was a legion of Rome - but that device on the shield eluded me. It was white and shaped like the radiating spokes of Helios on a deep field of crimson and even as we galloped up close to these legionaries I wracked my mind as to their origin. And the words of the Magister came again to me - to order these Romans back as though they were nothing more than errant schoolboys. It made no sense. The centre of the Twelfth was broken - any eunuch could see that - but in a moment of action, the commander of this newly-arrived legion had ordered his men into that breach and despite the odds plugged up that gap. Why would Lupicinus want to unstop that action? Like a mad whirlwind, these thoughts possessed me and so I barely remained aware of that larger arrival - those Armenian heavy cavalry all riding in a huge cloud of dust along the far bank of the Tigris, heading, I had no doubt, for the bridge over the river to put themselves into the lines of these Persians . . .

So we galloped up in among these Roman legionaries, lathered in dust and sudden sweat, the sounds of battle falling over me, and all about us I saw the detritus of the dead and the dying. Scores of slashed and crushed bodies lay around us. Many with deep cuts across the back of the head or the shoulders. Others were grievously wounded and now moaned or screamed on the hard ground. All, dead or dying, were coated in a thick glutinous mess - a foul mixture of the desert sand and their own blood - and it seemed to my mind as if each lost legionary was now being swallowed up in a dark cloak. Shattered weapons and shields lay everywhere. Over to my right and left, what remained of the Twelfth fought on amid the rearing horses and long stabbing contus blades - but here in the centre, these newly-arrived legionaries heaved forwards, their *hastae* striking hard into the flanks of the Persian horses before them. I heard a shout echo out again and again from their throats and in my astonishment recognised the Greek cry of *'Axios!'* These Romans were shouting out over and over that he is worthy and I wondered on who it was that had won that ancient accolade.

Then a dozen guardsmen were about us, their white sun symbols framing me, herding me in, and I shouted out as loud as I could that I was a courier from the Magister himself - I was Candidus, staff officer to Lupicinus, with orders for the *praepositus* in command of these Romans. But before anyone could heed my desperate words, even as we were hemmed in by those flashing shields and my mare reared up all anxious, neighing like a mad thing, the tenor about us all changed. The rhythmic shout of *'Axios'* suddenly swelled up and burst over all like that cry in the arena when a gladiator is bested against the odds and I knew in my heart that my order was too late . . .'

Unknown to Candidus, it appears that the shock of the sudden cessation of the storm, with that vast silence which it seems to have unleashed, brings the entire Persian advance to a halt. Even as the dust and wind vanishes and all along the lines of the Roman soldiers a sort of uneasy hesitation emerges, the Persian riders rein in and look about in astonishment. For not only has a new mass of Roman legionaries appeared right in the heart of what moments before had been a certain collapse and rout, there, across the Tigris, rides a long column of heavy cavalry, all framed in the banners and symbols of Christ. That shock seems to have stunned the lead Persians such that a certain stillness settles over all of them . . .

We will never truly divine the mind of Ardawan, the *Spahbad* of this Sassanian army, nor those aides and magi about him all lost in the swirl and flurry of battle. In the little hagiography which has grown up around the Siege of Amida and the Battle of the Hekatontarch's Mark, even less is known of the background to that confrontation between Lupicinus and Ardawan - and as such it is still shrouded in mystery and confusion. Was it propitious that the sandstorm arrived so suddenly and therefore allowed Artashemeh to secretly move her hidden regiments up to the Tigris to surprise the Persians? Or did the experienced Magister, perhaps through arcane soothsayers hiding old knowledge about weather patterns, know about the storm in advance and orchestrate her arrival accordingly? Why were most of the Roman officers kept in the dark and at a loss as to his plans to the extent that he is thought weak and dilatory - at least by Candidus, if not by many others? Why choose a disgraced legion to act as bait and not a more prestigious elite one? And finally, how did Lupicinus know – if indeed he did know – that Ardawan would turn tail and retreat at the sight of the endless Armenian 'snakes' advancing now down the far banks of the Tigris towards the nearby stone bridge - an advance and crossing which would put them all deep behind the Persians - a retreat, it seems, he desperately wished to forestall?

For retreat they did and in moments the entire Persian army, in its three great divisions, initiates a withdrawal.

'. . . Father, had you been there to see that rout, you would have yelled the old war-cry of our people and brandished your sword above your head as lightly a twig, for these Persians ran from the appearance of these Armenians like jackals from a lion-pack. I watched in awe as 'The Gorgon's Breath' vanished and in its wake vomited up column upon column of shining cavalry – tough nobles and princes from the mountains of the Taurus and the Zagros highlands. Alongside them, rode the *Azat* of their lesser nobles and minor families - men clad in scale and holding the lighter cavalry lances that we favoured as well as the recurve bow. And there, among her personal guard, all arrayed in bronze and framed by the images of saints, rode this Artashemeh, her face shining with the light of triumph and zeal even as she urged her horse on over that bridge. This brash woman is known among the Romans here in the north as a tough warrior-princess in the old mould of Zenobia and I swear I could hear in her wake the mocking laughter of her guards and favourites drift over the Tigris towards us all. She rode like a Eagle upon the tail of a sliding serpent and no matter how the sand shifted in the wind, her talons seemed to reach out to strike without mercy. Goaded by that appearance, I threw caution to the wind and, yelling a savage war-cry, I spurred my horse into the hesitating Persians and fell mercilessly upon them even as they attempted to wrest away their horses from this new sight. We fell in among them like white falcons then even as they fled, father, as snakes always do before the glorious rising of Helios, the bringer of light and harmony to the disordered dark world. That Persian lord, Ardawan, servant and slave to Shapur, fled into the deep desert back to his warrens and cunning paths, and in his wake lay the wreckage of Persian impudence and bravado . .'

Rhetoric aside, it is a complete withdrawal by all accounts. Even Candidus of Alexandria, still surrounded and hemmed in by Anicius' guards, writes of how the Armenian columns slid out of the desert in triumph and forced the Persians away like a mist before the sun, echoing in some small way Obedianus' words to his father. And there left upon the battlefield before Amida, in the wake of the retreating cavalry and elephants of the Persians stands the combined men of the two legions, shoulder to shoulder against each other, as the Tribune of one legion turns around, his face closed and frowning, while not too far away the commander of the other legion lowers that vicious gladius of his and begins to shake his head at the foible of the gods . . .

What absorbs most of the watchers however on those black walls is not this intermingling of legionary with legionary across that bloodied battlefield but the incongruous sight of a small tight *orbis* of Roman infantry seemingly stranded alone amid the retreating elephants and holding its ground even as those massed levy troops and allies drift backwards in a great heave of movement. There is something both forlorn and also magnificent about this solitary unit. There, not a mile from the parapets, beyond the exhausted lines and ranks of the two legions, stands this century of soldiers alone and apart from all the fighting and the movement. It is almost as if that *orbis* becomes poignant beyond the hundreds of other soldiers and officers mixed in now in that wine-press of battle simply because it remains there, waiting, and in that waiting seems to stand as a mocking coda to all the death and butchery about it. It falls to Candidus to remark upon them many years later that even after the long troop of Armenian horse has been sighted in amazement across the Tigris, moving south along its eastern banks, a high skirt of dust trailing up in its wake, that there remained something poetic not in that relief or arrival but instead in the little circle of men caught in that concentric ring of shields. Battle is chaos and ruin and blood, he writes. It is the eternal chorus of death aswirl with fear, daubed with frenzy, sculptured with harsh and unforgiving strokes - and rarely is it seen as a panoply in all its weight or frame. There, however, in that solitary knot of men it seems to Candidus that if ever one were to grasp at the futility and the heroism of battle, it is now in the sight of the century alone among the elephants and the spearmen and the Sassanian *Savaran* and the massed lines of the Persian foot troops and their auxiliary cavalry. And to the eye of Candidus, if not to others about him also, even as they see and divine the advance of the Armenian column down past the Persians, there comes the image of a flower trembling alone on a harsh floor as dark shadows reach out to drown it. A flower delicate and yet somehow vibrant wherein its beauty and order stand in contrast to all the blood and crowds and frenetic movement about it. A flower which, even as it is noted, is seen to tremble as that great mass of Persians retreat past it as if it did not even exist.

Barely ten minutes after the sand-storm has fallen away like a bad dream, the Fifth Century under Elias, that tall and thin Anatolian, is inundated by a retreating wave of Persians; a wave filled with fear and confusion. It is a sight which causes this thin Anatolian to begin laughing at the madness of it all in a rare moment of humour - a moment which prompts those legionaries about him to stare round in confusion. Elias laughs openly and honestly as the great bulk of the elephants turn about and pass them again, as the begrimed Sassanian cataphracts goad their Nissaean horses back away from the Roman lines, and even as those light skirmishers dash past, shaking their heads, all wondering on the fate of men and the games gods play. He laughs and grins and to many of the men of the Fifth about him his humour acts as a catalyst and soon more laughter rises up from that tiny *orbis*. Men laugh and smile and grin ruefully at Fate or Fortune or the whimsy of life itself while all about an entire army retreats past them and ignores them all as if they did not exist . . .

The Siege of Amida and the Battle of the Hekatontarch's Mark has never been a focal point for historians for a number of reasons: there has been little documentary evidence prior to our research and what there was is inconclusive and contradictory. It neither marks a major turning point in a war nor leads to any long-lasting change in the empire itself. It is usually glossed over in the histories and studies of this period as a footnote with most historians preferring to detail the siege and sack of Amida in 355 AD and again in 501 AD. The events here in May, 367 AD remain thus inconsequential and inconclusive - and for good reasons.

Was it a trap to bait the Persians and precipitate war, or did Lupicinus improvise after the fact of the emerging Sassanian force? How propitious was the sandstorm which shielded the advance of the Roman troops and why exactly did Ardawan retreat so quickly once he realised the army of Artashemeh was upon him? There is certainly the sense that the arrival of the Senior Sol Legion stalled the advance of the Persian troops while allowing the remaining Roman Cohorts to hold their desperately thin lines - however it is clear from the Magister's reaction and his orders to Candidus that this was the opposite of what he anticipated. Lupicinus did not want the Twelfth to hold. That much is clear. Not only that but Stygos too seems to have divined what was expected hence his insane order to half the lines. The Twelfth was nothing more than a trap and a lure - bait, as it were. A sacrifice. It was sent out to tempt the Persians into an attack - an attack designed to prevail over these demoralised troops. Was it that this Magister intended the Persians in their confidence to sweep onwards up to the walls of Amida, crushing the remaining legionaries under hoof? That by doing so, unknown to all and hidden by the sandstorm, the Armenian cavalry under the sister of Vashak Mamikonean would then manoeuvre in behind them over the stone bridge and so trap them all against those very walls? If that was the case, then it could be argued that perhaps Lupicinus himself had been bait all along - deliberately ensconcing himself in Amida in an attempt to lure the Persians onto Roman territory all the while hiding the Armenian troops on his far left flank over the Tigris for just such a purpose. Regardless, whilst such speculation is entertaining in its own manner it is nonetheless fruitless. The Twelfth did not collapse. They held despite the rout of the Second Cohort under Mascenius and they held not because of their valour or the arrival of some divine help but solely because another legion arrived without orders and on the hot temper of its commanding Tribune. And it was this Tribune's actions which, it may be argued, not only allowed the Twelfth to survive but also derailed the plans of the Magister Equitum and so allowed the Persians under Ardawan to retreat in a timely fashion back into Sassanian lands. In a sense, this Flavius Anicius, our 'Corbulo', if you will, upset so much more than the defeat of a single legion . . .

As the dust of the Persian retreat begins to settle and the soldiers and officers of both legions blink away their surprise at that fact, they see among themselves a curious effect. All up and down the broken lines of the Twelfth, even among the First and Third Cohorts, stand also now the dusty and bloodied *milites* of the Sol palatine legion. Soldier mingles with soldier and here and there the standards of both legions almost seem to twist together as if in an obscene embrace. Among the carnage, men look up and see not their brothers and tent-companions by their side - their *contubernales* - but instead strange men from different lands. For a moment, there is a distant almost wary response and all along the lines men look not to the men beside them but for those men who are *not* standing by them. This is no more in evidence than in the centre of that battle-line where once stood the Second Cohort but where now stands or rests the bulk of the legionaries of the Senior Sol Legion. It is here that the shields emblazoned with that white solar emblem seem to be most apparent while about them lie or kneel or crawl the wounded and the dying men of the Twelfth Legion. All across a carpet of shattered weapons, shields, and helmets, even as the dust drifts away, there is a quiet emptiness to it all; a silence different from that when the sand-storm ended. This silence is a bruised one. It is a peace in which each man stares almost angrily at each stranger by him as if by that presence alone he marks the absence of another. The line is long and ragged, broken and shattered here and there, but within all that long uneven redoubt of defence there is not one space which is not witness to this strange silence where men and shields and standards intermingle in uneasy silence.

In the wake of the retreating Persians, the Arabs with Obedianus at their head canter back towards this line of Roman soldiers and what their commander sees makes him draw his mount to a halt. His brothers and fellow Arabs fall in about him and too gaze all along that bloodied line. The dust drifts away to the east and the cool banks of the Tigris and what is left behind is something which strikes his desert eyes as unusual. There, all among the Roman soldiers, emerges an uneasy exhaustion and relief salted with a sort of muted hostility - as if each soldier alone among his peers resents or finds untrustworthy those about him. It causes Obedianus to turn to his old friend and companion, Jubyal, and remark laconically that if this is a victory he would not want to see these Romans in defeat. Before him, men and officers from both legions stand loosely and with dazed eyes watching that retreating Sassanid army fall back in haste and disarray. It is a moment in which order and cohesion is forgotten as each man steps forwards or kneels in the dust or rests the shield at his feet in relief, all the while his keen gaze remains upon that long and glittering mass retreating away into the distant deserts and oases to the south beyond the Masius mountains. Obedianus and those of his brothers and cousins of the Al Jawn who have survived that sudden and bloody fight rein in and pause before this line of men, watching them, assessing them, and see only a wary unease fill all their ranks.

It is Candidus, dismounting from his horse and handing the reins to his slave, who finds himself caught up in it all. That sudden retreat of the Persians under Ardawan brings a medley of activity all about him and the *principales* of the Sol legion. Before Candidus can place himself in front of the Tribune, however, the latter has brushed forwards and out into the now-empty space, followed by his eager and grinning staff officers. Guards fan out in a protective screen in their wake. Following them and beckoning Timoleus with the horses after him, he too moves past the front ranks of the legionaries and then is out into that killing ground, picking his way over shattered weapons and shields, stepping aside from the corpses of men and horses which litter the ground. It is then, as he moves to catch up with Flavius Anicius and those officers about him - all nodding and pointing out details with a satisfied air - that he sees, about a hundred paces down his right flank, a similar group emerge. This latter group, small and ragged, is one he recognises in an instant. All are dusty and covered in grime. One, Remus, his face easily picked out now by that swath around his head, hangs back scowling like a whipped cur. At their front walks the man called Stygos, the gladius still gripped in one fist, his dark gaze sweeping about everything with a thoroughness some might call obsessive. Candidus notes that the Eagle of the Legion has been passed into the hands of another and now the *Praefectus* of the Twelfth is looping that dark blade of his around his torso and pulling out the old vine stick. It is then - as he grasps the *vitus* and flexes his wrist as if testing it - that he sees the group Candidus is trailing and checks himself.

'. . . I swear by Mithras and the old gods, it was the first time I had seen this ancient *veteranus* smile - a true smile not that harsh leer which I had seen on him over the last two days. He smiled as he saw these officers emerge even as he too emerged - and then he was striding over to us, the others falling in behind him with a sort of wary and tired air. I heard laughter about me - the *praepositus* of this new legion nodded at the sight of the man walking towards him, and he too veered aside to meet him. He reached up and untied his cheek plates, pulling the fine crested helmet free, and I saw a youthful but worn face emerge - olive-dark with a neat trimmed beard. His face was cracked now by the desert sun and wind but in it still lay a Mediterranean softness. He pulled off his helmet, walking towards that old man who had usurped a legion's command - even as the latter smiled as if seeing an old friend. They met alone, their companions trailing behind them, amid all that wreckage of war, covered in dust and blood, and such sudden affection was shown in their mutual embrace that for one moment I wondered if Stygos was not a father to the other - except that I knew he bore no offspring that were still alive. His children were all dead as was his wife.

I have rarely seen an embrace of such affection and it clearly was as unexpected in the officers on either side as it was in me. These men hung back, watching, some smiling in the surprise of it and others frowning equally at it - these latter it must be said being mainly the veterans about the Eagle of the Twelfth. No one dared interrupt and for one long moment, these two commanders remained bound to each other in silence and affection. It was then that almost unseen the *Saraceni* federates under Obedianus cantered up and slowed to a halt about fifty paces ahead of us all. For one moment, I noted how sorely wounded they all looked but that a certain grim triumph lay on their desert faces. Obedianus urged his horse forwards a little then and seemed to be unsure of what to do next. By his side, an old *Saraceni*, loitered, twirling a Persian banner about his arm in a playful almost boastful manner.

The words of the Magister Equitum, Lupicinus, rose unbidden in my mind and so without thinking I found myself pushing past all these officers towards those two men. I saw if only for an instant Obedianus catch my move and dismount to join me. Clearly something in my face had intrigued him. I was through them all in a moment and then up towards where Stygos and this Tribune stood. Around and behind me, I could see a wide rough circle of *principales* from both legions almost eyeing each other warily. It struck me on how disparate both groups looked - one full of exhausted and shattered men, thin men in old tunicas and armour, their helmets dull and dented, the other filled with confident and alert men, men in bright armour, the sun flashing now from scutum and spatha. In this wide arena about me, I saw on one side, Gallic and Germanic and Illyrian veterans, their faces burnt by this harsh sun, while on the other stood the ancient stock of Cappadocian and Anatolian men, men beaten down by a tough remorseless land, whose blood was filled now by an uneasy mix of Christian superstition and oriental fatalism. And I did not know which side was the worse for it.

It was Stygos who sensed my arrival and broke from this legion officer in a brusque gesture. Together, they turned to face me, stepping apart, even as the *Saraceni* commander pulled up at my shoulder. The latter's white cloak was stained with blood and I noticed that he swayed a little with fatigue. Harsh words broke in on me then.

"The Magister is disappointed, I imagine," spat out Stygos and he twisted that vine stick in one impatient movement as he spoke. "Have we let him down, Tribune?"

The officer of the other legion - that legion encased in the symbol of Helios - frowned a little, looking between us. "Stygos?" he asked of him, and I saw how that youth of his, darkened now by the desert and other lines of care, had once been a soft thing; a rich thing, pampered and oiled. "We will be honoured by this. We have broken the coils of a Persian serpent at the very walls of Amida itself," he said, smiling, but I could see a certain frown gathering over his brow. "Why would Lupicinus be disappointed?"

"I have orders -" I began -

"Orders for the Tribune here?" broke in Stygos, spitting into the dust at his feet suddenly. "Orders to withdraw?"

I nodded into his old face and then added, "But it seems I am too late."

The *Praefectus* laughed at that. "Too late indeed! It seems, Tribune of the Magister, that the wine I ordered has been fruitlessly wasted! I hope you have more wine inside those dark walls for I fear it will be needed this night." I saw him check himself for a moment - this aged and cracked figure, all covered in scars and whose face presaged only death - and then he turned to glance quickly at the legion commander beside him. For an instant I saw again a certain affection in his eyes - an affection which seemed curiously out of place on his face - and then he shrugged. "Ani, you have saved nothing but a dead legion."

"A dead legion? What in Sol and Mithras are you talking about, Stygos?" Confusion and a certain frustration filled his face.

It was then that this Stygos turned to me and asked: "Will you tell him, Tribune? Or shall I?"

All the affection and humour was gone from him and again he was that harsh and chipped veteran; a man with too many years and too many lost comrades behind him. He turned to me and his face was closed and hard, all the scars on it white and in relief. I looked then at this other commander even as he too turned to face me, his frustration deepening, and all about us men stood and waited on me, silent and expectant. Far in the distance, I saw the arrival of the Armenian cavalry over the stone bridge and their long glittering columns fan out ahead of us, shielding us, forming a screen which cut-off the Sassanians from our sight. Thin veils of dust rose up in their wake even as the sun flashed from horse armour and contus tip. Behind me, I sensed rather than saw the exhausted lines of the legionaries all mixed up and wary of each other. Slaves and medici were moving forwards through their ranks and attending to the wounded all about, some binding up their wounds and moving them to the rear while others slowly and carefully put a stop to their pain and cries in the manner only the medici knew. I felt rather than saw this commander step closer to me, sensing his burning impatience on me. I saw then, among a mound of dead, the bloodied rag of a cohortal standard - that little vexillum flag - and it lay half-buried under the bulk of a black horse, its Persian rider nearby stretched out in the dust like a fallen statue. On a whim I pointed to it and shrugged.

"The Twelfth was a sacrifice and was meant to lie there in the dust as that standard now does," I said, not looking into his face.

The simplicity of it came to me in a moment of revelation. I knew now what Stygos had divined and I knew now what anger would be fermenting within the Black Walls of Amida. I knew because Stygos had prompted me and in doing so had torn away my naivety. For a moment, I remembered his demand for wine and also that moment this morning when he had stood before the legion with his officers all bruised and guilty about him. He and they had let blood and rooted out a canker - not to harden the legion but so that there would be none left to oppose that final march out into sacrifice and death. The Magister's face flashed before me and I saw again his anger. An anger we would soon feel.

I looked into the face of this Italian, at his almost desperate need to hear my words, and for one moment felt nothing but pity - pity for his wasted effort and toil and the loss of the men under his standards. Near me, the *Saraceni* commander sensed my mood and lowered his head but I caught a sudden flash of contempt from him and I could not blame him.

"In saving this legion, you have broken the plans of the Magister. Nothing more."

He laughed at that suddenly and turned back to Stygos. "Then this Magister is a fool! If in nothing else, I have saved you, Stygos. And to Hades with these orders!"

"The Twelfth was expected to fall," I broke in -

He rounded on me and the scorn in his face made me burn with shame. "*This* legion? This canker? It deserves to fall and be wiped away as if it had never existed! I didn't march here for the *legion*, Tribune. I came for Stygos."

And Stygos placed a hand on him then and said slowly, as if in a whisper: "But Ani, I am the legion now." . . .'

It is the sudden arrival of a score of imperial guardsmen which puts a stop to any further debate between Flavius Anicius and Stygos. These cavalry troopers, clad in jewel-encrusted helmets and richly-painted shields, arrive in a swirl of jingling harness and drumming hooves. High above them, floats the Labarum standard of the Magister Equitum adorned with a motto first conceived by the emperor Constantine - 'In This Sign, Conquer.' This sudden arrival, in which these guardsmen erupt from the ragged legion lines and curve about the officers almost as if imprisoning them, brings Stygos and Flavius Anicius about face and sees each one also instinctively drop a hand to the hilt of his sword. Candidus, caught off-guard, steps aside to find his slave, Timoleus, by him with both horses. There, amid these guardsmen, a silent officer nudges his mount slightly forwards, staring down at the assembled men before him. There is something incongruous in this moment wherein a tired and bloodied group of Romans stare suspiciously up at these mounted guardsmen - all dark Syrian troopers in silk and fine linens, their armour chased with silver and gold - who sit above them all, pristine and cold. Candidus later remarks that for one absurd moment he wondered on who the victors of the field truly were and thought that all were about to be imprisoned were it not for the distant sight of the Armenian cavalry drifting away towards the horizon, trailing the Persians. All about lay the detritus of battle: the dead and dying; shattered weapons and accoutrements; the smell of blood and excrement - all covered in a shroud of flies and dust. And the sight for him of those guardsmen on their fine horses seemed somehow offensive as if belying that scene. He watches these guardsmen as if not understanding their arrival and only dimly sees that the man urging his horse forwards is none other than Constans, of Damascus, his companion. This latter waits a moment, surveying all the officers below him, his dark face closed and distant, before reaching up to untie the cheek plates of his helmet and then remove it slowly. Black oiled locks fall about his face as he rests that helmet on one of the horns of his saddle.

'. . . I saw him nod to himself then and turn to look at me. I had travelled and served alongside him for almost a year here in the Oriens - at the beck and call of Lupicinus - and shared too many cups of wine to remember but now as he looked down upon me, I did not recognise him at all. I moved to step away from my groom and slave, to ask him why these troopers were all about us, but he silenced my move with a sudden hand. He turned to face the legion commander nearby and spoke then in pristine Latin:

"The Magister Equitum of the East, Lupicinus, Illustrious Consul, confident of the Augustus Flavius Julius Valens, demands your name and rank."

And this officer never hesitated for a moment. "Flavius Anicius Bassas, *Tribunus Legionis* and *Praepositus*, Senior Sol Legion, of the *Palatinae*, honoured by the Sacred Augustus, of the gens Anicii of Rome, son of Flavianus Anicius, once a Consul of Rome, and to whom you will address as *Dominus*."

Constans bowed his head slightly at that rebuke, barely hiding a smile. "Then, *Dominus*, permit me to pass on the orders of the Magister to one of an equally illustrious birth whose father has held the highest honour Rome and the Emperor can bestow - " He looked up then and swept his gaze about all the officers. "Know this: the Illustrious Magister desires you all to remain here in the heat and the sun and all this litter of battle. You are to remain here and await his orders and pray that the mercy and benevolence of Christ may fall on you all -

for assuredly, his will not." He looked down at Stygos by the side of this Tribune. "You have failed in your command and as death was your victory do not expect life now to be your reward or the reward of those *milites* at your back."

This Flavius Anicius stepped forward then and grabbed at his bridle. "You are talking madness! Does the Magister not understand that we have broken the Persians? What insanity is this?!"

It was Stygos who stopped further argument and I saw him reach up and break the former's grip before Constans could react. He loosened that grip and stepped in-between them, his face cold and harsh. And I saw then for the first time how he turned his menace and his scorn upon the other and all the familiarity and warmth drained from him. "Be quiet, you fool. You have marched your legion into something you know nothing of."

"Nothing? I know that when a friend is in danger, you march to his aid. I know that you never abandon a comrade to the swords of the enemy!" He tried to wrench his wrist away from the grip of the other but it was too strong.

"Ani, I am already a dead man - as are all these men of the Twelfth behind me. You cannot save what is already lost."

This rebuke seemed to baffle the legion Tribune. Nearby, a dozen of his officers and commanders stepped closer, all scowls and curses - one, a heavy-set man covered in reddish hair, his green eyes blazing with barely concealed contempt, spat into the dust and clenched his fist about the hilt of his spatha so that the knuckles turned white. This ruddy officer stepped up close to the Tribune, bristling like a boar on the hunt.

"*Dominus*, we are palatinae! Are we to let a perfumed Syrian on his fancy horse order us about? Remember our past! We are all veterans of the Gallic and Illyrian and Germanic lands. There are those among us who were there when the Sacred Julian was elevated to the Purple!"

Flavius Anicius spoke then without tearing his eyes from the *Praepositus* of the Twelfth and his voice was cold and unrelenting. "Asellus, you are nothing but what I command. Understand?"

I saw this Asellus redden even further and then a man by his side - a languid almost womanish figure in worn mail and who bore a curious tattoo along one side of his neck, all curved and circular as if a spiral of roots reached up to entangle his face, place a hand upon his shoulder. The effect was remarkable for almost as if by magic or a charm, this Asellus deflated at that touch, all his anger and temper draining from him.

The Tribune glanced once at this tattooed officer then and nodded. "Teutomeres."

"*Dominus*," nodded the other back in reply. He released his hand and stepped back as if his duty was done. Asellus glanced once at him and then glowered uneasily about as if unsure of what to do next.

It was Stygos who broke that impasse. He glanced up at Constans reclining in his saddle. "We obey the will of the Magister, in the name of the Augustus."

My companion nodded back to him. "Wait here then and judgement will come."

With that, he retrieved his helmet and signalled to the riders about him and then they all wheeled about and rode away in a flurry of dust, that large Labarum banner floating high above them all in glory and victory. In their wake, I saw bemused stares and heard angry, baffled, oaths being mouthed. Only this Flavius Anicius Bassas stood immobile and cold, as if unaware of the commotion about him and lost in some other world. He stood aloof and in his eyes I recognised a slight distant concern; a tremble so remote as almost not to be seen. He reached up then and rubbed his brow as if from waking and I saw him look about for the first time into the faces of the centurions nearby from the Twelfth - and I saw, too, how they gazed askance upon him and what fear and unease lay in their own bruised and bloodied faces . . .'

It is an awkward moment and one Candidus alone leaves a record of. There, deep in the wreckage of battle, among the dust and beaten-down earth of the Hekatontarch's Mark, the sun high and blazing now in a cobalt sky, a man who had once been the commander of this broken legion turns to face again those who in some way engineered his removal and in doing so shamed the Twelfth and left it rudderless and rotting. There, among the tired and wounded centurions, stands Strabonius, unable to look the Tribune of the Sol legion in the eye and who casts his gaze anywhere but at those men about him; nearby is Remus, his torn face eternally wrapped in a linen rag, the left-over of that face always scowling and bitter for this man once accounted himself - as all braggarts do - handsome and blessed; Cyrion stands apart, his bleak humour draining now and an empty smile plastered to his face, all the while he grabs his right wrist and twists it as if rubbing away an ache; ignored to one side leans Mascenius propped up on the shoulder of a comrade, one hand clasped against his side, his face white and streaked with blood and sweat. A rough bandage is wrapped about his waist and his hand presses against it even as fresh blood oozes from between his fingers. This last centurion gasps fitfully in pain and longs to rest his body down on the ground but dares not speak. There are others in among these officers of the Twelfth - newly promoted or transferred - who wonder and gaze upon the Tribune Flavius Anicius as if looking upon some marvel or myth never quite believed in or understood and these men now confront not just his presence but also that dark stain in a past beyond their experience which part of them had hoped was not real. A past previously only alluded to or slyly boasted of but somehow understood nonetheless. These men, all equally exhausted and wounded, stand back and stare both at the Tribune and also those centurions about them as if looking anew upon something they had once hoped was nothing but an idle boast.

Out beyond this pocket of unease, in which the officers of one legion stand apart from the officers of another and where the two commanders seem both intimate with each other but also now somehow separate in manner in which no easy embrace nor quip will mend, the surviving legionaries of the Twelfth and the Sol legions remain where they stand - some resting forwards upon the shaft of their spears, others removing their helmets to gain some respite from the heat, a few breaking ranks and kneeling down or squatting, too tired and exhausted to stand. To the rear, dash slaves and the weary medici, lying out the wounded regardless of which legion each one is from, or piling up the dead for the slaves to strip away their weapons and armour. Adjutants and notaries move among this latter pile, marking names and ranks and units in small waxen tablets for soon that awful litany and roll will be done where the dead are struck off and savings from the funeral funds will need to be requisitioned.

It is into this grim and uneasy silence that finally the eighty men under Elias return, all them still smiling slightly from the comedy of their stand out in the middle of the battlefield. The tall figure of Elias leads his men back into their position within the Second Cohort and only as they re-assemble and pace out their ranks within that mother-unit does it become apparent that of all the centuries within the Second, theirs is the only one still intact. These legionaries of the Fifth Century stand slowly under their standard and that mocking and desperate humour drains from them one by one as they look about them into strange faces - hard-bitten men each with the face of a Celt or a German or an Illyrian - and upon whose shields rests the ancient and revered symbol of Helios himself . . .

That wait under the harsh sun deep in the Hekatontarch's Mark is mercifully short. Within the hour, a long procession decants from the Mardin Gate of Amida and moves slowly out towards the ragged lines of the legionaries. It processes in a long curve around the right flank and then moves to form itself in an elegant line across the front of the Twelfth and Sol legions. Two columns of guard cavalry form up on the left and right flank, all glittering in embossed helmets and shields, while in the centre rests a small cadre of imperial officers and notaries, mounted on proud Arabian and Persian horses. High above these officers is the Labarum standard and next to it the painted icon of the Emperor, surmounted by angels and victory laurels. These two standards ripple out in a slight breeze as a solitary ensign trots forwards a little and then blows out a clear clarion signal which silences all the weary rumblings in the ranks. As that silver sound fades into the dry air, a sharp command breaks the silence and the order to lower standards rings out. One by one, the Eagles and then the maniple and cohort standards are dipped and in their wake all the legionaries and officers kneel in the presence of the Magister Equitum, Flavius Lupicinus, general of the East, and representative of the Augustus Valens himself. Heads are bowed and many soldiers whisper benedictions to preserve the majesty and justice of the emperor of Rome while others mumble prayers to Mithras and Sol to protect the honour of Rome and the *respublica*.

Lupicinus himself, astride a magnificent white stallion, its eyes flashing with pride and its head tossing as if desperate to be let loose on some heroic charge, emerges from that cadre of officers and advances forwards so that he is alone between these two ranged forces. For one long moment, he allows his gaze to move across the entire breadth of the intermingled legions and the small group of officers all now kneeling before him. There is a strange contrast between the solemnity of that gaze and the impatient horse below him. Candidus remembers years later that despite all their kneeling and bowed prostration - due to this high officer of the empire - all about him were eyeing Lupicinus beneath their brows and that there seemed to be an almost perverse fascination not with the Magister himself but with that white stallion and its eagerness to be away and absent. Finally, after a pause many find excruciating, Lupicinus nods once to himself and then speaks forth in a slow and clear voice the doom and decision of the legions. A solitary epistle addressed to Basil of Caesarea from Constans of Damascus allows us a rare insight into this moment and fills it with more detail than the pen of Candidus. For where the later is brusque and almost dismissive, as if eager to gloss over these events, his companion is more effusive and what he writes to that Christian bishop is the best illustration that we have of what follows:

'. . . I came upon these mixed men, reverend father, all lathered in the dust, beyond the wicker fences and ditches of the Persian encampment, out in a long stretch of the plain, now churned up by the passing of so many *milites*. The angry words of the Illustrious Magister, Lupicinus, still burned in my ears. I am an officer of Rome however and must do my duty no matter how troubling. As we traversed down the ranks of these men I saw again the newcomers from the Western provinces, all tall men in well-kept armour, who bore blue-eyes and open rough faces. They stood next to their brothers in arms of the Twelfth like incongruous statues all mixed up – blond and copper hair next to the dark shiny locks of the Anatolian and the Cappadocian, with their swarthy faces. I saw the shield of each legion rub against the other such that I could not see where one century stood apart from the other's counter-part in the line. Then my gaze found the Tribune of the newly-arrived legion next to Stygos, that Roman veteran, while Strabonius, who to my eyes always seemed to be expecting some new doom, hesitated next to them both. I knew the Magister would not disappoint this centurion's fearful eyes.

The orders of the Magister were unambiguous and he read them out despite the harsh look from Stygos and the bitter eyes of this young Tribune. He advanced his horse alone into that empty ground before us all and spoke out in a high loud voice - and his words fell upon them all like a *stigmata*: for disobeying the mandate of the Magister and marching into battle such that the Persians were able to retreat in full order and fight another day, the Tribune Flavius Anicius, of the gens Anicii, and all under the standards of the Senior Sol Legion, were to be demoted from the grade of the palatine ranks to that of the field army or the comitatenses, with attendant loss of status and pay. Furthermore, he continued, in honour of the courage and loyalty to the standards of their legion and its illustrious past the soldiers and officers of the Twelfth Fulminata Legion, of Melitene, are now to be reprieved from their shame and elevated into the ranks of the comitatenses, with all pay and privileges in accordance with that promotion. No longer is this legion to be considered a frontier legion only worthy to hunt bandits and patrol the *limes*. As it has stood today in battle so shall it again hold that honour.

As he read out those words, I sensed a mixed reception around me as the men in both legions absorbed their fate – some cheered and others cursed and a rare few seemed to frown at the injudicious nature of Fortune – and I wondered on those legionaries doomed and now reprieved and those others once lauded but now disgraced and how each now stood next to his opposite - but before this went on and murmurs might arise from the ranks into cheers or even indeed mutiny, the Magister read out the rest of his mandate – it was also to be ordered that as the Senior Sol Legion chose to stand in amongst the ranks of the disgraced Twelfth, once also commanded by Anicius, so then shall these two legions remain forever more bound upon the battlefield as twins of each other under his command. Let no force divide them from each other, he shouted out above the impatient head of his horse, and let what fate be theirs fall to all without let or discrimination – for now and forever more this will be their doom. It is to be entered into the *Notitia* as such and let no officer of the *respublica* sunder them from each other. For as one man moved to overturn the orders of the Magister so too shall this one man now stand above both legions as commander and *patricius*. And under him, shall the Eagles of these two legions now be bound together in chains so that all shall stand under an Eagle of Rome which shall look both forwards into redemption and backwards into ignominy, as these two legions marched both forwards into sacrifice and backwards from death and honour.

And he shouted out then for the aquilifers of both legions to rise and step forwards and I saw then both Eagles atop their poles brought out from the ranks. Each one was seized by his guards and then wrapped and locked together in a thin silver chain, one Eagle facing backwards and the other forwards, even as the key to that long silver chain was cast unceremoniously aside. Lupicinus nodded in satisfaction once this had been done and spoke again, saying that this 'Janus' Eagle shall cast nothing now but a double shadow and under that shadow shall stand all its soldiers . . .

And, reverend father, I looked down upon Candidus then, kneeling in the dust and blood, even as the Magister spoke the last of his orders assigning him alone from his staff to this bonded legion, stating that this unattached officer is no more to be a member of his *officium* but is now of this double-legion and placed at the whim and care of the Tribune Flavius Anicius, *Praepositus*, commander of the Twelfth and the Senior Sol Legions, as he sees fit. And I saw Candidus nod then and I swear that beneath the rim of his helmet I caught a secret smile. In the moments which followed, even as that bound Eagle was handed back to a standard-bearer of the Sol, I felt a strange and unnatural silence spread-out around the Magister, a silence which seemed as much a confusion as it was a sullen thing. Men seemed to glance warily about each other as if looking into a new and unwelcomed world. A world which was brought and imposed upon them and in which an unknown fate now resided. It was then that I saw this Italian Tribune rise up unbidden from his submission to the Magister and take a step towards him and his magnificent white stallion. It was a single step only but in it lay such anger and implacable defiance that I feared swords would be drawn. He took a single step, that privileged face of his tight and closed - and then in a flash he snatched at that silver-bound Eagle and raised it high in both hands, crying out that the Will of the Emperor be done and then he lowered this Janus Eagle into the dirt before the Magister and said in a low cold voice:

"*Axios, Dominus, axios . . .*" '

. . . Throughout the later empire, it seems to have been a practise of sorts to pair up legions into a brigade so that both fought together on the battlefield and while on campaign. Both Ammianus and Zosimus describe this process several times without detailing its origin or history. Again and again, pairs of legions or the elite auxilia palatinae fought side-by-side or were mentioned in terms which conjoined them. Nowhere however is there mention of two legions merging into a single bound legion in such a manner that the

Eagles themselves were entwined together. Only here and upon this long arid plain before Amida is such a thing done and it is a conjoining not of fellow legions or soldiers but the opposite - and before all these ranks and rudely twinned legionaries stands a single officer under the shadow now of a double Eagle looking backwards and forwards, that old Janus image which stands at the heart of Rome itself . . .

An officer who, even as the cavalcade of the Magister retreats back towards Amida and leaves him all alone before his men, turns and looks deep into the ranks before him, and asks in a low whisper for the centurion in command of the Second Cohort to step forwards . . .

CHAPTER ELEVEN

' . . . "Bring out that Centurion. Now."

I saw this officer and commander of two legions pull off his crested helmet and fling it dismissively towards a nearby slave. Around him clustered a small phalanx of senior officers and *principales*. For one moment, this Flavius Anicius looked up into the irregular outline of the double-Eagle above him and then he passed that standard over also giving it to the Aquilifer of the Senior Sol Legion.

This latter soldier grasped it between his hands and seemed to hold it in a careful fashion as if not quite believing what his eyes saw. The silver chain looped and looped about the twin poles of the standards and then curved up about those two Eagles, binding them both together, locking them against each other, one facing forwards, the other backwards - but then I saw this aquilifer spin the poles and reverse those Eagles even as uncertainty grew over his Gallic face. I knew then that a superstition was rooting in him even as he twisted the poles a second time, wondering on how the beaks and talons and stern gazes revolved and flashed above him in the sunlight. Nearby, I saw other *milites* and officers looking on in awe and perturbation - not knowing what to make of that revolving thing in his hands. The Eagles were gold and ancient and almost identical save that one bore scars and a deep chip across its brow as if some axe had attempted to split it centuries ago. But in that revolve, as this troubled standard-bearer twisted that silver-bound object again and again, I felt as if each Eagle merged into the other such that I could not tell one from the other.

Flies and heat fell over us all out there in the Hekatontarch's Mark. I remember a long trail of dust falling away back to Amida - the last of the train of the Magister - while to the south what was left of the advancing Armenian cataphracts disappeared into their own veil or gauze. All around us, everything seemed still and serene despite the wreckage of war and battle washed up about us. Up and down the long ranks of the soldiers of both legions, men were standing up from their submission to Lupicinus, wondering on the consequences of what had just been ordered. Many were wounded and exhausted. A few remained supported by their *commiliatones* in the files and lines. The shields of both legions flashed and echoed down those long lines and although most were splattered with blood or splintered or caked with dust something stirred in me as I let my gaze linger on that imperial symbol of Sol and beside it the old ancient thunderbolts of Jove surmounted now by the face of this Christian God - as if those ancient bolts were *his* bolts now. I smiled at that and knew that whether it was the face of this God of Abraham or Jupiter Himself, both were almighty gods with fierce countenances and unforgiving eyes.

He emerged, this Centurion that was so rudely called for, grabbing at his side and the wound which marked him. Men stood apart from him uneasily and I saw him look about at them even as a hunted look grew in his eyes. He swayed slightly, his face ashen with pain, and I saw the endless drip of blood stain the dust about his feet. In a moment, a score of legionaries from this Sol legion moved to contain him even as Flavius Anicius stepped in towards him. Was it fate or the whim of the gods that allowed the shadow of that newly-minted double-Eagle to fall across them both? I look back now to that moment and wonder if indeed it was neither but my own memory playing tricks with me. I know that my mind was still awhirl with the news that I had been reassigned as if in punishment for a deed not mine - but that also something about these two legions and all the bitter and weary men in them seemed to fascinate me. I could not tear my eyes from those oval shields and the disparate symbols painted on them. And something wild and passionate was moving in me. It was as if Mithras himself was marking me out with a daub of sacred blood. I remember thinking then, even as I stood up in the wake of this Tribune to see who this centurion was, of that terrible phrase penned by Virgil about Rome and Carthage which locked both forever in animosity and opposition: shore against shore, wave against wave, and arms against arms . . . *arma, armis,* came unbidden to my mind and is it now that I see that cursed Janus Eagle fall over Anicius and that centurion or did in fact that stain really exist? No doubt I will never know now. What I do remember is the silence within which these two stood as they faced each other.

Flavius Anicius, his face dark and scarred by the Cappadocian sun, a thin beard unnaturally grey, his eyes locked on this desperately wounded man, approached him under the shadow of the standard while all those other centurions of the Twelfth before them both stood back uneasily, leaving them in a little island of sand and blood and wreckage.

"Report, Centurion," said the Tribune, not taking his eyes from him.

The latter shrugged and grimaced back through his pain. "What is there to report, Tribune? The fucking Persians overran us all -"

It was then that the Tribune cuffed him savagely about the chin. I saw the edge of his chainmail sleeve catch that jaw and rip the skin. More blood fell at his feet as this Centurion staggered a little from the unexpected blow. His head snapped back up in a flash though and I saw that he was grinning now and a mad look was beginning to creep into his eyes.

"I won't repeat myself, Centurion."

"You *won't -*" A sudden laugh broke off his words and this Centurion shook his head. "Do you hear that, my *commilliatones*? He won't *repeat* himself!"

Anicius moved in again but the Centurion stepped back in haste, his head ducking suddenly, his side twisting in pain. " - Oh, we know you, don't we, we all know you - Flavius Anicius, that whelp who thought he could rule the Twelfth! Look, *commilliatones*, it is the pup who cried -"

This time it was Stygos who acted. In a flash, he was up against the side of this man and had rammed the pommel of that short-sword into his back. It was too much for the wounded Centurion and he slumped into the dust like a sack of rubbish, all the wind and bluster knocked out of him. For a moment, Anicius gazed down at him and I saw him smile slowly even as he frowned. It was a smile which chilled my heart.

"You - and you -" he said suddenly to two nearby Sol legionaries. "Lift him up and strip the military belt from him. Unbelt him and take his weapons. Listen, all of you, this is Mascenius, Primus Prior of the Second Cohort, that cohort which broke here at the centre of the battle-line. There is the remnant of the standard. This man failed to hold the line. He failed to obey the orders of the legion's *Praefectus* and allowed the men under his command to be slaughtered. I know this because my legion alone - these men here - dammed up that breach. He fled as his men died and the standard fell. Look at it! It lies in blood and death, broken, while this man dares to stand in my presence and still wear the military belt!"

"What orders?" cried out this Mascenius, even as the guards unbuckled his heavy belt and then flung it aside. "The orders of that old man? The orders of death? He wanted to doom the Twelfth! Nothing more! It was madness to obey him. Madness!" A sudden bout of pain contorted his features and I saw him spit up a stream of blood and vomit. "That man is nothing but a curse, I swear by the Forty!"

It was the coldness of the Tribune's reply which struck me. "For failing to follow your commander's orders, for allowing the Second Cohort to break the battle-line, for failing to save the Cohortal standard and so bringing shame upon the Twelfth, I, Flavius Anicius, *Praepositus* and Tribune of the Sol and the Twelfth legions hereby condemn you to summary execution as allowed under military jurisprudence. Said sentence to be carried out immediately and under the sight of these Eagles."

"You can't -"

It was Stygos who spoke next, his words dark and gravelly. "He can and he has."

Mascenius looked wildly about him even as he struggled with the two guards. "The order was madness! No Roman would ever follow it -"

"Strabonius and Cyrion did," replied Stygos, spitting at his feet.

"Then they were fools! All of you - listen to me! This Italian will bring shame to us all! Look at him - this is the same man who scorned us all - the man whom we broke! That fear we burned into him is still there! I can *smell* it - Remus, Strabonius, look, it is still there! Cyrion - don't let him do this!"

But those men he shouted out his words to did not look him back in the eye nor did they waver in the silence of their obedience. One, Remus, his face cruel and disfigured, bit his lip and I saw hatred flare up in what was left of that face but he held his peace even as this Mascenius raved like a madman.

It was then that Flavius Anicius, Tribune, turned to me and asked: "Do you know how to wield the *catena?*"

For a moment I did not understand him. I had been nothing but a spectator up until that moment and so when he turned to me and asked that question I did not realise - I could not realise - what it was he was asking. As though from afar I heard his words and found myself nodding back. Of course I knew how to wield that whip. I was an officer of Rome. I had seen enough men use it to break the backs of unruly soldiers and deserters. I had flexed it myself in anger if in nothing else to show my rank and impart discipline in those beneath me. I was a Tribune and up until a few precious moments ago a member of the military staff of Lupicinus. The *catena* was as comfortable to my grip as was the hilt of a spatha - but I had never used it on a man.

I had never needed to.

"Yes, *Dominus*," I found myself replying, "I know how to use the lead-weighted whip."

I heard my words as though I were divorced from them and felt a sudden violent tremor rush through me and then the world in all its unruly bedlam broke in upon me like a tumult; like a thunderstorm from the gods.

"Then wield it now, Tribune, wield it now."

In a moment, this Mascenius was stripped of his armour, the tunica underneath torn apart so that it fell from him like rags, even as he was dragged over to a small wicker fence - a remnant of the Persian defences here in the Hekatontarch's Mark. I saw them bind him, arms stretched apart, across that fence and before I knew what was happening some slave or orderly had thrust the bull-hide handle of the whip into my hands. Without thinking, my hand twisted reflexively about it, testing it, and I saw the long thin strips snake out from that handle, each one tipped with a vicious lead hook. The *catena*. That instrument used to instil terror and discipline into the subjects and soldiers of

Rome.

The words of Homer rose in my mind as I took a step towards this raving centurion and for one moment I allowed the beautiful Greek words to ripple through me like a breeze, like a balm, marvelling at their elegance and poetry, *heavy moves my heart within me* . . . All about me, men watched as I approached the bound man. Blood and a ravening of words fell from him as he twisted against his bonds. A thousand faces framed me, curious, detached. His alone consumed me as he twisted back over his shoulder to throw a despairing gaze at me. I saw as if from the corner of my eye that *Saraceni* commander nod once, his eyes agleam with a fierce light, even as his surviving desert warriors clustered up about him. The sun was high behind me and I saw my shadow leech over his form as I drew nearer. Of that I am certain. I cloaked his nakedness with my own shadow and a dozen dark serpents slid about him.

I turned to Flavius Anicius then and asked: "How many strokes?"

He did not answer. He did not need to.

I think it was then, as all the gods and fates bear witness, that I really saw him for the first time, this Roman of ancient blood, a man I later understood to be nicknamed 'Corbulo', both as a jest and as a mark of respect, a man whose dark face hid a deeper stain that was to torture us all though I knew it not then. A young man whose rigidity held nothing but the shattered pieces of a pride and honour beyond redemption. That early grey in his beard was pitiful and I remember wondering on why he had chosen not to dye it as many do out of vanity or affectation. I did not know him well enough, of course, to realise that Flavius Anicius of all men would never paint his face. His mask ran much deeper than that.

My shadow encompassed that poor Centurion and I whispered to him, "Man, if you have faith in your God, pray to him now in these your last moments."

He laughed back at me, his madness consuming him, and shouted out, "You talk to me of faith?! I am a man of God, blessed under Christ, and the Forty will bear me up to Heaven! Hear me, all of you," he cried out, even louder, "though this man whip me, the lashes fall on all of you of the Twelfth! My back is your back! My blood, your blood! My martyrdom, all your martyrdoms!"

Arma, armis, I thought, and brought the first lash across him as I had been taught - not hard or fast, but slow and even, like a stroke, like a kiss, so that each blow would be the same in its inevitable touch and pain and defilation. And the skin flayed from him like rotten parchment with ink so red, so red. Again and again my arm rose and fell and the long dark lines of the *catena* kissed his bloody back, slowly, endlessly, each last lead hook rising up even as the new first one kissed him again, and so the cycle continued, and his mad words tumbled gently into a whispered litany that only I could hear. The pain caused him to arc and tremble and so he crushed his lips, spitting out blood, as those words fell from him amid the kiss and tear of the whip. And those words I heard were names, one after the other, thrown forth from him as if each one were a grace and redemption for him - *"Hesychius, Meliton, Heraclius, Smaragdus, Domnus, Eunoicus, Valens, Vivianus, Claudius, Priscus, Theodulus, Euthychius, John, Xantheas, Helianus, Sisinius, Cyrion, Angius, Aetius, Flavius, Acacius, Ecditius, Lysimachus, Alexander, Elias, Theophilus, Dometian, Gaius, Gorgonius, Leontius, Athanasius, Cyril, Sacerdon, Nicholas, Valaerius, Philoctimon, Severian, Chudion, Aglaius -"* and the last he threw to me with eyes now beyond sanity and mortal concern *" - Candidus . . ."*

It was the last name he gave me in his pain and madness and it caused me to hesitate, my arm back and trembling, blood dripping into the dust about me. He gave me my name at the last and then he slumped down at the wicker fence, dead. I had struck him forty times and he had given me forty names and then his soul had left him as if that parcel of flesh was of no concern now.

And I pulled that dark shadow which had covered him away as I stood back and looked then to this Tribune - a mangled thing now at my feet - and I saw that his eyes were not on that corpse or on me nor were they on any of us but were hidden and deep within himself, as if lost and alone. I remember throwing that whip at his feet then on a whim and walking away from him though he did not look after me. I walked away along the files of the waiting legionaries, their faces dull and blank, towards an expectant Timoleus and I knew that far from executing a deserter and coward, this Tribune had done something more.

He had bound me now into his command in blood and death beneath a cursed standard . . .'

. . .The body of Mascenius is left where it lies for the civic authorities to bury later in the burgeoning Christian cemetery outside the North Gate. It is an irony of history, of course, that the body of the one cohort commander who refused the order to sacrifice and so indeed martyr the legion after the will of Lupicinus becomes the body of a new Martyr of the Twelfth. Whereas both Strabonius and Cyrion abandoned themselves to the doom of that order, expecting nothing but death, the indecision of Mascenius and his subsequent flight from the cohort standard - his sudden zeal for life, as it were - brought him into death and then upon the rolls of the martyrs of this legion. Saint Mascenius is still venerated in Diyarbakir to this day although both his grave and a subsequent shrine which sprang up in the years to come have long since vanished. His story in the martyrologies of the Church glosses over his cowardice naturally and makes of him a defiant centurion sacrificed to the pagan officers of a corrupt empire. Along with that first Martyr of the Twelfth, Polyeuctes, and those Forty condemned to that bitter icy lake to die, Mascenius becomes another name to buttress the deep Christian faith of the legionaries of the 'Thundering' legion . . .

It is as the two legions begin the tedious order of marshalling their lines and ranks into a march back into Amida and the Baths of Trajan, each man shouldering impatiently and in some cases with resentment up against his companion in the other legion, that a long file of cavalry rides hard back out from the dust of the south and the vanishing Persian and Armenian armies. It emerges in a gleam of iron and a thunder of hooves and sweeps hard upon the milling Roman legionaries almost as if to cut them down. A few barked-out orders sees several men leap aside even as these armoured riders career through them barely acknowledging any of them. It is a long file of some seventy riders - haggard men with wiry beards and cruel flashing eyes, all armoured in bronze scales and heavy iron helmets. At their head rides a woman, her head free and her dark hair loose and wild. One by one, the Roman soldiers stand up in amazement at this sight, this woman riding like an emperor past them all, noting her dented shield, the worn accoutrements of her belt fittings and harness, the Christian Chi-Rho symbol on her shield, now splashed with blood, and they remark on the manner in which her gaze ignores them all as she rides imperiously past. All the men in her wake smile above them also as if honouring her while disdaining the Romans below them and not one does not have a proud smile upon his face.

Artashemeh, the Mace of Arsaces, sister to Vashak Mamikonean, sweeps through the disorderly lines of the Sol and the Twelfth legions, her *Azat* guard in her wake, to the neighing of all their warhorses and the high resplendent flutter of the banners and heraldry of their Orthodox faith. She rides with a passion and a determination that causes the Roman file-leaders and century commanders to bark out swift orders to let her past even as the dust of that swift ride catches in their throats. Only at the last, as she urges her high black horse on, the white silk banner of Christ framing her, does she allow a curious glance into the worn men about her and for one lingering moment she looks long and pointedly into the faces of Flavius Anicius, Stygos, Candidus and Obedianus in turn - and then she is past them all and she and her troop of bodyguards are riding hard towards the opening Mardin Gate of Amida, even as a clear bucina cry echoes out to alert others inside of her arrival.

It is a moment in which the Arab chieftain of the Bani Al Jawn later writes that he sees a fate and destiny in her which he has never seen upon anyone before. A mark upon her face almost as if the grace and the *stigmata* of Christ himself has intertwined into a new and despotic sign. In the letter which he writes to his father we can read of his struggle to understand this revelation, the dust of her horse cloaking him, the jingle of harness deafening him, the endless trail and stream of silk blinding him, and there amid it all, her keen glance which penetrates them in a moment even as she is past them leaving that awful imprint upon his desert mind - that there in her face lies something dark and glorious . . .

' . . . She rode as the wind rides, father, as the sands themselves flow, over us all, and what I saw behind after she had gone was a thing in my mind that dazzled me. She saw me and in that seeing of me *understood* me as few have ever done. You remember when I emerged out of that Harra and the bosom of my foster-brother? You remember as I stood in the doorway of your camel-hair tent and I saw upon your face the *implicit* - the understanding of that which I had no need to say to you; of the desert; of Ailat Herself. You knew me - what I had become - and you said simply 'sit, drink', and we never spoke of my absence. That look you gave me *of myself* she gave me also and in the giving of it I *saw* in return - and, father, what I saw was as though a goddess sat upon her shoulder though she knew it not . . .'

This guard and troop of Artashemeh rides swiftly through the Roman lines as though they do not exist save for one swift and all-encompassing glance at the last from this Armenian noblewoman and cavalry commander. A glance which not only catches at all those whose fate is to soon become enmeshed with hers but which also leaves one, Obedianus, caught in the lash of an emerging feeling which will soon overwhelm his burning need for vengeance - that *tha'r* dear to the Arabs - and leave him stranded on a strange and beautiful shore . . .

That night, with the two legions now ensconced in the Baths of Trajan, an unusual *consilium* takes place. Deep in a dark chamber within the Baths, layered with a glorious mosaic of a herd of hippocampi, oil torches flaring uneasily along the cracked walls, Flavius Anicius assembles the staff and maniple officers of his legion together with Stygos and the leading centurions of the Twelfth. It is a tense and brooding meeting. The light from the torches renders everything into a dark and shifting world in which those mythical creatures underfoot - half horse and half-fish - seem to swim and move below them all with a mocking and jaded air. Wine is passed around but once the amphora is empty no more is allowed in and Anicius is heard to remark that if more drink is needed then let it be of words rather than wine. Within this *consilium*, Elias now appears as the leading centurion of what is left of the Second Cohort, its standard salvaged from the wreck of the Hekatontarch's Mark. He has been promoted to Primus Prior for his actions in charging the Persian cataphracts and bringing all his legionaries back to the line intact. It falls to Candidus to remark many years later that this Elias, his tall and rangy body somehow standing at odds to those of Strabonius and Cyrion around him, remains unmoved by his promotion and that the other two cohortal centurions step carefully about him as if avoiding a plague.

Far in the distance, beyond the walls of the Baths, all can hear a muted noise as the citizens of Amida celebrate their unusual victory and relief from the siege. There is much singing and dancing. Prayers and chants can be heard among the churches of Amida while others not of the Christian faith carouse in the streets with palm fronds, their faces daubed with lime or henna. It is a curious mixture of the sacred and the profane, with sexual licence and strict piety intermingling on an almost street-by-street basis. That sound washes up against all those inside the Baths and forms an uneasy reminder of a world and celebration they have neither been invited into nor are celebrated for.

The records of that meeting are preserved in a fragmented papyrus contained in a heterogeneous collection within the museum of Ankara. It is not known how these legion records became separated and were then preserved independently but what remains is a dry list of those attending and a brief mention of what was discussed. Candidus refers obliquely to this meeting in his later writings but remains circumspect and adds little to the record alas. Not unsurprisingly, it is evidently too tedious a topic for Obedianus to write to his father about.

It is to be lamented that little surviving detail remains about this meeting. It is clearly the first and is therefore the most important of this new combined legion command and one in which the Tribune Flavius Anicius will detail his first orders. Among the Twelfth's centurions - Strabonius, Elias, and Cyrion, stands also Remus and a score of other senior or veteran centurions. Obedianus is present along with his companion, Old Jubyal. Stygos corrals his officers with a harshness that is not lost on the officers and staff of the Senior Sol Legion.

Among these latter, of course, now stands Candidus, marked by the death of a centurion on his cloak, to use Late Roman military slang. Near him stands also one Asellus, the Campidoctor or Drill-Master of the legion, a huge porcupine figure with fiery hair and a temper to match, of ancient Gallic blood. Surviving comments about him emphasise his curly hair, prominent eyes, a scarred brow, and a swarthy face often coloured with the after-effects of wine. Many call him 'Cyclops' both for his appetite for wine and the beetling brows whose thunder - once set in motion - many are keen to avoid. Asellus is a man for whom both discipline and an appetite for wine stand in an equal if sometimes contradictory measure. It has been written about Asellus that once, upon a *campus* in some long obscure Gallic fort, after a night of riotous drinking he and his hung-over *milites* bested the pride of another legion in exercises only for him to then vomit ingloriously over the subsequently proffered victory laurels.

By his side, stands the second-in-command of the legion, the Primicerius, Teutomeres. This man is of Frankish extraction and we know a little of his background thanks to Ammianus Marcellinus and his *Res Gestae*. Originally, like Candidus, a Domestic Protector, he had fallen from grace after a prisoner under his care had committed suicide and he was subsequently exiled. Later, under the Augustus Julian, he had been reprieved and assigned as Primicerius of the Sol under its original commissioning Tribune, one Angelus, who subsequently went on to command the Fifth Macedonica Legion. This Teutomeres is a quiet and distinguished officer known for his patience and calm demeanour and bears all the hallmarks of a Roman officer of dignity - save that an ancient tattoo of Frankish design obscures much of his neck. This curious tattoo, many have remarked, including Libanius from whom much of this information is supplemented, is a design which seems to *grow* up about him as though he is caught in the grip of some ravenous vine or root. When queried about it, Teutomeres is often seen to dismiss it with an embarrassed shrug, commenting that wine, a woman, and a dark night by the banks of the Rhine whence he had been exiled had combined to give him this legacy . . .

Other officers of the Sol cluster about Anicius: the six maniple ducenarii - Marcellus, Septimio, Merobaudes, Decentius, Scorpianus and Bellovaedius - and various adjutants and orderlies. It is significant that the guards assigned to the doorways of this dark chamber with its hippocampi mosaics are all from the First Maniple of the Sol legion under command of the Ducenarius, Marcellus.

The *consilium* proceeds with the ratification of Elias as chief centurion of what is left of the Second Cohort. A casualty list is enumerated for both legions and while that of the Sol is brief and perfunctory that of the Twelfth is both long and heard with a deepening silence. Of the legionaries who marched out from Melitene over three days ago, barely two thirds remain. What is worse however is that of those roughly six hundred losses most are from the Second Cohort which can barely muster now enough unwounded soldiers to fill two centuries' worth of men. Elias is heard to remark that his promotion is like being handed an empty wine glass and being told to drink to the health of the *respublica*. No one laughs at that remark save Asellus who then reddens suddenly at his outburst. The three-day march back to Melitene is discussed in terms of rations and equipment, carts and supply animals. It is a discussion of logistics which is well-rehearsed and brief. Messengers are dispatched to Melitene to advise of the arrival of the Twelfth with the Sol alongside and that billeting within the legionary fortress is to be assigned forthwith. If necessary, hospitality and lodgings are to be sourced within the town itself now that both legions have been graded as comitatenses troops and allowed access to town and civilian facilities. There is much grumbling from the officers of the Twelfth about this who fear that the delicate balance between legionary and town-dweller will be upset but Anicius overrides their concerns with the stern warning that as Roman soldiers of the field army the town must and shall bend to their will now.

Obedianus is ordered to remain attached to the newly-combined legion brigade until further orders state otherwise and it is noted within the papyrus record that as barely sixty Arab riders have survived replacements should be sought, if possible. The chieftain of the Bani Al Jawn is heard to remark that there are no sons of the tribe left to bear arms save the crippled and the old now long since put out to the stars, as it were, in the deserts of the south. Those that remain are all that is left. Let it be so then, replies the Tribune, sixty will do as well as a hundred have done. It is a small comment which in another context may well have caused insult or a slight upon the honour of an Arab but clearly these words strike home in the heart of Obedianus for what is written next is nothing but the inclining of his head to the Tribune.

The fragments of the surviving papyrus break off at this point and we are left in the dark as to the remaining orders and procedures. A final fragment buried within another part of the collection of the Museum of Ankara allows us to understand that the *consilium* is in fact halted upon the arrival of a messenger from the Magister Lupicinus with a demand that the commanding officers of the two legions attend him without delay. Thus it is that moments later, Flavius Anicius, Stygos, and Obedianus with Candidus in tow offer themselves with all due ceremony and in full military garb into the presence of the Magister Equitum.

It is near midnight and the office of the Magister is nothing but a bare cell far from the carousal of the city. A solitary oil lamp illuminates a long worn desk of wood inlaid with pearls and amber flanked by two guards. Tapestries gild the walls but contain only geometric designs whose colours are faded and thread-bare in places. As the officers are admitted entrance into the presence of Lupicinus, the Bishop of Amida is seen to brush past them, a worried look upon his countenance, his fat hands pale and sweaty in the low light.

Lupicinus sits upon a light curial stool behind the desk, parchment and papyrus spread out about him, a massive inkstand of gold, a symbol of his office, thrust casually to one side. A plain spatha lies across that desk in a scabbard and all note as they arrive that the weapon has been half-drawn out of that scabbard. Apart from the two guards, the only other figure in the small cell is that of Artashemeh who is standing to one side of the desk and looking along with Lupicinus down into a roughly-drawn map.

It is the first moment that these officers and commanders are able to gaze upon her in full and both the pens of Candidus and Obedianus describe a woman who although not tall seems so. Her limbs are long and graceful, clad as they are now in a silk tunica and faded breeches after the Persian fashion. A riding cloak graces her shoulders with a wide hood thrown back. This cloak is designed with inbuilt sleeves which hang loose now down her sides. An ornamental belt around her waist bears a curious complicated knot at the front while hanging from that belt is a mace which is plain and unadorned by comparison to the girdle. Riding boots, again after the Persian fashion, complete her garb. What strikes both Candidus and Obedianus most though is not her bearing as she leans in over the Magister and the map before him but instead the pride and dignity in her face.

There is an instinctive reaction from these two writers - so apart in education and culture - which seems to ignite an almost reverential response from them. It is perhaps to be wondered on the novelty of seeing a woman garbed for war and occupying a position of familiarity in front of Lupicinus which provokes this response - this and the fact that this woman has ridden past all their own dust and blood and battle at the head of her warriors and guard without fear or hesitation. Both pens in encompassing this woman also allude to other women who stand further afield - as if this Armenian alone should not exist but in the shadow of other exemplars of her kind - Candidus wonders on the image of Zenobia, that queen and empress of Palmyra, who defied Rome and an Emperor until brought in chains and captivity to the Eternal City itself, and harks even as far back as to Cleopatra and Boudicca - both women of different casts. Obedianus however lacking that understanding of history remembers instead only Zenobia and also an Arab tribe once ruled by a fierce woman who bent all to her will as cubs are reared and trained by a mountain lioness. This woman, who fought and reigned for almost half a century, had spun about her the ancient diadem and shield of Ailat herself and so legitimised her rule under divine favour until toppled at the last by Christian warriors and monks in the deserts.

Both writers remain struck by her bearing now as she turns from that parchment map and gazes on all of them as they enter. They recall a wide dark face, worn with cares, whose eyes are somehow both gentle and also unforgiving. Tresses of black fall loosely about her forehead and there is a lack of jewellery or ostentation about her. Apart from the weave and design of her clothes and the ornate belt about her waist, she remains devoid of rings or torcs or armillae. It is inevitable that Candidus sees in her the echo of Athena perhaps or the ubiquitous visage of an Amazon whereas Obedianus wonders instead on that mountain kingdom of Armenia and its closeness to the Persian lands where it is not unknown for women nobles to ride to war or even indeed command armies or council kings.

It is Lupicinus however who breaks this spell as he throws that parchment map aside and invites Artashemeh to speak with an impatient gesture. What she says next dispels all thoughts of literary or mythological ruminations.

"Romans, Armenia has fallen," she says slowly, eyeing them all. "Arsaces, my King, has been taken."

CHAPTER TWELVE

Armenia is a tortured kingdom.

It is a pockmarked land of high mountain chains, alluvial valleys, and deep passes riddled with false turns and dead-ends. The mighty Araxes river cuts through it to the deep azure waters of the Hyrcanian Sea in the east. The Cyrus river to the north divides Armenia proper from the hill-tribes of the Albani and the Iberi. To the south, the two great chains of the Taurus and the Zagros mountains form a barrier to the green and lush fertile plains further south through which the long and eternal Tigris and Euphrates flow. Pontic mountains fringe the northerly edges of the country as it abuts up against the Euxine sea, with its ancient trading routes into Colchis and its echoes of the Golden Fleece and the Argonauts. Within this rocky kingdom lie three vast lakes swathed in legend and superstition and known as the 'Seas of Armenia': Arcesh or Van as it is called today, Sevan, and Urmia; all high mountain lochs whose surrounding pastures and hills remain cloaked in snow and ice during the harsh winters but whose own waters always remain ice-free. These 'seas' of Armenia provide little in the way of fish however due to the high saline content yet remain a potent wonder, standing within this rocky fastness as symbols of life and rebirth in all the ancient realms and dynasts which have claimed this land: ancient Urartu, Ararat, and Vaspurakan, for example. Now, in the deeply-Christian realm of Armenia, these vast lakes remain special as places of reverence for along all their shores monks and holy men wander using those waters to convert the hardy locals into the mysteries and grace of Christ.

There are those who say that this ancient and broken landscape - the jagged mountain chains, the twisted rivers, the mist-shrouded high plateaus, the long silent lochs - stands as an eternal reflection of the suffering and character of these remote and proud races of Armenia. As with the Persians to the south, Armenia holds many different peoples and clans within its realm: the dark and mysterious hill tribes who share their blood with the Cordueni to the west and who nurture feuds and hatreds never easily forgotten. The ancient kin of these hillmen fought and bested the Greeks under Xenophon over seven hundred years earlier. Separate from these scattered and morose tribes stand the large communities of Armenians proper whose blood and heritage goes back to the remote kingdom of Urartu which had challenged Assyrian hegemony a thousand years in the past. Under the kings and warlords of Urartu - Sarduri, Argishti and Menua, for example - this kingdom had checked the growing power to the south again and again. It was only the crushing invasions of the

Cimmerians and the Scythians from the north which eventually eroded the power of Urartu and led to its decline.

Year after year, invaders have crossed the high plateaus and river valleys from north to south and east to west, devastating the towns and fortresses of Armenia, for it is written that it is both the blessing and the curse of those peoples to live in a land which is both a warren and a prison. A warren for the maze of hills and passes and refuges hidden away and a prison for no matter where one flees it is never to freedom or salvation. In later years, with the deepening Christianization of the kingdom, this tortured aspect of Armenia is held onto with a hard desperate courage as if the land is in some way a *stigmata* from God. Indeed, there are those who claim that Armenia itself is akin to the body of Christ hung upon that bloody cross, pointing to its four boundaries as proof: the Euxine sea to the northwest, the Hyrcanian sea to the northeast, the Mediterranean to the southwest, and the Persian Sea to the southeast. Quarters which echo the four arms of the crucifix and upon which Armenia has been nailed from time immemorial . . .

Above these ancient memories and feuds then of the Assyrian and the Scyth and even of the Greek, all armoured in hoplite cuirass and shield, lies a prouder strain now - the clans and houses of the noble *Naxarar* within whose memories flow the ancient Armenian or *Hayk'* bloodline. These princely families however remain locked in bitter feuds over tatters of honour and prestige that date back to the days under the ancient Achaemenid Empire: Houses whose names recall the high royal power of an empire which vied with Greece and later Rome for suzerainty over the Mesopotamian heartlands. With the fall of that empire and the rise of the sons of Sassan, that old blood and honour resides now in craggy fortresses and remote hill-towns always looking enviously south into the fertile lands radiating out from the Tigris and the Euphrates rivers. Here, behind the mountains of the Taurus and the Zagros, lies the Mamikonean House, for example, whose scions always claim the hereditary title of *Sparapet* - the military commander or High Constable of the kingdom. Inland, around the Seas of Armenia, lies the Arsacid House itself, ancient dynasts and kings of the country whose bloodline extends as far back as the history of Persia. Further to the west is the Bagratuni House whose descendants always claim the ceremonial title of *Aspet* or Master of Horse and also *Tagadir* or the King's Crowner. Now with the rise of Christianity, the Gregorid House has emerged to claim the title of Patriarch or *Katholikos* of Armenia. There is also the House of the Kamsarakan, 'of the Six Hundred Horses', within whose blood runs the ancient ancestry of the Parthian Karen-Pahlavi and whose princes now stand beneath Arsaces as cousins. And finally the great House of the Gnuni whose eldest bears the title of *Hazarapet*, or Grand Vizier of the kingdom of Armenia. Titles and prestige and honours that remain fixed and immutable within each House. Beneath these great scions lie the inferior nobles and princes, the *Azat*, who bear titles and honours such as cupbearers, squires, and master of hounds, and who often break off to form companies of bitter riders or forlorn bodyguards.

These Houses and the march lords or satraps which accompany them are all deeply insular and competitive. Internecine war and feuds consume them over long generations with the result that these hereditary titles are bitterly defended and constantly eroded. A rugged land, insular in nature and with a patchwork of isolated Houses often cut-off from each other and defended by remote fortresses, has led to a kingdom which remains distinct from both the servile Persian lands to the south and the last echoes of republican or democratic law to the west in Rome. Here, in Armenia, as opposed to the over-arching King of Kings of Sassanid Persia with its despotic rule or the pedantic respect for law and the courtroom of the Roman Empire, we find a curiously proto-feudal country in which noble Houses inherit state titles and a king is proclaimed amid his nobles but who yet may never rule over them in the manner of a Persian *Shah* or a Roman *Imperator*. The centrifugal pull towards a single royal monarch is countered by the jealous rivalry of the different Armenian *Naxarar* lords and their remote mountain fiefdoms.

It is an irony however that within this fractious realm of competing Houses and broken landscapes, Armenia stands above all for the quality of its horses and as a consequence the martial dignity and prowess of its armoured riders. Here, high in the plateaus and rich alluvial soils of its valleys, roam the great herds of the Nissaean horses whose bloodline has spilled east down into the Mesopotamian heartland and west into the Cappadocian high plateau. The horses of Armenia are strong and wilful much as her riders are, it must be said. It is written that among the Persian court, that if a troop of Armenian *Naxarar* revolts from the rule of their King and turns its banners over to the *ShahanShan* then it will ride in the place of honour with the Sassanid army - such is its skill and valour - despite whether its lords and riders subscribe to the Christian creed or the Zoroastrian one or the older pagan mountain gods of Armenia: Hayk, founder of the Armenian people, Vahagn, god of thunder and lightning, Aramazd, supreme father of the gods, and Nane, goddess of war, to name but a few. It remains a constant source of wonder to those Greek and Syrian traders and travellers who penetrate the mountain fastness of Armenia that such a wracked landscape should produce that most aristocratic of warriors: the mounted lord on a proud steed, armed for war with the long contus, his body encased in mail and plate, the high silk heraldry of his House flowing back from him as he rides impetuously into battle.

These proud feudal Houses, each one marked by a distinct title or function in the Kingdom, occupy one of four tiers or steps of honour and are said to number in total now fifty where once in ages past there had been over four hundred. Merging bloodlines and feudal internecine warfare has eroded this number with some Houses assimilating peacefully while others have been wiped out in long wars of extinction. Now the fifty *Naxarar* Houses are being torn apart in a new and vicious cycle of warfare which pits Christian House against Zoroastrian House, princes and lords for Rome against those for Persia, all the while the Armenian King, Arsaces, carefully plays one side against the other for fear that invasion from either Rome or Persia looms on the horizon. This precarious balance has tipped dangerously over in recent years with the death of the Augustus Julian and a subsequent peace with Persia in which Rome has surrendered its claim to any involvement within the boundaries of Armenia itself.

This King, head and elder of the Arshakuni House, that ancient Parthian bloodline which dates back to Achaemenid times itself, girdled about by the emergent Christian faith, abandoned by Rome, has seen the princely Houses fall apart into competing factions along religious lines. It is a bloody mosaic which shudders and convulses in such a manner that few can follow it - and those that do so hold within themselves only the highest statecraft and cunning.

Among these fifty Houses, then, only four or perhaps five hold sway about Arsaces, and of these Houses, it is the Mamikoneans who hold the most power. One of the most ancient Houses of Armenia - there is a venerated legend within its families and princes that the first of the Mamikoneans were exiled brothers of the Han Emperor of China himself - this House holds the hereditary title of *Sparapet*. With the decline in the power of the Master of Horse, or *Aspet*, this title alone now wields supreme military power within Armenia. Arsaces may bear the jewelled diadem of Armenia upon his brow but it is the Mamikonean *Sparapet* alone who may summon the unruly *Naxarar* lords and princes with all their glittering retinues upon the ancient muster fields of this mountain kingdom. Yet this supreme title is a brittle one - no *Sparapet* may dare dream of claiming the crown, symbolic as that power is, for to do so would upset all the delicate bindings of feudal loyalty and privilege which alone allows Armenia to survive in a violent world. Hence these Mamikoneans, scattered about in the dark and rough hills of the province of Tayk, with its pine groves and wild eagles, and all ensconced in brooding fortresses and walled villages, are pragmatic and cunning in the extreme. The current head of the House, Vashak

Mamikonean, is recorded as saying before all the assembled *Naxarar* princes that it is better to wield a mace than it is a sceptre and what better mace to wield than one in defence of a sceptre? Now since the fall of Julian some five long years earlier and the surrender up to Shapur of the lower satrapies below the Taurus and Zagros mountains, this scarred and hoary old wardog has led the princes and lords of Armenia in border clashes against the Sassanians in a vain attempt to stall the *ShahanShah's* inevitable desire to wrest Armenia back into Persian control.

For four long years, Vashak Mamikonean has mustered the Houses still loyal to Arsaces in the old royal fields and led them south into the marchlands and satraps below the Taurus and the Zagros, harrying the Persian borders, leading his armoured nobles and *Azat* riders in deep raids, torching border towers and forts, massacring supply trains, surprising sleepy caravans and oasis settlements, and leaving nothing but devastation and blood and terror in his wake. The chroniclers and historians of Armenia call this period the 'Reaping' and refer to Vashak Mamikonean as the 'Lion' of Armenia - knowing all the while that no matter how glorious his victories or how bitter the betrayals of the Houses that defect from his banner to join the growing Persian sway nor how wasted and wounded are those *Naxarar* princes who ride back with him at the end of each campaigning season, it is all in vain. To the south, Persia rouses itself like an enormous serpent and its coils will soon slide and twist all about the mountain peaks and high crags of Armenia.

And so it comes to pass that on this final and fifth campaigning season, as the silk banners of Christ and His Saints are raised upon the royal muster fields about the Sea of Arcesh, with the brightly coloured tents and pavilions scattered about like monstrous blooms, and the herds of Nissaean horses thundering in the distance and echoing the royal trumpets and drums, that a great war *consilium* is held and all the *Naxarar* princes and lords sit - each upon a cushion according to his or her rank below the royal cushion of Arsaces - feasting and carousing as is the Armenian way, all the while Arsaces, his brow dark and fevered asks that eternal question: what will Armenia do between the rock of Rome and the desert of Persia? What will he, the King, the inheritor of a bloodline that goes back to the ancient Parthian Arsacids and whose ancestors once ruled lands greater than the Sassan dogs, what will he do now that Rome has held up its hands from Armenia and the Persians lick and nibble at the marchlands with all the persistence and inevitability of a jackal gnawing on the bones of the dying?

Those early chroniclers paint a vivid picture of the long debate which follows in which Vashak rises from his cushion, all embroidered with his

House's heroic deeds, dashing his goblet to the floor, shouting out that no Mamikonean has ever fallen back before the Sassanid dog and he will not do so now - even as the *Katholikos*, Narseh, soothes his anger with calm words and raises the issue that Rome has abandoned them with the shameful treaty after the death of Julian. How long, asks Narseh, the Patriarch of Armenia, a prince of the Gregorid House, how long can Armenia stand alone? Already, the princes of the eastern marches have dipped their banners in submission to Shapur in return for little or no abeyance. This Shapur woos them all with smooth words and smiles as is the Persian manner. Now the standards of the Houses of the Abeluni, the Droshakirn, the Hashtuni of the Endless Marches, and the Sagrasuni all ride with the Sassanid *Savaran* in places of honour. Do they not sit now upon cushions of equal rank with the great lords and satraps before Shapur despite their Christian faith? War will only prolong this bitter divide and allow Armenia to crumble House by House before the words of this *ShahanShah*. Surely it is better to accept the overtures of the Persian and keep Armenia free? These are well-rehearsed words and ones spoken many times by Narseh. This Patriarch is as much a pragmatist as he is a religious zealot and, as with many Armenian nobles, values the independence of his House as much as he does the integrity of Armenia or even the still-brittle veneer of Christianity now covering the kingdom. Other princes buttress his words, arguing that Shapur demands nothing but friendship and fealty in return for an amity of Armenian brother with Aryan brother. Has not Armenian and Persian always been kin and blood? Do not both sit on cushions of rank under the silk awning unlike the Romans who sit upon stools and ivory chairs?

Has not Armenia always looked east and south rather than west?

It falls to the head of the Bagratuni House, Ashot, Coronant of the King, his hair white like snow and his face cracked like a dry river valley, to rise from his cushion and shout back into the placating arguments of Narseh that this Shapur pours out words like wine and like all wine when drunk nothing remains but a broken head in the morning. Then he shouts out that *these* are the words of a Sassan and so thrusts his fist into his mouth, filling it with his fingers. The laughter which follows at his comic mask breaks the tension and allows Arsaces to smile under his heavy brow while ordering more roast meat and honeyed wine.

There, under the wide awnings of silk, all rippling to a gentle breeze by the Sea of Arcesh, the sound of its waves lapping along the pebbled shores, ever the thunder of hooves and distant drums in the background, the princely *Naxarars* forget their quarrels and feuds and feast the memory of their royal King and his ancestors all the while wondering on what this fifth season of war will bring now that the royal muster has brought them all again under the banners of battle and honour and Christ. Few sitting ensconced under that great royal pavilion, its silk awnings gaping wide under the azure sky, the sound of the waves upon the white pebbles of Arcesh, the distant neighing of the wild horses of the royal herds on the far slopes of the mountains, will realise that this will be the last mustering for Armenia.

It is early Spring under a placid sky and all about that muster field, amid the scattered tents and silk pavilions, all redolent with carousing and hot words of boasting and honour, few sense that the year will bring something other than more march warfare and deep raiding into the Persian fertile lands south of the Zagros and the Taurus mountains. Has not the 'Lion' of Arsaces led them in four long seasons of victory and honour in which Armenian nobles have bested their Sassanian counterparts? Has not the contus of Vashak himself shivered twelve times across the bronze breastplates of Sassanian lords and does he now not keep those shattered lances in his great hall and each one named after an Apostle of Christ? And why shall not this fifth mustering under the royal banner and standard of Arsaces here on the shores of the Sea of Arcesh bring yet more honour and glory for the princes and nobles of the *Naxarar* Houses?

And so the feasting and the boasting roars itself finally into a quiet time in the deep of night when the moon has risen and the wind has fallen and the long waves over the white pebbles only whisper now. The wild stallions and mares have gone higher up into the mountains to find sleep and peace. The silk tents and awnings hang limp and heavy under swollen torches and oil lamps whose light is muted and brittle. High, high above all, the harsh mountain peaks glitter with an icy rim and the glow from the moon echoes that coldness and throws it back upon the silent waters of Arcesh so that it seems as if silver and ice frame all.

And so it comes to pass, according to the ancient chroniclers of Armenia, that a small phalanx of nobles and guards drift like phantoms away from the assembled tents and move slowly along the white shore, in and out of the waters as if hesitating between this world and another - one insubstantial and seductive. Armoured in chain and iron scale, silk tabards flowing listlessly over that armour, great helms or cassis clasped in the crook of an arm, the long bejewelled spathas hanging from their belts bound in ornamental straps and buckles, each prince walks with his brother and sister through this gentle but cold surf whilst deep in their midst moves their King, Arsaces, aloof but troubled and speaking hesitant words to those few by him. Only once the royal pavilions and horse corrals are distant and almost unreal does Arsaces halt, the waters lapping about his armoured feet, the cold silver light cascading about him from above and from below, and then he turns to his fellow *Naxarar* warriors and tells them all that he will forbear blessing the royal standard when the dawn arrives. There will be no raiding nor battle with the Persians this Spring. No House will advance it banners and icons over the Zagros or Taurus mountains. In a silence of uncommon respect these princes and nobles of the Mamikoneans, the Bagratuni, the Gregorids, the Kamsarakani, and the Gnuni await their King and his words, all standing in the silvered waters of Arcesh as if on brittle glass. It is written then that the King gazed upon them all in turn with sad eyes and a gentle smile. His once dark brows and angry eyes were quiet now. He looked upon them all in turn and some he placed a hand upon their mail-clad shoulder and others he merely nodded to and only when he had encompassed them all thus one way or another did he stand apart and look back at them, saying that as Armenia is riven with conflict so now are his brothers and nobles also riven and split asunder. As the kingdom is falling into betrayal so too are those about him breaking apart. Brother will turn against sister. The Houses will turn into themselves to crack apart in fire and ruin. Where once there was but one Judas now there shall be cousins upon cousins of them. His words fall away into a grim silence then as each *Naxarar* lord looks long and hard into the faces of those about him or her - and it takes Vashak to step forward, silver arcs rippling out from him, to say with fierce words again that no Mamikonean will ever step away from the Arsacid House in betrayal - and in that moment alone does Arsaces step forwards towards him so that the waters of Arcesh clash about their feet and what he says next brings a silence that shatters all their souls . . .

' . . . "He knew that traitors were already in his midst."

It was Stygos who broke the spell which this Artashemeh had placed upon us all in that little chamber. His blunt words were spoken in an ugly and cold voice and he spoke them as if there was never any doubt in his mind. I remember glancing quickly into the face of this Artashemeh and seeing a sudden quickening in her eye and then she nodded in a sad almost neglectful manner.

"He was saying farewell, though we knew it not. Not yet. And each of us in our own way received from our King a final parting as we stood in those bitter waters at the edge of the Sea of Arcesh."

Flavius Anicius frowned at that. "A parting?"

And again Stygos spoke in his dark rough voice, all the scars on his carven face creasing in. "A hand was a blessing, a nod a curse. Isn't that so?"

She smiled in return. She reached out and ran a hand along the half-opened spatha on the desk as a troubled look came over her. "My brother, Vashak, as he stepped closer through those silver waters and uttered that fierce oath - that no Mamikonean would ever step away from the Arshakuni House - had seen only a King acknowledge each and everyone one of us in those waters. He had not noticed that we were all treated differently. I had. I can still feel his hand upon my shoulder, the squeeze of it, his troubled gaze on me, and then a little smile that told me so much of what was to come. Vashak at my side saw none of that. He was the 'Lion' of the King and we all know that lions roar and fight and rarely contemplate. It was his strength and his flaw in the end." She lifted up her hand and curled it up into a ball and I saw a sudden pain flare through her. A pain and an anger that almost made me step back in alarm. "And of course my brother never saw that even as he cracked the icy waters of Arcesh under the moon that between us stood our brother Vahan, the youngest of the three of us, he who we always shielded and protected like a cub, Vahan, his black hair always bound in copper fillets, who now smiled even as Vashak proclaimed our loyalty never noticing that our King had merely nodded to him as he had done to so many other princes and nobles about us all. Arsaces knew Vahan and the others were already under the Persian banner despite their presence here upon the royal muster field of Arcesh - and so he knew that even as Vashak swore an oath before him of the loyalty of the Mamikonean House that it was an oath already riven from within. It was what drove him to step in towards Vashak so that together they faced each other in a tiny swirl of silver ripples. He was trying to save his soul - all our souls . . ."

It was Obedianus who spoke next. There was something fierce and implacable in his face. Something akin to these Armenian nobles that told me that underneath his Roman deference and his clumsy Latin lurked a wilder heart. A heart which beat now in sympathy to this woman who stood before us and yet spoke as if she were a warrior and a man and one who knew all that could be known of loyalty and betrayal and valour. "Your King, this Arsaces, he was going to sacrifice himself to save them all, yes? To save you all from yourselves."

Artashemeh smiled at that but it was smile of such tragedy that it stilled his words. "Arabi, can you imagine a King who finds his true royalty only amid the deepest betrayal of his people? That is Arsaces. Yes, he was going to sacrifice himself to the Persians. Only that act might save his kingdom from itself." And I saw Artashemeh look almost without realising out of the small window into the night, her face falling into shadow, as her hand fell by her side like a dead thing . . .'

The words Arsaces uttered into the fierce but blind loyalty of Vashak have been inscribed in chronicle after chronicle of the Armenians though it is to be wondered on who precisely relayed those words for posterity. There, amid the lapping waters, the moon high above and the remote mountaintops all covered in snow, this King of ancient blood and nobility, turned into the passionate words of Vashak and stilled them for it is written that he told this head of the Mamikonean House, his *Sparapet* or High Constable, that when the wolves are already within the flock it is always best to seek sanctuary amid that which even the wolves fear. Arsaces said that he was nothing but a lamb under God and Christ and what did all lambs need? A shepherd. And so he would travel in the morning across the Zagros mountains into the ancient heartland of Mesopotamia with only a few companions and there throw himself and Armenia upon the friendship and amity of Shapur. And had not this descendant of Sassan and Ardashir himself sought him out in person as a brother and a royal colleague? Had not this Shapur extended him a cushion of rank equal to his own thus swearing peace and protection to him if he would but come unto Persia and end this rancorous divide of Armenian and Persian?

He would travel with the dawn and share salt with the Sassanian *arteshtar* and so seal a peace between the ancient Houses of Armenia and the Houses of Persia.

On the dawn of the first day of April, attended by a furious but dogged Vashak Mamikonean and a select guard of *Azat*, Arsaces rides south over the rough hills and tracks before the Zagros mountains, through the Great Zab pass, down into the fertile lands south of Armenia and the border marches. He passes slowly and with all due ceremony through the desolated towns and remote forts, honouring the minor *Naxarar* lords and satraps in these dangerous and unruly lands, and then once over the Zagros chain itself, he is met with an honour guard of *Savaran* under the banner and heraldry of the ancient Parthian lord, Perozes, of the House Mihran, ancestor to the Perozes later to lose against Belisarius outside the fortress-city of Daras. Here, amid the glittering armour and silk standards of the Persian cataphracts, Arsaces and his entourage are escorted with all pomp and ceremony to the revered walls of Nineveh to await the presence of Shapur himself. It is an uneasy wait as the Armenian nobles and guards under the watchful eyes of their Persian hosts in this one of the most ancient of Mesopotamian cities brood deep in the halls and walled gardens. The gentle fountains and rose-bordered walkways give them little solace and more than once Vashak is heard to scold the wisdom of Arsaces for allowing them all to be invited here into the arms of the enemy. Only the hallowed salt of peace given to Arsaces by Shapur mollifies him but as all know a lion is always restless and impatient of peace. Finally, towards the end of April, with the evenings lengthening and the purple shadows now all hazy with heat and flies, the King of Kings arrives with the combined nobles and satraps of his vast empire and bids the Armenian King to enter into his presence within a magnificent golden pavilion outside the marble walls of Nineveh.

It is a day few of the old chroniclers of Armenia pass over in silence or peace. It is midday and the golden pavilion is ringed by a triple-line of dismounted *Zhayedan* or 'Immortals', the elite royal bodyguards of the *ShahanShah* who always number ten thousand. The sun is hot and unrelenting despite the early month and as Arsaces and Vashak proceed through these armoured lines the light from their armour blinds them and causes them to look away with unease. Once at the portal into the golden pavilion, both are astonished to see two K'ushan elephants flanking that entrance, all decked out in silk and gold ornaments, standing like high ivory statues, immobile and silent. Thus suitably awed both Armenians are ushered by a gaggle of swarthy eunuchs from the fabled lands of Axum into the main chamber within and made to prostrate themselves upon silk carpets before the figure of Shapur himself seated on a massive gold cushion, with all his generals and nobles arrayed about him in order of precedence. It is a great hieratic frame of seated Persian and Parthian all sitting cross-legged, their arms folded and hidden within voluminous sleeves, their eyes masked in kohl, their faces fringed with oiled beards and the long dangling moustaches favoured by the Persian warrior-lords. Before this display of Sassanian power, both Arsaces and Vashak fall face down in the time-honoured fashion, offering up praise and devotion to the dignity and valour of the King of Kings.

And then a long silence fell over all in that golden pavilion . . .

' . . . "But it was a trap. A fateful lure which my King in his honour went to more in hope than expectation. . . ."

The silence which followed her words was broken only by the distant command of an officer changing the watch along the ramparts and bastion towers. Far in the distance, the shouts and cries of revelry had faded into nothing more insistent than a muted drone like the surf against a harbour wall. In that sudden silence we all, I think, paused to absorb her words. She had talked about events so close to our own that we stood confused by it all. It was if she narrated another world - a world of myth perhaps or tragedy penned by some obscure artist - and we struggled to piece it all together. Only Lupicinus, I saw, remained unmoved by it and I knew then that this was not news to him. The Magister reached out and span the stylus impatiently on his large desk, his pinched face frowning and his lips downturned. Already, plans and thoughts were boiling in him and I knew that he waited on us out of courtesy, nothing more. Stygos broke her silence first, looking quickly from Flavius Anicius and myself as he did so.

"This was, what, no more than eight days ago? Ardawan and his Persian troops must have already been massing for an attempt at Amida. What happened in that golden pavilion, Artashemeh? Is Arsaces still alive?"

Lupicinus nodded back. "Good. You are asking the right questions." He leaned back in his ivory chair and gestured with the stylus to the Armenian noblewoman standing by him. "Tell them. Tell them everything if they are to have a chance."

"The eunuchs seized them both," she continued, "and bound them in silver chains as a mark of respect. The sacred salt was tipped away without a second glance. My brother who had harried the Persian marches for four long years was dragged away without ceremony and flayed alive. The skin was stuffed with straw and hangs now from the high guy ropes of the pavilion. Arsaces, my King, was blinded even as that terrible fate was being meted out and then his sentence was pronounced - that for his rebellion and temerity in defying the King of Kings, he was to be transported to Anyush, which the Persians call the Prison of Oblivion. The next day a mighty Sassanian force marched north and crossed over into Armenia bringing with it fire and devastation."

Lupicinus grimaced at that and threw the stylus down upon the desk top. "Amida, it seems, *commiliatones*, was nothing but a feint to keep us preoccupied while this Sassanian oath-breaker moved north and west up into Armenia!"

Artashemeh nodded in return. "The muster fields were broken. Vahan, our younger brother, compelled the majority of the Houses to either go over to the Persian standards or abstain, in effect, surrendering. Our fortress outposts crumbled and within days - I suspect even as Ardawan encamped here at Amida - the Persian hosts were deep within Armenia. The royal town of Artaxata was taken in a night of fire and blood and the bones of the ancient Arsacid kings were disinterred from it and cast upon a dung heap. Four days ago, the Queen, Pharanjem, with her son, retreated to Artageressa, a secluded fortress with a thousand of her picked royal *Azat* guard and are even now under siege from Sassanian and Armenian forces. Under her orders, I rode with what is left of the loyal *Naxarar* princes and their retainers here over the rough tracks and little-known ways. Seek out the Roman Wolf, she ordered me, and closed the gates to Artageressa herself, seek out Lupicinus. And so we rode at night, our banners and standards bound up, our hooves muffled, our armour clothed in rags and cloaks, and by the grace of Christ and all the Martyrs under Him, we evaded the Persian patrols. Now we are here and have chased away a Persian army but I wonder if that army was defeated or indeed if we saved anything at all . . ."

Lupicinus snorted at that. "Indeed! You have this young Italian to thank for that!"

I saw Flavius Anicius move to step forward, anger and certain imperious disdain clouding his forehead - but Stygos grabbed his arm and pulled him back. It was a hold which brooked no disobedience and I remembered wondering again on what bound them like father and son. Together, they formed the oddest cast - an arrogant youth who shouldered a command not his to own yet and a *veteranus* who had sent men to death for so long that I suspect he now had forgotten what life really was. And I remembered thinking then even as Stygos pulled him back almost without thinking and Flavius Anicius responded without resistance that before me were the dual masks of Comedy and Tragedy but I could not tell which one was which . . .

It was Stygos, again, who asked the correct question: "Your Queen, Pharanjem - what was it that she asked you to do? Why the Magister?"

Artashemeh stepped in towards us then and I saw her look each of us in the eye. "Rome must come to our aid. She must. We are a Christian people under the Persian crop. Armenia is falling. Our King is in the Prison of Oblivion. My brother, Vashak, is mocked as nothing more than a grotesque figure of straw at the entrance of Shapur's pavilion. The Persian fire-temples of the magi will soon flare up across the mountains and plains of Armenia." She turned suddenly to face Lupicinus and the intensity in her face made her both beautiful and haunting. "Rome abandoned us when Julian fell and that fateful treaty was signed. This is the consequence. Persia flows now north up to the Euxine Sea. Soon Persian fleets will sail that sea and cross to Thrace and the Danube. Will you see Persian and Goth share salt? Will you see Constantinople crushed between them? Pharanjem saw this and closed the doors of Artageressa against me - bidding me take the last of the *Naxarar* lords west to Rome rather than face the Persians. I have a thousand Armenians under my standard! A thousand of the finest heavy cavalry this world has ever known - all Christian and all ready to ride back into Armenia and eject the Persian snakes! If you will but give us the legions to do it! Ride to the Wolf, she commanded, even as those gates closed on us, ride west and bring back the legions of Rome to save us - and, Lupicinus, Magister of your Augustus, Valens, do you not *owe* us this? Tear up that treaty now that Ardawan has broken the peace and assaulted Amida. Avenge your honour and let me guide a Roman army back into Armenia - let me save the Queen and the son of Arsaces! Let me relieve the siege of Artageressa and rally the *Naxarar* Houses of Armenia!"

And Lupicinus, his saturnine face frowning, his eyes in shadow, reached out and slowly grasped the hilt of the spatha. He closed his fist about it and then drew the blade out so that it lay naked and gleaming upon the desk of his office. For one moment, I thought he would raise it up and I saw Obedianus at least echo that gesture of the Magister as he too reached down and grasped the hilt of his own spatha. He did not, though. Instead, Lupicinus allowed a smile to cross his face as his eyes lingered on that naked blade. What he said next was something we all expected but still it shocked us.

"That is the thing with treaties, in all their fine words and delicate phrases, there is always a crack, a sliver, through which the tiniest worm can wriggle . . ."

And the look on his face then was one I had seen before and I knew then that a march into death and sacrifice was not over, merely postponed . . .'

CHAPTER THIRTEEN

It is only moments after this extraordinary announcement that Lupicinus bids Artashemeh to withdraw while he decides to talk in confidence to the legion commanders and officers about him.

I follow Candidus in the main here although a number of epistles from Lupicinus to both Libanius and Gregory of Nyssa allow me to embroider the Alexandrian's account somewhat - even if I use a little license in interpreting his words to those two luminaries. It is the sudden insight of Candidus previously - where he remarks that he has seen this look upon the Magister before and so allows him to understand that the Twelfth Legion remains bound upon a curious and sacrificial wheel - that colours our reading of what follows.

Lupicinus stands suddenly and bids this Armenian noblewoman of the Mamikonean House to retire. She, her gaze enigmatic, nods and moves to leave as if on cue. As she passes before these weary men of the two legions, she looks over them all again and smiles slowly as if knowing something that not even they are aware of. Obedianus later writes that this quality of hers - to look and in looking understand that which is not visible - reminds him of that moment in a dream when an unseen eye falls over you and all your hidden desires are lain bare. It is a moment which is both intimidating and also liberating. She leaves then and in the wake of her absence, the Magister waves his two guards away and bids them all to follow him a little out onto a stone balcony.

It is the dead of night and while the darkness above is complete and heavy like a shroud of the *lares,* torches and oil lamps below scatter and intermingle within the streets and forums of Amida. Laughter and rough curses drift up about them. Cymbals can be heard along with the faint strains of harps and lyres. Singing and praying clash against each other and somewhere in the distance angry voices collide all chorused with amusement and derision. The city in all its passion for life carouses secure in the knowledge that God and Christ and all the little Syrian and Greek Gods ever known have cast a protective net about those who live here. As Lupicinus, that 'Wolf' of the Emperor, gazes down upon the tumult of a city unexpectedly alive, it can be seen that his face is hidden in shadow and so very remote. He has fastened his spatha about him and one hand twists at the belt buckle again and again. It is a gesture which strikes Candidus as one both typical of his master and also one which makes him uneasy. He remembers another night not long ago in which this Magister approached him and laid an improbable burden upon him and it seems to Candidus that now after the battle of the Hekatontarch's Mark and the events which led up to it that somehow he looks upon Lupicinus with different eyes - as if he himself has somehow shifted. He remembers that bloody act only this afternoon in which by his own hand a man had been flayed alive and how at the last that dying man had thrown back at him his own name. Candidus the Alexandrian, his face a cast mixed from Aegyptian, Greek and Roman blood, shivers then atop that small balcony even as Lupicinus turns to face them, his back to the glitter of Amida, and scowls at them all.

' . . . "Her words are persuasive, are they not?"

It was Flavius Anicius who moved forwards a step and I saw that he was uneasy. "The Augustus Valens will not condone an invasion of Armenia, surely? You must write to him and inform him of what has happened here. No Roman legion will march into that country unless ordered to by the Emperor himself - "

"You think I do not understand that, Tribune?"

I spoke up then, desperate to salve a brewing discord. "It is not so simple now. Ardawan has broken the treaty ratified by the Sacred Jovian. Persian perfidy has torn up that accord. Do we wait until Valens decides our course of action or do we seize the initiative thrown to us by Artashemeh? Will we be Greeks or Trojans?"

Lupicinus laughed at that. "If I remember, the Amazons were on the side of the Trojans, Candidus! But you are correct. The treaty signed after the death of Julian at Samarra was always a divisive one. We surrendered up our right to intervene in Armenian affairs and pulled all our troops and officers out of that country. I still remember reading a copy of the wording once it was promulgated throughout the high *officia* of the empire. I was not the only Roman angered by that emperor's decision. Not only did the Empire surrender up Nisibis and those forts below the Zagros mountains, it also retreated from Armenia - a country we have always used as a bulwark to Persian aggression. Artashemeh is correct. We owe them all a debt of honour. And Ardawan has allowed that chain about our hands to be loosened."

"Loosened but not broken - is that it?"

Stygos leaned out against the balcony wall and gazed down into the revelry below. Although it was dark and little light touched his face, I sensed that he was scowling and that something black was moving through him.

Lupicinus nodded in return. "I cannot sanction a full Roman *excursus* into Armenia. That alone is the prerogative of the Sacred Valens. And it will take time for that action to happen - if it is willed to happen. Time that will see this Queen fall and what little resistance that remains in Armenia crumble and fade away. No, the legions will not march into Armenia."

Stygos turned from the balcony to face him. "But we will - is that it?"

And the Magister stepped in towards him, his face suddenly grim. "You owe me blood, Stygos. That legion is alive when it should be dead and all under its standards now martyrs and heroes. Instead, you have given me back a broken legion of cowards and deserters. You should be dead and your bones rotting in the Hekatontarch's Mark. That was the price for usurping a command that was not yours to take."

Stygos laughed suddenly at that. "You are a harsh man, Lupicinus! A harsh man - I remember when you persecuted the Euphemite heretics some years ago at Edessa and how you ordered me to root them all out and burn the lot of them."

"You were the rod I needed, Stygos. Nothing more. You always have been."

He nodded at that. "Perhaps. But I left the Eagles to claim something of a life. Perhaps that changed me."

"No. Men like you always come back. It is your curse. You left for a little peace but we both know it would never have claimed you. You would have drifted back in the end, that gladius in hand, whether your wife and sons died or not. In a way, their passing into God's hands was a blessing, Stygos. It saved them the shame of your betrayal -"

In a heartbeat, this scarred Roman was up against Lupicinus and I saw his hand curl around the hilt of that ancient gladius of his. Death appeared in his face and it was a pitiless mask, cold and remote. I knew then in a flash why there was no scabbard to sheath that dark blade and why it rested about his chest on a lanyard. It was a blade that needed no unsheathing and could be used to slash or stab in a moment. Stygos had slung a sword about him that was always already poised to strike. Now I saw his gnarled hand tighten about that hilt even as he moved up against the Magister and as I saw that movement I felt a sudden wash of fear envelop me.

It was a fear which did not seem to touch the Magister however. I saw him lean in then towards Stygos and slowly - so slowly as almost to a be a tender thing - he reached out and touched the scars on his ancient face. "Do you know what those heretics called you as they languished in the prisons and cells of Edessa? What tag they pinned to you with a black humour only those at the gates of death can know?" He turned suddenly to look at us all, his hand still on that scarred face more a mask than a living thing. And his words were soft and almost regretful. "They called him *manu ad ferrum* - 'sword in hand'. For the propensity with which he drew that old weapon. Some laughed when they called him that. Most wept. Stygos Sword-in-Hand - and I knew then that here was a man whose only object in life was to draw blood or die in the attempt." He stepped back and allowed his hand to fall away. "Draw that weapon now, Stygos, but not for yourself - draw it for me and for the Augustus and for Rome. It was what you were born to do. Command a legion for the final time and bring peace at the last to both you and the *milites* of the Twelfth. It was what tempted you to pick up that feeble offer from Strabonius in the first place, was it not?"

"To end all their shame?" The latter asked slowly and then nodded. "Yes."

"To bring them to death all on the fringe of your endless black cloak, yes."

I saw Stygos breathe in suddenly then and smile, tilting his head to one side. "How is it that I feel that in knowing me, you are also condemning me, Magister? Why is that?"

Lupicinus laughed quietly. "Condemn? Not at all! One does not judge or acquit a tool, Stygos. That is the thing about the man with the sword in his hand - it cuts or the edge dulls. That is all. The Euphemites were not wrong in their label of you -" And suddenly the Magister turned to Flavius Anicius, his voice hardening in the darkness. "And as for *you* - a Roman Tribune who marches into battle with no mandate - who throws his men onto the spears and swords of an enemy merely to save this blade, this old gladius of a Roman - be thankful that you have retained your command and I have not stripped you of your rank and title. Wonder that you remain under the standards. Think on that, Flavius Anicius, as you stand now before a Consul of Rome."

"Stygos was - is -"

"I know what Stygos is to you - what you are to each other. It was partly out of respect for Stygos that I hauled you out of that mess you created in the Twelfth! That and the fact that I respected your father - a past Consul of Rome. Do you think that I could allow an Anicii to wallow in such shame among such debauched legionaries? You made me salvage you from that and in order to quell the dissenters - and, yes, Flavius, there were many - I gave you command of a palatini legion instead. You shamed the blood of Rome by your folly - by your arrogance and stupidity. To think that you requested that posting to the Twelfth! And now, you little fool, you have blundered back into that cesspit of shame and ridicule. So be it. In throwing away the Sol Legion to save Stygos, you have fallen once again into the Fulminata. It is the Will of God and I shall not contest it." He paused then and smiled slowly. "And that is what I have now here in Amida - a pair of Janus fools in command of two disparate legions. And *that* gives me an opportunity. I cannot order an *excursus* into Armenia as Artashemeh wishes. Candidus here is correct. By the time Valens orders such a thing - if he does - the Queen will have fallen and the remaining Armenian nobles will be dead or have surrendered to Shapur. But I can do one thing that will neither break the treaty nor usurp Valen's authority here in the Oriens."

And it was Obedianus who spoke up then - this *Saraceni* who had remained silent so far on that little balcony overlooking Amida. He stepped forward inclining his head towards the office and dignity of the Magister, adjusting his white cloak as he did so. And I saw that his swarthy face was fierce now - almost eager - and that there was a barbaric cast to it that made me realise that here in the drifting borders of Rome and Persia and Armenia there lay ancient enmities and feuds few of us really understood.

Obedianus stepped forward and his voice was low and urgent and his eyes glittered in the darkness on that balcony. "You will order us into Armenia and disavow us at the same time. We will be a weapon thrown away and you will point to this battle here as proof that we were arrogant and uncontrollable. And we will fall deep in that ancient land at the last under Persian arrows fighting to relieve a Queen we neither know nor care for. And our sacrifice will unite the Armenian nobles and inspire their loyalty back to Rome. Our deaths will buy time until Valens holds up the standard to war against Persia. Isn't that so, Magister of Rome and Wolf of the Emperor?"

"As I said, the bonds are loosened but not broken . . ."

And I knew that this *Saraceni* had hit the mark. What use were we in this mangled legion of forgotten men save as a sacrifice? A lure and an offering deep in the wild snow-capped mountains of Armenia? He would throw us all into the serpent's lair and then wash his hands of us - calling us deserters and brigands and *latrunculi*. We would become a forlorn legion and our blood would be nothing but the knitting of waverers and the desperate inside that war-torn land. Our Eagles would fall into blood and chaos and no Rome would stand at our back. No legion or auxilia would come to our aid.

Lupicinus nodded towards me then and I knew he divined my thoughts. I remembered why he was known as the 'Wolf' and why Valens entrusted the Oriens to him while he warred and won glory far in the west over the Danube and deep among the forts and *vici* of the Goths. He nodded and the smile he gave me was both complicit and damning.

"Ardawan failed in his attempt on Amida and so Shapur will disavow him as a rebel or an opportunistic fool. I suspect we will even receive his head as a placating gesture. Shapur will use that disavowal to forestall a response from Valens while he consolidates his hold in Armenia. Well, *amici*, that is game for two players as well as one. March back to Melitene and recover what losses and equipment you can. Your wounded I will keep here and redistribute among my legions. They will be the favoured ones, I suspect. Gather as much supplies and *annonae* as the town can surrender. In a few days, I will send Artashemeh up to you with the last of her Armenian princes who are even now dribbling over the mountains here in her wake. Once she arrives, strike out east into Armenia to relieve their Queen, Pharanjem, at this Artageressa. You will stage this, Flavius Anicius, as an act of temper and rebellion, you understand? Your young head has been swayed by her beauty and nobility. Rouse those centurions under you with tales of her cause and the cruelty of Rome in abandoning her. Something of that ilk. Whip up the men to abandon the legion castra at Melitene and march with her east into the mountains and that great fortress -"

"Where will all die a forgotten death," broke in Stygos grimly.

"Forgotten? No. Quite the opposite. Your death will sway the remaining Armenian Houses back into the fold of Rome and buy us all time until Valens can order a full *excursus*. This is not a gesture, Stygos, it is a sacrifice. Remember that. And it is one you owe me."

"And Flavius Anicius and the legionaries of the Sol Legion? Do they owe you that?"

Lupicinus shrugged at that. "That legion is beyond its time. It should never have survived the Sacred Julian's death. It is filled with western Romans, pagan Romans, all honouring the memory of a man who fell too soon. They have been marching now under a darker shadow and it is only getting deeper and deeper. Perhaps the Sun will banish finally the Thunder and shame of the Twelfth or perhaps the Thunder of Christ and God will blot out at last that pagan Sun. Who knows? But remember this - all of you - those legions stood together today in blood and battle and what fate has brought together, *I will not tear asunder.* Your Eagles are bound now like mirrored totems and while I may order one fate to save Armenia or at least gain time - you yourselves have forged another fate quite apart from my own. *That* I have no command over."

The silence which followed his words was one I will never forget. In it lay a moment in which all those about me registered his decision and wherein each man both looked to the future while also laying aside whatever past claimed him. This Magister was asking us all to break our bonds with Rome, with our oath to the Emperor. It was a *sacrementum* dear to us all with the possible exception of the *Saraceni* but even he, I sensed, had already thrown in his lot with us. With him, I suspected it was the hot and impetuous words of Artashemeh which had swayed him - and I knew also that Stygos stood already condemned and owing a death. So it was to Flavius Anicius that I looked most in that long silence as we stood there upon that small balcony overlooking an uncaring Amida. He remained in silence and I saw that his dark olive-coloured face was still except for a small muscle which twitched at his jaw. Here was a Roman of ancient blood - one of the old *gens* of the Eternal City itself and whose bloodline I suspected was destined to outlive history itself - a man born of a

Consul of Rome and yet who had in some manner disgraced himself and allowed those under him to humiliate his name. Flavius Anicius stood alone now almost like a statue save for that muscle in his jaw and I wondered what it was that moved deep in his soul - Stygos ached to pass on into the shade of the underworld on a tide of blood to assuage his own remorseless life, that I sensed, and Obedianus rode the high steed of passion and poetry and sought fame or immortality in song - but this Italian shrouded in something dark which I could not fathom eluded me then. So I watched him silently while all about me the others absorbed their fate. I saw no emotion war in his face. No glitter in his eyes. No passion in the clench or unclench of fist. Only that tick within the speckled beard. So when he spoke, alone of us all, I must have looked as surprised as Lupicinus did . . .

"So it is *axios* at the last. When do we march from Amida, Magister?"

The latter nodded once, accepting his decision. "Why now, Tribune. The legions must march now. As darkness must cover your future actions so it should be fitting that you embrace it at the first. Be gone by dawn from Amida and use what little time I can give you at Melitene."

. . . I think back now upon that moment and know all those men as well as one can know any man, brother or soldier or friend, and see in that moment the seeds that later sprouted and doomed us all and only now - in the writing of this - do I fully understand finally what I wondered on at the time - why I never raised my voice against Lupicinus and his insane order to sacrifice two legions of Rome. I think I looked too long into those about me and failed to see into my own heart. Had I done so, perhaps I would have known that like Obedianus and his *Saraceni* blood or Stygos and his sacrificial temper or even indeed Flavius Anicius and his need to abolish a shame, that I too felt a lure; that perhaps in my own blood moved a destiny not unlike all their own. For what was I if nothing but the sum and memory of too many histories and annals and legends read or listened to under the porticos and atriums of Alexandria - that city founded by the greatest Greek of them all? I am Candidus and my eyes have seen marvels in scrolls as cracked as the face of Stygos, as stained with wine as the passion of Obedianus, and as brittle as the honour of Flavius Anicius. I was a man too lived in the past of words.

How could I not cling to the demand for sacrifice in the footsteps of these damned men? How could I not yearn to break free from those scrolls and begin my *own* story? . . .'

It is a poor monk hurrying towards Amida through the last of the night, eager to partake of the martyrdom of that city and who had not yet learnt of its deliverance, who alone stumbles into the long exhausted train of the two legions as they leave that city full of revelry and excess. Foot-sore and carrying nothing but a staff and a cloak rolled-up over one shoulder, this monk, Rabbula the Younger, pauses as the first wash of dawn lights his eyes while below stretches out the plain around Amida and the dark murky waters of the Tigris wending its way south into Mesopotamia and Assyria. Shadows reach out across that plain like long unravelling cloaks while the bulk of the city rises up cold and hard against that faint wash. It is as his eyes adjust both to the rising light and the emerging scene that a trio of dusty Arab riders appear and encircle him. These sons of the Bani Al-Jawn cast cold desert eyes over him and then urge their light ponies on without a second glance, leaving a trail of dust in their wake. And as that dust settles, more Arabs canter past riding picket before a long tight column of Roman soldiers. Amazed that these men are leaving Amida, this poor monk falls upon his knees in prayer, his hands clasped in the ancient manner, Aramaic words tumbling from him. He remains thus, earnestly beseeching them all to turn back to the doomed city as the long, worn, column passes him by. The description he has left us is a confused patchwork of Biblical quotation and rhetoric but buried within it one can read of a poor illiterate man overawed at the martial bearing passing him while unable to comprehend why these Romans are marching away from his doomed and soon-to-be martyred city.

With the Arabs of Obedianus riding picket ahead and on the flanks of the column, what emerges before the weeping eyes of Rabbula the Younger is the tight ordered maniples of the Senior Sol Legion under Marcellus, Septimio, and Merobaudes. Each of these three maniples is arrayed in a wide open marching column, with the century mules and the carts herded within the centre. To this monk's eyes, these Roman legionaries seem as saints, all armoured in scale cuirasses and iron helms, some crested or plumed and others adorned with gold sheaths or jewels. Their wide oval shields glitter with the emblem of the sun itself as if heralding God's glorious light while above them float the long vexillum standards of the centuries and the snarling *draco* heads of the Maniples themselves. One by one, these men from the West stare down at him as they march past, some smiling mirthlessly, others cracking crude jokes out of earshot of the centenarii and the ducenarii of each maniple. One *miles*, pausing at the last edge of his century, dips his hand into the leather wallet at his belt and then flings a copper coin to him, laughing carelessly as he does so. Others about him scowl at that and warn him that no god should be mocked whether Christian or pagan. Holy men are holy men no matter what spirit moves in them.

It is as the last of these Sol legionaries vanish into the dust of their march, that this Rabbula the Younger sees something almost miraculous. For there, in the wake of these soldiers with their Gallic and Illyrian faces, arrives the battered and wounded legionaries of the Twelfth - and even as a mumbled prayer falls from his cracked lips, his eyes alight for the first time upon that ancient and revered symbol on their shields. This monk, born out of a harsh desert discipline, cast adrift among the cells and caves of Cappadocia, transported now by the ritual of his words, opens his eyes and rather than saints in armour he sees instead the carven thunder of the Fulminata beneath the scowling visage of Jehovah Himself. It is a moment which transports him and allows his clasped hands to open out into the raised palms of supplication for he fears that Amida itself has been condemned like Sodom and Gomorrah and that God has used the rod of the Persian as chastisement upon those wicked and unclean inhabitants below. And to his amazement, as these legionaries of the Twelfth march past, century by century and cohort by cohort, many among them whisper back to him old prayers and praises to God and Christ and the Martyrs of the Twelfth. He notes the wounds and the blood upon them all and the darkness in their eyes - a weary stain which tells him that these men have witnessed shame and dishonour but like Job in the wilderness have burdened it all and are even now persevering in that darkness. And this Rabbula the Younger cries out to these soldiers and martyrs of the Twelfth that "Behold, I am of small account; what shall I answer Thee? I lay my hand upon my mouth," and each legionary as he passes this poor monk raving in the dust of that march answers back "Amen".

The last century of the Twelfth passes him by and in the gap which follows he sees yet more Romans emerging - and there appear before him the remaining maniples of the Sol Legion and again curious and dismissive glances are thrown down upon him. The sun is higher now and gilding the standards and dragons of these columns as they pass him and so Rabbula the Younger rises up into that light beseeching them all to honour God and His awful majesty no matter where his Will takes them. And the soldiers and file-leaders of the Sol Legion ignore his vagrant words, moving forwards under the stern gazes of the ducenarii of the maniples, dust and the squealing of the mules framing them all. Until, finally that is, this Rabbula the Younger, his voice shrill now, finds himself suddenly under the shadow of a large coarse man, his face ruddy and rough, who stares down at him with little humour in his face. Asellus, his gaze fierce and hot, listens as though to a child as Rabbula calls out for the Lord's mercy to cover them all like a shawl and then this bristling Gaul whispers down to him in a cold and angry voice: "They only knew how to pray!"

It is a rebuke which strikes this monk to the core and leaves him alone and shaken as the last of the two legions march away from Amida. Around him, a few remaining Arab riders drift, turning occasionally back over their horned saddles to scan the rear of that march. In his poor world, this monk is left uncertain of what has passed over him for within that long column marched men who beheld God with an open heart and men who mocked and scorned His majesty. And Rabbula the Younger looks back at the last into all their fading dust as the sun rises high behind him and knows not whether the Lord had cast out the unworthy from a reborn Amida or instead saved the righteous from a doomed city . . .

The papyrus which preserves this only writing of the monk is contained in a long collection of minor works by Gregory the Great. It sits more as an oddity than anything else but remains useful on two counts - it shows something of the confusions and passions of the times and how these emotions often sat side by side, and it also allows us a small glimpse into the mind of Flavius Anicius. For within these primitive and superstitious words lies the curious detail that the march out from Amida in the dead of night does not proceed with one legion leading another. Instead, the first three maniples under Marcellus, Septimio, and Merobaudes are tasked with in a sense *escorting* the Twelfth while the remaining three maniples under Decentius, Scorpianus and Bellovaedius bring up the rear of the Twelfth. Flavius Anicius is carefully guarding the Twelfth with his elite legion almost as if not trusting it to march where he wills it . . .

Obedianus, riding vedette with a small guard of companions, is the first to evacuate the *territorium* of Amida ahead of the main column and is in all probability one of the three Arab riders to surround and then abandon this poor monk. All about him, flung out on wide patrols, canter the remaining sons and brothers of his tribe. Of the original hundred or so, only some sixty now remain and of these not one does not bear some wound from a Persian contus or mace or *mashrafi* blade. Here and there, an Arab jogs alongside on foot, his hand on the rear horn of a saddle now that his mount lies dead on the field of battle. These dogged runners are unconcerned, though. New horses will be found at Melitene and soon they will all be mounted again.

The Bani Al-Jawn is less a tribe now than it is a memory in those riders about Obedianus. With scarcely sixty men, some past their prime, and the infirm and the women far to the south in distant deserts, this tribe is fading from the memory of other stronger tribes and with that fading will disappear all their past exploits and songs. It might be asked why Obedianus allows his brothers to ride under the standard of Rome so far from their ancestral home in the oases south of Palmyra and if such a question were to be posed to this Arab warrior then he would simply shrug at you and throw a handful of sand across his path - sooner know the will of the desert than fathom fate, he would seem to say with that gesture. However, behind that vague shrug would lie a deeper melancholy in Obedianus for in his heart lies the awful truth that what is left of his tribe is surrounded by stronger tribes all now fixing their eyes and hearts upon the icons of Christ. And the irony will overwhelm him that those icons of Christ are now at odds to the Emperor of Rome so that one by one those tribes are rising in rebellion against the lawful Roman authorities. War is brewing and Obedianus knows that soon Orthodox Arab will ride against an Heretical Rome. Within such a madness, he senses that the sons of the Bani Al-Jawn will fall unlooked for and unremembered. Hence their lonely ride north under the mantle of Roman protection far from those brewing deserts of discord.

It is why Obedianus, though he himself may not know it, writes so incessantly to his aging father who sits almost alone among mournful women in an open tent. These epistles, written in clumsy Greek, sprinkled with the after-print of a pagan Arab sensibility, while recording the past of his own exploits are also in some poor way an attempt to wrest a future from an obscurity Obedianus knows he can only ever defer never banish. And while these epistles are deeply personal and in many ways selfish, they are also perhaps the only legacy a dying tribe can leave now that all its poets and singers have faded away or fallen in battle.

It is why also that night, as the legionaries of the Twelfth and the Sol bed down in the ruins of an ancient hunting run, the stone walls nothing now but dribbles and cascades of ill-defined boundaries, that Obedianus pens yet another letter to his father and in it lies the first of what will be perhaps too many *ayyams*, or 'battle-days' - that peculiar Arabic poem which celebrates feats of arms and action. It is of course a celebration of the *ayyam* of the Hekatontarch's Mark and in its short and elliptical words, Obedianus alludes to past feuds and victories which will remain forever lost to us. And as with all epistles, no matter to whom, there is also a real sense that Obedianus writes not so much to a figure old and perhaps dying but instead as much to himself in the hope that one day he too will be old and fading away and re-reading these glorious exploits . . .

" . . . And I will tell you of a woman unlike any I have met and you will twitch that mouth of yours as if scolding me for you will not read these words for their truth but for my boasting. You would be wrong to scold me, father, for she is a woman yes but also a warrior and she has ridden past us all in the dust and heat of battle and, father, about her rode a guard and escort as brave as any I have seen about these Roman officers and *phylarchs*. And is not that a testament greater than any? That warriors ride willingly at her side? You will tell me that I am young and hot-headed like the lion-cub fresh from its mother's side but you will be wrong. We have fought a great battle and in that battle we have lost many sons of the Bani Al-Jawn and their blood alone tells me that I am not hot-headed. We won, father, in the heat and chaos of battle, in the wash of blood and the crying of horse, we won. And in that winning, the Persian serpent has been cut into many pieces so that it thrashes now from us, whipped and beaten. And this battle was a battle where we rode not alone as we have done so many times in the past but alongside others in joy and pain and exhaustion - we rode amid the standards of Romans and Armenians, alongside soldiers of the legion of the Sun and soldiers of the legion of the Thunder, together with those heavy cavalry of the Armenian nobles and lords, all armoured in iron and mail, like their Persian cousins, but who rode under Christian banners to the command of a woman who, father, swept her gaze about us all like a kestrel high upon its wing.

It was a battle-day the like of which the Bani Al-Jawn has rarely seen. Where in the past of memory and song have we fought blind and isolated? Where in the past have we struggled into a fierce storm as much our enemy as the Persians were? Where in the past have we splintered our lances among our foe only for that storm to cease and we all pause at the astonishment of that moment? And in that pause, as Persian lifted up his face-plate and Arab stayed his hand and Roman lowered his shield, did not the ground tremble at the arrival of these Armenians as they swept along the bridge over the Tigris itself? Take this *ayyam*, then, and know that through the charge of a woman upon whose shoulders Ailat Herself now rests we, the Bani Al-Jawn, rode victorious over the broken weapons and shields of our enemy . . .

> *When I saw the hard earth hollowed*
> *By this woman's flying steeds,*
> *And Ailat her face revealed -*
> *The full moon of the desert night -*
> *Then the matter was grim, dark -*
> *A tribe that has no song must soon decay,*
> *And chiefs fall away,*
> *No tent without poles stands long,*
> *And what pole can rise that is not*
> *Planted in the dust of battle?*
> *Rejoice! Cry out!*
> *The hollowed earth is planted again,*
> *The tent cracks and whips in the storm unbowed!*
> *She of the Night, of the Moon, of the Stars, shouts*
> *To horse! To horse! The deserts sigh and the deserts cry!*
> *And She I will follow though all will die!*

. . . Weep not, father. I know now what Rome holds forth. I know what tug lies in the blood under their Eagles and Dragons. I know what potency lies in their words and honour. I know now why you sent me with my brothers west and north. Rome is doom and glory and vanity. Rome is politics and expediency. Rome is the dust of too long a time but yet unwearied from the fight - and now, father, Rome is also one last gamble across a boundary over which no sanction has been given. Was it like this under Constantine against the Persians? I do not care, father. I have found Rome and it is the lonely gesture to follow a hidden goddess east into that land of snow and mountains and dark lakes . . .

For what are we, the Bani Al-Jawn, if not pledged to serve Her?"

In the rubble of an ancient hunting run, long-since disused and abandoned, as the evening fades into an inky wash, Obedianus puts stylus to parchment and both composes his first battle-day poem, his *ayyam*, and also seeks to justify a decision to throw in his lot with Flavius Anicius and to surrender to the mad whim of a 'Wolf' of Rome, all the while carving deep in his heart another reason. A reason whose countenance is nothing more than that of a woman's as she rides past and sees him and gives him the least smile.

Perhaps many moons later, under the cold silent night of a Palmyrean desert, his father, now blind and ailing, gives that parchment to his wife and as she reads it out to him, a dark breeze emerges from over an unseen horizon and this old man, the last true *phylarch* of the tribe, finds himself weeping, knowing that he has lost his son. He weeps and shivers at the edge of his camel-hair tent, soft words falling about him, and hears not the battle, the hooves, the cries, but instead the sound of his son drifting away, so far away, that he knows he will never see him again . . .

CHAPTER FOURTEEN

' . . . Work began on the Donellian Aqueduct ten miles from Melitene, on the Augustal Estates. Pamphilius, having refused the detail in his usual surly manner, remained in command of the castra while I took a body of four *conturburnia* from the century under Eligius. The aqueduct had cracked near the ravine which ran out of the Analaean Hills. The report from the Imperial notary of the Augustal Estates was correct in that the damage was natural and not the result of brigandage in the area. I ordered half the *milites* with Eligius to begin work on the repairs using local stone while the remainder under my own command provided a watch nearby. By midday, Eligius reported that the pipe nozzles had cracked and that new ones would be needed. I queried this and was informed that the lead nozzles needed to be of a certain volume - the ones we had brought up from the castra at Melitene were of the *quinaria* size whereas those needed here at the hills were of the *centenaria* type. These ones would have to be shaped personally as the flow from the hills here was severe.

It was too late to begin the march back to the castra so I detailed the men under Eligius to relax while those under my command were ordered to prepare a camp for the night. The afternoon was hot and dusty but water was plentiful from the springs nearby. Eligius sketched in the sand some more details about the aqueduct and advised me that once the new lead nozzles were shaped, it would be a simple matter to fit them now that the stone-work was repaired. He estimated that the Donellian Aqueduct would be flowing again within four days at most.

That evening we ate our rations about the fire and drank the remainder of the wine. It was a quiet time as the sun fell into a long low wash of purple and the cold settled about us so that we shrank into our sagum cloaks. The fire roared and spluttered while those *milites* not on watch or tending to the camp sang the old songs or the newer hymns to Christ and the Martyrs. I had put off writing up the daily report and had fallen back to enjoy the peace. It was as though we were all in a place cut-off from the cares of the wider world. Around us was nothing but deep shadows and the occasional distant cough of a mountain lion. We were alone under the stars and our fire was for us all the warmth and hospitality in the world. Lightly at first the little songs spread out around us, each one joining in, as we celebrated both the distant heroes of the legion, now so old that they were almost as mythic as Achilles or Aeneas, and then presently we drifted into the more recent hymns of those of us who had fallen under the great persecutions rather than surrender up their Christian faith. Around that crackling fire, moved and resonated those old names and then newer names and the only thing linking them together was their one origin - the Twelfth, the Fulminata, that legion we all called home, though it stood all shrivelled and twisted now with bitter roots and dry, cracked, branches . . .

> For we is Mules, we is Mules, and we bray the day away!
> We is Mules, we is Mules, and they feed us naught but hay!

. . . There, in the deepening dusk, with the shadows falling over us all, I looked up from those quiet voices and the sadness and defiance in them, and gazed on that high dark arch of the aqueduct which rose above us, seeming to frame us in the coming night, and wondered on how eternal was that scene I now gazed upon. The soldiers of Rome around me sat in a little pool of light beneath that mark of empire and civilisation working endlessly to restore and maintain it - and I think I smiled a bitter smile at that - at how pathetic it would have seemed to a traveller who might have stumbled over us in that night; the flames carving out a little edge of one arch about us while it would have seemed as if we squatted like beggars under the ruin of a once mighty empire, all the while we sang songs of past glories and forgotten feats.

So it was with surprise that even as I thought on that vagrant traveller, a sudden shout of alarm rang out deep in the darkness only to be answered with the retort of a Latin command and even as I rose I knew that the thing I had been dreading had finally arrived. We were five days away from the departure of the Twelfth for Amida and with no word of what had happened.

Until now, I suspected.

The rider was covered in dust and his mount - a hardy Cappadocian mare - was lathered with sweat but even as he was led in to the light of the fire with the legionaries about me rising up in expectation, I saw that he was not one of us. For a moment, this rider leaned forwards about his saddle horns and nodded then to us all before sliding down from his mount even as a *miles* reached up to grasp the bridle. I knew his type in a heartbeat. I had seen it many times before - those hardy Illyrian or Pannonian men who moved now within the higher circles of the Roman *exercitus*. Men bred deep in the mountains and valleys of those lands south of the Danube and who fought under emperors all equally bred from that land - Diocletian, Constantine, and now Valens and his brother Valentinian. Rough, brutal, men, uncultured and unlettered, but who formed a tough officer brothership within the army. Dust covered his mail shirt while the oval shield slung now over his back was battered and still bore marks of battle. I saw blazoned upon it the ancient symbol for Helios and found myself frowning, wondering on what legion this soldier had come from. A gilded helmet lay slung over one of the rear horns while a battered Pannonian cap rested upon his head at a slouched angle. He was exhausted and even as he dismounted he unwound the *forcale* scarf at his throat and wiped it across his brow, pushing that cap even further back on his head.

This legionary, this Illyrian or Pannonian, understood within a heartbeat that I was in command and advanced up to me without courtesy or ceremonial - and something in his gaze told me that his news was not to be welcomed.

"I have new orders for the legion from the Magister at Amida," he said, not waiting for my welcome. "Your centurion at the castra advised me to find you here and I have ridden without let to deliver the *mandata* of Lupicinus." He paused then and eyed the expectant legionaries about him. The smile he gave them as he re-knotted the *forcale* about his neck was a cold one. "Rejoice. The Twelfth has won a great victory on the plains south of Amida. The Persians have ran back towards their desert lands like camels in a stampede. The fame of your legion only grows, *amici*." And he spat then into the dust about his feet all the while still smiling.

I felt the shock in the men around me and saw how they tightened up about him, some wondering and others frowning at the obvious contempt in his voice. There is a saying about the soldiers of Illyria - in offering you a coin, they will take the rings from your fingers, and I knew that his words held another truth.

I gestured to the fire nearby. "You must be tired, *amicus*, come, sit. Drink what little wine we have left."

"It would be an honour to drink with the immortal heroes of the Twelfth," he nodded back, moving in to join us. Someone passed him a wineskin and he drank from it with all the gusto of a barbarian as he sat down, smacking his lips in the process. The fire carved out a bronzen mask from his face while behind him arose a wall of shades, all leaning in. I tore off a hunk of cheese and passed it to him.

"The Persians are broken, you say?"

He smiled back at me through a mouthful of that cheese. "Did I not say rejoice? Is not the Twelfth marked now by new honours and laurels at Amida?" He looked around him again into the faces arrayed about the fire and laughed in a way which made me tense suddenly inside. "Fear not, *amici* and *commilitones*, your comrades have been victorious! The standards of the Twelfth faced off the Persian serpent and saved Amida from rape and pillage! You are all honoured now with a new commander - and is this not what you have been yearning for all these months? Rejoice, your empty days are over!"

And this Illyrian soldier, his cap pushed back, the sweat and grime leaving long streaks across his bronzen face, sobered up then and all his humour and mockery vanished. He put aside the wineskin and leaned in towards me so that the flames hid no part of him.

"Your dishonour has been wiped away. You have a commander again. In fact, it would be true to say that *your* commander is in command again . . ."

His silence then as he remained staring deep into my astonished face was more damning than any laughter or humour he might have thrown at me - at us all . . .'

There is little remaining today of the Donellian Aqueduct north and slightly east of Melitene. A few pillars and the crumbled remnants of stone arches lay scattered here and there with most of the stone-work now long since re-used in old church walls or farmhouses nearby. The Analaean Hills rise suddenly as an outlier of the Taurus mountains and are characterised by craggy outcrops and dry scrub-like passes. In winter, always proverbially harsh in Cappadocia, these parts would have been inaccessible and very remote. To the immediate west lies a large expanse of grazing land and from these reports it is obvious that this was formerly one of the vast imperial estates given over to horse-breeding. Some five miles west of the last rump of the Analaean Hills, as they were once known, lie the remains of a vast villa-complex, later walled and turreted, and it has been reasonably concluded that this structure would have been the main administrative centre for the imperial estate or *res privata* here.

As a high massive plateau, Cappadocia in general has always been prone to earthquakes and it comes as no surprise to find a section of those legionaries remaining behind at work on repair - a time-honoured occupation of the soldiers of Rome when not at war for if they were not building ramparts and ditches or the solid buttress towers now characteristic of a Roman castra or a castellum then they would invariably have been involved with the ancient and huge engineering works of the empire: the aqueducts, the harbour moles, the canals, the city walls and provincial roads, for example. Tedium is always a rot to be avoided in any army in any period and Rome was not the first nor the last to exercise her soldiers in such activities to ward off that rot.

Here on this evening however that tedium had arisen not in anger or rebellion but instead in melancholy and whether it is something in all the legionaries under that huge arch or nothing more than a extension of our *Adjutor's* sensibility what is true is that as the darkness fell old songs and names rose among them all: the dry whispered names of legionaries long since fallen in distant wars and battles - under Caesar in Gaul or with Vespasian at Jerusalem - and also the whispered names of men who fell to execution and martyrdom rather than abandon the religion of Christ. And in those songs lay a subtle shift from the legionary hacked down beneath a Gallic axe or sword-edge, his shield-arm failing at the last, to that lonely legionary whose own body and soul has now become a battle-ground. Each name on its own lay wrapped in Roman *virtu* and yet that *virtu* differed through the ages from an outward expression of courage to an inner arena perhaps larger than any battlefield. This is the shift in the songs uttered under that huge arch in the night as the names of a Marcus or a Tullio fade into those of a Cyrius or a Lisimachus wherein Roman *virtu* moves from that last effort of defiance to one where the willing surrender to Christ becomes the highest ideal.

It is a *virtu* Optatus remains apart from and his pen records and notates but barely touches these emotions and desires. He remains alone on the fringes of a legion left apart and abandoned and remembers that he himself bears responsibility for a share of that. So that now, in this cold evening, that solitary fire illuminating not just the legionaries under his command but one giant curve of the aqueduct also, he hears and receives this news and something shivers deep inside him.

' . . . I stared hard at this Danubian soldier, seeing the worn edges to his face, the red line under his chin that marked where his helmet strap had lain, the flinty eyes that locked onto mine - and in that hard face I saw behind his mocking smile. I saw the truth he alluded to. And a shiver cut through me like a knife -

"Anicius?"

This soldier smiled like a wolf in the flickering firelight and nodded. "You name him 'Corbulo', also, I hear. And it is an apt name. He is worthy of it. Know that the Magister in his infinite wisdom has raised our Flavius Anicius over you all again as commander and *patricius* not just of your Twelfth but also our own legion, my legion, the legion he led into battle to save all your miserable hides - Mithras praise you all!" He snatched up the wineskin again and drank a toast to us.

"I thought you said the Twelfth saved Amida?" broke in Eligius beside him. A frown creased his brow.

"And they did - but the gods have a rare sense of humour, it seems!" And this soldier laughed again at us and the harshness of it struck us all around that campfire. "Did it never occur to you *why* Lupicinus summoned one lonely legion to Amida? Why the Twelfth was chosen to face an entire Persian army alone before the Black Walls?"

"For the honour -" I began but this soldier spat into the fire before him and something about the way he stared back at me stopped my words in my throat.

He shook his head slowly. "You poor fool, Centurion. There was no honour in that march and battle, only death. Lupicinus was using the legion as a lure and bait. All your deaths were to be nothing but the prologue to a trap." And here I saw him pause a little and something dark clouded his eyes. A canker or a bile which rose up from deep within him. "But as Sol Himself bears me witness, Fortune had a better design for you all. Our legion under Flavius Anicius intervened and so all you poor legionaries were saved despite the plans of the Magister. Ironic, isn't it? That now the man who once commanded you has saved you and stands once more over you all!" Again, his laughter was dark and mocking but something else lay in that laughter, something bitter, and I saw him glance about at the men crowding him like an insubstantial chorus in the shadows of the fire.

And I knew then what he was alluding to. I saw it in that laughter and the bitter glance he threw about him. I knew in a heartbeat.

"Lupicinus is punishing him, isn't he? This is not a promotion, is it?"

The Danubian rose then and hitched his military belt about him. I saw again his compact frame, his hard fighting form clothed in mail armour, so different from the thin men about me, and he looked down at me then and all the mockery and sarcasm drained from him. "Him? Not just him, *Adjutor*. All of us. We were palatini once - the elite of the legions - that was us. The Senior Sol Legion, raised under Julian himself, weren't we? Sol guides us and protects us on our shields and in our hearts as it did Julian, save at the last. We stood among the best of the legions. But not anymore. Thanks to Flavius Anicius and that foolish action before Amida we have been reduced to the grade of the field army. We are comitatenses now, no more. The Magister mocks us all, it seems, little man!"

And with that he grasped the horns on his saddle and swung himself up into it. All the men about him stood back warily. For a moment, he sat there, adjusting his cloak over the haunches of his mare, moving the shield on his back into a more comfortable position, before he looked down at me again.

"The legions will be here by mid-afternoon."

"The legions?"

"Your Twelfth, of course, and the Legion of the Sun, both under Flavius Anicius now. Detail provisions for another thousand men. Billeting will be arranged once the Tribune arrives but expect the townsfolk of Melitene to be rudely shocked!" He yanked the horse about with a harsh pull on the reins.

"Wait! What about the Twelfth?" I shouted out after him. "What are we now under Anicius?"

And he laughed as he rode off into the night under that high broken arch - he laughed and shouted back: "Rejoice, as I say! You are all comitatenses now! The Twelfth is a legion of Rome again!"

The darkness swallowed this Danubian rider up and I stood there by that small fire as the faces of the men under my command all turned to me in shock and surprise. A twig in the fire cracked suddenly and shelved in sending up a shower of sparks which vanished in an instant. In that halo of light, I saw worn faces, tired faces, the faces of men who had spent too long under a faded command. And I knew that this honour would be a cruel thing indeed . . .'

This is the first report from Optatus since the departure of the Twelfth under Stygos which delves into more than the long litany of duty rosters and punishment details. For five days, the papyri have remained dry and methodical but also somehow empty. Now, on that evening wherein this Danubian legionary from the Senior Sol Legion arrives with mixed news, the *Adjutor* finally allows his own reservations and thoughts to emerge once more. There, under that huge arch, illuminated by the fitful light of the campfire below, he looks about him and sees faces which are bewildered and uncertain. Faces which look to him as the acting-commander or senior officer and in whom they find perhaps an unease to equal their own . . .

Later, the next afternoon, under a leaden sky, the legionaries of the Twelfth and Sol Legions arrive back at the castra at Melitene. Optatus has ordered the remaining guard centuries to turn out in full armour and weapons while the slaves and servants have cleared away the detritus and rubbish which has accumulated about the place. Crowds of women and children are forced back into the barracks and the alleyways between them under orders to remain quiet. With a small core of notaries and centurions about him, Optatus waits nervously on a raised dais at the edge of the *praesidium* facing across the main open ground of the castra. All gaze out through the wide portals of the South Gate through which can be dimly seen the advancing dust and vague standards of the Roman column. Pamphilius at his side looks about and scowls as if bored by it all but it is noticed that his hand curls and uncurls tightly about the hilt of his spatha. The sky above is dark and a cold wind causes all the legionaries on the ramparts and bastion towers to huddle defensively into their sagum cloaks. There is the smell of rain upon the wind. The advancing lines and columns draw closer and the *Adjutor* sends a courier back into Melitene confirming the arrival of the legions and advising the town *curiales* that no doubt the new commander, Flavius Anicius, will once again want to greet them and that they should be prepared for his summons at a moment's notice.

It is the soldiers of the First, Second and Third Maniples of the Sun who enter first, slowly emerging from under the open portal of the gateway, marching in a practised rhythmic step, the long *hastae* slopped back over their shoulders, the wide oval shields swinging loosely at their sides. Yellow crested or plumed segmented helmets adorn them all and each legionary wears heavy mail hauberks or scale corselets, all covered in dust now. Held within the gap between the three maniples move the supply carts and mules with their attendant slaves. With the ease of a well-practised drill these men under their ducenarii and centenarii break right across the open ground and form up in ranks eight men deep under their dragon heads and century flags, with the baggage to their rear. Dust swirls and drifts across their ranks and files.

It is then that the first columns of the Twelfth drift like refugees out of the dust of that gateway and the sight which greets Optatus' eyes is a shocking one.

' . . . For a moment as the dust drifted apart a little I thought I saw nothing but the listless tramp of shades from the Underworld emerging from beneath that portal. Grey men and grey beasts of burden limped towards that gap formed by the first columns of this Legion of the Sun as it swivelled to the right. I saw the cohortal and century standards rising up out of that mass of refugees but somehow in my mind I did not register them as the marks of the Twelfth. Beside me, I heard Pamphilius snort like the bull he is likened to and heard him mutter that these were not legionaries but beaten men and I could not disagree with him. I saw in that drab crowd the indeterminate figure of Strabonius and noticed that in his face lay more than his usual wavering and evasion. He looked beaten; broken somehow. His gaze drifted about and one hand gripped the edge of a torn cloak and the knuckles were white like bone. Around him, marched the legionaries of the First Cohort and not a single one was not bloodied or wounded or bound now in linen bandages. I saw the oval shields and the dark thunderbolts on them, crowned always with the stern visage of God, all muted now and stained with crimson and dust and dirt. Not a few were splintered and several legionaries marched with no scutums at all.

The First Cohort under Strabonius followed in the wake of the Sol legionaries and formed up alongside them in a line eight men deep but before I could assess the state of the First Cohort, Pamphilius swore suddenly, uneasily, at my side. I am used to this centurion being angry and bullish. It is his mark, the dye-stamp of his coin as it were, but to hear him voice unease - that was something new to me.

"Christ and all the Martyrs," he breathed, his voice low, "what is Elias doing commanding the Second?"

That Anatolian, thin and hard like a worn practice post, was marching at the head of what was left of the Second Cohort. Behind him, marched scarcely two hundred legionaries under the six centurial flags. Less than half of the Second Cohort was marching into the castra - all six centuries under Elias I noticed were desperately short on men and those that met my eye were beaten men. The exception alone being the Fifth all of whom seemed to be standing apart in some way from their comrades. With a sharp command, Elias ordered the column to wheel right and form up on the centuries of the First Cohort and as he did so I saw his glance sweep past me and Pamphilius and the few other centurions about me and what I saw in that glance of his brought a cold knot into my stomach like a ball of ice.

"Optatus?"

"Mascenius is dead," I said slowly.

Pamphilius looked at me with a frown. "What in Hades are you talking about?"

I nodded to the Anatolian. "Elias is the new commanding centurion. Mascenius has fallen at Amida along with most of the Second. Look at how thin their ranks are."

I heard him swear under his breath again and knew that his unease had deepened.

There was something vaguely comforting in seeing Cyrion emerge next with the lads of the Third Cohort. Most were wounded or exhausted and bore marks of battle but nothing like the gutting of the Second Cohort. As with the First, this cohort had looked as if it had borne the brunt of bitter fighting but had not suffered in the way the legionaries under Mascenius must have. Again, with a sharp command ringing out, the Third now wheeled left and formed up as the final lines of the Twelfth Legion. As the last of the legionaries fell slowly into place, my mind raced like a chariot around an ever revolving track. In an instant I saw the losses the legion had borne - a third of the men were missing from the ranks: centurions, optios, file-closers, the devastation was encompassing. I swept my gaze about them all and saw in their eyes a tired and beaten thing; a spirit which had been broken though their standards remained upright in the detritus of battle. Even Cyrion refused to look me in the eye, all his usual boasting and thin bravado gone. Men I had known and fought with now seemed as strangers to me and I remembered the harsh tone of that Danubian legionary the evening before - of how he told us to rejoice all the while a black humour seemed to mock us. In the distance, I heard a thin wail rise up and knew that word was spreading through the women and their children that many of their men were missing.

It was then as the dust of the Twelfth finally began to settle that I saw something appear above their heads. It rose above and behind them, faint and indeterminate in that cold air, its light muted and a certain unevenness in its form confusing my eye. I frowned uneasily and I remember thinking that perhaps the dust was playing with me. It was an Eagle of Rome riding high above the ranks of the Twelfth, moving towards me in their rear, but it seemed as if in a moment of spite that it both bore down upon me and also fell back - that it seemed somehow to *tease* me with its presence.

"Pamphilius, do you see . . ." I began, raising up a hand to shade my brow - but before I could finish that sentence a loud command rang out and I saw the front ranks of what was left of the Second Cohort double up on themselves and in the gap thus created there strode forward not only that wavering Eagle but a tight knot of officers and adjutants. In their wake came the remaining men of this Sol legion in their ranks and files who peeled off to the left to complete the long line of the two legions.

And I saw him advance under the shadow of that wavering Eagle, cloistered tightly amongst his officers and *principales*, guarded almost by a phalanx it seemed, and I recognised him in a heartbeat. It felt as if all the years without him, in which we languished in shame and ignominy, fell away like an insubstantial mist. I looked upon Flavius Anicius, Tribune, once *Praefectus* of the Twelfth, a man who had bought his way into that commission, and who had brought with him something much more - and my heart contracted suddenly within me. He advanced now through the opening ranks of the Second Cohort straight towards us upon the dais all clad in full scale armour, leather pteruges flaring out from his shoulders and hips, a wide cloak trailing him like a shadow, while the men about him gazed at the castra about us all with practised eyes - taking in the bastion towers, the mural artillery, the state of the gateways, the repair or lack of the interior buildings - and I saw that among those men strode Stygos, that dark scarred face of his closed up, and that *Saraceni* Obedianus also. The latter seemed worn and unusually reserved.

Behind them all loomed that Eagle and it seemed to follow them as if emerging from a dream or a portent. The dust of all their march shrouded it but I could make out its shape and even as I did so it blurred again and the little grey light from above seemed to make it shiver uneasily as if it were vaporous somehow. Then I saw the gleam of silver around it. I frowned and looked harder and saw then what my mind could not comprehend. This was a *bound* Eagle. Silver chains lay wrapped all about it. And even as I saw that, the Aquilifer twisted the high ash pole of the standard and to my horror I saw *another* Eagle turnabout, its wings outspread, the talons grasping victory laurels, the stare imperious. I found myself stepping back on that dais in shock even as Pamphilius and a dozen other men about me gazed up at it, unbelieving. The Eagle of the Twelfth lay bound in chains to another - and I found myself staring back to Flavius Anicius at this sacrilege.

I had always remembered him as being pampered, spoilt even, a youth who had climbed too high too quickly on the backs of others - his father, the rich uncles of the Anicii, the favours owed and paid eagerly to all of his *gens*. He had been a young man who chose to stand among men he did not intuit and whose contempt he quickly earned. Of course, he had looked different. His smooth Italian cast broke him apart from us all here in the ancient lands of Cappadocia. Where we were twisted and worn by the harsh Winters - inured to toil and suffering - he was covered in the grace of oils and baths and bore a lithe frame that had spent too long in the gymnasiums and not enough under the sun or the rains. That alone would have been enough for us to despise him when he had first arrived - let alone that fatal mission which had brought him to us in the first place and had been the reason he had called in all the favours owed to him. Now, however, there was something different in him. All that softness and arrogance seemed to have been both beaten out of him and in the process to have hardened him up. This was Flavius Anicius but where once there had been a youth full of arrogance and ideals now there was a man who had seen those ideals broken and in that breaking had closed up on himself.

He mounted the dais without a glance to the other centurions and notaries about me and halted. For a moment, his eyes rested almost casually on me and I had the absurd notion he would actually embrace me. The stillness about us all was absolute and seemed to stretch forever. All I heard was the distant wailing of women and children, the braying of the odd mule, and the slight whisper of idle feet down among the ranks. Flavius Anicius stared at me, his face closed and distant.

"You stand relieved, Centurion," he said finally and I swear there was a faint hint of a smile in his face.

I found myself nodding back without thinking. "As the Augustus Wills, I stand ready to obey and at every command shall do my duty." Never had those words felt so hollow before. They tasted like dust in my mouth. Nearby I saw Pamphilius look askance at him with sweat breaking out across his brow.

He leaned in slightly and I saw a dark gleam in his eyes. "Your Eagle is another Eagle now, Optatus. Do you see?"

I did. It stood above us all in the hands of an Aquilifer I did not recognise and I saw that he too seemed in awe of that double Eagle above him. The silver chain looped about both these talismans of the legions, binding them, trapping then, one against the other, and even as this Aquilifer turned the ash pole again, I saw that the Eagle of the Twelfth - *our* Eagle - revolved and in its place emerged another, the Sol's. There, under that leaden sky, a cold wind wrapping me up in its embrace, the smell of rain on the soft air, I shivered as if a lonely god had reached down and uttered one last fatal prophecy before turning his back into the dark for all time.

"Probus?"

Flavius Anicius smiled then but there was no warmth in it.

By his side, that old Roman who had fought and killed under a dozen legions, laughed grimly and I saw the scars on his face crack and crease. "Let us say he fell in battle, Centurion."

The Tribune turned a little and gestured to the Aquilifer. "This is Nicias, Aquilifer of the Senior Sol Legion, and now honoured with the duty to hold aloft the Janus Eagle, gifted to us by the illustrious Magister."

The man was a Gaul, broad-boned and with an open face, clouded now with a faint superstition. He held that symbol high and even as he gazed up at it in the dull light I could see that his hands were tense. Without thinking, he swivelled the pole again and once more the Eagles revolved.

"Janus Eagle?" I echoed, my voice low, hesitant.

"The god of comings and goings, of portals, and arches, and those little steps we take forwards into the future and backwards into the past." I saw a shadow flit across his face then and almost without thinking, he reached up and tugged at the grey-speckled beard he sported now. "Lupicinus, it seems, has a sense of comedy as well as a sense of tragedy."

"The two legions have been conjoined?"

"Oh much more than that, much more! This Magister has condemned us all under the face of a god who looks both ways. And who has he placed in command of this condemned standard? A man who has ended up where he once began. This time however things will be different. Won't they, Optatus?"

And I saw him look along the ranks and files of the Sol Legion and more than that I saw how those *milites* and the officers among them gazed back up at him - in reverence, in respect, and many with a mocking glance that spoke to their affection for him, this 'Corbulo', this Italian who seemed so young and old at the same time. There, among all these Roman soldiers in their yellow crests and plumes, the symbol of Helios on all their shields, I saw only veterans and battle-scarred, men - men who had fought and marched for Rome for countless years. And such a contrast to the men of the Twelfth who stood now in-between these Sol legionaries! To my right and left stood the Sol maniples in tightly formed ranks whereas in the ragged centre stood what was left of the Fulminata - tired men, wounded men, men slouched under the century and cohortal standards - and even as I saw that contrast, I knew why the Sol was split and standing on either side of our men. I knew why this Flavius Anicius had formed the van from the first three maniples of the Sol and why the rear was brought up by the remaining three - and all the Twelfth were in the middle - and I knew why Flavius Anicius and his staff had marched not at the head of that long column but had instead marched within the last of the Sol at the rear.

This Tribune was not leading the Twelfth back into Melitene; he was herding them.

My eyes remained fixed on that strange conjoining of Eagles above us all and I remember thinking that if Christ was a god who redeemed then what was this Janus, this old and venerated god of Rome, whom some said was before all the other gods, even Romulus and Remus, those twins? What was this ancient two-faced god who presided over the past and the future and who only ever held up mirrors? And the sky above deepened in its grey hue so that I imagined that even that dome above us was silvering over into one huge mirror to mock us all below . . . And my arm rose up to that Janus Eagle, saluting it, honouring it, before all the men of the Twelfth and the Sol, before all the officers about Flavius Anicius, before whatever gods, two-faced or not, that still watched over us.

My arm rose up but in that thin light I seemed to be nothing but a grey man saluting his demise.'

CHAPTER FIFTEEN

That evening as the legionaries drift like wraiths into barrack blocks or take up duty rotas on the parapets and about the gateways, a thin drizzle of rain begins to cover the castra. It emerges from the dusk like a ragged cloak over the fort, a cloak ruffled by a desultory wind, and all along the walls and bastion towers men wrap themselves deeper into their heavy sagum cloaks. Oil lamps and braziers light up the interior and cast small islands of bronzen relief in the deepening gloom but the mood remains pensive despite the warm glow. Grief and anger cloud many of the barrack blocks as the losses of the Twelfth finally sink in. Men baffled at the death of their comrades rail at their fortune or turn that anger inside into a smouldering resentment. It has been a hard three days of marching back to Melitene and the castra - three days without pause or relief from Amida - and in many ways those survivors have yet to truly absorb the mockery of that day and the battle of the Hekatontarch's Mark. Word has soon filtered in among the legionaries and the centurions that the Magister had condemned them all to slaughter out on that plain as nothing more than an elaborate trap for the perfidy of the Persians. It was only the timely arrival of Flavius Anicius and the soldiers of the Sol Legion which had allowed those left to walk alive out of that dust and raging wind. Many men this night nurse festering wounds and an inner bitterness that the man who had once commanded them and who had been driven out had now alone saved their souls.

In amongst this black anger and pain, almost forgotten, also rises the weeping and the fear of the women of those *milites* fated now never to return. Fights break out over the remnants of possessions - purses of silver, precious gems, ornaments and jewellery - and those fights are often between wives and hidden lovers, each one claiming in some manner that those tiny objects are theirs by right now. Only the stern discipline of the centurions quell these bitter disputes and save them from escalating into blood and death. It is an evening fraught with tension under that thin gauze of rain; an evening of shock and sullenness and resentment. The legionaries alone upon the ramparts and towers look down upon it all and in some small way are thankful for being apart from it despite the rain soaking slowly into them.

Only in the centre of the castra, across the wide parade ground, lies order and calm for here the long neat lines of the Sol Legion's *papillio* tents can be seen. While the castra itself is uneven and bulked out with bastion towers, its insides crammed with huts and storehouses and barrack blocks, and seems more a small town than a fort, here within the centre lies almost by contrast another camp - the age-old ordered century and maniple lanes, all anchored by the dragon heads and century *vexilla*. It is as if one camp lies within another and neither will merge or conjoin. Here the sentries move slowly about the perimeter oblivious of those *milites* up upon the walls above them all and when the watch is changed in either place it is as if both legions are studiously ignorant of the other.

The evening drags on in deepening twilight and rain, the wind skirling about the growing puddles and causing the standards and dragon tails to flap anxiously. Small groups of women can be seen leaving the gateway towards Melitene, cloth or leather bundles over their shoulders, crying children clutching at their skirts, while hidden deep in their folds lies what little coin or gold can be salvaged from the legion funeral funds. These poor vagrants will walk like refugees through the rain and the dark into Melitene and throw themselves onto whatever Christian charity they can find now that they no longer have any right to reside in the legion fort. It can be seen that out of some unknown urge, Obedianus, of his own accord, has posted the last of his Arab riders along that road to Melitene as escort and guard to these families and that all through that rough night of wind and rain these desert sons encourage the women and children with soft words and a gentle patience - and in the eyes of these women, all desperate now, rises a strange respect that these distant barbarians from the fabled lands south of Damascus and Palmyra would show such care.

' . . . They moved, father, in small groups, one after the other, looking now towards the low walls of Melitene and whatever sanctuary they could find there. Some were weighed down with burdens - the sum of all they owned - while others walked barefoot with nothing but a dark frown upon them. Some trailed a ragged skirt of children and others scorned that baggage and moved alone, knowing that whatever the future brought, whatever the gods or fates threw at their feet, it was for them alone to grasp or reject. You would not have turned your back on them, father, either out of spite or scorn but instead shown them pity. For we have seen this procession before, you and I, have we not? Except, as Ailat alone knows, instead of rain and a rough wind, it was the eternal rasp of the desert sand which framed these footsteps - the footsteps of dispossessed families in the night. Instead of a dark and indistinct fort wrapped in fog and that coldness which seeps into your bones, it was the fires of an oasis put to the torch and the crackling of those adobe houses and towers we once called home. I saw under that rain, father, and watched as these families left that fort and all about me my brothers looked on and I knew that they did not see the rain nor feel the wind but instead remembered our home vanishing in light and fire . . .'

It is the look one such woman gives Obedianus, as the dusk finally sinks into night and the rain hardens almost as if response, that finally causes him to turn his mare about and canter back into the castra, leaving his Arab brothers and kinsmen to remain out in the night. This woman walks past, proud still, her hair a mess of loose curls and silk ribbons, the cast of her face defiant in the rain, and as she passes beneath him, her hands knotted about a large rough sack over her shoulder, she throws him a look - a look of loss and also defiance - a look that shows him the absence of a man who had earned her love; a man now gone but never forgotten - and Obedianus sees for one imaginary moment another woman's glance. An Armenian princess who looked so deep into his soul and who smiled so casually at the truth of it that he felt all the desert and all the songs of his tribe falter.

And this poor woman below him walks on even as Obedianus urges his mount about, leaving Old Jubyal to watch over them all. She walks on barely realising how her look has affected this Arab *praepositus*, for her thoughts hang upon that moment she last saw her man marching away, his face turning from her, his words rough and uncaring. And the rain falls in sheets now and the wind hangs upon her bundle, threatening to snatch it away . . .

Today that route to Melitene from the castra itself is now obscured by suburbs and parking lots. There is little that remains above ground save a few wall fragments and the corner section of the northwest of the legion fort. It was here of course that the bulk of the papyri was unearthed and whose discovery allowed a sizeable portion of funding to continue pouring in. It was these finds rather than the work we were doing within the modern town itself which attracted international attention - and that in turn led the Turkish and Polish academic bodies to devote more monies. We were fortunate I suppose in that had these papyri not been found by Jacek and his combined team that Summer then I expect we all would have packed up after a season or two and gone home to write up our findings never to return.

It was John Atkins who broached an observation one evening as we walked back from these ruins into the centre of Malatya, the ghosts of those women and their Arab escorts about us still in our minds. It was a short walk through the dusk and around us lay the small tavernae typical of the Turkish towns here as well as street kiosks and the long bedraggled sentries of poplar trees along the roadside. Behind us, lay that remaining corner of the legion castra now under electric footlights and scaffolding while ahead lay the bustle and colour of the town centre. We had spent the day mulling over the letters of Obedianus that Sally had recently translated and were now retiring for some much needed rest. And John turned to us as we walked - myself, Sally and Jacek, the brim of his hat pulled low against the sunset - and told us that Optatus alone redeemed them all. It was his pen, as it were, which dared to unveil a deeper matter than any legionary report or account had the right to record. Those finds changed everything - in a way without Optatus, he suggested, we would never have pieced all the rest together - not Candidus wriggling out of his books nor Obedianus with his curious gallantry. It was not that we had found his writings, in a sense, that was important but rather it was what he had *written* in them that mattered. He was the glue which bound all the rest together, you see.

I remembered thinking, as we walked slowly down that street, that he was wrong.

It was not Optatus who changed everything. It had been me. It was that moment I had knelt in the mud and dust of a trench and found the ostraka - that fragment of a pottery shard and on it the briefest sarcasm. Had I not read that inscription in its tiny Latin scrawl, I would never have promised to myself to seek out the truth behind that comment. I would never have persevered in linking, and exploring, and finally in bringing onboard these companions with all their insights and discoveries. Without that shard, we would never have de-camped one long hot Summer a few years later to head off into eastern Turkey and stand finally in a little vale of rock looking for that elusive final fragment of the story. It was not Optatus who had been the glue, it had been me. But I could not say that to John - or the others. It would have sounded like a monstrous boast. I know that. Even a boast, however, can be a truth.

So I remember walking that dusty road under the ragged shade of the poplar trees, tinny music blaring out from the tavernae, the growling engines of buses and cars hedging us in, and thinking that, yes, this *Adjutor* had penned more than his duty prescribed, as it were, but it was the least of his writings, that single sentence penned in mockery, which ironically had served as a catalyst to us all. I looked at my friends about me that evening - the writings of Obedianus still fresh in our minds and the unseen ghosts of widows and orphans trailing us under a cloak of rain - and I think it was then that I first felt truly apart from them all. Up until that Summer we had all pooled our finds and research in little ways almost as a hobby on the side. Yes, we worked and documented the ruins and fragments we unearthed on a daily basis but always in the evenings we gathered in a local bar and presented *other* findings - other research - and out of that gathering these lost characters were slowly emerging. This we had done casually and slowly. It was a sideline. On that evening, however, as I heard John pronounce our debt to Optatus, I knew something was still shifting in me. I knew that what for them was something that was perhaps anecdotal was for me intrinsic.

And it was that stubbornness in me which would later convince them all of that worth and would drag them all east towards that final portal of snow and darkness and death . . .

Under that evening then of rain and a blustery wind, as the wives and children of dead legionaries walk and stumble back towards Melitene with a guard and escort of Arabs, even while we drifted along that route and chatted carelessly about fate and excavation and I found myself standing apart from them all, another knot of figures walk, all huddled in great cloaks and felt hats.

These figures walk slowly about the parapets of the legion castra, a few slaves trailing them all, miserable in soaked tunicas, while at their head strides Flavius Anicius, his alert gaze picking over every detail. By his side walks Stygos, the rain running in tears and tiny runnels from his carven face, Candidus the Alexandrian, now cocooned in a dark cloak of Aegyptian wool, and finally Optatus uncomfortable and alone among these companions. The rain is heavy and constant now, falling in thick sheets so that few atop the parapets can make out the lights of Melitene in the distance. Sentries along the walls and the bastion towers crouch against the ramparts for what little shelter can be afforded but spring upright as this tight knot of men walk past them. They walk past and give them all not a second look though. Optatus is gesturing to a wall breach here, the cracked ramparts there, the rusty hinges and brackets on a ballista or the torn canvas coverings of an onager on the towers. It is a slow tour and the rain soaks them all but not once does Flavius Anicius hurry the report or put it off - quite the opposite. He seems to relish in Optatus' discomfit as the rain slices down in sheet after sheet. Indeed, it can be seen that on more than one occasion, he halts the tour and inquires of more details - why are the parapet blocks cracked exactly? When will the sinew replacements for the mural artillery arrive from Sebestae? Does not Brachius, the Dux, understand that these things cannot be put off? And so on as the rain grows deeper and the wind begins to howl over the castra walls.

Finally, above the western gateway, with the flanking towers on either side, this little knot of men halt and Flavius Anicius turns and looks out into the rain and the darkness. A few desultory lights can be seen sidling out of the gateway below but these soon disappear into the night and the wind. Behind them, rough commands and a faint tuba cry can be heard alerting the sentries to a change in watch. A rider canters impatiently back into the castra, his white cloak trailing him like a wraith.

' . . . I recognised that *Saraceni* Obedianus as we all looked down over the eroded parapet walls. He glanced up at us and I saw a scowl cloud his features and then he was under the gateway and gone. I shivered beneath the heavy cloak and wrapped it deeper about me. The wool was fine and prepared with oils from the old Jewish district in Alexandria but still the rains got in and dampened my bones like a curse from Dis Himself. *A cloud dimmed heaven*, as a poet once wrote, *and drew the darkness down*. And this Tribune stood there against the parapet in silence looking out into the gods only knew what. The tour had been long and I sensed that a secret amusement lurked in his breast at it. This Optatus was a man who dutifully followed him in all his questions and queries, hanging at his side like a reluctant slave, but I did not like him. There was something cold and remote about him as if he were here under sentence of some kind. The man was Punic by ancestry - I could see it in his dark face and the tight curls of hair and his almond eyes, the prominent nose. There was in him that other African, the African apart from the mixed wine of we Greeks and Aegyptians and Romans in the east. In him, lay the decadence and rancour of a defeated people. Those ancients who had built Carthage and seen it obliterated under the boot of Rome. This Optatus was a man in whose blood lay defeat and a history which had promised so much and delivered in the end so little. He was small of stature but wiry and alert yet there lay in his eyes something missing - and I sensed that like these other centurions in this broken legion that this Optatus was not immune from the stain of that past which seemed to bind the legion - a Gordian knot which had this Tribune in the centre in some fashion - a knot which teased and evaded me, as I was painfully aware.

After what seemed too long a time, the Tribune turned from the parapet and looked this Optatus in the eye.

"Where is he?" he asked finally, his words as cold as the rain.

I saw Optatus blink suddenly and then a reserved look came over him. "Him, *Dominus?*"

"You know who I mean. Are we to jump about each other like gladiators in the arena? Where is he?"

There is a fatalism in those of the Punic stamp - a weary resignation which you will always see if you push them too much or heckle them too far. It comes from the loss of that great empire opposed to Rome and indeed the loss of that white city that was once the greatest save for Alexandria in all the world before Rome grew. All Africa fell to the *respublica* in the end - Aegypt, Libya and the shores of Carthage - except that with us we were protected, valued, as it were. Not so with Carthage. Her people were vanquished worse than the Trojans. Her fleets burned. Her lands savaged. And finally that city, that metropolis with its arsenals and its high walls and its wonder of a harbour, was salted from the earth forever. And so in a sense the Punic people now are dispossessed not only of their history and their future, they are also dispossessed of their home. It has left them all wrapped up in a great dark cloak of fatalism and if one looks deeply enough in each face one will see it in all of them. I saw it now in this Optatus as Flavius Anicius pressed him atop that wall, the rain sheeting down, the wind grabbing at us all. The *Adjutor* hid within himself, within that Punic cast of his face, and shrugged then.

"You must understand, Tribune, he chose this -"

"I am not looking for a report, Optatus. Must I ask again?"

He shook his head slowly in reply. "No, he is there, where he lies every day and every night." He pointed out a small shack built behind one of the grain *horrae* down along the inner south wall. A dim murky light could be seen through a small aperture shuttered now against the weather. "He lives down there and shuns us all, Tribune."

The laugh that Flavius Anicius gave back then was sharp and ugly. "And so he should, Optatus, so he should!"

"He is still *Magister Armorum* of the Fulminata, Tribune. Though all know that title is nothing more than an honorary one now. He will not stir from there -"

"You mean no one has had the courage to strip him of the title?" The mockery in Flavius Anicius' voice was undisguised and again I saw this Optatus seem to shrink in on himself, his eyes veiled and his voice low.

"Courage? No, perhaps not. Or is it perhaps that what he is is more a testament than any of us can ever be to the Twelfth?"

I saw the Tribune smile at that and exchange a swift glance with Stygos.

"Who is this *Magister?*" I asked suddenly, curious, looking between them.

Again, it struck me that there was much about this Tribune and his history that I did not understand. There was a deep bond between him and this old Roman with the carved face of an idol - that was obvious and apparent to all. And the 'Wolf' had acknowledged that this bond alone had saved Flavius Anicius from a harsher penalty than the one he was now enduring - almost as if Lupicinus was allowing his respect and affection for Stygos to colour his actions. Clearly, Stygos and Anicius were intimates from the past but in what matter I had no idea - and clearly also whatever had happened here in this castra that had left the legion rudderless and Anicius promoted out of disgrace was *after* Stygos and Flavius Anicius had separated in some manner. Their meeting in the aftermath of the battle outside Amida was a meeting of two men long parted. Now something else was emerging that hinted to that disgrace and my keen curiosity seized me.

"Why was this man not commanded to march with the Twelfth to Amida?" I asked, impatient to know more.

Stygos shrugged back, his face blank. "I was told he was incapacitated. Nothing more."

"You will see, Tribune, you will see," replied Flavius Anicius, with a sardonic light in his eye.

The rain swirled about us as we descended down to the long grain depot. The ground underfoot was turning slowly into mud and I saw rats scurry deeper into the shadows under the wooden *horreum*. Their fur was slick and seemed to glisten with an unhealthy light even as they vanished from my sight. At the end of the supply depot was a flimsy hut tacked on as an afterthought. It was shoddily built and reminded me of the shacks I had seen crammed up against the walls of the Jewish quarter in Alexandria where those too poor to work or carry errands ended their days scavenging wood or canvas. It was less a hut than it was a last refuge, I remembered thinking, and even as we approached I could smell a stink coming from it that made me step back in surprise.

"Sol and Mithras, it smells like a cesspit."

"Or a brothel in the morning," added Stygos, frowning, that dark look appearing on his face. "You have a friend in there?"

Anicius shook his head. "A friend? No, more than that." He looked to Optatus at his side. "Is she still with him?"

The latter nodded back. "Every day. She has never left him. More a slave than a wife, less a wife, more a whore, the men say. She won't be happy to see you."

"I expect not, no."

The stench grew as we stood before the entrance. It had a sour smell to it that reminded me of rank sweat and urine stewed too long in a man's clothes. A stench found in those who have scouted and fought in the field for too long and who now ache for the baths and the oils the slaves carry in their ungent jars. I raised the hem of my cloak and covered my nostrils. "This will make sick men of us all, *Dominus*," I said in a muffled voice.

He ignored me and I saw him reach out a hand for the latch. He paused and turned to Optatus, a strange look in his eyes, as if he were assessing him. That latter looked back and I thought I saw a flicker of unease pass through him. "Only you, Optatus. Not Strabonius or the others - Remus or Cyrion and the rest. Only you I allow in now with us. Do you understand why?"

For a moment, Optatus frowned, his eyes remote. Rain cascaded over him and I sensed that a part of him enjoyed its undiluted wash. He smiled at Flavius Anicius but it was perfunctory and distant. "Me? Or my stylus?"

"Is there a difference, Centurion? Can shame exorcise itself or can only another do that? Let us say that I am allowing both faces to look."

And with that, he raised the latch and disappeared within.

The interior was dank and mildewed. All around in the cramped space lay broken pottery and smashed wood. It was as if a violent tempest had suddenly charged through the room and vanished just as quickly leaving only the wreckage in its wake. The smell, if anything, was stronger inside and even

Stygos stepped back a little at it. A small oil lamp, a little clay thing greasy with use, lay on a straw matt on the floor, its wick throwing out a weak haze of light. The roof came down almost to our heads, sloping in from the high wooden wall of the grain depot that formed one side of this shack. Against that wall, lay a trestle cot and heaped on it was the tallest man I have ever seen, all wrapped up now in torn blankets and an old sagum cloak. His feet poked out from the edge of the cot and appeared huge and shockingly white in the pale light, like the carven feet of a marble statue. At the other end there fell back a great sculptured head more a mask or a helmet than a face. It was barbaric in its splendour, framed by a long braided beard now all matted and dirty with food and spittle, while crowning it was a thick shock of wiry yellow hair the colour of rancid butter. The brows were heavy-set. The lips wide and cruel. There was a scar down one side of this cast of a face and its was ragged, uneven, and I saw that no medicus or surgeon had ever healed that wound, It was something which had reknitted itself under rough hands and using thorns found in the wild. In that light, as we stood there about the doorway, this giant figure muffled in rags and what was left of a military cloak, looked for all the world as if it were not a man but a Titan laid out in the earth. In any other place men would have wondered upon him such was his size but here on that cot with that stench about us all what I saw was the ruin of Man and not his apotheosis.

What Stygos said next echoed what I was thinking. "By all the old gods, what is this?"

"This, Stygos, is Cniva, a Goth, Artillery Commander of the Twelfth, *Magister Armorum,* and the only officer of this legion to honour my command."

"And much good it did him, you arrogant bastard!"

She emerged suddenly from a mass of shadows and rags in the corner of the room, an unkempt figure clothed more in darkness than wool or linen. Her hair was wild and filthy and there was something worn about her, as if she had toiled for too long in the fields under a harsh sun. I could not tell her age - indeed I could not tell her race or tribe or blood, such was the filth on her. Rotting teeth filled her mouth and her eyes were dim and bloodshot. The only relief on her was a gold bracelet on her arm studded with rubies - a few of which were missing, I noticed.

She crouched before us in that hovel and a wild anger blazed up in her. "Leave, Anicii, or by all the dark gods of the Underworld I will have your eyes out on my nails before you can call for help!"

"I have no choice, woman, he is my officer and I will see him."

"Your officer, is it?" she snapped back, and made as if to strike him - but in an instant I saw Stygos step forward and grab her arm. He twisted it and forced her back a step even as she hissed at him. "Let me go, you bastard! Get out, all of you! You have no place here!"

The old *veteranus* looked back at Flavius Anicius with a quizzical expression. "She's a spitter, this one. You want me to throw her outside into the rain and the mud, Ani?"

She struggled harder against him but I could see that her efforts were in vain.

"No, her anger is not her fault." He stepped closer to her, his voice low. "Listen, Sunilda, if you have any faith in your gods then give me leave to speak to him. That is all. I will ask no thing of him that he will not freely give me. I ask no act from him, only words. Will you give me that?"

Her laugh was more a growl than a thing of pleasure. "That is what I am afraid of! Your *words*, little pup, were what did for him in the first place. Get this bastard dog off me, you hear?"

"Stygos, unhand her."

"She may just claw your face off. I have met her kind before - she would sooner piss on you in the gutter than give you a draught of water or wine."

"Fuck you, you old mongrel!" she snapped back, twisting in his grasp. I saw the golden bracelet slip down her arm. "The Furies feast on your soul -"

He shrugged. "Of that I have no doubt, woman, no doubt at all." He released her arm and stood back into the darkness of the shack.

This woman, this Sunilda, glanced warily at his retreating form and then she massaged her arm. I saw a faint bruise emerging where Stygos had gripped her. She looked up from it and then at the Tribune - and all the anger and the harshness faded from her. For a moment, underneath the dirt and the lines of anger, something soft, regretful, emerged.

"Please, I beg of you -"

It was then that the giant figure all wrapped up in rags on that cot stirred. A voice thick and guttural spoke out in broken Latin and although it seemed groggy the timbre of it filled the shack.

"Sunilda? Is that you yapping, by all the gods?"

She slumped then and I saw all the defiance bleed out of her. She turned to look at the figure. "Cniva, don't let him -"

"Gods, woman, get me a drink. All the *waelcyrge* in the skies above will not match you for your temper. Get me a drink, curse you!" His voice boomed about the shack but it was slurry and hesitant.

And he rose up, the rags sliding from him in a pool of black. Cniva sat up slowly and I swear I almost looked up at him, he was so tall. That head of his with the fierce scar and the shock of wild hair and the long braided beard swung unevenly around to gaze out even as he reached up one hand to clasp his temple. "Gods above, I have a plague of elephants in my head. Get me drink, woman." I saw old saliva on his chin and gobbets of dried mucus about the corners of his mouth. He swivelled about and brought his feet down upon the packed earth of the floor and I saw that under those rags and that torn cloak, he was naked and shockingly white. "I told you never to let me fall asleep sober enough to dream."

She reached out a hand and touched his shoulder. "You are not dreaming, my love, my warrior, Cniva, of the Charini. The *Praefectus* has returned." The sadness in her voice was touching.

"Anicius? Back?" He blinked slowly and in a way that was almost comical.

I saw him try to look about in that gloom but his eyes were unfocused and dull. I understood then what I suspected the others knew in that room before that giant of a Goth - the man was drunk and almost insensate. I could see it in the manner in which he swayed and seemed unable to see into what was before him. A dribble of spit ran slowly down his chin and when he reached up to wipe it away, the effort was casual and incomplete. The reek of sweat and excrement and stale wine rose up from him.

"Magister Armorum."

The words were spoken slowly by Flavius Anicius as one would speak to a staff officer about a campaign table. I saw Optatus hanging back in the shadows along with Stygos and realised that he was watching them both with a keen eye.

Flavius Anicius stepped in then and reached out to grasp the face of this Goth. "I am back."

"Back?" He tried to focus on the figure before him but I saw that the effort was too much. "Wine, woman, I told you -"

"Hear me, old friend."

Something strange happened then. It was as if we in that dank and rotten place fell away and all that was left was the tiny space where Flavius Anicius and this Cniva lay. Darkness seemed to embrace us and leave only them in a little light - or is it that I remember it that way? I suspect the latter, of course - and yet in my memory even as I write this now all these years later with the image of these men still bright in me but tainted now by blood and death, I do wonder if I am not remembering it in its true form. Flavius Anicius leaned in towards this barbaric giant in his rags, the hands still on his face, and seemed to whisper to him in a quiet place apart from us all - and it felt as if we were looking in from a great distance, that we were an audience to these two. Even Sunilda hung upon the edge of that darkness, her eyes downcast, her hands twisting about each other in a wretched fashion. And I remember how odd it was for the Tribune to hold this Goth's face in his hands as if a boy was cradling the head of an uncle or father all the while soothing him with his words.

"I am back, Cniva."

"Not a dream, then?"

"No, not a dream, or a drunken stupor."

"Ha, the bastards gave in, then?"

"Worse, they have cursed me with the fate I desired."

"Fuck them all, then. You're really back?"

"Hear my voice. This is no dream."

"I never thought - it has been so long."

"They have given me the Fulminata again."

"Fuck them all, then, fuck them all in their skulls."

"I need you, Cniva, do you understand? I need you."

"Me? Fuck that. I am useless. I always was."

"Useless? You were the only one who stood by me."

"Ha, I did, didn't I?"

"I need my artillery commander."

"I stood by you - and it was the worst day of my life."

"Will you stand again, Cniva?"

"The worst fucking day . . . If I don't, what was the point of it all, eh? Fuck them. It is on all their heads, eh? All of it."

Flavius Anicius released that cast of a face then and allowed the great frame to fall slowly back onto the crumpled rags. The marble of his flesh seemed somehow obscene in the sordid light from the oil lamp. I saw this Goth's eyes flicker uneasily and then fall into sleep. One knotted arm swung down from the edge of that cot and rested on the earth as if it had been thrown aside in neglect. For a moment, the Tribune stood by his side, looking down at him and I thought I saw a moment's sad reflection in that olive face of his. Silver sparks coloured his beard. He spoke to Sunilda without taking that gaze from Cniva.

"If he wants wine, give it to him. All he can drink, do you understand?"

She nodded back, all her anger and rebellion now fled.

"Pay for it, barter for it, steal it, if you have to. You will be his cup now."

"Nothing new then," she shrugged back.

He turned to face her. "No, I expect not. If he sobers up, his pain will come back. Drink is his mercy."

Flavius Anicius turned then and moved to leave the shack and its ruin behind and we, like dutiful children, followed him into the rain and the darkness.

Outside, we paused a little near the last of a row of *papillio* tents. Sheets of rain fell over us and we heard around us and above us on the ramparts the sound of men at work or on patrol or arguing over dice and board games. Two sentries walked past, their shields slung over their backs, heavy cloaks thrown over their helmeted heads against the downpour. I noticed that one was playing with a pair of bone dice in one hand and knew that he was eager to finish his watch and sit among his tent-mates to gamble his silver coin. Up on the ramparts, I heard sullen voices in the darkness. I quickened my pace to catch up with Flavius Anicius.

"Tribune, that Goth is a drunk," I began. "He is of no use to us. The Magister will not condone -"

"Condone, is it?" He turned to look at me, his face cold and arrogant. "You speak of something you have no understanding of. Be careful."

To my surprise, Stygos spoke up beside me. "Candidus is right, Ani. What use is this barbarian? The smell alone on him will cause a panic in our men. Let alone the mules. He is drowning in wine and you want him with us?"

For a moment, I saw Flavius Anicius look between us, weighing us up, and then he nodded once. "Follow me - you, too, Optatus." And then he strode off into the rain and the wind. With a quick look to the *Praefectus*, I followed him and we walked into the rows of low leather tents, past the tall standards and up towards another supply shed against one wall. It was an open depot fronted with a long line of wooden portico columns, all roughly carved. On each column lay an iron brazier lit now and throwing distorted shadows back and forth into the interior. Inside, as we approached, I glimpsed various bundles and crates. One half seemed to be filled with carts or small wagons of some kind. As we crossed under that portico, out of the rain and into its shelter, the Tribune halted and turned to face Optatus.

"Tell them," he said in a brusque tone.

The *Adjutor* hesitated a little and then gestured into the interior. "This is the artillery supply depot of the Twelfth. From here we maintain the mural engines on the ramparts. Spares and all the bolts are kept in here. Once a month a ballista or onager is dismantled in turn and moved down here for renovation or repairs. We have eight of the stone-throwers on the walls above and four bolt-throwers. In here are spares and parts to repair half that number. There is a small fabrica at the rear for more complicated metal-work. Slaves maintain this depot while all the artillery crews are seconded from various centuries as needed." He turned then and moved closer to the small carts that filled up one half of the open shed. "These however are something different - something we have little use for and something Cniva alone has a knack for."

The cart was a small light two-wheeled type with a hitch for a pair of mules. The wheels were large and heavily spoked which told me that they were designed to travel fast over rough ground. Iron hoops and bolts testified to the solidness of the construction. The board at the front was wide enough for two men while in the cart itself lay a large object covered now in a leather sheet.

Optatus moved up to the nearest cart and pulled the sheet away. As the dust settled, I saw the gleaming outline of a powerful bolt-thrower, its torsion mechanism partially dismantled. Slots along the inner sides of the cart held dozens of small vicious bolts all bearing flanged heads. Oil gleamed in the light from the braziers.

The Punic *Adjutor* turned to face us. "There are six of these carroballistae. No one knows how the Twelfth inherited them. There are stories told among some of the tents that these are the remnants of the artillery lost to the Judeans over three hundred years ago and won back at Jerusalem. Others mock that as the superstition it is. Some old *milites* claim that a legion passing through down to Antioch and then on to Damascus had them and left them here as being too much trouble. No one knows. They have remained in this depot for as long as I have been stationed here. Six carroballistae and all ours now."

Flavius Anicius reached out a hand and rested it along the edge of a cart. "Mobile field artillery, *commilitones*. And that Goth back there in that hovel is the only one who can handle them."

"That man is a drunk!" I protested, feeling that this was madness. "What use have we for these?"

It was Optatus who replied. "Yes, he is a drunk. Wine is his damnation and his salvation. You saw him back there. Stinking of it and little able to get dressed let alone command men or respect. But, Aegyptian, I have never known anyone understand artillery or siege weapons better. There is something broken up *here* in him. It has left him a cripple except for that one talent. That man is touched in the head by whatever gods he prays to and that touch has left him a genius in that alone."

"But he is a Goth," I insisted. "What knack have they ever had for these things? We cannot risk this all over a few ballistae on carts!"

"We can," replied Flavius Anicius, "and we will."

It was Stygos who smiled then and I saw him spit slowly into the dust at his feet. He smiled and the look he gave the Tribune was fierce. "Corbulo to the last, is that it?"

"Listen to me, all of you. We are to be abandoned by Rome and sent east into a realm as ancient as anywhere in the orient. A realm studded with mountains and high passes and deep bitter lakes. A realm riven with betrayal and endless feuds. And all to die forlorn under a storm of Persian arrows so that these Armenian *Naxarar* lords will keep their faith with Rome - a Rome which has abandoned them as it is now abandoning us. Our blood is to be spilt for nothing more than time, *commilitones*. Time for an emperor to decide on the fate of that realm. Our deaths buy over the waverers and the fickle among mountains long since stained with treachery and broken alliances. I do not know about you but that does not sit easily with me."

"It is what the Magister commanded of us, Ani. We owe him."

Flavius Anicius scowled at that. "*Owe?* Did not Lupicinus himself say that the bonds have been loosened? Did he not say that Rome would disavow us? And does that not work both ways? Where lies our worth now, I ask?"

"The Twelfth is to be sacrificed -"

"*I* decide now what happens to the Twelfth. No other. Is that not right, Optatus?"

The *Adjutor* shrugged in the wavering light. "Is that what you ask of us?"

"It is what you all owe me." His voice was hard, unrelenting.

"Then so be it. As Corbulo wishes."

I knew then what he was doing and I sensed more than understood why it was he was doing it. This man in whose blood ran one of the oldest names of Rome would not stand by and see his destiny dictated by another. There was something in him that demanded not vengeance but something else - something deeper - a settling of a debt owed. A debt which lay not in the hands of a single man but instead in an entire legion. This Anicii stood before us, shadows flickering over him, the bulk of these carroballistae behind him, all hard-edges and cruel lines, and that harshness in his face, the coldness in his eyes that others saw as haughtiness, became something else then. Like a faceplate closing up, Flavius Anicius stepped back into that past which had shattered his illusions to the dark place he now found comfort in.

"That name was given to me in jest but cannot a thing of mockery become also a standard to rally to? And here I am where I always wanted to be. And there to the east lies Armenia whom Corbulo alone tamed and brought under the dominion of Rome. I take up a rag of a jest then and wind it about me into my standard. I am Corbulo returned and I march again into Armenia and this time I will take the Twelfth across that divide it had once sworn under its very Eagle never to enter. I will march up to Artageressa and that queen who lies entombed within it and we will not fall at the last, *commiliatones*. We will not stumble and die under Persian arrows. We will not sacrifice ourselves for a Rome that lacks honour or courage. This I vow as your commander."

"And what will you do, Ani?"

He looked us all in the eye and his words were cold and distant. "We will break that siege and escort this Pharanjem out in triumph over the dead bodies of the Persians and the Armenians who have sided with Shapur. We will trample that shattered land under foot as Rome has always done. We carry a double Eagle now - a Janus Eagle - and like all doors that swing forwards and backwards we will march and fight to the fate of our own choosing. Why else did Lupicinus hold up above us this double thing? As he cut us from Rome, he also has allowed us to cut ourselves from *him*."

"You think he has sanctioned this?" I asked in disbelief.

"He as much as told us that. Remember, he said what fate had brought together, he would not put aside. He said that though he bound the eagles together, what followed was all our own."

"Those were just words, Tribune!"

"Do you think so? I think he knew exactly what he was saying. Stygos? You know him better than all of us. What do you say?"

The old Roman didn't hesitate for a moment. Here, in this open depot, the flaring braziers casting bars of light over us all, he stood half in darkness and half in fire and the scars all across that carven face seemed deep and impenetrable. "That man," he said slowly, his voice gravelly, "does not throw dice so much as carve them and let others risk a throw. That I will tell you for nothing. He asked us to abandon Rome, to break our vows to the Augustus, so that we may serve Valens and Rome. That is a curious thing. To ask of us sacrifice *and* sacrilege. And we agreed, did we not? Blood is owed and that debt was called in. And yet . . ."

I saw Flavius Anicius nod. "His words allowed a deeper meaning, did they not?"

"If they did, it was a meaning we can never hold him to. You know that, Ani."

"We are *damnatio* in any case, old man. Let us be so in victory rather than death."

"This is all moot," I broke in. "We will never triumph over the Persians in any case. What you propose is folly. We are nothing but two legions against Shapur himself."

"And a thousand heavy cataphracts, Candidus. Armenians lashed by vengeance and honour under a woman whose brother has been flayed alive and whose king has been blinded and lies now in the Prison of Oblivion. How can we not triumph? This is the last thing the King of Kings will be expecting, is not? A sudden thrust of heavy infantry and cavalry back into Armenia towards Artageressa? No, those Persian hosts and their Armenian allies will be sitting in the ruins of that land drunk and replete on the spoils of the Arsacid House. We will advance over them like thunder across the mountains - and I need these," he said suddenly, turning to face the shadowy bulk of the carroballistae. "I need Cniva. That Goth will allow us to break a siege."

I looked between Flavius Anicius and Stygos and saw that whatever bond existed between them allowed no dispute now. These two were bound upon a rack of friendship that no words from me would break. I tried one last attempt to dissuade them from this out of desperation, if nothing else.

"I have been seconded to you, Tribune, from the Magister. He is still my superior as he is yours. He would want me to write to him of this -"

"But you won't."

"I am his subordinate -" I protested.

"No, you are mine now, Tribune. You are on my staff. You are one of my *principes*. But more than that, Candidus, I have bloodied you, have I not? I have written you into my fate and if I could see into your soul, would I not find you grateful for that? I think I would."

He turned to leave, walking past me as if I were nothing but a soldier on guard and he was doing the rounds of the vallum and fossa. He turned to go and Stygos fell in behind him, a smirk on his face.

"You will replace me one day, Candidus. You know that? I write you in but there will come a time when you alone will pick up that pen. Is that not what you have been looking for all along?"

He was gone into the darkness and the rain but his words hung about me like chains. For a moment, I remember gaping after him, watching him and that old Roman with him disappear into the downpour, hearing their footsteps vanish into a dull commotion of sounds outside, even as the rain lashed down and drummed from the wooden timbers above. The light in the braziers hissed and spluttered. The shadows about me rippled like black cloaks. And like phantoms, they vanished into a dark world outside, those two Romans who stood at opposite ends of youth and old age looking in towards each other.

It was Optatus who brought me to my senses as he touched the hem of my cloak. "He has not changed, Tribune, he has only hardened."

I found myself reaching out and grasping his shoulders with an urgency I had not expected. "What happened here? What happened that we are all echoing that moment like poorly played puppets? Tell me!"

But that cursed Punic face of his closed up and he too broke from me. For a moment, he hesitated on the threshold, caught among the fires and the darkness which fluttered around him - and this Optatus half-turned back to me. "It was Cniva alone who stood apart from us that night - the night we broke this youth of his folly and arrogance. He alone rallied to him but we spurned him for it as the drunken barbarian he always is. Do not think for a moment that this artillery is of any significance, Tribune. It is not. It is nothing more than a shield. Flavius Anicius will stand by him not out of honour or debt. Nothing so noble, I am afraid. He will stand by him to mock us. That is all. That is what Sunilda back there is afraid of, you see. That Goth will be hoisted out of his cot and *flaunted* before us all as a reminder. A reminder that we failed the legion - that we failed him."

"Who is he that holds you all in such a grip?" I asked, my voice a whisper.

He looked back at me from that threshold, his shoulders slumped, his eyes evasive. "Oh, Candidus, do you not know? Has he not told you? He is Flavius Anicius Bassas, the last of the first of the Fulminata." He gave a sour laugh. "I thought you knew . . ."

And with that he walked away from me and I stood alone in that shed. The fires hissed and spat upon the columns. Darkness ebbed and flowed about me. I looked back at those carriages with their deadly artillery on them and wondered on them. This Optatus was right. We would be marching into mountains and high passes - into a land renowned for its remoteness. What use would we have for these antiquated machines? But something stirred in me as I let my gaze linger on them. These were things no legions used anymore in the desperate and evasive wars we fought now on the borders of the empire. These belonged to an earlier age - the age of Trajan and Marcus Aurelius - that age wherein Rome lit the borders with fire and victory and triumph. In those days the ancient legions were larger and more cumbersome but all the more fiercesome because of it. Ancient writers tell of those legions and the artillery which accompanied them and how these light carriage-driven ballistae ranged up and down the flanks of the enemy line, pouring on fire like iron hailstones from the gods themselves. But those days were long over. Now the legions fought in a leaner and more flexible form. The frontier was shattered in a thousand places and the field armies of the *respublica* could no longer sustain those bloated legions as this Fulminata had once been. And with that change had come the loss of these field batteries along with so much else. Yet here they waited, covered in dust-sheets, hidden in a cavernous shed, wrapped up in the dark.

I reached out a hand and ran it along the torsion housing of the ballista that Optatus had uncovered. It was cold to my touch. There was a brutal stark quality to the craftsmanship of the housing. It had no decoration on it. No lettering of ownership or unit identity. The metal was harsh in its simplicity and yet also wonderfully apt. All the design and the craftsmanship was devoted solely to efficiency and power-ratio. Nothing more. The ballista was well-oiled, I saw. On the floor of the cart itself lay a scattering of leather containers no doubt holding the dismantled parts - the levers and nuts and bolts used to assemble this machine for battle. I counted at least forty wide-tipped bolts stowed along the inner rim of the cart.

I looked upon the past of Rome - the legacy of an old legion now long since moved on or disbanded or fallen in the dust - and despite the words of Optatus, I found myself smiling in that underworld of light and dark, of flame and blackness. I smiled as I touched the past.

The Tribune was correct, of course. I never did write to the Magister. He knew me better than I knew myself then. Or was it that Lupicinus knew us all better than we suspected? Was it only this 'Wolf' who understood the wider game being played? I still do not know and now of course have no one to ask. We are all shades lost in eternity caught in a little light. A light which allows us to stand for one moment in glory or shame and then we fall away forgotten and lost. In that shed, as I stood there my hand upon that ballistae, feeling its deadly cold, a smile wreathing my face, I felt as if for the first time all the parchment and all the vellum I had ever read was falling apart from me, that I was tearing it asunder, that my hand was pushing through it, through all the old lines of ink, the cracked ages in which I had drowned myself, and before me lay a naked world cruel and more real than anything I had ever read about before. And the words of this Tribune rose again in me - that one day I would command; that one day the pen would be mine . . .

It was a light of glory to come; a light of shame, too. And at the end, it was a light that left me alone amid a hollow of shadows and though the pen in my hand now is a heavy one and the ink from it dark with blood, that smile I found in that depot remains with me still . . .

> *This terror, then, this darkness of the mind,*
> *Not sunrise with its flaring spokes of light,*
> *Nor glittering arrows of morning can disperse,*
> *But only Nature's aspect and her law,*
> *Which, teaching us, hath this exordium:*
> *Nothing from nothing ever yet was born.*

EPILOGUE

'A hollow of shadows . . .'

Those words remained with me in the days after John's funeral back in Britain. Had I known then that they were a portend of things to come perhaps I would not have relished them so much. Like Candidus, however, who remained unaware at the time of what battles and betrayals were to come, those words nested in me and seemed to speak more to me and my loss than anything else. And so we buried him in a little affair with a few of us about him on that final day as the coffin was lowered into the earth.

Jacek and Sally remained aloof from me, of course. I did not blame them. Neither could look me in the eye.

So it was that a few weeks later I returned alone to that remote valley. The team had been dissolved, of course, all the equipment packed up and stowed away at Istanbul. I hired Akil, that ineffectual soldier, using a few favours from the military garrison nearby and together we drove in an old battered jeep up into the valley. I let it be known that I was returning to pay my last respects and I suppose that in a way I was. Akil sensed something was different, though, but he left me alone.

We reached the valley late in the afternoon and to my surprise much of the scaffolding was still intact. I expect the area was too remote for thieves to bother with. We parked the jeep at the foot of the slope and I told him to wait below while I scrambled up to that ledge. I had a backpack on and I knew he was eyeing it uneasily but I was off before he could enquire further in his broken English. Winter was arriving in all its harshness here in eastern Turkey now and the higher slopes of the peaks about us were white with snow. Ice glittered in long runnels from cliff edges and boulders. The scramble up took longer than I expected and that surprised me. No doubt that first time was coloured by emotion. When I finally reached the ledge, I had half been expecting Jacek to be there to greet me but all I found was ice, a cold wind, the smell of dampness on the air.

It stood there as I remembered it - massive, absolute and ancient. The rubble about it was covered now in thin snow and so this portal stood out more in contrast - as if it had been lifted a little from the world about it. The sheer size of it impressed me again and I remember putting the backpack down not taking my eyes off it. Down below, I could see that Akil had drifted a little from the jeep, trying to keep an eye on me but he was too far away to see what I was doing. The backpack held few items but none of them to do with funerals or paying one's respects. In moments, I had retrieved a light chisel, hammer and a stiff brush. I had to work fast and I had to work methodically before Akil grew restless and called me back down.

They say that when you are focused on something, time changes, your mind narrows down into a smaller world, and so it was with me. I cleared away the remaining loose stone, breaking up the accumulation of rock and debris, brushing the fragments carefully aside once the larger pieces had been disposed of. It was cold up there on that ledge before that portal but I didn't notice. I worked as if in a fever. Once I caught a faint whiff of sour cigarette smoke and half expected Sally to nudge my elbow but instead it was only Akil down below chasing time away out of boredom and no doubt the cold. I worked as carefully as I could knowing that my time was limited. The portal was deeply incised into the rock about it and the fit was almost perfect. Whoever had engineered this work had known what they were doing. Only that central hole and the lever that went with it would have been able to rotate the stone disc aside. I had no hope of opening it now and besides that was not my intent.

I found it at last even as Akil below was calling up in a hesitant voice. It was faint and scarred by time but there it lay so close to that portal as almost to be a part of it. I brushed away the dirt and lichen and saw emerging from underneath it the faint eroded lines of Latin. The words lay at chest height and were immediately recognisable. A single word in Late Roman uncial Latin now so faint as almost to be invisible. I remember leaning in and that my lips moved as I mouthed that word, one finger tracing the letters almost as if writing them for the first time.

I laughed then and I knew that no matter what Sally thought, or Jacek believed, we would all be back - that neither of them would be able to resist - and that despite what funding problems might arise, no matter the academic frowns or the peer hostility, the three of us would stand before this portal as it opened for the first time in over a thousand years and we would descend into the darkness that lay behind it. That 'hollow of shadows' which Candidus alone had alluded to. I laughed and traced that single Latin word again even as Akil shouted up from below not expecting my humour to echo down the stone walls.

And within that laughter I heard my voice whisper that word: 'Fulminata' . . .